THE ISLAND OF APPLES

D0492427

This book is due for return on or before

6 SEP 2005

WITHDRAWN

The Island
of
Apples

GLYN JONES

with an introduction
by
Belinda Humfrey

CARDIFF
UNIVERSITY OF WALES PRESS
1992

First published 1965 by J.M. Dent & Sons

New edition, with revisions by Glyn Jones, published 1992
Reprinted 1998

British Library Cataloguing in Publication Data

A catalogue record for this book is available from the British Library.

ISBN 0-7083-1176-8   paperback
0-7083-1177-6   hardback

Published with the financial support of the Arts Council of Wales

New material typeset in Wales by Megaron, Cardiff.
Printed by Gwasg Dinefwr Ltd., Llandybïe, Carmarthenshire

CONTENTS

THE ISLAND OF APPLES:
AN INTRODUCTORY DISCUSSION

> But now farewell, I am going a long way...
> To the island-valley of Avilion;
> Where falls not hail, or rain, or any snow,
> Nor ever wind blows loudly; but it lies
> Deep-meadowed, happy, fair with orchard lawns
> And bowery hollows crowned with summer sea,
> Where I will heal me of my grievous wound.[1]

Thus speaks the dying or 'passing' King Arthur in Tennyson's
Idylls of the King (1869). One of Tennyson's main inspirations for
this story was Lady Charlotte Guest's translation, *The Mabinogion*
(1846), made in Dowlais, Merthyr Tydfil, and dedicated to her
infant sons, Ivor and Merthyr with the words,

> May you become early imbued with the chivalric and exalted
> sense of honour, and the fervent patriotism for which [Wales's]
> sons have ever been celebrated.

Lady Guest was the wife of a master of Dowlais Iron Works, the
Guests being involved with the Works from 1763-1900. Her 'real'
situation by life and marriage was clearly not for her ironically at
odds with the aspiration or dreams she expressed through her
translation of, and annotation to, the Welsh Red Book of Hergest
(1375–1425). The story of Arthur, 'his exploits, whether fabulous
or real', ending with his being carried off 'to the Island of Avalon,
in Fairy-land', is told in her notes to the first story of *The
Mabinogion*, 'The Lady of the Fountain'.[2] The island paradise,
rich in apple trees, appeared in Welsh and Irish stories, known to
Giraldus Cambrensis (*c*.1146–1223) and others before and after
him,[3] a Hesperides apparently without a dragon. (The winterless,
healing, fruitful island was, of course, not the only destination

given to the wounded King.)

I draw attention to the title of Glyn Jones's novel first of all because, for the reader, the title might be one of the novel's greatest puzzles or problems. The blurb on the dust-jacket of the original English edition (by J.M.Dent) begins,

> Who is the handsome, accomplished young stranger who comes to Avalon, or, as the setting is a Welsh Valley, Ynys Afallon, the Island of Apples?

And the pre-title page carries the explanation,

> 'The Island of Apples' is Avallon, or Avilion, or Ynys Afallon, in the Celtic mythology the island of eternal youth. The story deals with the arrival in a beautifully situated Welsh valley of a handsome, accomplished, glamorous and fantastically brave young stranger, and the effect of his presence on a group of boys who become his friends.

This association of Avallon with the land of youth was seized upon by Glyn Jones's many newspaper and periodical reviewers in 1965,[4] and accepted as describing the schoolboy world of the novel with no, or very little, analysis of the relationship of the title and the novel itself. Avallon is mythically the island which keeps King Arthur alive with the potential to return to the 'real' world, but it does not sound like *Tir na n-Óg*, the Land of Youth. Glyn Jones himself, however, provides the novel's epigraph, *Ynys Afallon ei hun sy felly*, a line from T. Gwynn Jones's poem 'Ymadawiad Arthur', The Passing of Arthur, resembling Tennyson's poem; the line means 'The island of Avallon itself is thus' and reads like an interpretation of the novel. So to what in the novel can the title, the name, *The Island of Apples*, be attached? Does it describe Ystrad, the Valley, the fictional name for Merthyr Tydfil, which is the setting for much of the action of the novel, the world of the group of schoolboys who are its central characters? Does it describe the boys' experience of Ystrad, or their perception or conception of it (if they perceive or conceive, rather than just experience – a question I shall come to)? And if they are on the Island of Apples already, where do we place the 'young stranger' who visits it? His name, we might note, is Karl Anthony, not a remarkable name, except perhaps in its foreign first name, but bearing the same initials, KA, as King Arthur. This Karl Anthony arrives on the island of the boys' consciousness by river. The opening sentence of the novel is, 'The first time I ever saw Karl Anthony he was floating down past our house in the river.' Yet he leaves the novel at its end, drowned from a wrecked boat on a larger river, a lost hero but no King Arthur. His wrecked 'beautiful white sailing yacht... graceful and light as a great snowy sea-bird', intended to carry away over the sea both him and the boy-narrator, is named *Tir na n-Óg* (250–51).[5]

The Island of Apples is an enchanting title, resonant of seclusion, primitive Edenic freshness, idyll, fruitfulness and chivalric romance. In a note-book (now in the National Library of Wales),[6] in which Glyn Jones jotted down plans and structures for his novel as he wrote it, charted its development, and collected possibly useful words and images, there appear two earlier titles, 'Black and Purple' which suggests both darkness and splendour, but obviously refers primarily to the colours of the Ystrad school uniform (and Glyn Jones even drew the round school cap with its two colours, 'half and half'), and 'Goodbye Brewery Square'. This last title is quite unlike *The Island of Apples*. It sets the novel in a precise historical time, the first quarter of the twentieth century, perhaps the period of the First World War (1914–18), by its half-echo of the song 'Tipperary' and its 'Goodbye Piccadilly, Farewell Leicester Square'. (The War is not mentioned in the novel, though the Boer War (1899–1902) is still a memory; but neither do the boys seem to notice the Cyfarthfa Steel works which, although they had been run down in 1902, were revived in 1915–19, and would have dominated the townscape seen from their Cyfarthfa Castle School, fictionalized as the grammar school of the novel. They ignore events and places which do not impinge upon their own lives.) 'Goodbye Brewery Square' while suggesting escape, sets the novel in a real world, in a town where beer is brewed and fathers may get drunk. The actual 'Brewery Square, the *cul-de-sac* where our factory stood', the home of the narrator, is described with vivid precision (19). And what a 'real' world we are plunged into in the first pages of the novel, far from remote and romantic.

The very first paragraph (after the dramatic opening sentence already quoted), presents schoolboys 'dawdling about in the High Street looking for something to make fun of', looking into the newspaper offices' window at 'carnival kids dressed up in paper' and 'wedding photographs dotted with fly marks and the corners curling into tubes in the sun', having 'a bit of chat' with 'six dotty old men let out from the workhouse… sitting in a row against the black railings of the churchyard wall', one dribbling yellow shag, 'all of them smelly in their boiled suits' and getting them 'to curse and swear'. Every stage of man's 'real' life is here, from carnival children to old men and death, all deflated, flymarked, shabby, suggesting a poverty highlighted by sunshine, with no consolation from social or religious institutions or ceremony (the wedding photographs and churchyard railings). The world of black and yellow continues as the narrator, the 'I' of the opening sentence, introduces us to his few school friends. We soon see the first, Jeffy, 'a very thin yellow sort of boy with something twitchy the matter with his nerves', kneeling on a tea-table, 'squeezing blackheads out of the back of his [hunchback] father's neck with a number eight watch-key and wiping them off on the lip of the slop basin.' (8, 10)

This is just a beginning of the narrator's long-sustained, copious description of streets, buildings, houses, rooms, the appearances and activities of their inhabitants. To select a few details robs the writing of its cumulative power. It also breaks apart the double text which we are given; for although the reader might interpret what the boy is describing, all detail is of an acceptable surface for him, rich, astounding or exciting in itself alone. The Ystrad (Merthyr) and later Abergarth (Carmarthen) streets, countryside and their houses and people, are fascinating to him, fascinating to his eye (and tongue) but rarely to his thoughts or emotions.

So Glyn Jones's novel has a romantic title but a realistic setting and characters. In fact, the novel, although not centrally autobiographical, draws heavily on his re-creation of his own experience. He was born and brought up in Merthyr Tydfil and educated at its newly opened Cyfarthfa Castle Grammar School. The history of Merthyr Tydfil, industrialized in the nineteenth century so that its population increased from 7,000 in 1801 to 70,000 in 1901, Glyn Jones outlines in the chapter called 'Autobiography' in his *The Dragon Has Two Tongues* (1968), distinguishing Merthyr from the 'squalid, drunken, turbulent township' of Jack Jones's novels by stressing its 'considerable intellectual ferment and artistic activity'.[7] He shows the town's history as involved with his family's history from a great grand-father who largely derived from the original rural Merthyr and one who moved there from a farm at Llanybri overlooking the Towy estuary south of Carmarthen (the place of Glyn Jones's own annual school holidays). His own boyhood home, with a mother of 'active piety' and 'awesome good looks' who was a teacher from 1900 and during the First World War, with a father serving as a soldier then working for the post office (his teaching career having been frustrated by meningitis and the threat of poverty), and plenty of books – his mother's literary, his father's social, economic and political – is not drawn upon for the novel; although the character of his father 'at once a great sceptic and a romantic dreamer'[8] might seem a general inspiration. But, clearly, other relatives and Merthyr inhabitants are there in disguise (as the working note-book also proves) within Merthyr and Carmarthen as seen with the limitations of a boy's eye view. As Glyn Jones was born in 1905, the narrator of the novel, who eventually we discover to be called Dewi Davies, and his three Ystrad grammar school friends all aged about twelve to thirteen, certainly pre-adolescent, are his contemporaries. They come from equivalently 'comfortable' home backgrounds, though with the dingy austerity typical of such homes in the first quarter, indeed the first half of the twentieth century, their four, self-employed fathers being the owner of a small woollen factory, a jeweller, the owner of a drapery shop, and a small farmer (who also sells sewing machines).

After school, Glyn Jones's life kept him in touch with schoolboys. After training at St Paul's College, Cheltenham, he returned to live in Wales and taught here throughout his career. His first teaching was in a slum area of Cardiff where 'direct contact with the conjunction of poverty, vice and crime was new to [him] and [he] found the experience deeply shocking and distressing'.[9] Having lost that job in the war because of his conscientious objection, he taught at Bridgend; after the war he taught at Caerphilly and eventually at the then English-speaking Glantaf County Secondary School in Cardiff, until 1965, the year of his retirement and the publication of *The Island of Apples*. From forty years' daily life with boys, he knew his subject.

His own memories from boyhood had also been quite well cultivated, especially in his prose writings. Glyn Jones's first published works – poems – were in the *Dublin Magazine* in 1931, and he considers himself a poet primarily. There followed a collection of stories, *The Blue Bed* (1937), thirty-one *Poems* (1939) and then yet more stories, *The Water Music* (1944). It is here, twenty years earlier, that we meet the originals of Dewi Davies, and certainly of his friends of *The Island of Apples*, in two brilliant stories of quite distinct styles, 'Bowen, Morgan and Williams' and 'The Water Music', a sort of coda to it. After this collection of stories, Glyn Jones produced no book for ten years. Then came twenty-one poems, *The Dream of Jake Hopkins* (1954) and the first of his three novels, *The Valley, The City, The Village* (1956). The first part of this novel deals with childhood in Merthyr again with similar and even the same boy characters and households but spread out over several years to the sixth form. There followed *The Learning Lark* (1960), a satiric depiction of school life from the adult point of view; and then *The Island of Apples* which Glyn Jones's fellow poet and critic, Leslie Norris, described in 1973, as 'unique, a little masterpiece and surely the high point of his work'.[10]

As in *The Island of Apples*, the earlier treatments of groups of schoolboys use first-person narrative, and comparison shows Glyn Jones's variety of experiment with this elementary fictional device. In 'Bowen, Morgan and Williams' from *The Water Music*, the first-person schoolboy narration of the tragi-comic disruptive impact of a few boys, and a dog, on the both tidy and untidy everyday life of Merthyr households, comes close to the style of *The Island*. But, by comparison, the narrator is a self-conscious story teller. 'The Water Music' is an experimental, exhibitionist, lyrical piece, full of the schoolboy narrator's internalized, meditative, literary allusions, and even translations, as distantly, affectionately and admiringly he watches his friends as they swim unselfconsciously in a river pool into which he does not dive until the story is finished – or dives only in his imagination. The fiction on the surface is a somewhat literary debate about symbolic writing, as the clever schoolboy, thinking of symbolic free-expression of the kind of Rimbaud's *Bateau Ivre*, as he, the boy, attempts to transform himself into a gull, is held back by the comedy of his own human history and actual situation. A romantic view of oneself as a flying boat or bird is difficult to sustain, as Dewi Davies is to discover at the end of *The Island of Apples*.[11]

Here, in 'The Water Music', we see the influence on Glyn Jones of his friend Dylan Thomas, but in a work unlike any of Dylan Thomas's in its own exotic exploration of words, its own form of self-mocking humour. Much of the power of this story lies in its tensions between 'real' or 'down-to-earth' and romantic experience, while both kinds of experience are equally productive of comedy and wonder, all observation and experience being accepted on equal terms by the schoolboy soliloquist/narrator.

Glyn Jones remarked recently that the difference between poetry and prose is 'that one can have more jokes in prose'.[12] Glyn Jones certainly has plenty of jokes in his prose, even unextraordinary, schoolboy, Eng. Lit. jokes.

> The butcher's cart and bill-heads of Dai's father bear the slogan, 'Let Badger be your Butcher', which seven-syllabled line in the opinion of that erratic but pithy critic Evan Williams, contains more poetry and *cynghanedd* than the similarly hortatory but more famous words of the High Priest of Lakery urging us to take Nature for our Teacher. For Evan, who always hears of such things, has solved the riddle of Hamlet. The clue lies, he maintains, with the hidden character called Pat, addressed directly only once and that in the tortured reflection of young Denmark – 'Now might I do it, Pat, now he is

praying,' but whose machinations and subtle influence have confounded three hundred years of criticism.[13]

The quotation shows, by contrast, what sort of schoolboy narrator is not to be found in *The Island of Apples*: Dewi Davies in the novel is a natural, unselfconscious storyteller anxious to convey information, not to entertain or impress. (He does tell funny stories, but he does not laugh at himself.) But the quotation also shows the sort of game of implicit contrasts Glyn Jones can play. The bookish townee boy who, when not romanticizing himself as bard or bird-spirit, is concerned jokingly with hidden characters in *Hamlet*, can debunk Wordsworth, 'the High Priest of Lakery' while his creator is in fact supporting Wordsworth and letting Nature be his Teacher in the form of sunlight and a 'boy-bodied' river.

In *The Valley, The City, The Village*, the recollection of childhood in first-person narration is closely detailed and sympathetic but distanced, the writing of an adult looking back. The first few pages start with boys playing truant but soon, from observing as a boy his grandmother's 'mangled hands', the narrator tells of his adult thoughts about that grandmother's 'bitter childhood' and how, when in winter she took daily from Ystrad a pail of pigs' wash to the 'pigsties isolated on the colliery refuse tips', she would often put 'her frozen hands deep in the warm slop of pigs' food.' This is also the 'warm and visionary' granny, 'radiant... my glossy one, whose harsh fingers lay gently and sweet as a harp-hand upon my curls.'[14]

This narrator has sympathies and a social conscience absent from the actual schoolboy of *The Island of Apples*: he is concerned to understand sympathy and other feelings; he knows, thinks, and feels about growth, suffering, development of character. Though relating funny incidents and conversations in the boys' lives, such as of Benja Bowen boasting about his information on 'bro-thels', he shows himself quite alien in his starchily florid comments: 'I felt at such times in my mutable and bewildered blood both repulsion and the awakening of some new authoritative power which impelled me to listen. The desired hold of innocency was still then powerful upon me.'[15] Dewi Davies of *The Island* is in a process of early growth, and unconscious of it; his style gives the reader the illusion of listening to or reading the schoolboy's narration just after his adventure. He is in the close grip of recent events.

There is clear difference between the kinds of statement made by Glyn Jones's narrator Dewi Davies, early and late in his story. For example, there is his comic account (narrated as matter of fact, not comedy) of his father's having become furry from using 'that electric box for his rheumatism' while the hair on the top of his head got thinner despite a variety of attempts with restorers. It ends:

> I watched him uncorking the test-tube and pouring some of the white liquid on to his head, massaging it into his hair with his fingers and examining the steam over his *pince-nez*. This was his latest restorer, a Red Indian had given the recipe to the chap who had sent it direct to the Dragon Mills. Standing before the mirror on the little stool, naked to the half, very bony, his hanging skin covered with thick red hairs, his head steaming faintly like a sucked thumb – that was the way my father looked the last time I saw him alive. (47)

This contrasts with something like this:

> But we loved the windy nights best of all, watching the huge masses of cloud crossing the clear sky; or instead we made, for a change, those dark charging tons of darkness stop dead, and we let the moon swim out far into the open blue, and we loosed the small stars and sent them whippeting across from cloud to cloud. It was lovely to watch this in the dark on the mountain, crouching together, and the air pouring over us as though we were stones lodged at the bottom of a torrent, listening to the wind rushing upon us as it pushed itself shrieking through the holly hedge. But often when I got back to Academy House again I couldn't sleep, I thought of the moon bright on the mountainside, and the circling stars, and I wondered why anything was, why the stars in their millions existed, and the people of flesh and blood, and myself; I lay in bed often gripping the mattress, because when I thought like this for a little time my mind seemed to reel, I felt as if I was becoming faint and

> unconscious with the swirling mystery around me, as though I
> was slipping overwhelmed into everlasting oblivion. When I
> told Karl about the vastness and the terror of my thoughts he
> smiled at me, and nodded, and patted me in a comforting way on
> my back. (196)

Or with this:

> I walked back to the fire in confusion and sat down. I thought of
> all the trouble we were in, Growler's home burnt to cinders,
> Growler dead, Karl in flight, and pursued by mysterious
> watchers and bloodthirsty dogs. And myself his accomplice in
> everything that had been done. Could all this have happened?
> Was it true, was it real, or only a dream? (250)

Or with this:

> What if Karl had been captured?... He would never tell them I
> was with him, he was too honourable, but what would I do
> without him? Without Karl I didn't feel as though I lived at all,
> not even existed... (253)

Yet, the highly romantic pitch of Dewi's obsessional declarations
such as the last, in the climactic ending of the novel, is given reality
and balance because the small frightened boy, about to sail away in
the *Tir na n-Óg*, comforts himself by memory of the stability of
his most recent home in Ystrad, a household of wild children
which is simply amusing and interesting and has had no emotional
impact on him:

> Karl spoke to me about what we would do abroad, but I was
> soothed as much by our talk of the Powells, Tally trying to
> cadge a penny ha'penny each off us to buy fags, Mendy picking
> his nose with the button-hook, Luther at the dinner table
> dipping his hair in the broth pretending to wash it, Mr Powell
> collecting the pennies from all the public dubliws and the boys
> in school ragging Tally he was a son of one of the copper kings.
> (251)

Moreover, memory of the 'real' schoolboy world makes acceptable the poetry of Dewi's heightened observation of the natural
world (which itself is sustained by a series of domestic images,

such as the velvet, boiling, marble and bundles in the following extract):

> All around us were the high trees with solid masses of green leaves in the sunshine draped over their branches like displayed velvet. With the blood boiling beneath his feathers a thrush sang endlessly in the little lemon-leaved oak. The night had left the perfect pearl-shine of a moon behind hanging over our heads as we lay on the grass, marble white and dry, but fragile as a bubble, and transparent, and the gulls sailed round over the river, and over the trees, and in a great ring out over the sea; or they came dropping down with their wings curved, as though they were bringing us huge bundles carried under their arms. I thought waking and sleeping about Tom and Charley and Jeffy, and wondered where they would be on a hot afternoon like this. Had Jeffy tried to get a ram's horn for us to call our club together? Had he stood on the wall up the mountain and dropped a brick on to the head of the old big-horned ram, hoping to hit one of the horns off? The ram was still lying on his side unconscious when we came back down the mountain two hours later, but when we went to examine him he got up and ran away. (251–2)

The last three sentences of this paragraph with their elision of time sequences show speculation blurring into present dream, as Dewi falls asleep. They convey Dewi's confused or delirious mental state. Nevertheless, here is still the same, unselfconscious voice, urgently telling us of truths.

As narrator of his story, Dewi changes pace and style as his pages move on: this has psychological plausibility. Early in the story, when his life has stability, he describes characters, central and peripheral, at a leisurely pace through close visual observation and anecdotes. As he moves more deeply into his obsession with Karl and into a consequent loosening of imaginative self-control and into physical danger, his account of the plot accelerates, action is fast, major events following in swift succession, and his control of sentences appears to sharpen. Ironically, in the last part of the story, when dream and reality are not always distinguishable, his style has clarity and surface simplicity. Thus some authorial tricks

of transference or transformation in language are barely percept-
ible, such as a reference to a 'frightened birch' (252) and the
change of 'pursuers' to 'rescuers' in the very last sentence of the
novel (256). The consistency of the voice is much helped because
the narrator is always telling a story, not analysing himself,
describing not interpreting his experience, not analysing others or
the significance of events (except when, finally, they endanger
Karl). This is so even in the last half of the novel when he does say
occasionally that he is happy, worried or in terror. Usually his
emotional or mental state is indicated by events, like his sleep-
walking or not sleeping, his getting scabs on his belly or a boil on
his face.

*   *   *

But, given that Glyn Jones achieves the illusion of a consistent
schoolboy voice in a precise time and place, in his narrator, what
sort of novel is he writing? Does he aim for or achieve more than
that? The single, retrospective chronological account of an adventure by an extremely observant and sensitive thirteen year old,
powerful though it is in itself, and likely *per se* to have appeal,
especially to secondary school children, seems surprising for a
novelist who started writing in the thirties, was deeply aware of
the revolution in the novel in the inter-war years, moving on, as he
indicates in *The Dragon has Two Tongues*, from admiration of
D.H.Lawrence to Virginia Woolf,[16] and himself exploring tech-
niques of poetry, stream of consciousness and other 'anti-novel'
devices in his stories and his previous three-part novel, *The
Valley, The City, The Village*.

In explaining the novel himself, Glyn Jones tends to begin by
referring first to facts, in answer to one of the first questions
usually asked by his readers: Is Karl Anthony a real person? – the
supposition being that he is a figment of Dewi Davies's imagination. Leslie Norris quotes a letter from Glyn Jones beginning,
'What sparked off *The Island of Apples* was the actual appearance in
Castle School of a boy who gave me, so many years later, the idea
for Karl', and ending 'Karl was a real boy, he is really supposed to

exist.'[17] Glyn Jones has provided helpful information for this Introduction and has written similarly of the provenance of 'the idea for' Karl, 'a creature of flesh and blood', with further amplifications.

> At that time the Merthyr community was a static one; that is, the great influx of population of the last century was over and the exodus of the thirties had not yet begun. The advent of a stranger, therefore, was something unusual, an event. We – my grammar school friends and I – used to gather often after homework at the end of our street where we used to meet a boy a bit older than we were, who obviously came from a world very different from ours. He used to cycle down from wherever he was staying to see us, because he knew no one apparently in Merthyr. He was English, a relation of one of the owners of the steel works, and he had come to Wales to begin his sort of apprenticeship in steel works management. We got to like him very much and to look forward to our talks with him. Another stranger, a boy who briefly attended our grammar school, was aloof, a loner, who in the evenings walked about town wearing a sombrero. [17.7.90][18] My mother rather deflated me and diminished my great interest in him by remarking, 'Oh I know who he is – Mary Angell's boy, I used to teach with his mother'. A strange outsider figure, there called Gwydion, or Dion, appears also in *The Valley, The City, The Village*. [25.9.86]

And Glyn Jones has explained other facts and events:

> I think it is important to realize that the novel is far from being just fantasy; much of it, actual events, are firmly based on fact. [2.4.86] Everything – well nearly everything – in *The Island* is based on fact. Yes, there was a schoolboy 'strike' when I was in about form four... [25.9.86]. The headmaster of our grammar school, a tall and dignified scholar (quite unlike Growler therefore)[19] *was* a butterfly and moth collector, a walker of the night hills, who received gifts of the creatures from friends around the world; and his house *was* burned down in mysterious circumstances [17.7.90], but some years before he became our headmaster. [25.9.86] The factory of *The Island of Apples*, what I call the Dragon Mills, was, of course in Merthyr, and was owned by my cousin's grandmother... and was a place

my cousin and I used to go to play in when we were boys. It's at the bottom of a very short lane opposite the large yellow YMCA building at the top end of the town. [16.9.90][20]

Abergarth is, in general, Carmarthen town and the Vaughan Arms [48–9] is a mixture of the Golden Lion [Lammas Street] and the Angel Vaults, a pub in Nott Square kept by my aunt [Polly Anthony]. She appears in her true physical aspect [except that she was never in a wheelchair] as 'my Auntie Rosa' in pp. 282–3 of *The Valley, The City, The Village*. [26.9.86] [21]

Of course, 'facts' like these do not accommodate even the creative transformation of them by a combination of Glyn Jones and Dewi Davies. For example, the narrow slate roof of the Angel Vaults is replaced on the Vaughan Arms by a remarkable weighty one 'of the thickest and heaviest tiles I had ever seen, it looked as though it was roofed with moss and hymn-books' (49).

Nor do facts explain the symbolic impact of real places in the context of fiction. For example, 'the Nannies', the ruined viaduct, originally with ten support pillars (which, says Glyn Jones, are drawn not from one of the several viaducts over the Taff valley of Merthyr but from north of Caerphilly, over the Rhymney valley) provides a 'lonely and isolated' tower for the courageous Karl to climb: 'Majestic, he called it, and mysterious.' (125–34) 'This [climb] could quite well have happened [says Glyn Jones in a letter, 2.4.86]... and the fire on the top seen by Dewi could have been the glare from opening furnaces somewhere in the valley.' But a ruined tower is a romantic symbol of isolation, mortal aspiration, a romantic poet himself, and much else (such as Yeats explored in his *The Tower*); and this one, a means of Karl's self-elevation in his and his friends' eyes, has a dramatic crack in it.

> [E]ven the most bizarre episodes are capable of natural explanations, [says Glyn Jones of his novel 2.4.86]. 'The reality of Growler? His mind is obviously breaking down and I see him dying of a heart attack while out after moths again. Neither his death nor his house fire have probably anything to do with Karl except in Dewi's over-active imagination. [2.4.86]

There are, however, unexplained facts or events within the story told by Dewi. There is no explanation as to how the snake-handled dagger with which Dewi and Karl swore a blood-oath (228), *after* Karl had announced his discovery of Growler's body, was later found protruding from the body by Karl and all four younger boys; it is a reality there, causing the three friends, Jeffy, Charley and Tom, to see Karl as a murderer and to run away from him (233–5). The plot itself has its mysteries, with sometimes no apparent authorial direction as to what we should label fact or fiction within its own fiction.

Glyn Jones remarked to me that the novel was written in 'a state of excitement' which is no doubt true. Nevertheless, the working note-book and the manuscripts in the National Library of Wales, showing considerable rewriting and rearrangement within the novel, indicate his having most trouble with events. Clearly he knew how he wanted the novel to end, with two boys attempting to sail away over the sea, apparently to France, but it took time for him to find acceptable motivation. He played with ideas of their wanting to reach a French master, a 'princesse lointaine', or other girl friend, a French ancestral family, even an archaeological dig, although early in the planning stage, when Karl was 'Roger' in the notebook, Glyn Jones had thoughts of a murdered body, an unknown victim.

In the final version, with some of these ideas built into Karl's fantasies about his foreign origins, the motivation, the propulsion into the escape, is superb. For Karl, the fantasist, there is the escape from what he labels ordinary, drab life, a making of fantasy into reality, a quest for another world.

> I hate everything about my life here, this madhouse, Growler's paltry school, the valley, everything. I am homesick for nobility, and honour, Dewi, weary of the pettiness, of all that is common and vulgar, and the small satisfactions, do you know what I mean? – parched for a glimpse of the mysterious brightness burning at the back of the sun. That world is my home. (203)

There is also the possibly real escape from the police, as the result of his steadily built up confrontation of Growler the headmaster, making him suspect of arson and murder. For Dewi's motivation, there is hero-worship and notions of loyal friendship. But, with the comic deflation which dogs him from his first encounter with Karl (when he has to wear his mother's itchy bathing costume at night – his nightshirt having been given to his father who is potentially ill from having plunged into filthy water to rescue Karl, (31–2), it is his having broken his uncle's armlets while playing with them which prompts him to run away (240, 242).

The National Library of Wales note-book shows how Glyn Jones assembled a mass of material for use in his novel. In this book he draws on other, observational, note-books (apparently the size of small diaries, one always carried with him) in which he had jotted incidents, anecdotes, dreams and sights: dates referring to these observations go back to 1950. (For example, one of his dreams (dated January 1957) provides Karl's dream of entering the crater of a volcano, narrated for (and by) Dewi on the evening of his arrival to live with Karl at the Powells (164) – another symbolic placing!) He can also be seen sorting out symmetries and patterns of events in the novel, such as the to and fro of Karl's and Growler's confrontations, the loss of parents by the other three schoolboys, the punctuation of Dewi's life by deaths: at the end of Part One, his father's, at the end of Part Two his mother's, and finally Karl's.

If written in excitement, the novel is tightly structured. The tone of the novel is buoyant, but the events in the life of Dewi Davies are grim and stressful, dominated by a series of deaths. The fast-paced last section includes the hideous death of Mr Powell (218–21) and the attempted cremation of the dead headmaster, Growler (236–7). Physical descriptions of these last two horrors are given by Dewi without apparent emotional reaction. But then, his father's illness in the cottage hospital at Abergarth was a nuisance to the boy because he couldn't swim, boat or go fishing (48) and his father's death went almost unnoticed because he was preoccupied with his first meetings with Karl. He does show signs of fear and loss at the second, his mother's death, which prompts some slender memories of her, including her reactions to his father's death (171–4). Here the phrasing of his indifference to the loss of family and home, the sale of Dragon Mills, sounds somewhat like a defiant effort of will.

> I didn't care at all. I was glad. I never wanted to go near Brewery Square again. I loved it in the Powells', living up there in the attic with Karl. It was like a holiday all the time, alone in our tent, camping out on the mountain or up the woods. (174)

'What I tried to do in it... was to give a picture of a mental–spiritual state, of the way a boy on the verge of adolescence, sensitive, imaginative, would react in certain circumstances', wrote Glyn Jones to a puzzled reader of *The Island*, Mrs Jackson in 1972. And to me:

> The novel is, in one aspect, about things coming to an end. Dewi is a boy on the verge of adolescence. This is the time when our parents begin to 'die' to us and the figures of authority are also diminished... [2.4.86]
>
> [Karl] is Dewi's creation. We create... out of what we observe and learn of a person, an image of that person which satisfies us in our dealings with him or her. That image is always of necessity partial, sometimes inaccurate, sometimes completely false. So in a sense there are two Karls in the book; on the one hand is the young poseur, the line-shooter, moody, unreliable; on the other the handsome, fearless romantic, who, although having a certain measure of truth, is created in Dewi's imagination from what he sees and knows of Karl. No one, surely, could be such a person as Dewi imagines Karl to be. He is a noble creation, a compensation to Dewi for the – as he sees it – humdrum, pedestrian, even squalid life around him. Everything concerning Karl becomes for Dewi distorted, magnified, suffused with powerful romantic light; he is unable to see Karl as another human being but always as someone living outside our ordinary existence, always handsome and fearless, always victorious, always untroubled by doubts, untouched by failure, suffering or disaster.
>
> ... *The Island of Apples* is a sort of study of early romanticism, a romanticism that is yet without sex and its accompanying *angst*. [17.7.90]

Here are Glyn Jones's schoolmasterly, clear explications of his novel in retrospect. The actual work must appear to us richer, subtler, more sophisticated in its revelations and explorations. In 'The Water Music' Glyn Jones uses the words 'in the pleats of my meaning' and this is clearly a novel with pleats. 'The way a boy... would react in certain circumstances': the last is an interesting phrase. Inevitably the reader asks why Dewi accepts Karl's self-romanticizing and adds to it (in fact perhaps debasing Karl's concept of himself, in suspecting him guilty of vengeance by arson and murder). A passing sentence shows Dewi's mother and granny make Karl sound 'ordinary' and 'common' (137). Dewi's three friends, who also lose home stability, a 'dying' of parents, are not so entranced by Karl, as is made clear in Dewi's narration. For example, there is Tom's laughing at Karl's story of his seeing a sabre duel in Serbia, Charley's arguing with him (136–7) and Jeffy deriding his assumption of magical powers (224). This distinction Glyn Jones points out in a letter (2.4.86), explaining, 'their natures are different, Tom being solid and (usually) sensible, Charley shallow and conceited and Jeffy neurotic, wilful and destructive' (a harsher view of them than Dewi presents in the novel). Of course Karl appears mysteriously in Dewi's life first of all, leaves his glamorous dagger for him, and throughout makes a special appeal to him. But there is an astonishing change in character from the Dewi who sits in the overgrown orchard behind the house, in a glass coach provided by his father for him to play in, reading a novel about a schoolboy, Rex, who when travelling abroad, is captured by bandits, substituted in error for a king, and eventually becomes a friend of the king;[22] for here Dewi comments, 'This book was a lot of guff really, nobody could have all the luck this Rex had' (40). Yet, soon (after the death of his father) he accepts without question Karl's stories of his own travels and unlikely adventures in various parts of Europe, stories of oppression, rescue and escape, which clearly derive from romantic fiction. For example, there is the story of the foreign princess, his *fiancée* who was in exile on a beautiful island, having been helped 'to escape through the sewers of the city' past thousands of rats (185), or the story of his wronged friend Victor, in their school in a French château, and of the evil town they visited, where a woman had given birth to a bull's monstrous offspring (165–8). In this last, Dewi blends the landscape of Ystrad and the French town as he falls asleep in Karl's room, blending his dream with Karl's story; but he also takes into the story-dream a 'terrible screaming' from one of the Powell household, Karl's real household, into which he has just arrived.

In his recent explanations of the novel, Glyn Jones's stress on Dewi is interesting, for the novelist has clearly invented two main characters in *The Island of Apples*, Karl and Dewi. The one needs to impress with his courage, heroism, extravagance and cool leadership, and carefully stage-manages his self-drama; the other needs to be impressed, indeed to be dazzled. The reader might well be tempted to search for the causes of Karl's behaviour and self-created romantic image, separate from that given him by Dewi. He is quite a few years older than Dewi, should be in the upper sixth but is in the fifth year (201), and, as elements of his conversation, stories, and interests in Ystrad (the visits to the music hall and the clinker tips) show, he is aware of girls and perhaps of human suffering, as Dewi is not. Karl's receptivity to the wonder and beauty of the natural world, his study of bark, insect wings and leaves ('He was fed by his eyes, he told me', 183–4), Dewi sees as being given newly to him, although his narration has shown him initially having knowledge of plants and quite an eye for landscape and skyscape. (Indeed it is when Dewi *remembers* seeing from a hill a dark cloud 'sweep back like a theatre curtain off the grass of the plain' to reveal the valley containing Abergarth (41–2) that a reader might well temporarily suspend belief in the truth of his reminiscent narrative.) All the same, for psychological study, Karl, another orphan (138), is perhaps more interesting than Dewi, with his mixture of adult competence and cultivated mysteriousness (139), in his own stressful Ystrad world. Possibly Karl too is being healed of 'grievous wounds' by escape into fantasy.

But within Dewi's story, Karl introduces nasty ironies. Dewi sees him as bringing beginnings, awakenings, an ecstatic freedom. But he is destructive, as shown in the irony that it is Dewi's father's courageous rescue of Karl from the river which produces the pneumonia, possibly typhoid, which kills him. Clearly, with his truancy, quiet disobedience and assumption of authority, at school Karl would be disruptive of normal procedures, a subversive. But finally his involvement of a younger boy in his adventures is dangerous. This is anticipated in the ascent of the Bryngwyn in mist (189–94). At the climax of the novel Dewi narrowly escapes drowning in a storm, and but for his transformation of 'pursuers' to 'rescuers' in his final sentence, perhaps a reader would fear for Karl's lasting effects on him. Leslie Norris, with praise of the reviewer Irving Wardle's evaluation, sees 'sad, stubborn' Dewi Davies as a hero at the end of the novel, a hero who 'gets rid of Karl' having waited 'until he is strong enough to take the world on its own terms, who knows... that the weather is going to be bleak and grey.'[23] There is much observation of real weather in *The Island of Apples* and it is noticeable that in his working note-book Glyn Jones collected his past descriptions of weather. The final storm is both physical and symbolic of painful mental severance. But it incorporates opposites; 'The lightning *burned*, it jigged and throbbed in the heavens like an *unceasing* agony pushing through my flesh... I saw the *green* rain falling *cold*.' (256) Glyn Jones wrote in his note-book, in capitals, 'Was Karl dead when he fell overboard? No! He lives for ever!'

Do we have the impression that the imaginative quest, the romantic view of life, if achieved only temporarily, has unceasing power? Or does *The Island of Apples* have power because of the lack within it of a clear authorial direction (a characteristic of English Romantic poetry from, say, Blake's *Songs of Innocence and Experience* and Wordsworth's and Coleridge's *Lyrical Ballads*)? Are we presented with a world within the novel where the dividing line between dream and reality, fiction and life, is so difficult to discover, that creative imagination is too strong for the exercise of direction, normal or judgmental? The mind of the pre-adolescent child, a world where associative power is rampant (a world of similes) but comparing power is absent,[24] has obvious attraction for a poet, even when writing prose; for there the imagination has free rein, the creative process itself can be explored. A poet is unlikely to condemn the liberating power of a Karl.

'The High Priest of Lakery', Wordsworth, is not far from *The Island of Apples*. It would be ridiculous to see here a transformed, even parodic or ironic version, of the childhood parts of *The Prelude*, the 'circumstances' of the growing boy being a mining and steel town in Wales, instead of an untouched Lake District; even though one could argue for a comparison of the boy in the novel with the one in the poem, both with their parental 'props' taken away, having to form their own minds. But, in this novel Glyn Jones seems to share Wordsworth's sympathy for 'real children' who share the experience of 'dreamers', 'forgers of lawless tales', romancers 'who make our wish our power, our thought a deed'.[25] But *The Island of Apples* also has kinship with the English Romantic poets' more constructive explorations of the disparities between vision and reality, their inter-relation and sometimes sustenance of one another. Apparently looking to the end of the novel as a summary of its discovery, Leslie Norris, with Irving Wardle, plumps it into the very different Romantic world of 'La Belle Dame Sans Merci', the bewilderment of the lonely, cheated knight on the bare hillside. Keats's poem of that name sits uncomfortably with the rest of his work, which tends to celebrate all-inclusive, not excluded, experience. Something of Norris's link is understandable. There is an element of the discomforting in Glyn Jones's *Island*, as in his other prose fiction, but perhaps this comes mostly through his often writing on the verge of the comic grotesque (an alienating style) even in his affectionate portraits of people, as much as from his leaving his reader to assemble his images and interpret them. In considering the Romantic poets' exploration of the disparities between vision and reality and their sustenance one of another, think of Wordsworth's transformation of the old leechgatherer to a figure of a 'dream', 'a man from some far region sent' to persist in his 'mind's eye' when he himself, like the old man, requires 'Resolution and Independence'. Or think of Keats's ability to escape to the song of the nightingale, the 'immortal bird' in 'full-throated ease' yet also to dismiss it as a 'deceiving elf' as he returns to his mortal 'sole self'. In its form and in its discoveries, Glyn Jones's *Island of Apples*, raising questions about the sources and nature of creative vision in a world of death, has much in common with these.

The ending of the story stays with the reader, but afterwards, thinking back, what stays in the memory after the excitement and mysteries of Dewi's narration, after the celebration of places with concentrated pictures of them, after the diffused but detailed impression of a mining town community, after the vivid characterization of adults and children (which I have hardly looked at in this discussion), and after the perplexities of Dewi Davies's (and Karl's) mental confusing of fiction and fact, and everything which that opens up in our consideration of the novel as a philosophic artefact? (The novel itself is a fruitful *Island of Apples*!)

Dewi Davies is given not only the clarity and other qualities of an ideal story teller but the associative eye of a poet. His writing (or speaking), a mixture of rich slang and colloquialisms, of racy talk and dialogue, and of vigorous description, is illuminated with similes drawn not from illusion, dreams or romance but from 'ordinary' life. Some of these I have already quoted, such as 'his head steaming faintly like a sucked thumb'. Here is a list of a few. Some are inventive: a board and easel crash 'like ten cartloads of coat-hangers tipped together from a gallery in an empty chapel' (71); others are just striking: 'there was more meat on a bike than there was on Jeffy.' (97) But usually they come from visual observation. Here are three on the face of Growler: his mouth was 'like a public oven' (65) and his skin 'pitted all over with holes as though he slept every night on knitting' (67); when he was angry, 'it had the threatening bulged-up look of a saucepanful of milk just before it boils over on to the fire.' (99). Some similes come from country knowledge: the tangles in Auntie Mag's hair under her net looked 'like black bunches of sopping bladder-wrack' (51). Here are others from a few consecutive pages: 'goose-droppings like cheroots' (51); the face of Walter Lloyd 'so round and flat and big... it would have done fine for the face of a town clock', the face and neck 'covered with invisible ginger hair, all in swirls, like the fur of a pig' (57-8); a sky had 'solid fillets of radiant cloud... flaky and bright, yellow in the sunset, like golden haddock'; rooks circling were 'black as stirred tea-leaves' and air 'turned the colour of marmalade' (59). Another randomly chosen group of pages provides images of Growler's dead face which 'gleamed back at us in the moonlight like gun-metal' (236), a heart 'bucking fiercely like a frightened pony on the end of a halter' (242), fields 'reaped and ridgy as the cane work of a chair' (249) and the sound of rain in grasses 'like mice among paper' (252). Such similes might make one wonder if the writer needs any escape from the real world into fantasy: this narrator is given the creative associative power which makes 'common' life joyous or at least exciting.

BELINDA HUMFREY

NOTES

1   C. Ricks, ed., *The Poems of Tennyson* (London: Longmans, 1969), p.1753.

2   1877 (2nd) edn., (London: Bernard Quaritch), pp.b + 31-3. (Facsimile, Cardiff: J. Jones, 1977.)

3   See R. S. Loomis, ed., *Arthurian Literature in the Middle Ages* (Oxford: Clarendon Press, 1959), 'The Legend of Arthur's Survival', pp. 65-7.

4   Of some fifty reviews collected by Glyn Jones's publisher (largely of April 1965, a few later) those which make some distinct, valuable critical observation, albeit briefly, include the following: *Yorkshire Post* (1st), *Western Mail* (3rd) *The Observer* (4th: Irving Wardle), *Merthyr Express* (8th), *TLS* (8th), *Cork Examiner* (22nd), *Huddersfield Examiner* (24th), *The Countryman* (Summer: Ronald Blythe), *Anglo-Welsh Review* (Summer: Roy Thomas); and in the USA: *New York Herald Tribune* (3rd), *New York Times* (5th), *The Plain Dealer*, Cleveland, Ohio (25th), *Detroit Press* (30 May), *The Chattanooga Times* (18th July), *Waukegan News* (24th July) *Detroit News* (5 Sept).

5   Numbers in parentheses within my text refer to forthcoming pages.

6   National Library of Wales MS 20715C.

7   Glyn Jones, *The Dragon Has Two Tongues* (London: Dent, 1968) p. 22

8   Ibid., pp. 10, 11, 21-2.

9   Ibid., p. 29. Also quoted in Leslie Norris, 'Glyn Jones', *Dictionary of Literary Biography, vol. 15, British Novelists, 1930-59*, ed. B. Oldsey (Detroit: Gale, 1983), p. 227.

10 Leslie Norris, *Glyn Jones*, Writers of Wales Series (Cardiff: University of Wales Press, 1973) p.49.

11 I was led to this association and interpretation by the note in Glyn Jones's *Island* note-book, NLW: 'Reread *Bateau Ivre*'.

12 Interviewed by Robert Minhinnick, *The New Welsh Review*, No 1, Summer 1988, p.9.

13 *The Water Music* (London: Routledge, 1944), p. 158.

14 *The Valley, The City, The Village* (1956) (London: Severn House, 1980), pp. 10, 12.

15 Ibid., p. 33.

16 Ibid., pp. 30, 31.

17 *Glyn Jones*, pp. 49-50.

18 Letters to Belinda Humfrey, 1986 to 1990: date references are in the text.

19 The NLW note-book shows that at least one schoolmaster was modelled on one of Glyn Jones's teachers – a chemistry master with the bardic name of Sarnicol who is mentioned in *The Dragon Has Two Tongues*, p. 26.

20 *Merthyr*

Quite a number of the roads in Merthyr, from Commercial Street to Church Street, which are mentioned in the novel, may be found there today, as are several of the buildings described in the novel, but with some changed names such as Libanus for Soar Chapel. Maps old and new, together with books of old photographs, such as the series of *Valley Views* obtainable from Merthyr Heritage Trust, are interesting to compare with the novel's descriptions.

21 *Carmarthen*

Some of Glyn Jones's now surprising observations are true: horses were taken out from the shafts of their carts or traps and taken into the pubs with their owners to the stables at the backs. But though some visual description of place is sound, such as of Carmarthen castle ruins, other sights are altered for no apparent reason. There was never a park with boating lake close to the river in the centre of Carmarthen: for this perhaps Glyn Jones remembered Builth Wells. Dewi's statue of 'some old curly general... wearing a bullet-proof vest and a big sword... [made of] white marble on a base of black granite... behind railings of outsize muskets' is a bronze statue with sword but no armour, on granite. The railings of muskets have been transported by the novelist from another war memorial in Carmarthen. Glyn Jones is not interested in photographic likenesses.

22 Glyn Jones derived the basic plot of this story from a book he used to read when staying on his uncle's farm at Llanybri, near Llansteffan, Carms., in his school holidays (*c.*1917): *The Little Hour of Peter Wells* by David Whitelaw (London: Hodder and Stoughton, 1913).

23 *Glyn Jones*, p. 55.

24 See S. T. Coleridge, 'Use of Works of Fiction in the Education of Children', *Miscellanies, Works*, ed. T. Ashe, 5 Vols., 1892, p. 161. Coleridge sees the comparing power, judgement, as absent in children (as so, apparently does Wordsworth).

Some sentences in *The Dragon Has Two Tongues* (p.45) may be interesting in relation to Glyn Jones's experiment with an adolescent's use of language, if he views an adolescent as seeing (that is, using only the physical eye) from his own amoral world; 'words are in some way intimately connected with the human psyche, with ethics and convictions and attitudes, in a way paint, which is without adjectives, is not; words involve us in judgement and often cannot remain morally neutral as paint is able to do.'

25 *The Prelude*, 1805, V, see ll. 540-57; in the 1850 version: 'daring tales'.

26 'Ode to a Nightingale': it ends, 'Was it a vision, or a waking dream? / Fled is that music: Do I wake or sleep?'

GLOSSARY OF WELSH WORDS AND PHRASES AND ANGLO-WELSH DIALECT FORMS APPEARING IN THE TEXT

(supplied by Glyn Jones)

146   *talu-pump* – bomberino, a team game played by schoolchildren

147   *cochyn* – ginger, red-head

148   *'Oes gafr eto?'* – title of a Welsh folk-song usually translated as 'Counting the goats'

157   *yr hen fochyn* – the old pig

161   jibbons – spring onions

162   *cymanfa* – a hymn-singing festival

179   jontomus – pizzle

180   *didoreth* – feckless

240   yorks – leather straps worn by workmen below the knees

251   *Tir na n'Og* – (Irish) the Land of the Young Ones

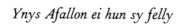

Ynys Afallon ei hun sy felly

PART ONE

overview.

① Narrative voice - Demi Revies.

- how consistent is this voice.
- where + why are the deviations.
- there are echoes of other voices.
- are we these Demi throughout.
- distinguish between young man Demi
+ adult Demi. Who can rearrange his
thoughts.

Composite voice.

② Karl - mystery of this figure - Does
he exist - how does he exist - real
or imaginary - What is the overall
function of Karl.

③ is the novel an allegory (symbol/image)
is the novel a rite of passage.

I

THE first time I ever saw Karl Anthony he was floating down past our house in the river.

It was the day we broke up, the last afternoon before the summer holidays, and I was a good bit later than usual, even, getting home, because after school we went dawdling about in High Street looking for something to make fun of. It was bright and hot and we didn't have our school bags to carry, we stood a long time outside the *News and Banner* offices going through the pictures, the schools' sports, and the carnival kids dressed up in paper, and the wedding photographs dotted with fly-marks and the corners curling into tubes in the sun. Across the street were the big folding windows of the new shop, Ystrad Motors, and there we had a good look at the brand-new motor-bikes, the royal-blue two-stroke Charley fancied and Jeffy's big red American twin cylinder among them, although Jeffy didn't even have a push-bike. Lower down High Street, their caps over their eyes and the points of their walking-sticks resting on the pavement, six dotty old men let out from the workhouse were sitting in a row against the black railings of the churchyard wall, most of them were bright red in the sun, and polished, one smoking a clay pipe, another dribbling yellow shag, all of them smelly in their boiled suits, and we had a bit of chat with them; we got them to curse and swear about the workhouse food, and the no smoking, and fat old Annie Francis the bossy matron.

When we came to Guidi's, Jeffy Urquhart led us all straight into the shop and through the bead curtains into the inner room, he treated us to a dandelion and burdock each and a plate of chips swimming in vinegar. The man behind the counter brought us forks, Guidi's special, solid lead, but we used our fingers, and Jeffy bent the forks into sort of bangles, and then made a chain out of them. There were four of us altogether, Jeffy, Tom

7

Griffiths Pugh that everybody called Tom Stiff, and Charley Llewellyn, and we had just that afternoon finished our second year in the grammar school.

Jeffy was a very thin, yellow sort of boy with something twitchy the matter with his nerves, he was the same colour all over, and even the holes in his stockings were yellow, unless he had inked them over black. His hair was two or three different yellows, and thick, and coarse as box-rope, and his eyes were yellowish too and always very glittering, they looked like flat rings of brass, but a bit greenish as well, hard and solid, like a goat's. One of the things we used to do on the way home from school was go up the *gwli* at the side of the Tiger and touch the big black downpipe fastened to the side wall of the pub, because the overhead wires were sagging on to the Tiger troughing, and the pipe would give you an electric shock. Most of us just gave the thing a flip as we were passing, or shoved somebody against it, or got some kid a bit off the latch to stroke it. But what Jeffy used to do was spit on his palms and grip hold of it hard with both hands, and then stand there by the entrance to the *gwli* yelping out loud like a dry-hinged door, and writhing in agony, until the landlord came round from the front entrance and bawled us all away. Jeffy was a bit mad, and sometimes he would sit down on a high kerb at the side of the road and laugh and laugh at the top of his voice although none of us knew what he was laughing at.

Jeffy's father was a jeweller with half a shop in Church Street, a dark poky little place painted black as tar and so narrow you could hardly make out his name, *Sanderson McK. Urquhart*, painted squeezed up tight on the board above the door and window. Day and night, summer and winter, you could see Mr Urquhart's sad bony face in the little shop window, with the black magnifier stuck in his eye and a shrub of bleeding wadding growing out of each ear, he sat there repairing his watches, with only his head in sight, frowning in the light of the green-shaded lamp, never looking up, showing the few black hairs drifting wavy as a Gulf Stream across the yellow of his bald head. He was

8

a short man, a hunchback, he didn't have a nice smooth hump but one of those with a sharp edge to it, his coat curved out between his shoulder-blades as though he had put it on over a big back-fin; and he leaned forward from his waist in a sort of half-bow walking, he seemed to have no thighs and his knees were fastened straight on to his bum. In the house he always looked yellow and cantankerous, as though he had a bad back, or a boil, or aching teeth, and I was afraid to talk to him.

When Jeffy and I were studying for the grammar school, and before my mother found out what sort of a boy Jeffy was, I used to go up to their house regularly so that we could do our homework together; and sometimes I saw things there I didn't understand until a long time after. I did think of asking Charley about them, because his mother used to let him have girls in the house, and he knew about women and that, but I thought I'd be clecking on Jeffy, so I didn't.

'Hawthornden' the Urquharts' house was called, a big shabby heap of a place in its own grounds, all covered with thick creeper so that you couldn't see the outside walls anywhere; from the hill behind, it looked like a huge mound of ivy leaves piled up into a sort of solid rick or haystack, with little windows cut in it, and roofed with red tilings. There were a lot of black gloomy old fir trees all around, and beds and beds of stiff flag-flower plants, like half-opened umbrellas pushed into the earth.

Inside you would think it was an empty house, it looked at first glance from the front door as though the people had just moved out. The rooms were cold and gloomy, and bare and hollow-sounding, they had black ceilings mostly, or brown, and wallpaper faded white, and they were always dead silent and smelling of damp. The Urquharts had a piano and a dusty horn gramophone, but I never heard any music coming out of either of them. Half the keys of the piano had collapsed anyway, and once just as I was coming into the room I saw the Captain opening the lid and lifting a couple of flagons out of it. Jeffy promised to show me their gramophone records one day and when he did there they were, a whole cupboardful, all cracked or

9

smashed up, and later on when we started camping out on Charley's farm with Karl Anthony, Jeffy used to bring them up the mountain in his school-bag, a pile at a time, to keep the fire going.

In another room they had the top of a miniature billiard table up-ended in the fireplace, and a bunch of broken cues by the side of it stuck in a drain-pipe painted with arum lilies. I asked Jeffy several times if we could have a game on it but he always put me off. The Urquharts never seemed to have a proper fire in any of their rooms, or any washing on the line, or a line. And they didn't seem to have many proper meals either. I only ever had anything to eat there once, Mrs Urquhart gave me a sort of cup of soup; it was red, like quarry water, and half cold, all I could taste was the spoon. I always thought their house was very peculiar compared with ours and my granny's, because I never even *smelt* anything tidy to eat there, not bread baking, or bloaters on the gridiron, or boiling jam.

One day just after I started going to 'Hawthornden' Mrs Urquhart told me I would find Jeffy in the parlour with his father. When I went in Mr Urquhart was in his shirt-sleeves leaning across the tea table with his elbows on it, and I could hear his hard hoarse chest creaking like a cane chair at every breath. The baggy sleeves of his shirt were cream flannel with black stripes, and his jacket and big wing collar and bow tie were heaped on the piano beside him. Jeffy was on the tea table, kneeling across the tea-things, squeezing blackheads out of the back of his father's neck with a number eight watch-key, and wiping them off on the lip of the slop-basin. 'I won't be long, Dewi,' he said when I came in. 'I've only got five or six more behind his ears now.'

I stood waiting by the door. There was no sound in the room except the loud grit in Mr Urquhart's breathing, harsh and dry, like grinding earthenware. I watched Jeffy fascinated, I couldn't take my eyes off his yellow hands, the finger-nails invisible, bitten down to nothing, and the skin growing up over what was left of them; and on the back of his left hand was a raw scab

10

about the size of half a crown; he called it foxbite, he had caused it himself by rubbing garden dirt into a criss-cross cut he had made in his skin with his rusty jack-knife. I hated what he was doing to his father, it turned my stomach up even to think about it, but if I hadn't been so much afraid of Mr Urquhart I would have asked Jeffy for a go.

At last Jeffy said, 'That's the lot, Mac. Thruppence is the charge', and he handed back the little brass key.

Mr Urquhart hung it on his watch-chain, alongside the shiny green hook Jeffy said was a lion's claw, and then put on his coat and wing collar. He didn't say a word, and everything he did seemed slow and clumsy and impatient. While Jeffy was buckling his bow on for him he took a little leather purse out of his trousers pocket, opened it and put a thruppenny bit from it on the table. Then he went out of the parlour in silence, stooping as though he was going to creep down a low tunnel, and closed the door behind him. Jeffy made a long nose and put the money in his pocket.

'Is he your father, Jeffy,' I asked him, 'or your grandfather?'

Jeffy looked at me in a very funny way. The expression in his yellow eyes was pretty wild, I thought, or perhaps awkward, I couldn't tell which. I didn't know at all what I had said wrong. If it had been me I would have blushed, but Jeffy was too yellow.

'He's my father, you fool,' he said.

'I thought he must be your mam's father,' I said. 'How does he look so old?'

'How could he be my mother's father if his name's Urquhart?' he said. 'He'd have to be my father's father. And he can't be my father's father because he *is* my father.'

'I only asked,' I said, a bit taken aback.

'I only asked,' he mimicked me, making a jib. 'I only asked.'

I looked at him without saying a word, half expecting him to try to give me a biff, but he only stood staring at me with his eyes glittering in his brazen way.

At last he turned away. 'Oh, shut your mouth,' he said. 'Shut your flaming mouth.'

He went and opened the recess cupboard filled with tattered piano music, and after a bit of rummaging he took out the ledger he used as a homework book. When he turned round again he didn't look so wild and nasty. 'Come on,' he said, 'let's go on with these cowing fractions so that we can have a game up the workshop.'

I seldom saw Jeffy's mother and when I did she hardly ever spoke. Once I went to 'Hawthornden' in the middle of a snow-storm, but although she was staring out of the window at me struggling through it she didn't say a word about it when I got into the house. She never seemed to know what she was doing. If Jeffy and I happened to come into the parlour and she was there, she would begin to tread about the place like a sleepwalker with the lids of her staring eyes wide open, and surrounded with the straw-coloured fur of her lashes; she looked straight in front of her, she would shake the curtains or alter the cushions without a glance at them, or she would just go on gazing out of the window at the pine trees as though she didn't even know what day it was. She had a lot of bright yellowish curls, and wet red lips, and her wide-open blue eyes with the long close-together lashes, all the same length, looked like the big china eyes of a sleeping doll. Her veins showed through her white skin, they were blue, but faint, like words scrawled on the other side of writing paper. I never saw my mother lying down at all, let alone smoking, but often when I passed the parlour door in 'Haw-thornden' I would see Mrs Urquhart through the crack stretched out full length on the couch in her dressing-gown, with her head back, blowing cigarette smoke into the air. When I told my mother she said, '*Ach y fi*', but she asked me what else.

The Urquharts had a lodger, a big, heavy, red-faced man with dense fair hair in firm grooves so deep it looked like tree-fungus, and a big fluffy bunch of loofah for a moustache. He always smoked a pipe and wore thick hairy suits with big squares on them, and there was always a strong smell to him; sometimes it was homely, like the handle of my father's cherrywood walking-stick warm from his kid gloves, but other times he stank strong

12

and stale, he reminded me of the Vaughan Arms, or the beery cellar-niff coming up through the Tiger grating. Everybody called him the Captain. He used to give Jeffy old ledgers to scribble in, and pencils with the name of the brewery he travelled for stamped in gold on them. Sometimes Jeffy got money out of him, and one Christmas he drank so many of the Captain's samples, so he said, he got blind drunk, he threw the cat out of the upstairs window and then he messed himself up and his father had to bath him and put him to bed.

One evening in the summer when I came up to 'Hawthornden' to do my homework, instead of knocking at the front door I went in at the side entrance as Jeffy had told me in school, and round into the garden at the back of the house. At the top of the garden Mr Urquhart had a long low shed, a sort of workshop, and Jeffy wanted to show me the new jeweller's lathe his father had bought for it. I was on the garden path above the dining-room, and when I glanced down I could see the Captain and Mrs Urquhart inside. She was lying back on the couch. It was dim in the room but I could see by the whiteness that her arms were bare. The Captain was on his knees, leaning over her with his back to the window. The only thing like that I had ever seen before was up the Coedcae tips with Charley Llewellyn when we were kids in about standard two or three; we saw a man lying on top of a woman on the grass, making a baby Charley said they were, they had to do it nine times every night for nine months. I didn't stop to watch what they were doing down there in the dining-room, but I did see the Captain biting Mrs Urquhart's arms, and she let him do it. I heard the door of the shed creaking open, it was tarred outside but painted scarlet inside, and Jeffy came out. I went off up the path towards him quickly so that he wouldn't see what was happening to his mother through the window.

The workshop was a long wooden shed with shutters over all the windows. Inside the noise was startling, it sounded like an aviary, there were about twenty or thirty clocks of all shapes and sizes standing and lying on the benches and hanging from the red-painted walls, all of them showing different times, and all pecking and clucking away loud enough to deafen you. The only light came from two dazzling, green-shaded electric lamps, like the ones in the little Church Street shop, they were bolted to the work benches where I could see lots of midget screwdrivers spread about, and stacks of watch-glasses, and papers with the little hands of watches stuck in them like the froggings on the tunics of the hussars; and I could also see several wineglasses turned upside down, they were all different, some of cut glass, some tinted pink, but all had their legs or bases snapped off. Jeffy told me these were to put over the watches brought in for repair, to keep the case and the guts together until his father had finished working on them. The new lathe was pretty, about a foot long, the steel in it glittering and polished like silver in the dazzling light, and the cast parts painted bright blue; Jeffy knew how to work it, but all the time the felt wheel was spinning round I couldn't help thinking about what I had seen from the garden, Mrs Urquhart leaning back on the sofa and the Captain nibbling up and down her bare arms.

The two other boys with Jeffy and me the afternoon we broke up were Tom Griffiths Pugh and Charley Llewellyn. Tom was pretty big, very dark and hairy, he had a big shabby head full of a lot of old bones, and covered with dead-straight hair sticking out like black catskin from under his little school cap. If you didn't know he was in the lower school, he was so lanky you would guess him to be a form sixer. His father kept the Bon Marché, a big gents' outfitters in Commercial Street, the shop had been in the family for years, started by Tom's grandfather Griffiths. They had handled a lot of money in their time, my granny said, but everybody knew Tom's father was a proper fool, his name had been in the *News and Banner* for drinking in the Ystrad pubs after hours, the police had caught him two or three times, once huddled with half a dozen other boozers under the table in the Boot bar, and another time singing a hymn in the Tiger lavatory with a double whisky still in his hand. But he was a nice man all the same, he could make you laugh, and sometimes

14

when I went to call for Tom I could hear him on the couch in the next room tickling Mrs Pugh until she was helpless.

But to see old Tom nobody would think he belonged to a family connected with the outfitting trade. He had to have long trousers when his voice went like a foghorn in form one, and he had grown so fast ever since that he never seemed to have everyday clothes to fit him. One of the sights of our playground last winter, I always used to think, was Tom leading our form two into school from the yard, all of us about half his size, and he wearing his little shrunk overcoat above his knees, and his school cap like a pudding basin on top of his head, the peak well down over his glasses. But at the beginning of the summer term he had looked all right, so long as he didn't button the coat up, in a black suit he had been wearing for chapel until then; but by now the cuffs were up near his elbows, and he had lowered his braces so much that the fork of the trousers was half way down to his knees, and a frill of white shirt bloused out all the way around his waist below his waistcoat. Another thing Tom was always having to do was to slit the stud-holes of his collar a bit more to get it round his neck. Tom's hands were huge, very damp and bony, and his feet were enormous too, he always showed about twice as much bootlace between his lace-holes as anybody else in school, his flat wide laces made the fronts of his boots look like those little black stays the shepherdesses used to wear outside their blouses in the cantatas we had in Libanus chapel.

Whatever you did, or whatever you told Tom, he just stood staring down at you through his thick glasses with his mouth slightly open, the spittle gathering a glitter on his parched bottom lip, and the old whistle coming out through his nose as though he had a tin nostril; he never said much, he was pretty slow and stolid always, sometimes when his thick glasses stared down at me, his fat sore lips hanging apart, his look reminded me of a big-boned cart-horse. Because it doesn't matter what you tell a horse like that, you can say anything you like about him to his face, or give him good news or anything, but he never looks surprised or ratty, only a bit downhearted all the time, and Tom was just the same. But before coming out of school earlier that day Growler Roderick our headmaster had shaken hands with him again before the whole school for being top of the form, as he had done after every exam now for the last two years.

The third boy was fussy Llewellyn, the famous arguer. The initials on everything belonging to Charley were C. D. Ll., and whenever I went to call for him at Grosvenor Gardens where he lived I heard his mother calling him Denzil. But everybody knew Mrs Llewellyn was funny, a bit noncompos really. Tom and I went there to tea once or twice, and she had everything so polite and swanky, with all the crockery covered with roses of the same rosy pattern, and wide lace on the tablecloth, and a servant, we were afraid to eat anything, we sat there with our tongues hanging down to our knees. Phoebe Rees the servant was, a girl from by us in Iron Lane, all the boys down there called her Feelme, she came in carrying the silver jug and teapot, wearing a little lace cap on her head, and a white apron. The cakes Mrs Llewellyn gave us were so small, and Tom's eyesight was so bad, he had his face nearly on the plate looking for them. And she was the same with the tea, we never got more than half a cup at a time because she never liked a cup full to vulgarity she told us. She was enough to turn you inside out, but Tom didn't show it much, not until we were shaking hands goodbye with her, and he began wiping his feet on the doormat on his way out.

Charley was pretty brilliant too, a real know-all in maths and physics and that stuff, he had learned four-figure logs on his own, he said, and he could remember chemistry formulae for Sheepy Upton without a hitch, not only easy things like CO_2 and Pb_3O_4 but really hard ones without any swing to them, or alliteration—things most of us had never even heard of. Charley could do them all flying. His father was a farmer and he also sold sewing-machines, you could see him about the town, a fat, red-faced man in breeches and green knitted stockings, and a brown bowler so hard it looked as though even the wheels of his own gambo wouldn't crack it.

If you wanted to make Charley mad all you had to do was to

16

say, 'Horse-dung' to him. Charley had girls on the brain and even in the elementary school he liked a bit of clutching. He used to be in love with a kid called Judith, Richards the scholarship teacher's daughter she was. Richards had a big garden, and when this Judith's birthday came round Charley took her a bar of chocolate for a present, and a bucket of horse-dung off the farm.

Charley was short and squareish, with a round rosy face, blue eyes, and black shiny kid-glove hair, all solid and lacquered in lovely waves, he loved it so much he always carried his school cap in his pocket to show it off. When Lucas gave us our French oral, every boy in our form knew the answer to the question: 'Quel est le plus bel élève de la deuxième classe?' It was: 'Charley Llewellyn est le plus bel élève de la deuxième classe.' Charley's face used to go red as a roadman's when somebody said that, but he loved it really, he used to grin round the class delighted, his little beamers sparkling bright blue and long-lashed, and all his lovely white teeth in view. Charley always thought he was *it*, he was always spick and span in school, no dandruff on his shoulders, his pocket-flaps always out, his two socks the same colour, he reminded me of those waxy little smilers with barley-sugar wigs Tom's father had in the Bon Marché windows. His suits, with the little white handkerchief showing in his breast pocket, always fitted him to a hair, his trousers always had good creases in them and his boots were always shining. In fact, if you happened to be sitting next to Charley in school and you bent down to pick a ruler or something up off the floor, you could smell the boot-polish coming up in waves off his boots. But Phillips the new junior English used to tease him; when he went through *A Midsummer Night's Dream* he gave Charley Helena's part to read so that he would have to say: 'I am as ugly as a bear.'

In the middle of Ystrad, the main road through the town widened out a lot, the crossroads there were called Ystrad Square, there were shops and offices and banks and that all round it, and the underground lavatories in the middle; and it was here in the square, just by Islwyn the *News and Banner*'s pitch, that the four of us used to separate every afternoon after school. Jeffy Urquhart

17

went left along Station Place towards the narrow lane with the posts in it that would bring him out just below 'Hawthornden'. Charley turned right into Grosvenor Street, to get to Grosvenor Gardens, a sort of crescent of swanky painted-up houses with red-tiled roofs and long lawns and flower beds in the fronts, and names like 'Buckingham Villa' hanging on fancy logs of wood over the front doors, instead of numbers. Charley's mother, I heard my own mother saying, was a woman who used to *buy* bread, she wouldn't stay on their farm up there on the mountain because it was too mucky, or too cold, or too far from town, she had to have a house called 'Collingwood Lodge' in those Gardens where all the women drank coffee and wore long earrings and played cards in the parlour with the gaslight on and the curtains open.

When Jeffy and Charley had gone Tom and I went on across the Square and down Commercial Street a little way together until we came to the Bon Marché. Tom's family lived in the big rooms over the shop, so at the side door we shook hands, and I left with Tom the lead fork Jeffy had pressed into my hand when he said goodbye to me in the Square.

'See you soon,' I said, 'if not sooner.'

When I looked back Tom was still standing in the middle of the pavement outside the shop, staring down through his thick glasses at the ring of lead fork in his hand.

2

WE LIVED in a house in the yard behind our disused factory, the Dragon Mills, down there in the middle of the crowded houses at the bottom of the town, the rough dirty part; so after leaving Tom I went down Commercial Street by myself until I came in sight of the level crossing, where the coal-trucks and the miners' train went over the road from the pits to the sidings. There, by the pawnbroker's on the corner of Iron Lane, I turned off into a couple of narrow side streets made up of pubs and eating houses and workmen's lodgings mostly, and half way along Industrial Terrace I reached Brewery Square, the *cul-de-sac* where our factory stood. This square was old, a pretty shabby sort of place, it seemed to get smaller and smellier all the time, there was always dried horse-dung all over the road, and torn-up newspapers, and bottles, and broken boxes; it was surrounded by scabby buildings, some of them empty and boarded up, and offices and warehouses and that. At the far end were the railway sidings where the coal-carts came to load up. We had a timber yard on one side of our factory which helped to give us a decent smell anyway, and Simonds' sand and gravel order office on the other. Opposite us were the Tubal Foundries, and Price the undertaker, and the tin mission, and Martyr's beer, the little brewery with the high chimney they had named the Square after.

Our mill stood higher than Simonds' or the timber yard, in fact it was the most conspicuous building in the whole Square, and since I had been in the grammar school I always wished it wouldn't look so shabby and terrible from the road. The whole mill seemed as though it hadn't been painted since my grandfather, I think it was, put it up. It was one of the things my father and mother used to argue about, my mother loved everything to be smart and bright as jaspers, she was a bit mad like that, and every spring she even used to pull all the oilcloth in our house off the floor and scrub the boards underneath it. But my father didn't bother, the house and the factory could go to dust for all he cared.

The front of the factory, facing the Square, was built of some dirty brown stone with currants in it, very lumpy and knobbly, like dusty pudding. Half way up this wall there was a green door under a wooden hoist, and down on the level of the pavement a big archway. All the glass panes in the three rows of windows there were thick with the dust and cobwebs inside the mill, or else smashed and stuffed with black rags or filled with boot-box cardboard. Before I started school, my mother used to give me the lids of old hat-boxes to draw on, and when I did the factory I always crayoned in a couple of hundred windows for the front of it; but really there were only thirteen facing the Square, three rows of four and an extra one on the top storey. The main entrance, that big archway on ground level, was closed by heavy green double doors smudged black with wool-oil; but you could still just make out part of the red dragon on them, standing on his hind legs, and the name, Dragon Mills, painted in a curve above him.

No flannel, not even yarn, had been made in our factory since before I was born, and I had never seen the double doors open to let the wool-wagons into our yard to unload. Only the coal-cart came down the archway now, and the railway wagons every time they brought a crate of boots or clothes for our stockrooms from the goods yards. We ourselves, my father and mother and the rest of us, went in and out through the little door cut in the big one, and so did Price the milkman, and Mr Powell the insurance, and Morgan the butcher, and all our customers of course, coming to buy hats and boots and to order suits and costumes in the factory.

The top floor of the mill was completely cleared of machinery, it was quite bare and empty now, and in wet weather I was allowed to go up there to play if I wanted to, and take other boys with me. Mostly we played soft-ball cricket with my double-skin, because of the windows, but the smaller kids liked having a go on the rope swing old Rees had tied to the rafters, or else climbing up and down the ladders through the trapdoors, from one floor to another, pretending they were on board ship. And what Jeffy Urquhart got me to do once was haul him up to the roof from the ground floor with his foot in the pulley-hook, although I wasn't supposed to touch any of the lifting tackle at all, because it wasn't safe. But I didn't go up the factory much now, except to have a smoke, I preferred the glass coach in the orchard, especially in the summer, because the whole factory was smothered in fluff and dust, and the floorboards were thick with the grit coming down the chimney, and blowing in through the broken roof-slates. And I couldn't stand the stale fatty smell there either, like goose-grease, and the strong niff of old machine oil, and the rancid sheep's grease soaked black and slimy into every bit of woodwork you touched.

The ground floor, divided into two by the archway running through it from the double doors into the yard, was almost pitch dark, you'd have to be clever to get into it at all through the door because it was packed to the walls and the ceilings with machinery; all the old machines from the whole factory had been brought down and stored there, I don't know what for, ancient looms, even hand-looms, devils, big coils of belting, mules, spinners, carding machines, the lot broken and out of date, black and oily some of it, some rusty, all covered with thick dust and heavy cobwebs, and piled up in the dark of those ground-floor rooms where nobody ever looked at it.

Only the middle one of the three storeys of the mill was in use now. It was our stockroom. Soon after my grandfather died my father gave up, first weaving flannel, and then spinning yarn, he couldn't bear being cooped up in the mill, my mother said; he started a round with a couple of johnny-fortnights to help him, selling woollen goods up and down the valleys—vests, under-pants, drovers, knitted stockings, blankets, tweed lengths for suitings. He was in his oils doing that. By now we sold every-thing you could think of for wearing, including hats, and boots and shoes for men, women and children. We didn't have a proper shop, but all our goods, all our stock and samples, were kept on the middle floor of our factory, there was plenty of room there, and it was our warehouse and showroom. Every-body in Ystrad knew about us because we advertised every week in the *News and Banner* under a picture of a dragon on his hind legs. Jeffy told the boys in our form that he had seen one of our adverts that said: 'Dragon Mills. Great reductions! Davies's trousers down again!' But Jeffy was a proper cow for making fun, although he couldn't bear anybody to make fun of him. Oh no!

No shop in town could supply complete mourning outfits for the whole family faster than our factory. My mother saw to that. She thought the flame wouldn't burn upright if people didn't have their black a couple of days before the funeral. Everything delivered from stock in forty-eight hours, and no worry. That's what we guaranteed. Not like that Pugh the Bon Marché, Tom's father, you didn't know where you were with him, or Evans the Realm, he was worse, you'd see his boy going down the street carrying a hat-box when they were bringing the body out on to the pavement.

I lifted the latch of our little door, went along the dark archway under the mill, and came out into the sunshine again in our factory yard at the back. This yard was whitish, or more light grey in colour, and it sloped down gradually from the back of the mill to the river. Our house, the front covered with thick ivy, stood on the left-hand side of the yard at right angles to the back of the factory, and my granny's house faced us. So surrounding our yard we had the river and the factory on the long sides and the two houses on the shorter sides.

Down there, on a wooden packing-case by the edge of the water, a bearded old man in a straw hat was sitting in the sun with his back to me, smoking a clay pipe. He was Rees Mawr, the tattooed old soldier my father had for a warehouseman, a grumpy old chap unless you buttered him up a bit. I knew I wouldn't get tea for another half-hour at least because it was Thursday, and my mother was in chapel in sewing class, so I chucked a stone and hit the box Rees was sitting on a loud bang, and then stood back against the wall of the archway.

Old Rees looked round cross and grumpy, and started swearing under his breath, most likely he was still sulking after some row with my mother, dinner-time perhaps, for cleaning his bike when he ought to have been in the bootroom, or coming back late from the Bell after dinner; or with my granny for sitting on the yard dubliw with the door wide open.

I hit the box again, but Rees didn't look round this time although I could still hear him grumbling and swearing to himself.

Rees— I didn't know what his other name was, or if Rees was his Christian name or his surname, everybody called him Rees, or Rees Mawr—Rees was a tall thin old man, he never had a shirt or a coat on, he always wore a black jersey with a low round neck under his braces, and his postman's trousers came up comfy under his armpits. He had a white beard, very thin, you could see his face through it, and a straw hat the colour of copper wire with age. The first time Jeffy and Charley came down our factory yard they noticed there was something the matter with Rees, Jeffy kept on nudging me and pointing to the hanging bag you could see swollen up inside the leg of his trousers, and he wanted me to let about half our scholarship class into the yard some time to see it. But bag or no bag, people said Rees had been the best cyclist in town in his day, he had ridden up Bryn Road which was practically vertical, so steep the pavements had to be in steps, with handrails alongside to help you up. He still had a heavy old solid-tyred monster, a fixed wheeler, very high, and dull black in colour, that my father used to borrow to ride about on in town sometimes, the fool.

To get Rees into a good mood it was best to question him about South Africa, or ask after his new boy, because he had a son aged about two or three, that he used to *cwtch* with a shawl around him up and down the back lane. Or you could start him on about his silver cups and when he was a track racer. Then he would let you time him on his bike, he would wheel the thing into the middle of the yard, mount it from the step on the back hub, turn the handlebars sideways and sit there while you counted out loud—one, two, three, four—balancing for ages without moving. My mother and I were going on our holidays to Abergarth tomorrow by train, but my father intended cycling down there on this old bike of Rees's. It was mad. After what I had seen of him on the thing it would take him the best part of a fortnight to get there.

When I tossed the third pebble Rees shot off the box so fast I froze against the wall, I thought I must have hit him. But he didn't look round, he put his pipe down and began going off up the bank of the river at his hobble, looking very excited, and after three or four yards he started shouting for my father. 'Mr Davies,' he yelled at the house in his thin old-man's voice. 'Mr Davies, come quick-o, there's a body in the river.'

Our house was at one end of the yard and my granny's house at the other. On the fourth side was this river, not the Ystrad itself but only one of its tributaries, the Nant, that flowed into the Ystrad farther down the valley. I liked the Nant all right, although the water in it was black as ink with coal-dust; but my father and mother used to worry about it, especially when I was smaller, mostly, I think, in case I fell in. Fair play, there was nothing to stop me. Also sometimes in summer it dried up bright brown, and stank, and my mother went mad and called in to see Russ Price the inspector of nuisances, and in winter it overflowed. The water came rushing rough and pitch-black out of a sort of huge tunnel under the road about fifty yards above our factory, and just below my granny's garden it went into another tunnel with a big iron grating over the mouth. On the opposite bank to our mill were the backyard walls of Coffin's Court, a street of pretty rough pubs and lodging-houses, and the people living there often chucked their lousy bedding over the walls into the water at night, or sheets of oilcloth or broken linoleum, or straw mattresses, and all this got plastered against the bars of the grating from time to time, with smashed-up prams, and tins and bottles, and sometimes even old sugar sacks with a couple of bricks and a dead dog in them, or three or four cats with their kittens perhaps. Then the water rose and flooded our yard, and when I came home from school I had to take my boots and stockings off to paddle from the archway to our front door, and climb into the passage over the special boards plastered with red clay my mother used to fix in the doorway to keep the water out of the porch and the rooms in the front of the house.

'Mr Davies, Mr Davies,' Rees Mawr kept on shouting, 'come quick-o, there's a man in the river, I tell you.'

I thought most likely old Rees couldn't see straight, perhaps it was only a log of wood, or even a lot of old rags or papers, so I ran down the yard and looked up the river towards the tunnel myself. Sure enough, whatever was floating down looked exactly like a body; it came on, rising and falling rapidly on the water, which was pretty full in the river that year because the summer was wet, it was floating on the far side close under the backyard walls of Coffin's Court. Almost as soon as I got to the river bank I found my father standing beside me, his moustache waxed out thin like opened dividers, he had hurried out of the house and his red ledger pen was still in his ear. In one hand he was holding a cup of cocoa and with the other he was scratching his seat. He squinted up the river through his *pince-nez* and said in his fussy way, without turning round: 'Better get the clothes-line, Rees. Go on, Dewi, help him, boy.' He never looked me in the face now because he was so short he had to glance up at me, and he couldn't bear doing that. We weren't going to Abergarth till tomorrow, but he looked forward to his fishing for weeks, and he was wearing his holiday clothes already, 'to air them', he said, his brown Norfolk suit with the leather buttons, and his brown cap to match, and his yellow boots and leggings and his high hard collar.

There were two separate drying-lines stretched between the posts in our yard and I ran to the nearer of them, but it was my granny's, with a few things drying on it, and I heard Rees behind me shouting: 'Not hers, I'm not touching hers-o. Not likely.' He had been in the Bell all right, or the Ship & Castle, standing beside him I could smell him. I hurried to my mother's line, but tug as we would we couldn't get the rope through the pulleys because of the knots, so I had to run across to the house to get the bread-knife from the kitchen drawer. When I got back Rees was by the river again, down on his hands and knees this time, but all of my father I could see was his cup of cocoa steaming on a stone on the bank. I ran forward towards Rees.

What a shock! There was my father, fully clothed, out in the middle of the river, he was so short he was up to his chest already, steadily struggling forward across the current with his arms stretched out sideways to keep his balance, because the river bed was paved with a mass of sunk rubbish that could easily put him over.

I saw the body coming on very fast, head first, towards him, rising and falling on the waves like a motor-boat, but sometimes turning right over. When it was nearly opposite him my father adjusted his *pince-nez*, stretched out his hands towards it, made a jumping grab, missed, overbalanced, and disappeared under the water. In no time at all there were two bodies floating down the river, and a few seconds later they were rolling about together against the grating over the mouth of the tunnel below my granny's garden.

But whatever was the matter with the other chap, my father was conscious. As soon as his head was above water again he shouted: 'Throw us . . . that clothes-line . . . Rees.' His wind seemed all gone and he was breathing hard. He began climbing up the iron grating, clinging on to the bars with one hand and with the other trying to hold the chap's head above water by the collar. Between us Rees and I chopped the rope free from the line-posts with the bread-knife, and then, standing on my granny's garden wall, I slung the loose end of it down to them, clothes-pegs and all. My father let himself down into the river again, to have both his hands free, and after a big struggle there up to his neck in water, he managed to get the clothes-line knotted round the chest of the other chap hanging limp in his arms. Then while Rees and I stood on the bank and tugged together against the strength of the current, he struggled forward towards us, holding the body floating up on the rough surface of the river as best he could.

At last we got them both out of the water and on to the bank. There the three of us together managed to lay the young chap flat on his face on the ground; he was a big weight to carry, sopping with water, and I watched his clothes and his whole body oozing, beginning to stream off rivers of black liquid like mushroom gravy, his brown boots, his trousers, his shoulders, his face; it was as though his body was made all of sponges, and somebody was kneeling hard on them, and all the water was being slowly squeezed out of him over the ground. He lay there quite still on his belly where we had put him, his face turned to one side and his bent arms in the shape of a soldier surrendering, and in the ear turned towards me I noticed something pretty unusual—a thin ring of wire, a little silver earring. But he looked terrible all the same, his face as pale as death and his snow-white hair cut down almost to the bone. I wondered what was best to do for him, but before I could decide I saw my father sitting down right beside him very suddenly with the clothes-line still in his hands. He sat down in a rush, lay back on the yard in his wet, gave a loud bather's belch, and fainted with his head on one side. I looked at Rees, but all he could think of doing was taking his straw hat off and fanning my father's face with it. Two men unconscious side by side in our yard, I thought. I had no idea at all what to do myself, and neither had old Rees Mawr either.

But just then I heard the little door leading into our yard from the Square clicking open, and presently who should come out of the archway into the sun but my mother, with my granny behind her; they looked lovely in the clothes they wore for sewing class in the summer, my mother with her parasol, stately, and tall as a policeman, in her big hat, and the long high-necked dress plastered with tea roses; and my granny, her contralto bosom fat in her grey costume, wearing her stiff collar and velvet tie and leaning heavily on her ebony walking-stick. I was pretty glad to see them, and afraid of a row, too, off my mother, because although my father had everything under the sun wrong with him, and it wasn't the first time I had seen him fainting, I couldn't think what I ought to do to bring him round.

'Here, what's happening?' my mother said, very bossy and domineering as usual, marching down the yard towards us. 'What's going on here?' She sounded cranky and awkward, she used to be a headmistress before she got married, I heard, and she liked everything to go on what she thought was normal. When anything a bit out of the ordinary happened she went mad.

'What are these two doing here?' she went on.

I thought she meant my father and the other chap lying side by side on the ground, but when I looked up her parasol was pointing to the cup of cocoa and the bread-knife.

'Dewi,' she shouted, 'have you been doing anything wrong after school? What's happened to these men? Come on, out with it. What have you done to the clothes-line?'

You couldn't blame her really, because lying down there on his back, sopping wet, with the water running off him back into the river, my father didn't look anything like himself; for one thing he was much stumpier even than when he was standing up, and as well as his Norfolk suit being black with water his waxed-out moustaches were drooping, he had lost his cap and his long ginger hair was plastered down over his shut eyes. His mouth flew open when he fell on his back, and the skin of his whole face had turned a greyish bluish tinge under the wet, the colour of blackboard chalk dipped in school ink, with a bit of puce mixed in with it on the cheeks and the nose.

'It's our dad, Mam,' I told her. 'He saved the man's life in the river.'

Her colour flew up crimson. 'He must be mad,' she said. She dropped down on the ground beside him, opened her handbag, took out her purple bottle of smelling-salts and held it close to his nose. 'Rub his hands,' she said. 'Rub them.' She looked beautiful with her cameo and her big round hat, and her eyes flashing black as a gipsy queen's, but she was so angry I was afraid to say anything to her.

My granny had reached us by this after her long hobble across the yard, she was lame and fat, with her arms reaching down to her knees, and she leaned hard on her black stick. 'Hold his head up,' my mother said as my granny knelt down agonizing, with all her joints going off like pistol shots, and she supported his head on her skirt. Rees and I sat each side and rubbed his wet hands, while my mother laid the bottle down and undid his soaking tie, and pulled the stud out of his shirt and collar. It was easy, the collar had had all the starch washed out of it and had gone limp as a rag. She opened my father's shirt. He must have had the bushiest chest for his height of any man in Ystrad. It was the electric machine he had bought for his rheumatism that did it, the thing didn't touch his joints and swellings but it made thick hairs gush out all over him, he grew hair everywhere, he was covered with long red and white fur like a forest monkey. All but his head, that is, the sandy hair on his head was long but very thin and getting thinner.

The next time my mother pushed the smelling-salts under his nose he opened his speckled eyes quite wide and for a time he lay there staring straight at the sky through his hair, he didn't even blink although he must have had the sun right in his eyes. His skin was solid and glassy and cold as oilcloth. I thought he was dead. But suddenly loud stiff noises began going off inside his belly like moving iron. And then, after one or two poor attempts he closed his mouth, pulled his hand away from Rees and put his fingers to the bridge of his nose, feeling for his *pince-nez*, and he gave one side of his moustache a twirl.

My mother pushed the red hair away from his eyes. Underneath, his brow was like brickwork, and she smoothed it with the stick of menthol from her bag. Gradually we got him to his feet and began to help him across the yard to the house; but after a step or two I could see the clothes-line twisted round his leg, so he had to stand, supported by the others and still dropping water like a watering-can, while I tried to untangle the thing and free him. When I turned round I had the shock of my life. I couldn't believe my eyes. There was nobody tied to the other end of the rope. The loop my father had made to go round the young chap's chest in the river had been cut clean through with a knife, the rope circle was on the soaking ground where the two bodies had been lying a minute ago, but there was no sign of the chap himself. Only something stuck in the softened ground in the centre of the broken ring that I had the sense to shove fast as a fish-flick inside my coat before anybody saw it.

'Stop, Rees,' I said. 'Rees, where is he? What's happened to the chap? He's not here.'

They all stopped and turned round. They had forgotten all about him. Everybody looked pretty blank and sheepish, even my mother. All we could see was a trail of dark wet footprints from the river bank up into the archway, and hundreds of black dots and dribbles around them on the white earth, as though somebody had been carrying water across the yard in a colander.

Rees left us and went up the slope to the arch to look out into Brewery Square for any trace of him, and by the time he came back we had got my father into the kitchen. He was shivering like mad by now and sneezing, and my mother made him sit close to the fire, on top of the hob almost, and drink half a cupful of hot whisky and sugar before even taking his clothes off; he sat there in the fireplace shaking all over and with his teeth rattling, and steaming so much you could hardly see him, and every now and then belching wind that sounded solid after all the water he'd swallowed.

'No sign of anybody,' Rees said, coming back into the kitchen. 'No sign at all-o. I can't understand it myself, there's ungrateful, Mr Davies, after you saved his life, for the boy to go off without so much as boo, bah or kiss——'

'That will do, Rees,' my mother interrupted him, sharp as a razor. 'Show a bit of respect, will you? No need for tavern vulgarity. And I wish you wouldn't breathe that Ship & Castle smell all over the kitchen.'

Before long, when my auntie Bronny came home from her shop, they got my father between them up the back stairs. Under the window at the far end of the landing I could see our tin trunks roped up for our holiday, and I wondered whether we would see Abergarth the next day. Between the three of them they washed all the river muck and the stink off my father in the bathroom, and then they put him to bed, and before the night was out everything in the house for heating was in there with him, the three flat-irons, a stone jar of boiling water, a hot brick, and the iron oven-shelf from the kitchen range, almost red hot and wrapped in some old flannel comms of my granny's.

When all this was going on I was sitting on the window-cill of my own bedroom next door. I took out the knife I had found stuck in the yard and dried it on the bedclothes and then I put it under some of my things on top of the wardrobe standing in the little room behind my bedroom. A lot of the walls in our house were really only matchwood covered with about ten lots of wall-paper, and as I was doing this I could hear my mother in the next room chewing wind about my father in his state of health going into the water. The next time a body came down the tunnel he was to call Simonds the gravel next door, or some of the men from the timber yard, a lot of thanks he'd got for risking his life, not a word of gratitude, nothing at all, the ungrateful scamp, going off without so much as thank you. I couldn't hear my father answering a word, most likely he was hiding under the bedclothes shivering and trying not to listen.

Suddenly, just after I had slipped the knife away, I heard my mother coming along the landing. I had been sitting down dreaming about it, but by the time she came in I had the right expression on my face. She wanted my nightshirt.

'My nightshirt? What for?' I asked her.

'For your father,' she said. 'Quite big enough. Where is it?'

'Where's his then?'

'In the trunks. I packed it. I thought he could sleep in his shirt and drovers for one night. But with all this confloption he's caused me, goodness knows, I might have to fetch the doctor to him before the morning. Come on.'

I handed her my nightshirt from under the pillow. 'What am I going to do?' I asked her.

'You can have this,' she said.

It was her bathing-costume, the one she used to wear on holidays before she got married. It was made of thick navy-blue serge, like men's suiting, the bodice and the baggy trousers all in one piece, with a deep frill round the waist, and rows of frills round the sleeves and the bloomer-legs all trimmed with white tape. I would look a sight in it, it was so baggy, and besides that my mother was about a foot taller than I was. She always enjoyed making a fool of me, I was sure of that. But it wasn't only the way I looked that worried me, it was the way I felt. This bathing-costume was as rough on my bare skin as sacking, as soon as I put it on I knew I would never be able to sleep a wink in it. But my mother wouldn't care about that, she would think it was good for me.

And that's what happened. What with going to stay at the Vaughan Arms the next day, and wondering about what I had seen in our yard, and the bathing-drawers, I couldn't sleep properly for hours. I lay in bed itching all over, and on fire, hearing the Nant outside and thinking of the silver knife and wondering about the stranger my father had rescued from the river. Sometimes, half awake in the pitch darkness, I heard talking from the bedroom next door. 'I'm coughing, Carrie,' I heard my father moaning in the middle of the night. 'I'm coughing.'

'Well cough then, name of God,' my mother answered, sick of him, and wanting to go to sleep.

But all the time my thoughts came back to the young man. Who was he? Where had he come from? How did he come to be in the tunnel? Rees called him a boy, but I thought he was a man. He looked a good bit longer than my father lying beside him on the ground anyhow. But then my father was one of the stumpiest men in Ystrad. The chap had looked pale and his white hair was cropped right off. I noticed a broad collier-boy sash around his waist when we carried him on to the bank, a silk crimson one. Did that mean he was a young miner? I wondered. But his high boots, what about them? And I hadn't noticed any blue scars on his head or his hands like the colliers had. Where had he gone to once he was out in the Square? How could he walk through Commercial Street soaking wet? I had never seen him before, myself, and I don't think any of the others had either. Why had he run away without a word when my father had risked his life to save him? It was a sort of insult to do that, my mother was sure to be right there. And yet I felt sure the young man hadn't meant to be insulting towards us. He had left me his knife anyway, a wonderful present, I was certain he meant it as a reward, or in gratitude. We would have been kind to him, we would have dried his clothes and given him something to eat and drink if he had let us. Although I hadn't seen much of him I liked him, I liked the little silver earrings, and the tender groove in the nape of his neck, and the soft brown boots without laces that looked like riding-boots worn under his trousers. I kept dozing and waking up, hearing my father and mother arguing next door, and thinking about the man all the time, trying to puzzle out who he was, and where he had come from, and whether I should ever see him again.

3

THIS house we lived in in the yard was really my grandfather's old woollen-mill converted, it was a long low building with a thick rug of bright green ivy growing all over the front of it. Here the old man had woven tweed suitings and shirt flannel by hand before he built the big factory facing the Square, that he called the Dragon Mills. That's what I heard my father and mother saying anyhow. In my grandfather's days our river, the Nant, had turned a water-wheel for him, you could still see the big green circles coming through the whitewash on the pine-end of our house, and the blocked-up shaft-hole, and it was this wheel that had supplied the power for the mill and driven all the machinery in it. The cottage opposite us on the other end of the yard, where my granny and my auntie Bronwen now lived, had been the home of my grandfather when our present house was still used as a mill, before the big building had been put up in Brewery Square.

We had two lots of stairs in our house, a carpeted one going down into the hall in the front, and a bare wooden one, very steep and narrow and twisty, into the scullery behind the back kitchen; this back stairway was about the only bit of timber in our house without paint on it, it was bare and the treads were pitted with thousands of little holes made by the naily boots of the workmen using it when the building was still a factory.

Our rooms seemed to be all shapes and sizes; some, like our kitchen, were huge and low, but mostly very dark. In fact the only sunny room downstairs, the only one to get a real bit of strong morning sun, was the pantry. Others, my own bedroom was one, were tiny little places, so small they were more like deep cupboards than real rooms; and some of these had thin little doors themselves in the walls, very low and narrow and wall-papered over, but if you stooped and went through them you would find yourself in another little room again on the other side, usually with no window and with only a skylight in the roof.

But never mind the size, what my mother fancied was real glossy graining everywhere, inside and out; almost every bit of woodwork seen in our house, doors, stairs, surrounds, banisters, shelves, skirtings, window-frames, cupboards, fireplaces, chair-rails, dressers, everything had to be grained all over with brown and yellow paint, and then varnished shiny as a coffin lid. Sometimes the graining was in dead straight vertical lines, tight as harp-strings, or corduroy, or the yellow downpour of unblown rain; sometimes it was thick and wavy, in the crocus-golden bends of a mermaid's hair. Dark curved lines, other times, very thin and clear, were painted like brown isotherms, in widely spaced out ovals, on a landscape the pale honey of sunlight. Our painter was my father's uncle Dan, and if Dan wanted to make a job last out because he didn't have another booking, he would put two lots of graining on at different angles; he would make the wood look exactly as though he had been painting it with golden syrup and then stuck a glazed yellow gauze right over it. Or he would use shading, and bring up lonely, cow-red hills here and there, smooth and rounded, towering up from a desert

34

flat and dusty in the sun as the land of the cowboys. Sometimes he would cover the timber of an absolutely smooth door-panel with painted-on wood-knots, chestnut or red brown, and complete with black splits and beads of resin; or do one side of a fireplace in wide, bold tawny sweeps, and then spend ages on the opposite panel with all his combs and brushes in his hands, mottling it inch by inch with stipples and hundreds of little bird's-eyes. And on top of all the painting, my mother always had Uncle Dan's latest book of wallpaper patterns on the table, every spring you'd see huge sheets of stripped-off wallpaper and what looked like miles of paper selvedge going in big tangled armfuls out of our house into the river.

When I woke up the morning after the rescue I could see at once my father was going to have a lovely day to cycle down to Abergarth, because when I opened the curtains a big gold placard of sunlight sprang on to the bedroom wall. I wondered how he was, in the next room. He must be better because although I had been awake scratching myself most of the night I hadn't heard him making a sound for hours.

I slipped out of bed, and the first thing I did after getting that terrible itchy bathing-costume off was to go into my little room and take the knife down off the top of the wardrobe. I hadn't had a chance to have a look at it without interference in daylight before, not a real look. Was it a knife or a dagger? What was the difference? If it wouldn't shut, did that make it a dagger? Or was it the size? This knife wasn't very big, the handle only just fitted my hand, or very heavy, but it was a lovely shape, and brand-new, without a mark or a scratch on it anywhere, the blade long and slender and polished, the shape of a beautiful narrow leaf, with a raised rib on each surface running down the middle from the handle to near the point; and it shone as though it were made of pure silver. But the handle—as I was looking at it I thought for sure *hilt* was the proper name—was marvellous. It was made of some darkish unshining gold, what you gripped hold of were the bodies of two slender serpents, their skins covered with lovely smooth scales, twining closely belly to belly round and round each other, the heads meeting at the top with the under-jaws flat against each other, and the four deep red eyes glittering and flashing like rubies. The protection for the hand was made by the tails of the two serpents, a slender metal tail swept out tapering each side, and curved downwards beautifully in a guard from where the hilt was joined on to the blade.

I carried the knife to the window overlooking our orchard in the back, and there the sunlight came bouncing back off the blade into my eyes as though it were a mirror, I was blinded by the dazzle of it and I saw its light jumping about golden on the ceiling of my bedroom. It was a beautiful knife, one of the best I had ever seen. Why had the young man left it behind? He couldn't have forgotten it, because he had stuck the blade right into the ground of the yard. Did he really leave it to show us how grateful he was? I wondered where he had got it from. I wanted to look at it all the time, and handle it, but I didn't want to use it much, or let anybody else use it, or even see it.

Suddenly I smelt the bacon I liked, smoked streaky with a lot of *sâm* most likely, frying in the scullery underneath me, and I heard my mother turning the tap on and off outside the back door; so I put my knife back in its place on top of the wardrobe, dressed, and went down the back stairs to the kitchen.

There I could see my mother by the table loading a tray with used breakfast dishes to carry them out to the scullery, and I knew by the black look on her face and the masterful way she was banging the crockery about that she was in one of her tantrums over something or other. Over going to Abergarth, most likely. It was my father who always wanted to go to the place for our holidays; he was a native of Ystrad, but he believed there were seven special winds meeting in Abergarth that would always cure him whatever was wrong with him. Seven winds! My mother was born down there, and my auntie Mag the Vaughan Arms where we always stayed was her sister, or her half-sister or something; but she couldn't bear the place. For one thing, in spite of all those marvellous seven winds, my father's rheumatism was always worse there because he spent so much time in the Garth river fishing. For another, the place she always wanted to go to was London, where she could visit the warehouses, and see the latest styles and ideas in ladies' hats and costumes and that, for the factory. She was always pretty crabby the day we went away, and as I was coming in through the kitchen door she suddenly stopped filling the tray. She was beautiful, but when she was in one of her moods her hooked nose always seemed to come well out of her face, it looked somehow as though it was going to make a nasty snatch at you. 'What have you got those on for?' she said in her headmistress's voice. 'Go back up and change this minute.'

I had put my best suit on because I always wore it when we were going on our holidays.

'I thought we'd be going as soon as we'd had our breakfast,' I said.

'The cab won't be here for another couple of hours yet,' she answered, very short and sour. 'So you can get them off. Go on.'

My mother used to give me the worms with her bossiness; but I managed to ask her if my father was better.

'I don't know,' she said, shooting off into the scullery with the dishes, 'and I don't care.' There was a lovely smell of frying coming from out there, and the bacon was making a nice sizzling noise like bike tyres on a sopping road.

I was worried though. What did my mother mean? Why didn't she know if my father was better? I hadn't thought much about him and how bad he had looked the day before, my mind had been filled with the man from the river and his left-behind knife. When she came back in I said: 'Is dad up yet?'

She started cutting bread and butter with her lids pulled down carefully over her eyes.

'He's up and gone,' she said. 'It's wonderful you didn't hear him. He made plenty of noise. He was coughing and sneezing plenty.'

I laughed, but it sounded hollow, like loud laughing in the empty baths. 'Gone?' I said. 'How did he go? To Abergarth, you mean? On Rees's bike?'

She dropped the bread-knife and went back out to the scullery without even answering. 'He'll be a lot older before I try to tell him anything again,' she shouted back in, and the bacon began a furious spluttering as she pronged it down in the frying-pan in her temper. '*Wfft* to him and his old machine.'

That was my father all over, half dead in the night, and the next morning, because it was sunny, waxing his moustaches and off to Abergarth on Rees's boneshaker for the fishing, and him suffering, supposed to be anyway, from rheumatism, gall stones and gastritis, chronic. After all he had been through yesterday. No wonder my mother was mad. When I laughed she gave me one look and it went right into my chest hot and out behind me. I made up my mind it was best to keep out of her way for a bit. I slipped back upstairs, changed into my old Saturday ganzy, my boots and my corduroy trousers, and sat down on the bedroom window ledge to look at my knife again, waiting for her to come up to strip the beds. When I heard her beginning to climb the back stairs I slipped the knife away, hurried across the landing to the front of the house, went down into the hall and then through the house back into the kitchen. My bacon was on the table waiting for me, smoked short-back, not streaky, and as I chewed it I could hear my mother just above me banging the furniture into the walls in her temper. I wasn't afraid she would find my knife up there, I knew that even if she took it into her head to go into the little room and look on top of the wardrobe for something, all she would see would be my dried-up paint-box, and my cloth box-kite with a ball of string attached to it, wound round and round a garden dibble.

When I had finished eating I went out through the back door into what we called our orchard. This was a long narrow strip of ground behind our house where my grandfather used to have his lade, and his millpond, and all his outhouses. But it was all dry land now, a real wilderness, running along between the river on one side and the back walls of the Brewery Square warehouses on the other; all that remained there of my grandfather's buildings were a couple of yards of stone wall held up by very powerful ivy trunks, and a few rusty dyeing vats with the colours still deep and rich in them. At one time we used the patch for keeping chickens, and my granny told me that the day I was born we had three hundred and sixty-five eggs in the house, one for every day of the year. But in the end the river-rats were too much for us and we had to put all the hens under the chopper. I went there to keep out of my mother's way until it was time for the cab. Some time or other I would have to go across the yard to say goodbye to my granny, because I was sure of half a crown there, if I could wait for her to get it out from under about twenty skirts; but if I went too early she would think up a few messages for me to do in Ystrad before we left.

Our orchard was overgrown with tall stiff grass, a lot of it as high as I was, and the air there in the summer was full of buzzing insects, and heavy with the sweet stink of elder flowers, and the beery smell of old roses, and the uncut hedges of privet gone to seed. There were one or two decayed fruit trees about the place too, white-limed up to the armpits, old, and the branches covered with curly blue fur, but all we ever got off them were a few cracked apples tasting like corks. I liked sitting out there in the glass coach my father had bought for me to play in when I was small, a bishop's coach he said it was, although you couldn't believe him; because when I told Jeffy this he said his uncle had a good few coaches in the garden too, emperors' coaches they were, twenty or thirty of them in fact, or more, he had emperors' coaches two deep all round the garden wall. My father had taken the wheels and the shafts off and stored them in the factory, and there it stood, black and shiny in the long grass, like a little glass summer-house, the ivy growing up inside it, and a lot of the woodwork covered with bright orange pinheads of damp, or as soft as paper, and gradually dropping to pieces in the weather. But because of the grass and a couple of apple trees, it couldn't be seen from the back of the house, and I still used to go there some-times, mostly to dodge my granny, and to hide from that terrible scream of my mother's that seemed to reach me all over Ystrad, and that used to make me sweat in my dreams—'Dewi!

Dewi!' a screech louder than the old caca-hawk's in the Pantglas woods.

I had a book in the leather door-pocket, one the mad woman in the Ystrad library told me I could keep, so I sat down with my feet on the mouldy leather opposite, shook the spiders out of the spine, and tried to have a read. It was an exciting book, but mad, and I couldn't keep my mind on it, I kept dreaming all the time about the young man from the river, hearing the Nant rushing past the orchard on one side of me, and every now and then the mounting scream from the big saw in the timber yard the other side of the wall. And mixed up with the reading and the noise was the memory of the knife, and the earringed young man, and the wet track across the yard from the rope ring. The book was about a schoolboy from England, Rex something or other his name was, he didn't have a mother and he was travelling abroad by train to see his father, who was an engineer building bridges over the deep ravines in some wild mountainous country. Well, at one of the frontier stops this Rex, because of his name I think it was, gets mistaken for the prince of that country by some fierce rebels on the look-out for him. They kidnap his train and want to put him on the throne instead of the king his uncle, who spends all his time gambling, and on yachts, and going about with actresses and that. The rebels are pretty mad when they find their mistake, because Rex hasn't got the royal birth-mark on his shoulder, but he's heard all their plans, and they take him to their hiding-place, a ruined castle on top of a hill, with a raven sailing round it, where they are going to shoot him. But I had had a look at the end and I could see everything was all right; this king, Rudolph his name was, falls overboard, trying to escape when the rebels capture the count's yacht, he'd had too much champagne to drink anyway, and the real Prince Carl is found and made king, and he and Rex become big friends, because somewhere between where I'd got to and the end Rex had saved his life, and risked his own life for him more than once. This book was a lot of guff really, nobody could have all the luck this Rex had, every day he had plenty of it; but it was good, I liked it better than those stories about the boarding-school boys I read. I always fancied reading about horsemen in red cloaks riding up and down the roads in the rain, and secret passages in the castle walls, and duels with swords, nine against two, and the two winning.

I must have gone fast asleep. The next thing I knew was my mother, ratty and red in the face, tapping at the glass window of the coach with her ring finger, and shouting for me to come in and change, she had been looking everywhere for me, the cab was waiting at the factory doors.

4

THE place I always liked going to in Abergarth was a hill behind the town called the Allt, it looked green and roundish from the bottom, something like a flabby plush balloon half blown up and held down by a sort of net or rope-work of grey paths; and I always liked looking down over the Garth plain from up there, and at the fields spread out on the hills surrounding it, they were like a patchwork quilt with an outsize herd of long-horned cows lying *cwtched* up asleep underneath it. But I didn't make my first visit there until almost a week after we arrived in Abergarth because of serious illness. I came up the Allt at last because I had had a big shock outside the Vaughan Arms that afternoon, and I wanted to think about it a bit without my mother moithering me all the time to go and visit my father.

From the breast of the Allt, woolly with a deep green wool of bracken, I saw far below me the huge dark shadow of a cloud sweep back like a theatre curtain off the grass of the plain, letting in the bright sunshine, and showing the broad green valley where the town of Abergarth stood, and the field-covered hills around it, some full of little oblong cows, some sprinkled with sheep no bigger than their own droppings; and here and there were the tiny whitewashed farm-buildings, like painted toy houses put down on the mat. The town itself was small, more or less a gammy oval in shape, it stood grey in the middle of the glare of the grass, and the wide Garth river flowed black round half of it, and then went on making big loops out on the plain, writing its own name in silver, people said, but that was all guff. There was faint smoke breathing up from the red chimneys of the town, and clumps of green trees bulged up like burst padding among the grey brickwork here and there; and, as I watched, the sun caught somebody's glasshouse and lit a big white-hot bonfire on the roof, blazing bright enough to blind you. The railway and three or four roads and their hedges ran out of the town into the fields, one went over the river on a grey humpbacked bridge curved in the bend of a bag-handle. The little Abergarth park was in the castle grounds, I could see the grey ruins, and the bowling-green, and the circular boating-lake no bigger than a dish of washing-blue. The tall thin spire of the parish church rose in the middle of the town, hairy with dead ivy stalks, although you couldn't see those from this distance, and right out at the edge of the fields I could pick out the converted country mansion standing in its own grounds, the cottage hospital where my father was most likely dying of pneumonia after two soakings in two days.

When my granny and Rees Mawr waved our cab off outside the factory the morning we left Ystrad, the weather was still warm, and the sun was shining as my mother and I drove through Brewery Square and out at last into Commercial Street. But by the time we had got up town to Ystrad station the glare of the whole morning seemed to have dimmed down, the big blue bum of a cloud hung right above the roofs, very ragged and close to the chimneys. And as soon as our train moved off up the valley towards Pencwm I saw the slope of the first raindrop falling like a fencing-scar across the glass of our window. Within a few yards the compartment went black and cold, and the icy hail crashed harsh as shovelfuls of cinders chucked hard against the window-glass, so that I couldn't see out. We were in the middle of a cloud-burst. Every now and then the pitch-black country outside the train lit up bright in the lightning with the clear mauve glare of methylated spirits, and after every flash I could feel the thunder crashing heavily on the coaches as well as hear it. Anybody out in this would be drenched to the skin in no time at all.

My mother didn't say a word, she sat there in her best purple costume and her big purple hat like velvet machinery, where two large spread-out seagulls had dropped down dead. She sat up slanting in the corner all the way without touching the back of her seat, her stays so tight on her the springs in them creaked with every breath and with every lurch of the train. She wasn't only thinking about what my father had done, I knew that. She was always crabby and worried when she was away from our house and it was raining, she was afraid the Nant would flood the yard, and pour into our passage and front rooms before my granny could hobble across to put the boards up and plug them with the red clay. But there was one thing nice about her, she filled the compartment with her rich holiday smell of sweet biscuits, and lavender water, and bag leather.

It took us the best part of an hour to reach Pencwm, where we had to change trains for Abergarth. It was still emptying when we got there, although the lightning had stopped, and the grumble of the thunder was a long way off. As we crossed the railway bridge I could hear the solid rain sweeping like showers of ball-bearings across the curved corrugated iron roof. I jumped up to see, between the roof and the iron-panelled sides of the bridge, if our connection was waiting. I got a nasty shock. Our train for Abergarth was backing slowly into the station in the middle of a lot of blown-about smoke, and I could see as usual we were going to have plenty of room on it, because the platform was almost empty. The Ystrad people called this the pigeon special because of the big baskets of homers always filling the guard's van on it, it was very slow between Pencwm and Abergarth and usually there was hardly anybody on it except these pigeons, and two or three old men carrying rods and waders, and with fishing-flies stuck on their dai-caps.

I jumped again to make sure. 'You go on,' I said to my mother, 'my bootlace is undone. I'll catch you up.'

For cycling my father wore a little cloth cap, brown boots, and leggings held on with corkscrew straps. I couldn't see what suit he had on instead of the one soaked in the river, because the long grey dust-coat he always wore in the warehouse covered him. It was soaking wet, in fact there couldn't have been a dry thread on him from cap to boots, and his feet were in a puddle of water he had dripped himself. Across his back he carried his fishing-rods. The cloud-burst must have daunted him and he had given up his ride to Abergarth to catch the train.

When I jumped the first time on the bridge, I spotted him on the covered platform standing beside Rees's monster, watching our train backing into the station. By the third jump he must have seen my mother because he was hurrying down the platform wheeling the bike, the saddle up to his shoulder, rising up on his toes at every step as he always did when he wanted to show he was in a cocky mood, and every now and then giving his moustaches a twirl. The rain was heavy out there where the platform was without a roof, it dropped around him upright as wallpaper and he knew my mother in her velvet most likely wouldn't follow him out into it. When he got to the guard's van he took a quick look round over his shoulder, pushed the bike inside, and disappeared in after it.

My mother had seen him too by this time, she guessed he wasn't going to come out again so she climbed into the nearest compartment and I ran down the bridge steps and got in after her.

At last the train started and she hardly opened her mouth all the way to Abergarth. She could do this fine; once she didn't talk to my father for a week, it was the time he was about with a big black eye, he had banged into the latch of the bootroom door in the dark. She sat all the way without a word, every now and then rubbing her stick of menthol across her forehead to make her stop worrying so much. Her gipsy face was pale and crotchety, and a bright raggedy blotch burned like red paint on each of her cheeks. My father stayed out of the way, most likely he was busy in the guard's van wringing his shirt and drovers out among the pigeons.

It was dull with nothing to do, and nothing to eat, and nobody to talk to, just watching the hills and the soaking fields moving round and round on their turntables for miles and miles. Out here in the country everything passed by slowly and far away from the train, it wasn't exciting like travelling up the valley, where the bridges and trucks, and whole rows of houses suddenly hurtled past the carriage windows as though they were chucked at you, and were missing you by inches. There were a lot of good bends in the line, though, and you could look out of the window and see the sunlit side of the engine and the coaches of our train curving round in front of us, and the smoke bending down into the fields and disappearing. As I sat on the seat opposite my mother I got so bored I even began to wish I was one of the Powell kids, because then most likely I'd be under it, travelling without a ticket, and dodging the ticket collector in the lavatory; and that would have been more exciting than just looking out of the window. I had noticed my father had his *pince-nez* on on the platform, although he had come out of the river the day before without them. He had found them that morning, my mother said. She didn't want to tell me about it but I moithered her a bit for something to do. When he went out into the yard early to go off on the machine, she said, he saw half a tree stuck fast in the grating in our river, it had floated down during the night; the top half, and dead; no leaves or bark on it; only the lost pair of *pince-nez*, dangling from one of the twigs like a leaf on a cobweb, hanging by its chain, and flashing round and round in the sunlight and the little breeze. She started to smile, and then she looked at me and stopped suddenly and gave me a sour look instead, and stared out of the window again.

When we reached Abergarth at last the rain was over, but it

was cold, and all the pavements were still soaking. Myrddin Tŷ-coch, my auntie's half-daft odd-job boy, was on the platform waiting for us, grinning, clean and tidy for once except for his teeth, his boots newly greased and his cloth cap on his head the right way round. He had brought the iron hand-truck they used for the barrels in the pub to carry our luggage. I never liked talking to Myrddin when my father and mother could hear, because he was always on about girls and babies and that, and about dogs stuck together under the bridge so that all the horses and carts had to go round them. He told me years ago he was a bastard, before I was sure what a bastard was, and now as he wheeled the truck from the station he started on about the same thing again. Born in a cowshed, he'd been, he said, his mother gave birth to him the same minute as the cow dropped her calf in the next stall. He told me he didn't mind anybody calling him a bastard, but he wouldn't let didn't matter who it was call him a sod. Did I know what a sod was? I would be daft to let anybody call me a sod, he could tell me that. And then all the way to the Vaughan Arms I worried because I couldn't think how I was going to stop them.

So we walked on through the streets from the station to my auntie's, me and Myrddin at the back wheeling our roped-up luggage on the truck, and my father and mother in front with the bike between them, my mother the height of a policeman and her purple costume going in at the waist like a bed-spring, and my father in his long dust-coat, trying to make himself taller by rising on the toes of his boots at every step. They didn't say a word to each other all the way, they looked pretty peculiar together always, walking, because even without her big hat on she was about a head and a half taller than he was.

WHEN I woke up in my bedroom in the Vaughan Arms the next morning the first thing I saw was my father, stripped to the waist, standing very skinny and furry on the footstool in front of the fireplace, examining the top of his head in the mirror. He had moved the chalk dogs and the other ornaments to the side of the mantelpiece so that he could do this easier, and his inside-out vest he had tossed on to the bed beside me. Since he had been using that electric box for his rheumatism he had become so shaggy that the vest was covered with a thick mat of red fur inside, it looked exactly like the harness-flannel of a chestnut horse, under the saddle, or the inside of the collar. But in spite of that, the hair on the top of his head, although he kept it pretty long, got thinner and thinner, and he sent away for everything he saw advertised in the paper to try to stop it; a green ointment out of a tin stinking like goose-grease he had at one time, and a blue oil that oozed through a rubber massager; even a special soft soap and a sort of head-razor for shaving the thin parts to encourage the growth—he had tried them all. This morning he had a test-tube of what looked like thick milk in his hand, and on the mantelpiece was the narrow little cardboard box with our Ystrad address on it that it had come by post in. I watched him uncorking the test-tube and pouring some of the white liquid on to his head, massaging it into his hair with his fingers and examining the steam over his *pince-nez*. This was his latest restorer, a Red Indian had given the recipe to the chap who had sent it direct to the Dragon Mills. Standing before the mirror on the little stool, naked to the half, very bony, his hanging skin covered with thick red hairs, his head steaming faintly like a sucked thumb—that was the way my father looked the last time I saw him alive.

Because after breakfast, to show big, he went out for a ride on the bike, wearing his new straw boater with the red silk ribbon. He was burning to do a bit of fishing, he said. We heard, after, that as he was coming fast round the corner by the cottage hospital he failed to take the turn and fell off on top of Rice the roadman, using his hook on a bit of low trashing in the hedge. Rice had a big fright, and a bigger one when he saw the bike in a heap on the road with the front wheel still spinning, and my father collapsed half in the ditch, stretched out on his back as though he was dead, and the straw-benjy rolling in through the hospital gates. He called his mate, and between them they carried him after it inside the building. The doctor took one look at him and said he was in the middle of pneumonia, and he would have to stay in bed until the crisis was over.

Every day of the holiday, usually two or three times, I had to go down through Abergarth and out to that cottage hospital to ask about my father. I could hardly ever go swimming because of it, or boating on the lake, or fishing, all I did was tramp to and fro three times a day, because it was too far for my mother in the heat. I never saw my father once, I wasn't old enough they said, but I had to go and sit in the semi-darkness and the strong iodine smell of that creepy old entrance hall, and wait until one of the nurses came down the corridor so that I could ask her how he was.

The Vaughan Arms, the pub kept by my auntie where we were staying in Abergarth, was right in the middle of the town, opposite the monument and the drinking-troughs, half way along the main street where it widened out into a sort of square, the place where the farmers left their carts and gambos tilted in rows on mart days and Saturdays, with their shafts on the cobbles. There were so many public houses in Abergarth they were some-times next door to each other, and the Vaughan Arms was the middle one of three in a row, with the Plough on one side and the Rock and Fountain on the other. It was one of the oldest pubs in town, people said, built on top of a cave, and the walls were about a yard thick, so that the small windows were very deep set. I often used to feel frightened there in the night, I heard scratchings and creepy sounds, because it was haunted. Myrddin told me that once when he put his hand out to open a door in the

48

cellar a white hand appeared in front of his and opened it for him. For a long time after that I used to grab all the door-knobs suddenly before the white hand had time to turn them. And when I was upstairs in bed on my own in the dark, I often used to hear those noises in the wall, sometimes a whirring sound, or a chair being rubbed across the floor to and fro, to and fro, or someone handling a heavy chain stealthily as though they didn't want to make a noise. That was one of the things I didn't like about the Vaughan Arms, and I don't think my father and mother liked the noises they heard either.

The first thing I noticed about the pub every time we went there was the colour of the outside, and the second was the smell of the inside. From the street it was a square whitewashed building under the biggest roof of the thickest and heaviest tiles I had ever seen, it looked as though it was roofed with moss and hymn-books, the ridge dipping under the weight and gone into the sag of a slack clothes-line. The whitewash on the walls wasn't very white, it was a dirty vegetable green, it must have had a few bucketfuls of fresh cow-dung mixed in it, and as well as growing lovely puffs of ragwort and red valerian in every crack, it gave the walls a seaweedy look as though they'd been wiped over with laver bread. You could tell how old the pub was as well by the mounting block near one of the windows and the tethering rings one each side of the door.

You noticed the smell of the pub as soon as you went in through the front door and along the slate slabs of the passage, it was like masses of dead flowers gone strong, I always thought, or the hoppy smell of the Martyr's opposite us in the Square when they were brewing, but a lot staler; it was made up of strong beer, and old vomit, and tobacco smoke, and spit, and horse-piss, and sweaty harness from the stables out the back. But mostly it was the stale stink of old beer, it had spread every-where in the building in the three hundred years or whatever it was the pub had been up; it met you in the bar and the smoke-room, in the living-room upstairs, down the basement, and right up to the second floor and the attic where our bedrooms were. I

49

was always a bit afraid I'd have the niff of it soaking into my clothes, like Davito the chip-shop's boy in our scholarship class: you couldn't sit next to Johnny Davito in the summer because of the niff of fish and chips coming warm and stale off his corduroys and his greasy hands.

My auntie Mag the Vaughan Arms, the one who kept the pub, was a short fat woman, a waddler, always about the bar in a flowery overall and a white hair-net that looked as though it was on to stop the birds pecking the titbits hidden in her mop. She was a thick, five-foot-high trunk of solid lead to bump into, she didn't shift an inch, but all the soft flesh of her body, her big bosoms, her cheeks, her dangling nose, the skin-pouch under her chin—their whole weight hung down heavy and helpless on her, as though they were being tugged down very hard towards the floor by something or other pretty powerful. She served meals in the pub basement, and when I saw her standing in her packed overall in the middle of the long tables down there, or frying ham and eggs by the big black fireplace, it looked to me as though the force of gravity was dragging a lot harder at what was hanging inside her overall than at the timber and the iron-work standing upright and rigid all round her.

The pub was usually very quiet all the week, my auntie Mag didn't believe in strong drink, but on mart days and Saturdays, according to her, she didn't have time to spit, the farmers were in and out of the place all the time, not only in the bar, but leading their horses in through the front door and along the passage to the stabling out the back, and using the private room for writing, and going down the corkscrew steps to the basement for a meal. This basement was a long narrow room dug out of the rock right under the pub, the walls were covered with thin dirty whitewash and there was a skylight at each end. When my father took me out fishing, sometimes, early in the morning, I often used to lie on the table there in semi-darkness, waiting for him to come down from bed, watching my auntie Mag having a shave under the dim skylight, and when the place was empty like this it looked terrible, very shabby and gloomy under the low rock roof, exactly like a dungeon, with the dust and the heavy cobwebs everywhere and the cinders piled up high in the grate. But by dinner time it was crowded with farmers eating their dinners round the long tables, and talking and laughing under the hanging oil lamps, and then there was nothing wrong with it.

My auntie did the cooking by the fireplace, she stood there red and sweating in her stockinged feet, there was so much sweat and so many tangles in her hair it looked under her net like black bunches of sopping bladder-wrack. She must have been the sweatiest publican in Abergarth, and every now and then you'd see her pushing her towel down inside her overall to wipe under her armpits. The farmers didn't seem to notice the stale fat smell of her cooking, but it used to turn my stomach up. I liked my auntie Mag, but although there was always a tableful in the Vaughan Arms I couldn't stand anything she made—even if she gave you a cup of tea it was like gravy, with coins of fat floating on it, and she used to put so much beer in her cake you couldn't cut it.

But this was Monday afternoon, and quiet, the weather was sunny and very hot, and I had been spending my time after dinner down the hospital as usual, waiting to hear how my father was. On the way back to the Vaughan Arms I stood for a bit at the end of the Abergarth High Street, leaning against the warm-blooded wall and looking along it, and I thought about Ystrad, and I wished I could be back there and up the butts, or in the long grass with Tom and Charley and Jeffy Urquhart. Although it was the middle of the afternoon there wasn't a single person in sight in the whole length of the main street in front of me, everything from one end to the other was dead still, and silent, and deserted, it was exactly like a coloured picture post-card, showing all the striped shop blinds out over the pavements, and the sun pouring down hot on the empty road, baking up one side of the street and blackening the other with shadows. Only one living thing was to be seen, and that was too hot to move— the Rock and Fountain's retriever bitch lying fast asleep among the horse-tods in the middle of the road.

I dawdled up the pavement, kicking the wall, on the opposite side from the Vaughan Arms, because it was a bit cooler walking the street in the long blue prism of shade than in the sun, and also because I always liked looking at the brand-new riding harness, and the spurs shining like silver, and the wrinkled, bone-handled riding-crops in the saddler's window. I knew Thomas the saddler well, his house above the shop was one of the places my mother and father always went to to supper every time we stayed at Abergarth, and I did think once of asking him to sew me up a leather sheath for my knife. But I was afraid it would cost too much, and Thomas might blab about it to my mother or my auntie Mag.

Thomas's shop was right opposite the Vaughan Arms; and standing in the middle of the wide main street, the sort of square, between them, was the statue of some old curly general from Abergarth, wearing a bullet-proof chest and a big sword. He was made of white marble and he stood on a square shiny base of black granite. Around him were railings formed of out-size rifles, or most likely they were muskets, criss-crossed and with hanging slings and fixed bayonets, all solid iron and painted brown. There were two long horse-troughs there as well, filled with drinking water, one against the muskets facing Thomas the saddler's and one right opposite the Vaughan Arms.

All the blinds of the High Street shops seemed to be down against the sun, including the saddler's, so I crossed into the middle of the road where the statue was, and looked down into the water filling the drinking-trough on the Vaughan Arms side. It was fresh and clear, and full of sunlight, the horses hadn't started drinking from it yet and there was no chaff floated off their muzzles to be seen on the surface. With my back to the inn, I leaned my elbow on the edge of the iron trough, and ran my fingers to and fro in the lovely cool water. Then suddenly I heard a shout behind me from the Vaughan Arms.

I was right opposite the entrance to the inn, only half the width of the road and the pebble pavement separated me from the front door of it. When I turned round I saw the sunlight pouring in through the open doorway on to the large mat and the slate flagstones at the entrance to the passage. Beyond this glaring square, the long passage itself leading to the yard at the rear was pitch-black, it was impossible to make out anything in the darkness of it. But at the far end again I could see an upright oblong of bright sunlight—the open door leading out into the stable yard at the back of the inn.

As I looked from the street along the dark passage, I saw something out in the yard at the far end that I couldn't believe. Standing dark against the brilliant white of the stable wall, and looking out towards me, was the young man my father had rescued from the river the week before, he stood there facing me, the dazzling light falling over his face like a golden visor, smiling down the passage for a moment or two as though he meant to come along it and out into the bright sunlight of High Street.

I didn't know what to do. I stood leaning back against the horse-trough, weak, and excited, and happy. I wanted more than anything to speak to him, I knew he would be friendly, and yet I was afraid at the same time. I waited a bit, just staring. I didn't know what I was waiting for, and then I ran across the road, in through the open door and along the passage towards him, my heart thumping as though it would beat out a great hole in the front of my chest. Half way along I saw the door at the far end slam, and everything went black, and the next moment I was sprawling on the broken flagstones of the passage. I lay there a moment or two dazed, and then I sprang to my feet and battled on again to the door in the darkness. After a bit of groping I managed to throw it open and look out into the fresh air of the yard.

There was no sign of the young man. Near the wall at the far end I could see Myrddin the odd-job boy wheeling a loaded muck-barrow out of the stable across to the dung-heap in the corner. About sixteen Myrddin was, I think, he was very strong and half daft, and filthy now through forking horse-muck, his boots and his khaki breeches covered with old mud and dung;

he had no coat or waistcoat on over his grey flannel shirt, and the peak of his cap was on the nape of his neck. He put down the barrow when he saw me, came across the yard, and hit me a hard blow in the chest with his fist. 'Hallo, Dewi,' he said, shoving his brown saw-teeth and the long-end smell of his grin into my face. 'How's your daddy today, *bach*?'

It was always best not to show Myrddin you wanted to know something because if you did he wouldn't tell you. Everybody knew he was one of the biggest liars in Abergarth, anyway, so I said my father was just the same, and I asked him if there were any horses in the stable.

'Pity, *bach*, pity,' he said. 'Not on a Monday, mun,' he went on in a different voice. He took a few pages of a book and one hard cover out of the back pocket of his khaki breeches. 'Have you ever read about them Russians, Dewi?' he asked me.

'What?' I said.

'Blackguards, *bach*,' he said, 'them Russians. Blackguards.'

'Was anybody in the yard a minute ago, Myrddin?'

He put on his daft grin again. 'I was,' he said.

In the end I went round the stables myself, although he tried to keep me back describing how his mother gave birth to him in the train on the way to the farmers' exhibition; I searched through all the sheds and outhouses in the yard and looked into all the mounds of shadow heaped like rubbish behind the walls, but I couldn't find a trace of the young man. In the end I left Myrddin sitting in the muck-barrow smoking a home-made fag and pretending to read about the Russians, and I went to give my mother the message from the hospital. Then I climbed up the Allt by myself to have a quiet think for a bit and to look at the knife. I had it hanging low round my neck on a piece of tape with the blade in my old blue marble-bag, under my shirt. It seemed by far the most beautiful thing I had ever owned, I had never seen anything half so lovely and so beautifully designed and made, the polished silver of the steel blade and the slim scale-netted serpents forming the hilt with their ruby eyes and the snaky-slender out-sweeping tails of the guard. I sat in the bracken turning it sharply in the sunlight, making the blade shine like a flashing-glass, thinking of the silver-haired boy with the ear-rings and the brown riding-boots who had left it for me. Where had he got it from? I thought of the adventures he had won it in, perhaps, through his bravery, coming out victorious in the end after defeats, and all sorts of dangers. Would I ever see him again? Although I had missed him that afternoon I felt sure I was going to, and although I had never spoken to him he filled my thoughts all the time, he was like someone I had already known for years, who had always been there, ever since my childhood.

6

EVERY morning when I woke up in the Vaughan Arms with the blue dagger of the daylight between the curtains, I began thinking of what I had seen that afternoon in the stable yard through the passage downstairs. What had I seen? I imagined the happening dozens of time every day, I was haunted by it, sometimes I got into a fever thinking time after time after time of every detail that had taken place. I hadn't enjoyed the first few days of the holiday but now I hated the thought of going home, I wanted to stay in Abergarth in the hope of catching a glimpse of the young man again, or perhaps a real look, perhaps even to see him long enough for him to notice me, and give me a chance to speak to him.

As I sat in the entrance hall of the hospital a day or two after, the nurse came and told me my father had passed the crisis during the night, he was weak, but he was going to get better for certain. Back in the Vaughan Arms I could hear my mother in the bar telling my auntie at the top of her voice the best way to run the pub, and when I gave her the message the first thing she said was: 'That will give me a chance to do a bit of visiting at last. And there's no need for you to stay here any longer, Dewi. You can return to your granny tomorrow.'

I didn't want to go home, not now, and I started arguing with her, but she stared with iron eyes when she wanted to daunt me and I gave up. I had a real feeling I wouldn't see the young man in Ystrad, he was here, about me, in Abergarth, I was conscious of him all the time, but I thought perhaps it wouldn't be so bad if I called for Charley and Jeffy as soon as I got home and we'd go up the Swamp for a swim, or light a fire on the mountain. My mother went out of the empty bar, and as I was thinking what else we could do I heard her filling the pub, and most of Abergarth High Street, too, by the loudness of her voice, with 'Praise God from whom all blessings flow', accompanying herself to *Hen Ganfed* on the upstairs harmonium.

I knew the cottage hospital waiting-room pretty well after all the time I had spent in it, and I hated it. It was the entrance hall to the old mansion really, a pretty dark and gloomy sort of a place even in bright sunshine, very enclosed so that I always felt trapped in it, with three or four dusty stained-glass windows around it high up, letting in hardly any light; and with red and yellow tiles with coats of arms covering the floor, and carved wooden panelling of dark kitchen-door brown reaching half way up the brick walls. There was a very wide wooden staircase, all carved and varnished, coming down into the hall from upstairs, and carved wooden benches like chapel pews, for visitors, stood against the panelled walls. All the woodwork, and this entrance hall was mostly woodwork, was old and brown, nearly black with age, and as I waited there I used to listen to it creaking out loud in the heat all the time, or making tapping noises; at first I got a bit frightened, sitting there by myself in semi-darkness, because in the dead silence the noises sounded very uncanny, as though there was something pretty ghostly and furtive moving there, slowly creeping down the stairs in the semi-darkness and prowling towards me over the floor.

My mother had come to the hospital with me, but she had

gone down the corridor and into the ward to see my father. That afternoon we had been to visit my uncle Walter Lloyd, my mother's stepbrother or something I think he was, a no-good old soak living by himself out over the river bridge in the country. We walked the dusty road until we came to two little cottages standing right at the grass verge of the roadway, miles from anywhere, and the dirty one was uncle Walter's. It was no good knocking at the front door, it had thick ivy growing across it, so we went in through the squealing iron gate at the side and around to the back. There we came into a yard that was under a thick covering of ashes and tarry goose-droppings like cheroots, and in the middle of it we saw a little red-necked man sitting on a flagon-case by the pump with his back to us. 'Hallo, Walter,' my mother said to him, and at that he worked himself round slowly on the box so that he could face us.

He was a short stout man with a red-hot face, so round and flat and big it looked as though it ought to have fingers going round on it, it would have done fine for the face of a town clock, it glowed in a flat disc and a thin cloth cap, black in colour, lay dead straight on top of it. He didn't answer my mother, he just sat staring at us as we came towards him over the dung and ashes, his boot and sock beside him on the ground, and a dirty roller towel hanging down over his right knee. I could see that his leg behind it and his foot were bare.

When we reached him my mother said: 'Hallo, Walter,' again. 'How are you, boy?'

'Good day, mum,' he said, touching his cap to her.

'Good day, mum!' she shouted. 'What do you mean, "Good day, mum"? Don't you know me, Walter?'

'No, mum,' he answered, touching his cap again. He was so drunk he could hardly talk.

'Now, none of your manœuvres, Walter,' she said. 'You know me well enough. I'm Carrie, your sister, Jack Davies's wife from Ystrad.'

While she was explaining I was looking at this uncle Walter Lloyd's inflamed face and neck, and I could see they were covered with invisible ginger hair, all in swirls, like the fur of a pig. He remembered my mother at last, one day when she was a little girl she ran out into the snow in her nightshirt. He took the towel off his knee and showed us his leg. It nearly made me faint. There was a huge gash along the side of the calf that looked as though a deep groove had been lifted out of the flesh, it was the bright red of butcher's meat, very wide and deep and wet looking, and the shape of a smooth potato-furrow. The cut had a wide braid of black scabs around it, and outside that the flesh was a greenish plum-colour, and the rest of the leg was saffron. All the time he was telling us about the fall that had caused it he kept touching it, and squeezing it with his dirty fingers. It didn't seem to hurt him at all, but I could hardly bear to watch him and all I wanted was for him to put the towel back over it to hide it.

My mother began a big argument with him, ordering him to do this and that. Why didn't he see the doctor, why didn't he do something about the garden, why didn't he go nearer the town to live, and not bury himself in a wilderness like this? Why didn't he go and stay with his sister in the Vaughan Arms until he could look after himself again?

'And live on tea and titty?' he growled at her. 'She'd never spare me so much as a pint. And have you ever tried eating our Mag's dinners?'

What was he doing for the cut? she wanted to know. Wasn't he afraid it would turn septic? He must see the doctor at once.

'This is what I'm doing,' he answered. He turned round on the box, put his bare leg under the spout of the pump and started pumping water into the groove. Although he wasn't willing at all for her to interfere, she tidied the cottage up a bit, and washed out a few rags for him, and spread them on the black-currant bushes round the garden to dry. When we got him up off the box to go back into the cottage he was so lame and drunk he could hardly walk, we had to help him across the back yard and put him in his armchair by the fireplace. But before we got him there he was sick, the beer made hardly any sound coming out of him, or any struggle, he just opened his mouth and let it pour up quietly, he was so used to it, and all we heard was the loud splash it made on the ashes of the yard.

We were very late coming away from my uncle Walter's after that, and we weren't able to go back to the Vaughan Arms; it was evening visiting time at the cottage hospital, so we went on past the old church and down the footpath to the hospital that way. The sky was pretty peculiar, but nice, very clear and a warm blue, and there were long solid fillets of radiant cloud laid out on it, flaky and bright, yellow in the sunset, like golden haddock. The iron clock on the church struck eight. The tower and the spire rising out of it were covered with the leafless stalks of some thick dead creeper, there were masses of them, the spire had an unshaved look because of them. As we passed, it appeared furry against the clear light of the evening, pointed like a magician's cap, only very hairy, and the rooks kept sailing round and round it, black as stirred tea-leaves in the sunlight, cawing out loud as though they were being disturbed.

My mother went in to see my father as soon as we reached the hospital and I sat in the entrance hall again by myself, to wait for her. It had started to get a bit dusky in that place already and I hoped she wouldn't be long. I began to think a lot about spewing, and how stinking it was, about my granny back in Ystrad trying to throw up for hours when she had the bile, and making so much noise we could hear her retching across the yard; and then I pictured uncle Walter spewing from his hip without a sound, just letting it pour up like a bottle of water turned upside-down. I hoped my mother wouldn't be long, I was hungry and I knew my auntie had pie with a bit of burnt on the crust for supper, the only really nice supper she made.

As I sat there waiting I began to hear the sound of slow heavy boots crunching on the gravel drive outside. I turned and looked out through the wide-open double doors. The air there had turned the colour of marmalade, but there was nobody to be seen. The sound drew nearer and nearer, and presently a policeman came into the entrance hall followed by two men carrying a shabby old house door between them like a stretcher. There was a body on it covered over with a brown blanket.

'Stay here in the hall, boys,' the policeman said in Welsh to the two bearers. 'I'll go round and find the matron. I won't be a second.'

He went off past me making a big noise with his nails on the tiled corridor, he seemed to be quite at home as though he knew all about the place. The two men came in and stood, still holding the door, right in front of the pew I was sitting in. I recognized one of them, the one in front wearing the blue overalls, when I was small he used to be Ffonso, our milkman in Ystrad, but he had left our valley years ago to live with his sister here in Abergarth; now he was the odd-job man of the place, sometimes he carried the post, or dragged the furniture to the front in the auction-rooms, but mostly he worked about the church, he pulled the bell and dug the graves and cut the grass in the burial-ground. I remembered him because my father was always talking about him, and saying what a marvellous fly-fisherman Ffonso was, wet or dry, he could toss a matchbox into the Garth river, so my father said, and then stand on the bank with his rod and drop a fly right on top of it as it was floating down the current. I didn't know the other man for certain but I thought most likely by the look and the smell of him he was Rice the roadman; he had no coat on, I noticed, his boots were clayey and he wore straps below the knees of his corduroys. Both Ffonso and Rice were sweating with the heat and the weight.

When Ffonso recognized me he nodded and grinned. '*Duw*, this bloke's a weight, aye,' he said.

'Who is he, Ffonso?' I said.

'Don't know, mun,' he answered. 'Find him we did, like. Me and Davy by here. In the grass. Fell off the roof, must have.'

'What roof, Ffonso?'

'The church, mun. Must have been climbing the steeple, and the creeper come away. Bloody mad, aye.'

'Have you carried him here from the church?'

'Too true we have. Haven't us, Davy?'

Davy nodded but he didn't say anything. I remembered him for sure now. One night I had seen from the upstairs windows at the back of the Vaughan Arms a large cluster of brilliant red lights, like warm, ruby-coloured glow-worms, floating smooth as the lights of a boat in the darkness across the fields between the river and the back wall of the pub. They were so beautiful, and creepy as well, I had to stand and watch them. They came nearer and nearer as though they were afloat on the flood of darkness, and when they were a few yards from the wall I could see what they were: this Davy Rice the roadman was wheeling a barrow full of red oil-lamps out on to a job on the road; he had had them in his cottage, cleaning them and filling them up for the night, and lighting all the wicks. And he was the man, must be, my father had fallen on top of when Rees Mawr's bike failed to take the turning by the cottage hospital.

'Is he hurt much?' I asked Ffonso.

'Unconscious, whatever. *Duw*, I wish that bobby would hurry. Wonder he's alive, aye.'

'Do you know him?'

'Never seen him before, mun. Complete stranger everybody do say. Nobody don't know him. That's why the bobby told us to bring him in by here, like. Nowhere else to put him. For the night, he said.'

Just then I could hear the policeman coming back along the corridor, and someone walking with him. When the two rounded the corner into the entrance hall I recognized the matron in her white cap and cuffs. They came up to the body without a word, and the matron turned back the end of the blanket. At what I saw I felt the hair on my head coming alive, as though there was a powerful electric current shooting through it. The face under the blanket was yellow, very ill looking, the flesh in the dim light the sickly colour of thin custard; the eyes, closed, and dark with bruises, were concealed under black and purple, shaped like a highwayman's mask, or one of those masqueraders' in a domino ball. There was dried blood sticking the short hair together and spread all over the skin down one side of the face, right on to the collar. I had seen this face before, and in this lying-down position. I recognized the white cut-down hair and the silver earrings. It was the face of the young man my father had rescued from the river, and that I had seen for a second in the stable yard of the Vaughan Arms a day or two before.

What the matron had been saying while I was staring at the young man I don't know, but the next thing I realized was that the face was covered over again, and the bearers were moving off down one of the corridors, carrying the door with the body on it, and I saw my mother marching towards me across the hall.

'A lot better again,' she said. 'There's a blessing. Come on. You must have a good night's sleep before you go home in the morning.'

'Am I bound to go home?' I asked her.

She looked startled and angry. 'I thought you were dying to,' she said. 'You must go in any case, and take that machine of Rees's with you on the train.'

I wanted more than anything to stay to talk with Ffonso after he had carried the young man into the ward. Or perhaps I could find him working in the graveyard tomorrow. I wouldn't have minded coming to the hospital every day to see the young man, and to find out more about him, and thank him for the silver knife. The thought of him, whenever I remembered him suddenly, was like a warm glow, and very comfortable, the memory of his face was like being cold in winter and putting on a coat hot from in front of the fire.

PART TWO

I

THE first morning assembly in the school hall after the summer holidays, we saw almost the same old gang as before the break hobbling and limping in their gowns on to the staff platform— Beynon geogger was up there chewing his false teeth already, Pegger Armstrong swinging his clicking limp, Tossy English, his head like a cottage with the thatch on fire, and Roderick the headmaster, Growler we called him, the thick wide lips of his purple face in a frog's turn-down, and his belly so swollen he looked like a woman going to have a couple of heavy babies. He was starting the term well. Whenever he sat down he had the habit of hitching his trousers up higher and higher at the fork and he came on to the platform with his trouser legs up near his knees, showing his fat calves and his white underpants and his suspenders holding up his woollen stockings.

None of us could bear this Growler. In school he would often roll top-heavy into a classroom, stop the teacher, and take the lesson himself. He had no more manners than a ram. He fancied he was the best teacher in school, doesn't matter what the subject was, even woodwork. And singing. When Cooper our music teacher taught the whole school part-songs in the hall on Friday afternoons, Growler would roll round among us with a five-shilling piece between his fingers; when we were standing there singing our parts he would push the coin into our mouths vertical, right in between our teeth and half way down our throats, to make us open our mouths wider. And to show us what he meant he used to shove his fist and the five bob down his own throat as well, and that was a lot easier for him than for us because he had an opening like a public oven, and his whole gob was slack and flabby as well, as though he'd had too much dumtit as a baby. But the sound he made when he really started singing himself was tremendous, he had a bass voice that shook the flooring under your feet when he really poured it out, it was thrilling to hear him, and you could feel everything humming and vibrating with the power and the volume, yourself from the boots up included.

If you couldn't answer Growler's questions in any subject he would get his hair off and bully you, although he was a dab-hand at mixing you up, and half the time it was hard to make out what he was talking about. He was the most deadening teacher in school, everybody said that. He used to make jokes and the only one to laugh at them was Growler himself, and usually the teacher standing in the corner would manage to work up a weak sort of grin if Growler turned round and looked at him. You never knew what he meant, or what he was going to do, or what he was thinking. For one thing he had his own private language, a sort of special double-Dutch, and he used words that none of us had ever heard of before except in a book. If it was raining cats and dogs, or the whole valley was under one sheet of ice, he always called that 'inclement weather'; and if you were really hopeless in a subject, according to him you were 'woefully weak'. 'Deplorable' was another word he used and 'offices' for dubliws. Some of the boys spent every break playing bobby-slops round the school dubs, chasing each other with their belts or their scarves twisted into slashers, and one day Jonno Nicholas pulled the corner of the wall off when he was swinging round it in a hurry, a huge chunk of Bath stone most likely weighing a couple of hundredweights fell off. Growler had the whole school in the hall next morning to find out who'd done it, and the first words he boomed out when we were all settled were, 'Which of us bit a lump out of the offices?' One or two boys tittered a bit, but he bawled at them so much they got frightened and shut up. Growler was a sort of savage when he got really narky, he growled and bellowed about the school raving like a great mad pipe-organ, like Watkins the organist in a *hwyl* palavering on the thunder-pedals in Libanus after chapel, shaking the building, and if the news went around he had his rag out everybody crept about the corridors without saying a word.

Sometimes when you expected a good dose of the strap for something, Growler would only whip his glasses off, cough his chesty old laugh up at the ceiling and then rock off down the corridor. But any time he was in the classroom with you, you could feel him right up to the walls, and there were five or six boys in our form, Growler had shattered them as to their nerves, he had only got to give them half a look to make them start pulling their ties round like mad, and flattening their hair, and trying to look a bit more interested or intelligent, because you never knew for sure what he would start getting into a rage about.

Growler looked pretty funny in school, short and fat in his darned pawnshop clothes, all frayed and dyed and baggy, and his tattered acid-stained gown over them, big enough to make a couple of suits and an overcoat for him. But in his moth-hunting get-up he looked terrible. Because that's what his hobby was, moths and butterflies. Sometimes he used to terrify the people living up the Ystrad mountain, he used to hide among the trees in the dark by the side of the road, with a white sheet over him to attract the moths. He had about the best collection in the whole country, people said, he often gave the school stamp club postage stamps he got on letters from all over the world asking about it. He was a short man, not much taller than my father used to be, but a lot heavier and fatter in the belly. And uglier. Everybody's temples as far as I could see, went *in*, but Growler had a big lump of fat stuffed in there on each side of his head, so that his came *out*. He had a huge top-heavy head, bald, but with washed yellow hair spread lightly across it like a layer of marzipan. He had a low spread-out nose too, and a mouth so wide you expected it to join up at the back of his neck when he grinned: and deep winy skin the colour of a purple apple, pitted all over with holes as though he slept every night on knitting.

All the teachers were present the first day back, except Sheepy Upton. Sheepy was missing. Everybody said thank God. Everybody but Charley Llewellyn, that is. Charley always got good marks off Sheepy for ordering horse-manure for him cheap

67

off the farm. By playtime, the rumour was going round the yard Sheepy had committed suicide. Growler had given him the shove for being hopeless and he had gone up England somewhere and put his head in a gas oven. Everybody said that showed what a peculiar sort of bloke Upton was, because it was taken for granted that if anybody from Ystrad wanted to commit suicide he drowned himself in the Swamp, the pond we had up the mountain. The boys who started the buzz about the suicide were Bleddyn and Alcwyn, their father was Reynolds the chief constable of Ystrad, and they used to listen behind the door if he was on the phone about our masters or anybody special we knew.

This Sheepy was always a bit mental anyway. At one time he would never go home after school without locking up all the chem cupboards three or four times, and wandering round the lab touching everything and muttering—the taps and the benches and the blackboards, to make sure they were all there. The first winter we were in the grammar school he taught us chem wearing woollen gloves and a long scarf wound round and round his neck, and two or three waistcoats. He kept all the Bunsen burners in the lab alight to warm him up a bit and he had a boy doing sentry-go at the end of the science corridor to signal him if Growler was parading so that he could give us the wink to turn them all out. And now everybody said he had gassed himself.

My father was dead too. He was getting on fine after the pneumonia in Abergarth, but according to what Doctor Lilley said some disease you catch from a dowsing in rat-infested water finished him. My mother took over the business pretty soon. Goodbye cartwheel hats and big puff sleeves and plush and purple costumes; she hardly ever went out now except up town to chapel, she wore her black flannel skirt and bodice and her pinafore all the time and she left all the dressing up to my auntie Bronny. She looked grumpier than ever, and more disgusted, snapping at everybody all the time—'Leave off at once', 'Give over, will you?'—that's how she governed me all day long, and 'Get out of my way, you're dull as shop bread', or 'There it is,

68

if it had teeth it would bite you'. And she was mingier than ever, I couldn't get a penny out of her, and if I grumbled she would say: 'You get plenty. Too much pudding will choke the dog. Go on with your homework.' But she slaved like an engine herself and she loved managing the business really. When my father was alive she always used to argue with him about what we ought to do to sell more clothing and footwear, and she grumbled he was more cut out for gallivanting the valleys than for being tied down to the business. But now she was her own boss and she didn't have to say ay, ay, and amen to him or any-body else. Fair play, everybody knew she was straight as a die, she'd force a receipt for tuppence on you, people said. One of the first things she decided to do was to sack old Rees Mawr, our warehouseman. She got my auntie Bronny to give up the millinery workroom where she was first hand, and take his job over, part of it anyway, as well as a bit of my father's collecting round. My mother had always been pestering my father to give Rees the push, but he wouldn't, because Rees had been raised with my grandfather, and he had water-trouble, and a boy still on the breast, and he had been wounded in the behind in South Africa. My mother said she was surprised the Boers had been able to wound him there, because whenever she saw him he was sitting on it. My granny and old Rees were always arguing and quarrelling too, but my granny was the one who said my mother oughtn't to give Rees the sack, and she brought up all my father's excuses. In the end my mother let him stay on part-time.

One of the schemes my father thought up a few weeks before he died was to buy a pony and trap to deliver our suits and foot-wear and that to our customers who lived too far down the valley to call and fetch them. His idea was—at last—to sell all the old, broken, worn-out machinery collected in the ground floor of the factory, and make a stable there on one side of the arch, and what he called a coach-house on the other. I looked forward to this, I fancied myself driving the Welsh pony and trap up and down the valley like Mog Morgan the butcher's grandson, with a grey whippet running under the axle, or perhaps riding the little black mare that I was going to name Lark or Princess up the mountain for a gallop with a saddle on her. But when I mentioned the pony to my mother a couple of weeks after my father died she looked at me as though I had gone mad. She didn't even bother to answer. She had a temper that went up like a fire of shavings all the time, so I got out of the office fast without saying another word.

Our school was two-storeyed, and built of yellow brick, and it stood on a grassy tump above the main road through the town. The playing-fields were on the opposite side of the road, sloping gradually down to the Ystrad river. In the middle of the front lot of school buildings we had a large square of asphalt courtyard, with a ring of grass in the centre. There was a big sort of cement cauldron full of earth and geraniums standing on this grass, held up by four fat little Bath stone boys with broken tuppences. The masters complained a lot about our 3A formroom up there on the first floor of one of the wings overlooking this front courtyard. It was only a converted stockroom really, and they said it was too dark to do any work in; but all the boys in our form thought it was the best classroom in school. For one thing it was very isolated, at the far end of a hollow, resounding passage with only storerooms and stock cupboards in it, it was too far from the rest of the school and up too many steps for any teacher on duty to come along at break or dinner time to see what we were up to, and chuck us all out. Some of the boys in our form used to practically camp there in winter, they kept food in the empty desks at the back, you could smell it, and pets, and a couple of packs of cards; they hid their fags and spanish-root in a hole dug out under a slash in the green baize of the notice board, and Tosh Lewis had a gas-ring as well, and a little saucepan, and his soldering-iron, hidden among the solid geometry on top of the map cupboard.

When we looked out of our classroom windows there wasn't much we could see except that patch of grass in the middle of the asphalt square below us, and the yellow brick walls surrounding the quadrangle, and the corridor windows and the classrooms all round. But on the ground floor, over in that wing directly opposite us, was Growler's private corridor, and his private door into school, and three semicircular steps outside leading up to it from the quad. We could see every visitor Growler had in school, and every master he sent for we were able to watch passing the windows on his way down the corridor; and we could see Growler himself, we could see the burnt-looking lid of hair laid on top of his head anyway, when he left his room and started rolling around on one of his spying visits through the school.

One afternoon when we had been back in school about a fort-night, we were waiting in the classroom for Lucas, our French master, to come in to look after us. The lesson on the time-table was chemistry really, but because Sheepy hadn't turned up this term the teachers who happened to be free had to supervise us. Most of the boys were shouting and larking about and cribbing homework, and it wasn't long before Tosh and Jonno began wrestling as usual, and the board and easel went over on the hollow floor with them on top of it, crashing like ten cart-loads of coat-hangers tipped together from the gallery in an empty chapel. There was dead silence for a bit after the crash, but nothing happened.

Jeffy Urquhart and Charley Llewellyn were looking out of the formroom window across the yard, keeping an eye on Growler's corridor. They could see him standing outside his room, as he often did when he had sent for somebody, and they were watch-ing him, black-faced behind the big glass doors at the top of the quad steps, meditating hard, picking his nose and flipping it away.

Tom and I were playing golf. We had a hole in the floor-boards by the map cupboard at the back of our classroom, a small one where a knot had dropped out of the timber flooring, and we had invented a putting game for it, we used to try to pot the small roundish ends of blackboard chalk into it in turn with our rulers. Tom was marvellous at it. You couldn't say he was extra good at games, he was too big and stiff, and all the time he had to wear those thick glasses that were so powerful they made you want to spew if you slipped them on when Tom was having a swill; but at this special golf, and billiards, or snooker more like, and at gobbing over the rafters in the school shelters, nobody in our form could touch him.

About a quarter of an hour went past. Lucas had gone down Growler's corridor, Jeffy and Charley told us. Most likely he was having a telling-off off Growler. As a teacher this Lucas was pretty hopeless too, almost as bad as Upton, even the kids in form one used to rag him, although he was big enough to eat them. There was so much noise in our room now it was a wonder Stevens, droning Latin through his nose on the floor below, didn't hop up and hand out a few hundred lines, or shove a few of us into detention. The winner of three games between me and Tom was to play Jeffy Urquhart. Tom won the first two as usual in about five shots and I made my way up to the window to tell Jeffy it was his turn. Then Charley and I leaned together on the cill talking, and looked out of the window down into the quad. I hadn't been with him more than a couple of minutes when I saw two men coming in through the front gates of the school and walking across the wet asphalt towards the steps leading up to Growler's corridor. The one in the top hat and frock coat I recognized immediately as Powell the insurance, Mr Titus Powell, a friend of my father, the conductor of the singing in our chapel. I remembered at once the scenty, warm, man's smell of the inside of that silk hat he was wearing, because I had put it on more than once after Mr Powell had left it in our parlour, and gone into the kitchen to have a talk with my father and my granny. At the sight of the other man something seemed to happen to me, I felt queer and very light, weightless all of a sudden, as if all my flesh had suddenly drifted away from my bones and floated out of the window. It was the young man I had last seen lying unconscious on the house-door in the Abergarth cottage hospital.

I had told Jeffy, Tom and Charley during the holidays what

72

had happened in the factory yard the day we broke up for the summer holidays, and about glimpsing the young man again in hospital. But I had a feeling that Jeffy, anyway, didn't believe me, and as I was telling them about it on the way up for a swim in the pond on Charley's farm, I was looking out of the small of my eyes at him and I could see his face working, making awful shapes and jibs that showed he thought I was telling a big lot of lies. Tom didn't say anything, as usual, his glasses just stared at the ground as we walked up the road, he took it all in as though he heard every day of his life about somebody being pulled out of the river and then suddenly vanishing half drowned, or nearly braining himself falling off the church steeple. Charley didn't believe me either, he put a very haughty look on his face as I was telling them, trying to daunt me, but he didn't look as haughty as he thought he did because he had a long black booggy hanging out of his nose. But I didn't go on, I didn't tell them anything about the silver knife in my bedroom, or about seeing the ghost of the young man or whatever it was at the end of the Vaughan Arms passage. One day I was going to show them the knife when they had got me to tell them the story again. I was going to carry it round my neck under my shirt and bring it out before them when they were all ragging me about what I had said.

'Ay, Charley,' I said, 'you know that chap I was telling you about the other day, the one my old man pulled out of the river?'

I said it as calmly as I could but I felt so strange and excited inside I could sense my colour going up in my face, hot, the way it did when somebody caught me telling lies.

'What about him?' Charley said. He sounded pretty cool and indifferent, I could tell he didn't want to hear any more.

'There he is,' I said, nodding down at the two men standing together on the top step outside the head's door.

Nobody who knew much about our school would have stood there like that, people just turned the door-knob and walked in and waited in the corridor until the head could see them. But these two were knocking on the outside door, at least Mr Powell was, expecting somebody to come and open it for him.

And soon somebody did. As Charley and I leaned there looking across the quad the head's door inside the corridor opened and Lucas came out. He saw Mr Powell and the stranger on the steps outside and took them into Growler's study and soon Lucas's head began bobbing past the corridor windows opposite us in a hurry, so we left our look-out and got back to our seats. 'Lucas,' we said to the boys nearest us, and by the time he had crossed the hall and climbed the steps to our class-room everybody had drifted back to their seats.

We just went on doing what work we fancied with Lucas looking after us, homework or anything. I felt excited at the idea of the young man being so near in the school building, I couldn't concentrate on anything, but somehow after the first shock I wasn't really surprised to see him again, I had thought all the time so much about him that it seemed natural now to catch sight of him almost anywhere. As far as I could see he was all right again after his fall from the steeple. How was it he hadn't killed himself? What did he want the head for, I wondered. And what had he got to do with Mr Titus Powell? Somehow I couldn't imagine him in Academy House with all those dotty Powells, and the cracked walls, and the smells, and the meals I used to see there, rabbit with blood on it, and beef dripping, and skim milk, and the salty broth Buddug made out of potatoes and parsley and scrag end, most likely bought on strap.

When my father was alive this Mr Powell was one of the best friends he had in Libanus chapel, and my granny thought the world of him too, because once she had been in his ladies' choir. He was a tall big-bodied man, very stout and important looking, with an untidy beard, grey, and often with what looked like cobwebs of dried snot on it, as though he had cleaned his fingers in it after wiping his nose with them. He had a very large, pale, bulby nose under a network of prominent veins, scarlet and hard and shiny as threads of sealing-wax. He had a huge bare forehead too and the back of his head was covered with a

74

tight-fitting cap of hair of a bright auburn colour that I thought must be a wig, although my father and mother always grinned and denied it. He was often dressed up like that in his shabby top hat and frock coat and spats over his heavy cracked boots, he was about the only man in Ystrad who didn't keep those clothes for best and funerals. He lived in a row of little houses called Edwards Terrace, behind the tramroad, up near the workhouse. But his house was the big one on the end, a tall, narrow, ramshackle old building with tin cocoa-adverts nearly covering the pine-end, and huge black timber balks leaning against all the front bay windows to stop them falling off into the garden. It was called Academy House. He had a brass plate on the front door with 'T. Powell, L.T.S.C., Professor of Music', on it. Mr Powell seemed to do a bit of everything. Although he was supposed to be Libanus's leader of the singing he often wasn't in chapel on Sunday because he had gone away preaching. Every week in the *News and Banner* the 'Hope of Ystrad' lodge report ended with the words, 'Harmony was provided by Worshipful Brother Powell', and when my father took me to the annual lodge concert I heard Mr Powell on the platform reciting in a big bass voice from *Rhys Lewis* in Welsh, and then in English a piece about old Fagin in jail and waiting for the rope. The day I went up to the grammar school from standard four to sit the scholarship, who should come into the hall with Roderick the headmaster, carrying the big envelope of question papers under his arm, but Mr Powell, and he sat at the table right in front of us all through the exam, scowling round very fierce between his glasses and his bushy eyebrows to stop us copying. At one time, a few years ago, he began going from house to house taking orders for some new kind of tea he was selling, cheap, he said it was, and extra strong, and another time he had his children pushing leaflets through the doors telling us he was now a coal merchant. The Powell kids were a pretty dotty lot though, and that wet night, after they had been round the streets, there were more leaflets plastered all over the pavements than had ever got in through the letter-boxes. My mother told my granny she didn't mind buying Powell's tea so much, although she couldn't understand why there had to be so much timber floating about on the surface of it, and she would even put up with his coal, that spread more smuts and stife in our kitchen than anything else we had ever burnt in our range, as well as pouring such masses of black smoke out through our chimneys, and my granny's, that from the factory yard we looked like a couple of cruisers steaming neck and neck full speed ahead. But when it came to *Brewcaff*, Powell's special dandelion coffee, my mother just wouldn't go on taking it. The stuff smelt strong, like hot mud, and once when my father left a cupful standing a bit on the hob it turned so solid he couldn't get the sugar into it. But it didn't matter how insulting and bossy my mother was to Mr Powell about his tea and his coal and this coffee muck, he still called on us regularly once a fortnight, carrying his stumpy insurance book and his little indelible lead, his cuffs rattling and the bright auburn skull-cap of hen's feathers gleaming on the back of his head. Sometimes he was very happy, and he would step out of the archway and cross our yard humming to himself, and then talk to my father and mother for ages in our kitchen; other times, especially if something sad had happened in the valley, like an explosion, or a fall in the pit, or a suicide, he cried into his red handkerchief.

My granny was the one who was really partial to Mr Powell, she wouldn't say a word against him and she was often in our kitchen by the time he got there on his visits, or else she came hobbling across the yard on her stick soon after. She had always been keen on singing, Rees Mawr told me, that was why she had such a big bosom in her blouse, and she liked to talk to Mr Powell about his concerts and the time she toured America with his ladies' choir. She couldn't belong to any choir now except the Libanus one, she was too old, but sometimes when I was over in her house on a Sunday evening, instead of going to chapel, she would get the score of some oratorio she'd been in under Mr Powell out of the cupboard and hum the choruses from it to herself by the fire.

I started going to Mr Powell for piano lessons when I was small, but once I got into the scholarship class my mother had a good excuse to stop me. I liked Academy House all right, apart from the piano lessons and the strong smell of pee everywhere it was all right. You never knew for sure what would happen there. One Saturday morning when I went for my lesson the Powell kids told me they couldn't find their father anywhere in the house, and then at last Luther came into the studio grinning and beckoned me up the first flight of stairs. He couldn't speak, poor dab, not unless you waited about half an hour for him to get his gulping and stammering over. He pointed to one of the cracks in the panel of the bathroom door, and there inside I could see Mr Powell in his top hat, stripped to the waist, washing his trombone in a bath full of water. He was so ugly, so fat and covered with long black hairs, that I ran downstairs and home without my music lesson.

Mrs Powell was dead years, but there were eight or nine children still at home, and because they didn't have a mother, and because they lived on the thin most of the time, my granny was very sorry for them, she was always preaching about those three hundred and sixty-five eggs we had in our house the day I was born and comparing us with the Powells who had to live very close to the ground, although they were every bit as respectable as we were. She got my mother and father to invite the children down to the factory for the day, one at a time. My mother didn't want to because she couldn't bear them, but she did it. But when she caught Luther up the plum tree in our orchard showing me his bare behind, she said she was having no more Powells, the tin-buttoned, flea-marked lot, she'd had a bellyful. All the Powell kids seemed to have something the matter with them. Buddug, the eldest girl, had slitty eyes and a puffed yellow face, and some sort of twist in her back under her spread-out curls. Mendy—Mr Powell always called him Mendelssohn—was a kind of cripple with terrible bandy legs and two thumbs on his hand. Luther's stammer was so bad he could hardly talk at all by now, and Eben had fits that made him lean against the wall and neigh like a horse. Taliesin, the eldest one still at home, was in the sixth form of our school now, he was brilliant, everybody said he had read more biology books even than the head, but he was always dirty, and by himself, and his face was a mass of blackheads.

Presently Charley woke me up pitching a note on my desk from behind. 'That bloke must be our chemmy master,' it said. 'Instead of Sheepy. Bet you.'

He meant the young chap we had seen with Mr Powell, did he? I didn't know what to think of that. Was he old enough? I didn't believe he was. He seemed very young to me, especially standing by the side of Mr Powell. But when the bell rang for play Charley went round the yard telling everybody he knew what the new chemmy master was like, he had seen him going into the head's room, a tall chap, sunburnt, with white hair, living in Edwards Terrace, young, most likely this was his first job. Charley was a real know-all like that. But when Armstrong limped out into the yard to ring the handbell at the end of play-time he had a big suck-in, and he didn't know what to say. Because there was the young chap mister bumptious had been telling everybody was the new master standing at the end of the form Growler shoved every new boy over fourteen into—the bottom of the 5B line, partnering Dodger Quant. You couldn't miss him among all the black and purple school caps, with his short white hair and the brown-sugar sunburn of his face. He had his arms folded, and he was gazing about him over the school as though he was looking for something. Jeffy and I spotted him when we ran round the corner into the yard from the fives court where we'd been having a bounce about. 'Look who's over there, fly-me,' Jeffy said to Charley as we got into line. Charley said something dirty and Jeffy tried to give him dead-leg back.

Whatever the young chap was looking for he didn't find it, and in a few seconds he had gone into school with the rest of 5B.

2

THAT evening, on the way up to Charley's farm, I found out the young chap's name.

I didn't see him after school but perhaps 5B had gone over the playing-field last lesson or perhaps the head had let them out early or something. After homework I was going up Commercial Street to meet Tom and Jeffy where we had agreed in Ystrad Square when I saw Arthur Price the milk, his hands in his trousers pockets, riding his father's yellow pony without any harness down the road. Mostly people called him Arf, but he didn't like that.

'Ay, Pricey,' I shouted across to him. 'New bloke in your form.' Pricey was bottom of 5B and anybody could cheek him.

He nodded but didn't stop the horse.

'What's his name?' I asked him.

He turned up the whites of his eyes. 'Er—Anthony,' he said, 'I think.'

'Anthony what?'

'Karl, or something, he told Tossy.'

'Where's he from?'

Pricey lowered the corners of his mouth, lifted his eyebrows and shrugged his shoulders. 'Search me,' he said.

The pony kept moving on. Then Pricey turned round. 'Funny bloke,' he said. 'He've got earrings, aye.'

Anthony Karl. That couldn't be right. Must be Karl Anthony. There were half a dozen lots called Anthony in Ystrad and there were some more in Abergarth, plenty of them. And Karl—I had only ever seen that name in a book. He wasn't one of the Powell lot then. How was it Mr Powell had brought him to school? Soon ahead of me Ystrad Square came in sight and I could see Jeffy there, talking to Islwyn the *News and Banner* paper man on his pitch outside the Commercial Hotel. Islwyn was a good runner once, or he thought he was, and Jeffy always used to rag him about the time he came last in the Cambrian Dash and the Welsh Powderhall.

When I reached the side door of the Bon Marché I opened it, went along the dark passage, put my fingers between my teeth and whistled up the stairs for Tom Stiff, until Pincher began barking up in the rooms. I came out and left the door open and Jeffy and I went down Grosvenor Gardens to call for Charley. We never expected Tom to hurry after us so we stopped and looked at the football boots in the boot-shop window. I noticed Jeffy was queer, very jumpy and wound up, there was something the matter with him and his eyes were red. We saw the corn-stores horse and cart coming up Grosvenor Street with a load of hay on it so huge you could hardly see the cart at all, and only a bit of the little horse, his head and his tiny little hoofs. Jeffy began shouting at the driver and pointing to the top of the load as though he could see something wrong up there. The driver stopped the horse and got down and began walking round the cart looking upwards, but Tom turned up just then wearing his school cap like a pudding basin and we did a bunk round the corner into Grosvenor Gardens. There we knocked at the tradesmen's entrance of Charley's house and the four of us went past Grosvenor Park and up the road to Pantglas, the farm Charley's father had on the mountain.

3

I HAD been on a good few farms, especially up in Abergarth, but I had never seen one like Pantglas, the one on the Ystrad mountain belonging to Charley Llewellyn's father. There was a coal-mine right in the middle of it, and the chap living in the farmhouse wasn't a farmer at all, he drove the little winding-engine belonging to the mine, a bit of a level it was, in the woods half way up the mountain, with only three or four men working in it, and a couple of boys. Everybody in Ystrad knew about that level, we could see the coal-tip belonging to it among the wild hay high up on the slope, and if we were ever able to hear that little winding-engine chuffing away up there when we were down in Ystrad it was a sure sign of rain.

All the farm buildings in Pantglas were stuck together in one untidy lump, the place looked terrible, Jeffy used to kid Charley Llewellyn the only way to tell the farmhouse from the pigsties was by the geranium in the window.

At the far end of the farm the Territorials came for firing in the summer, their rifle butts were in the rocky bed of a dried-up stream on the moors, miles from everywhere. Charley said his father's land reached right up to the dry-built wall we could see along the crest of the mountain, but Jeffy and I didn't believe him. The farm wasn't old Llewellyn's anyway, my father always said, he was only renting it from the colliery company. But Pantglas was a fine place to go to, there were plenty of woods there, and a bottomless air shaft, and a couple of stagnant ponds, and an old tunnel with an echo, and a long lake with a suck-pool called the Swamp. Sometimes we took our slings and hid in the bracken, we shot at the mountain ponies and tried to make them gallop into the water. Other times in the summer holidays we potched about with our shirts off and tickled for fish in the streams; but what I liked best was lighting a huge fire after dark in our camp and roasting ourselves around it, eating sugar and cocoa, and tiger-nuts, and listening to Jeffy acting the goat, getting us to shout, 'Shut the shutters and sit in the shop' and that, and mocking Growler, his rocking walk and his talks about our bad habits and our bowels, and his big voice bawling: 'On with your task, wretched youth.' Jeffy used to sing to us up there too, falsetto, he was an atheist and he had a lot of songs that sounded like hymns, 'At the cross, at the cross' and that, only the words were dirty.

In a very lonely and secret part of the woods we knew a sort of grassy platform, a flat square of turf sticking out level from the slope of the mountain, not far from the rocky cart-track that led up from the farm, past the powder-house and over into the next valley. There we had our camp, the paths up to it through the bracken blocked with mounds of dead thorn bushes. The trees were thick as a jungle around us there, and the grass was very tall; it was hard to find it because of this, and because of the deep bracken surrounding it. Although the square platform itself was covered with very close turf we always called our camp the long grass. We had built a cave on one side of the platform out of old pit tramlines; we had upended a ring of them into a sort of wigwam shape, and covered them outside with thick branches, so that we had a hut big enough to hold the four of us if it happened to come to rain. And it was handy to keep our stuff in, an old bucket and a frying-pan and that, and matches and cigarettes, and Jeffy's clay pipe and tobacco.

Once on a Saturday afternoon when we got there we found half a dozen dirty kids from the British school with snobby noses and donkey-cropped heads messing about on our turf, they were out for the day and they had their fishing-nets and their home-made cricket bats and their lunch in newspaper with them. They were pulling branches out of the huge heap of kindling we always collected to keep our fire going, and they had turned the flat stones we used to sit on upside-down, showing the white grass underneath, and the worms writhing, and the wood-lice trotting about. One of them was even swaying up and down in the branches of the sloping tree Jeffy used to walk up to drink his soup in, and that made him mad. He rounded the kids up and told them this camp was private property, but now, because they had found out our secret hiding-place, they all had to join our gang. And to join they must bend over and have three whacks across their ragged arses with their own cricket bat. The kids were too frightened to refuse and Jeffy got them into line, the four of them, touching their toes. He brought the bat slowly up to the first kid's trousers and then drew it back again, getting his

eye in for the clout, he did this three times, counting out loud—
one—two—meaning to give the kid a real stinger when it came
up to three. But he never got there. The next thing we saw was
Jeffy staggering back and the bat flying out of his hand. The big
fat sister of one of the kids, a girl about thirteen, had rushed mad
out of the woods with her bubs jumping about in her blouse and
given him a hefty welt on the side of the head that nearly put him
down on the grass.

'What do you think you're doing, you big bully?' she
shouted at him, red in the face and cock-eyed with temper.

Jeffy was too startled for once to say anything. She picked up
the bat and came on at him with it over her head, but when she
saw all the little kids scampering away into the trees in different
directions, she stopped.

'Wait for me,' she shouted out after them. 'Moncrieff and
Sylvester, wait a minute or you'll get lost.'

But they wouldn't stop running, they went on shouting back,
'Four-eyes', and, 'Ginger, you're barmy' at Tom and me, and
she had nothing to do but run off into the woods after them.

Charley rolled on the grass helpless, and so did I, and even
Tom Stiff had his mouth open wide laughing although he wasn't
making a sound.

'Moncrieff and Sylvester,' I shouted to Charley, although I
could hardly get the words out, and we said to each other, when
we could manage it for laughing, the other kids' names that used
to make us helpless—Vince and Jabez in form one, and Punter
Thomas and Archie Sproule whose middle name we found out
was Keepence, and the big fat Shadbolt twins with pimples and
glasses next door to Charley in Grosvenor Gardens, Martha
Serena and Aggie Superba. But Jeffy wouldn't laugh, he had
pouted, he went off by himself sulking into the bracken because
the fat girl had simpled him in front of us all.

That night, the night after we had caught a glimpse of Karl
Anthony in school, we were up Pantglas woods sitting around
our fire, Charley, Tom and I with our backs to the cave, and

Jeffy roosting by himself on the other side of the blaze, right on the very edge of our grass platform. All the evening he had been very queer, very jumpy and touchy, even his look was queer, his eyes red, as though he had been crying, although you couldn't imagine Jeffy crying, and his face yellow as butter. If he stopped talking for a minute I noticed he began tearing his nails off until they began to bleed, and digging, digging hard into the turf with a stick held in his hand like a dagger. The others kidded him to tell me how he had got boozed up again during the holidays, and how he had sat in the bath and drunk the bath water and eaten the skin he had pulled off his feet. But he kept putting us off, digging and digging and getting up and going into the cave every whip-stitch for firewood, restless as if he had the worms, bringing out the wooden wedges he had kicked out of the colliers' railway line running below the farm and tossing them on to the blaze, and smoking a home-made cigarette sopping up to the half.

I ought to have been enjoying myself fine because our fire was huge, roaring by now, and smelling beautifully of the tar on the railway blocks, and the night was warm, and the woods silent and pitch-dark all around us. But I felt uneasy, as though something was going to happen, and watching Jeffy made me on edge. It was twilight by the time we were coming up the cart-track towards our cave, in the blue sky were only a few broken lumps of gold, and as we passed the Swamp we could see through the trees the daylight still lying on the surface of the lake with the low shine of serge. We were in single file because of the thickness of the undergrowth, Tom walking in front. Suddenly he stopped. Ahead we had spotted smoke rising into the air above the long grass and the bracken, just where our camp would be. And we could smell a strong niff of burning. Somebody was in our camp. We went quietly forward through the ferns and climbed up the bank on to our platform, wondering what we would find. Although the smoke column was still going up thick from the ring of charred stones in the middle of the patch, no one was there, and the fire itself was nearly out. I felt disturbed after that all the time. I never liked to think that someone had been in our camp when we weren't there. I didn't want to go home, but I wished Jeffy would be quieter, and that some uneasy feeling inside me would go slack so that I would be able to laugh at him a little better.

'I was in Church Street one morning,' he began telling us at last from the other side of the fire, 'in my old man's shop, arsing around with the burnisher, and this old bloke Bartlett from the Wern down the valley came in, pretty drunk he must have been —do you know him?—he'd suddenly remembered about the American clock he'd brought in for repairs a couple of years ago. He was wearing the oldest coat in Ystrad, it was so old all the stripes had disappeared from it. He wanted the clock back any-way, most likely to try and pawn it for beer money. He had the horse and gambo outside in Church Street and he invited me down the Wern for the day if I felt like coming. Well, it was a lovely morning, very hot, and I went with him. Have you ever been down the Wern? The farmhouse is a sort of hovel, like a broken-down ruin. When we got inside the kitchen he asked me if I'd like something to drink, sherbet or a glass of wine. Home made the wine was, he said. There was a dirty old woman sitting in the corner by the fire, I didn't notice her at first because it was so dark in there, the windows boarded up like a dungeon; she looked about two hundred, all wrinkles and thick hairs, and she nodded for me to say yes when he offered the wine—although what I really like is a drop of the old port, or burgundy, not this home-made horse-piss with a lot of potatoes in it, and stingy nettles, and all that muck. Bartlett goes into the pantry and fetches back a flagon sopping wet, and three ancient-looking wineglasses, opaque I thought they were, special antiques, but when he had used his muffler on them a bit I could see they were ordinary glass. He pours us a wineglass each, parsnip wine it was, he said, as white as milk, and sweet. And lovely. Ever tasted it? It made me boiling hot and I laughed all the time. When he had finished his glassful Bartlett banged a nail into the wall and hung the clock on it and then he asked me if I would read the Bible to his mother. He left me the flagon and went out. I read a bit but it was baking in the kitchen, what with the weather and the fire and the booze, and when the old woman began snoring I picked the flagon up and went outside to cool off a bit, they had a little bench and a round table in the garden by the back door. Soon Bartlett comes back. He laughs again when he sees me. "Don't drink too much of that stuff," he says. But it was nice, lovely and sweet, and cold, Bartlett told me he had a deep well of spring water under the pantry floor to keep the bottles in. He went away again and the next time he came back the flagon was empty. I thought perhaps he would ask me if I wanted some more, but he didn't. He was going to feed the pigs, he told me, he had over forty, saddlebacks. I said I'd help him. He laughed and told me I'd better go and lie down in the kitchen, or read the Bible a bit more to his mother, Jonah and the whale was her favourite story, he told me. I said no, I felt great inside, I was going to give him a hand. If he wouldn't let me do it I'd fight him. I tapped him on the shoulder to challenge him and then I put my dukes up in his face. Pity help me if he had taken me on, I'd have had a proper lamping, but he only laughed again and put the yoke on my shoulders, and hooked a couple of buckets of barley meal on to the chains.'

Jeffy started reeling and staggering round the fire, making us laugh acting a drunken man with a yoke across his shoulders carrying two heavy buckets full of pigs'-slop.

'In one of the pigsties there was a sow with a litter of ten,' he said. '"Pour the buckets in the trough in there," Bartlett told me. I managed to open the door and go in stooping. I bent down to pour the stuff in the trough and the next thing I was flat on the floor in the pigs' muck with two buckets of barley meal all over me. Old Bartlett managed to pick me up, I was soaking and covered with slop and pigs' muck. Bartlett couldn't stop laughing. "You go and dry yourself and fetch the cows," he said. "I'll do this."

'Well, I went from the pigsties up to the stack yard to unfasten the collie from the anvil. On the way I tried running. I put my foot in a blooming rabbit-hole and came a cropper. I fell flat on my face, and I had to start clutching the grass of the yard with both hands to stop the world going round. I was stunned. And then in a minute or two I went out to the wide, stretched on the grass unconscious half an hour—an hour, more like. The cows mooing to be milked brought me round. I sat up and began to be sick. It poured out of me when I got to the dubliw, I thought I was going to spew my ring up. And then all of a sudden I was better, and I thought: "Thank God I'm sober now." I got up off the grass and went to get the sheep-dog off the chain. When I was doing it I turned back to look at Bartlett coming in through the gate of the yard, and the next minute I was running backwards full speed past him towards the dung-heap, I couldn't help myself, I went like old boots . . .'

Suddenly Jeffy disappeared right in front of our eyes, it was exactly like a conjuring trick, only there was no flash and explosion and no puff of smoke. One second we were watching him running backwards across the grass in the firelight with his shirt out, and the next he had vanished arse over tip into the darkness.

We all sat there grinning, staring before us over the blaze into the blackness, waiting for him to climb back up into the firelight again, but nothing happened.

There was dead silence as we all listened, straining our eyes and ears but catching no sound or movement anywhere, only the soft creaking of the air above the fire. And then suddenly, without any warning, a terrible screech broke out in the darkness right above our heads, for a second or two I went icy all over, and I felt freezing electric shocks shoot one after the other through my head-skin and my hair. But I knew in no time what it was, the old screech-owl, the one we called the caca-hawk because of the big soft dollops he splashed on the branches, was at it again, trying to frighten us out of his woods before fluffing off into the darkness. I saw Charley, sitting next to me, turning round suddenly at the screech, looking pretty surprised and frightened, peering up into the trees where the noise came from;

as he did it I happened to be watching him, and what I saw as the owl fluffed off over us was his expression changing like a flash. Because instead of looking up he began staring over my head into the blackness of the trees behind me, he wasn't just frightened of the screech-owl now, suddenly he looked absolutely terrified; anyone else's hair but Charley's would have been on end to go with that look; and his eyes, although they were little really, seemed to be bulging out of his head with terror, and his mouth had opened into a square, like the time in standard four he bawled his eyeballs out when the Pantglas sheep-dog got among his rabbits, and tore his Snowball and Thumper in pieces. Whatever he was staring at was scaring him to death, and yet his forehead was wrinkled as though he couldn't really believe it either. '*Duw*, Dewi,' he said, dropping off his stone on to his knees and pointing over my shoulder. 'What's that in the woods? Look at it! A light! O, *Iesu*, it's moving!'

When I looked back myself I could see in the darkness over the bracken a large shapeless glare glowing like bright phosphorescence in the woods about twenty yards behind our cave, it was absolutely still by then and dead silent. At first glance it made me think of the incandescent gas mantle we had in our kitchen, but it was huge and shapeless and ghostly, and at the sight of it I jumped up too, I dare say I was just as frightened as Charley. I could feel the hair on my head alive again as it had been a few seconds before, and in spite of the fire the fright iced me up like Swamp water through and through. Once before, farther up the mountain, we had seen a light like that in the woods, a sort of greenish smudge floating slowly in and out among the tree trunks, and then disappearing. We had all run away from it down the mountain road, and when we got home we heard that Ernie Hughes from our form had been found dead on the railway line, it was a mystery, there wasn't a mark on him, only a little round bruise, red, the size of a threepenny bit, right in the middle of his forehead. It flashed through my mind that the best thing to do now was to creep over to the far side of the fire and hide there below the level of the platform, perhaps the ghost hadn't spotted us and we could spy on it without being seen ourselves. But my heart was still thumping like a hammer and before I could bring myself to move the light suddenly disappeared completely. The branches of the trees were growing together thickly just there, black, and dense as cauliflowers, and it was pitch-dark. I couldn't take my eyes off the place. Then I heard somebody treading through the bushes on our right, and after a bit the figure of a man came into the light of the fire, a coloured man, short, he seemed, compared with the height of the bracken, wearing a large white hat on his head. As he got nearer he found the path through the undergrowth our side of the thorn barrier, and he began to trample easier. And then his chest gave out a long rumble, and he coughed, and we all recognized him at once. It was Growler Roderick, our headmaster, he had been standing beneath the trees with his sheet over his head and his lamp alight under it to attract the moths, the silly old fool, the silly old flamer.

Charley and I must have been as white as sheets as we got to our feet to meet him. Tom looked much as usual, peering ahead through his short-sighted glasses, the lining of his little school cap down like another poke at the back of his head. The first thing I thought was thank God it's only old Growler, although he was bad enough, and thank God none of us happened to be smoking. And then I began to worry because Charley and I didn't have our school caps on, and I wondered if there was anything about on the grass we ought to have hidden in the cave, like fag-ends, or matches, or empty 'Black Cat' packets.

'Well, boys,' Growler said, coming at his slow fat rock out from the bracken, his broad face, with a grin all over it, shining and the colour of cocoa in the firelight. 'Are we enjoying ourselves?' he asked us. He must have known he had frightened the life out of us, standing there behind us in the darkness like a lit-up ghost. Most likely he had done it on purpose, the cunning old crawn.

We all mumbled yes, sir, wondering, now that our fright was over, how long he'd been listening there in the woods, and how

89

much he'd heard of what Jeffy had been telling us. Everybody in school believed Growler was a spy, he always wore rubber heels and he had been seen listening in the yard outside the ground-floor classroom windows, trying to hear what was going on during the lessons.

Standing there, his big face dark in the glow and flickering of the fire, he looked a sight. There was something daft about a fat grown-up man dressed up in the darkness like that to catch a few butterflies. He had the big, white, wide-brimmed hat of thick straw on his head, it must have belonged to his wife once, he had split the front of the crown to get it on, and a tight blue boiler-suit, the two breast pockets stuffed with notebooks, swelling out like the bosom bulges of a fat woman, and the trousers tucked into a pair of black leggings. These overalls, with a metal buckle like a brass tobacco-box on the front of the belly, gave him a terrible bulgy blown-up look round the middle and the bum, because he was wearing them on top of his ordinary clothes, and they were always baggy enough to begin with. On the boy scout's lanyard round where his neck ought to be he carried his special carbide lamp, a bicycle lamp it was with a shutter fitted on to it, and over his shoulder hung a fishing-basket, most likely holding his killing-bottles and those things. He gripped the long cane handle of his mothing net in one hand and over his other arm hung the white bed-sheet. He looked a proper freak standing there fat and heavy and clumsy and ballooned up in the flickering firelight. He had shown us all this stuff, the lamp, the net, the treacle-bottle, the gassing jars and the blue fitter's overalls covered with bird droppings in school in the biology society. But we had been frightened at the first glimpse of him standing lit up in the dark wood because we had never seen him actually dressed in this terrible get-up before. Fair play, Growler was ugly enough to frighten anybody any time, he didn't have to wait till dark and have a white sheet over his head.

He began to come up to the fire grinning, and he shook hands with each one of us in turn. It was horrible touching him, he was cold and he felt wet somehow, and sucky, like stuffing your hand in a clayhole. But his voice was magnificent when he spoke to you near by, you could feel yourself vibrating.

'I know you all,' he said. 'Who are you? Form two, is it?'

'No, sir, form three, sir,' Charley said, patting the white handkerchief sticking out of his breast pocket to show Growler he'd got one. Somehow or other he'd managed to get his cap on to the back of his head. We always had to make fun of mister bumptious Charley or he would have been a proper creeper. It was because of his mother, she was always on to him to be polite and touch his cap and be a gentleman right from his toes up. Before we started going to the Swamp for a swim she even used to come to the baths with him, because she heard a lot of the boys going there were rough and Charley might learn bad manners swimming with them. 'Chase me, Charley,' we used to whisper behind his back when he started acting a bit advanced. And Jeffy would go on saying anything that came into his head—round the fowl-house, up the leg of my drawers—and that made Charley blush and cry quiet for a bit.

'Of course,' Growler grinned. 'Form three. Let us see now. Hughes Griffiths?' he said, nodding to Tom.

Hughes Griffiths! And it wasn't so long ago he had been shaking hands with Tom on the platform before the whole school, telling us what a marvel he was, and a big example to us all to follow—top of his form four times in a row, ever since he'd been in the grammar school. Hughes Griffiths!

'Griffiths Pugh, sir,' old Tom said.

'Tom Griffiths Pugh, sir,' said Charley.

'Evans, isn't it?' Growler said to me.

Good. I liked that. He'd got my name wrong. I didn't want him to know anything about me. Not old Growler. Not likely!

'Dewi Davies, sir,' said Charley.

'And you?' Growler said, suddenly turning to mister important Charley. 'Cavanagh? Taverner? Who are you?'

Charley was a bit taken aback.

'Llewellyn, sir,' was all he said, muttering, blushing because

Growler didn't know him, his red cheeks shiny as hat-fruit in the firelight.

Growler nodded and grinned all round, looking very satisfied, as pleased as if he'd got all our names right first time. And then I had an idea that made me hot and set me back a bit. Did he say them wrong on purpose? Perhaps he was up to his games again, pretending not to know us when he'd been spying on us all the time. 'We usually have another boy with us, don't we?' he said after a long grin. 'We have another member in our club.' And the moment he said that I knew for certain he'd been listening to Jeffy, the creeping sneak. 'A very inky boy,' he went on. 'With fair hair. Let's see now. Irvine? Erskine?'

'Urquhart, sir,' said Charley.

'Ah, yes, Urquhart. Jeffrey Urquhart. That's the boy.' He looked round the grass patch. 'And where's Jeffrey Urquhart this evening?'

Nobody answered him. We stood there awkward and feeling diddled and most likely blushing. We realized, even Charley, that Growler must have overheard every word Jeffy had said, Jeffy was so excited telling his story, like somebody half hysterical, talking at the top of his voice. At last Charley walked away around the fire to the edge of the platform above the slope. 'Urquhart's over here somewhere, sir,' he said. 'He was with us just now.'

He was wearing his school cap on the back of his hair to show his crinkles, and because he wanted a haircut he had to walk with his face down to keep it on, as though he was holding a sheet of paper under his chin. Then with his back to us he bent down and peered out of the firelight into the pitch darkness of the woods.

'Jeffy!' he shouted out loud. 'Jeffy-o!'

Charley was a proper flaming fool. If Jeffy didn't happen to know Growler was with us he would be sure to bawl something pretty dirty back for Charley to do to himself. And Growler would be bound to hear it. I felt hot and very uncomfortable waiting, listening anxiously for an answer to float back out of the darkness. But no answer came, the echo of Charley's voice lasted a second or two and then the woods were absolutely silent around us again. Perhaps Jeffy had spotted Growler standing under the trees and was keeping out of the way until he was gone. 'Did you want him special, sir?' Charley asked, coming back.

'Not special,' Growler said, grinning again. He dropped his sheet and his net on to the grass at his feet, slung his fishing-creel behind him and suddenly leaned over towards Tom, who was standing nearest to him, and grabbed hold of him by the throat as if he meant to throttle him. Tom jumped for once as though he had touched hot iron, but Growler had him tight, he seemed to throw all his heavy weight on top of him, and then, clawing at Tom's clothes, he managed with a lot of puffing and bone-cracking and a big struggle to lower himself gradually to the grass, to get all his fat down on to one of the big flat stones we had around the fire. It was lucky Tom was pretty solid and always stiff as a poker, or he would have collapsed on top of Growler, and we would have seen the two of them on the grass one on top of the other. As I watched all this palaver I was glad Growler hadn't picked on me to catch hold of. I couldn't bear the touch of him, and he always seemed to want to do it. The first time he shook hands with me was after a school concert, it went through me like the sound of chalk squeaking on the blackboard, or tugging dry wadding between my teeth. His hand was soft and cold, and lumpy, like a heavy dollop of wet chewing-gum. I rubbed my palm on my trousers after it, and my tongue kept coming out between my lips, making me want to spit.

'Sit down, boys,' Growler said, from down there on the grass when he had recovered his puff a bit. As he waved his hand to the other flat stone near him I noticed his straw hat was down in the crust like a cake taken too soon out of the oven. But what the devil were we going to talk about to a crank like Growler? And what if we said something wrong, or something he didn't like, and he turned nasty? It was all right for Tom, he was always top of the form, and not so bad for Charley, either, because he always had plenty of kidney, and he knew about mantissas and characteristics and that muck, and he could sing as well, and argue as long as water flows, the big know-all. But what about me? And Jeffy, he was worse. I was wishing Jeffy would stop his clowning, wherever he was, and come out of hiding for me to have a bit of company.

Growler's pipe was about the size of a bowler hat and he began packing tobacco into it with his sawn-off-square fingers, and hawking and coughing. Everybody was dead silent apart from him, no sound anywhere except this deep coughing coming full of phlegm from Growler's guts and, once he got his pipe going, his breath bubbling in and out, loud and wet, through the suck of his disgusting fat chops. I would rather hear the old screech-owl shrieking or splashing his caca on the branches any day than listen to Growler breathing.

Charley said at last: 'After butterflies, sir?'

'Moths,' Growler said without looking up.

I didn't mean to say a word if I could help it. And Tom didn't open his mouth either, he just stared out of his shining glasses at Growler with his mouth wide open. His specs were not at all like Growler's really, although both lots were very thick and round and powerful. When you looked straight through Tom's glasses into his eyes he seemed to have two deep holes in his head, with little bright pin-heads at the bottom of them, like something glittering at the far end of a corridor; but Growler's eyes were magnified behind his glasses, they were huge and swollen, the thick glass swelled his eyeballs up until they bulged out of his head like the eyes of a frog.

We all sat in dead silence again after Growler's answer, watching his stumpy fingers, two with gold bands on them, holding his pipe, we were feeling sad and uneasy and desperate. Mostly Growler's chopsy face was hidden from us by the shadow of his big hat-brim, but we could feel he was watching us all the time, and every now and then he looked up into the firelight and grinned round his horrible cold, fat, frog's grin. What was he trying to do, the silly old fool? Was he ragging us again? Sitting with us just to annoy us because he knew he was spoiling our camp? Or did he have some other wheeze up his sleeve? I began to sweat thinking of that. And still there was no sound anywhere, except that wet piggish sucking noise of Growler's smoking, and from time to time his coughing, that I didn't mind so much because, fair dooz, he was a pretty majestic cougher, deep and rich and heavy, he sounded like a full-sized organ coughing. Why the devil didn't Jeffy come?

After what seemed about two hours without a word, Charley started again. 'Nice evening, sir,' he said, the fat-head.

Growler looked up and grinned and nodded. 'I am sorry Urquhart is not present,' he said. 'I would very much like to speak to him. Mr Beynon has been kind enough to bring his homework essay along and show it to me. I read it this afternoon with very great interest. A composition on the Balkans. I expect we all did one, did we? A meritorious attempt indeed by Jeffrey Urquhart. It might be a good idea to ask Mr Beynon to read it to us all, as a form, if he hasn't already done so.'

Growler had us all squirming on our stones by now, the old hypocrite. If Jeffy had been with us Growler would most likely have flayed him, not only for barefaced copying, but for the scribble in his homework book, and for making a proper bug of the whole thing with blots and smudges and crossings out. Geogger Beynon had read the essay to our form anyway, stopping to chew his false teeth, and jeering, at every other word. He had asked Jeffy to hand him his geogger textbook so that he could show him what it said in it about the Balkans, because according to Beynon everything Jeffy had written was wrong. When he opened the textbook he noticed Jeffy's name wasn't written inside it, only 'If my name you want to see, turn to page forty-three.' Beynon was sarky again over this, but he was dull enough to turn to page forty-three all the same. There it said: 'Get out—I'm dressing.' That finished Beynon. He went suddenly crimson and started to squawk like a trodden-on duck, he called Jeffy everything he'd heard Growler bawling when he had his hair off, a donkey, a *bwbach*—anything, and, when Jeffy had given him a mouthful back, we watched them marching off down to Growler's corridor, Jeffy in front with his homework book open in his hand. Growler happened to be out, so Beynon left it on his table. Jeffy still hadn't had it back, but Beynon—a proper sneak Beynon was—must have spoken to Growler about it, and explained what had happened. All of us in 3A had seen the essay before Growler or Beynon anyway. We had watched Jeffy copying it out of the weekly paper we had in Ystrad, the *Workers' Clarion*. 'The Balkans!' was the first sentence in the article. 'The Balkans! The Devil's back door to the East!' Unluckily for Jeffy, the landlord in Beynon's lodgings took the *Clarion* and Beynon spotted where Jeffy had got it from.

Growler looked up again and grinned. And then, before he could say any more about Jeffy, his face went serious and puzzled. He scowled, staring hard in front of him. He stopped sucking his pipe and pointed with it across the fire at the spot where Jeffy had gone over the edge of the platform.

'Who's that, boys?' he said, whipping off his glasses. 'There seems to be someone waving to us. Is there somebody there? Not Urquhart, is it?'

Yes, he could see Jeffy climbing back, I thought in a flash before glancing across myself. When we all looked in the same direction we saw that a head had appeared there in the firelight, only a head, the chin on a level with the grass. A head much handsomer than Jeffy's, the cropped hair and the sunburnt face of the boy Pricey said was called Karl Anthony.

I felt stabbed hot through and through my breast when I saw him. One of his hands appeared rosy in the firelight and beckoned us towards him. Tom, Charley and I sprang up and hurried over, only too glad of a chance to get away from Growler. Below the edge of the platform the ground sloped outwards steeply, making a drop of ten or twelve feet. We found Karl lying among the bracken on the grass and soil there, in the darkness, holding Jeffy in his arms.

'Help me, please,' he said. 'Let us get this boy to the fire. He has just fainted.' Or it sounded something like that. I had never heard him saying anything before. He had some sort of foreign accent, he sounded like a Frenchman, or a North-Walian, or a German perhaps, but not guttural at all.

Between us we managed to get both Karl and Jeffy up on to the grass. Tom had his arms under Jeffy's armpits and his hands on his chest and Charley and I carried his legs. There was more meat on a bike than there was on Jeffy and he felt light as a feather. His eyes were closed, he was sagging between us and unconscious, out to the wide, and his face, with a gash across the forehead, was pale, as yellow and bloodless as flesh pressed against a window; but I wasn't frightened to see him like that at all, it seemed natural and ordinary. As we were carrying him limp across the grass to lay him down by the fire we could see that old Growler had recognized him; he knocked his pipe out, but instead of coming towards us he went the other way, he began crawling on his hands and knees across the camp in the other direction, making for the trees near the cave. What a bum he had, moving away from us like that, the biggest in Ystrad, sure to be, the bum beautiful, swollen and hanging in his overalls like the baggish trousers of an elephant or an extra wide cow. And when he reached the trees he tugged his heavy weight upright slowly against one of the trunks and shouted across to us. 'This way, boys,' he called. 'It's Urquhart, isn't it? What's the matter with him? Bring him this way, boys, so that we can carry him home to his mother.'

He began motioning us towards the path through the bracken that led out on to the mountain road.

Karl took no notice of his shouting, he ignored him as completely as if Growler hadn't been there or said a word. 'Lay him down near the fire,' he said to us quietly. 'He will soon be well. I have already been speaking to him. We must always keep him warm.'

When Growler saw we weren't doing anything like what he told us he waddled across from the trees to our side of the fire. I don't think it was his belly that made him sway like that when he was walking, it was the weight of his big head, it rocked him right over from side to side, the way my metronome dodged with the weight up near the top; if it hadn't been for the ballast of his big boots, heavy enough for a diver they looked, he would have gone right over sideways on to the grass.

'Didn't you hear me?' he said, puzzled, when he reached us. 'This boy must be put in the care of his family at once. Can't you see he's ill? Lift him up, please. Come on, bring him this way. I will accompany you.'

That was just like Growler, he thought he knew everything about everything, first aid and hygiene included; he used to stop boys in the corridor in school and talk to them about their teeth, and their blackheads and pimples, and every chance he had he would tell the whole school how much we ought to do every morning after breakfast, enough to fill a sugar-basin, and that diarrhoea meant *flowing through*, and all that stuff. He was a dirty old crawn like that.

Karl rose suddenly, bowed, and with a couple of steps across the grass went and stood up against Growler's belly, and stared down into his fat face. He looked thin, and high, and not real, about two or three feet taller than Growler. He seemed to belong lovely in the firelight and he gave me a feeling of glory just to look at him.

'This young boy lives quite near here, does he?' he asked him.

Growler looked round at us, quite taken aback for the moment, but bossy again in no time. 'Ystrad,' he said, 'I think. Urquhart lives somewhere in Ystrad, doesn't he? You boys know.'

Charley nodded. 'By the park, sir,' he said.

'Ystrad is three kilometres away,' said Karl. 'To carry him that distance might be dangerous. Soon he will be well.'

'How do you know?' Growler bawled out suddenly, the old bully.

Karl's head jerked back, he looked as though he had been struck or insulted. 'I have examined him, sir,' he said. 'No bones are broken.'

It wasn't only old Tom's mouth was open by now. We had never heard anybody talking to Growler like that before, nobody at all, not even Dodger Quant the gin-shop, who would cheek practically any teacher in school. But Karl didn't sound cheeky, only sure what he said was right, and grown-up, and he spoke in a very polite and swanky way. When he said *sir*, it wasn't like us saying *sir*, it was more like one of those dead-shot duellers in the library books, being polite to a chap they're sure they're going to put a bullet through in a few minutes' time.

'Examined him!' Growler bellowed again. 'Perhaps you are mistaken, foolish boy.'

'Indeed it is possible I am mistaken,' Karl said quietly. 'But if so, we shall be moving a great distance a person with a fracture. Perhaps with more fractures than one.'

Growler was pretty mad but he couldn't do anything; he looked sulky and angry, his dark face sultry somehow, it had the threatening bulged-up look of a saucepanful of milk just before it boils over on to the fire. He turned away from Karl as though he had finished with him, and came up to us. 'You lads,' he said shortly. 'Lift the boy up. Bring him this way at once. Come along now.'

None of us moved, the three of us just went on kneeling on the grass beside Jeffy as if we were magnetized there. Growler glared down at us very surprised, angrier and uglier than I had ever seen him in school, the purple skin of his wide face flushed and damp and swollen, looking like a face bloated from water too hot for washing. He had become so fierce and glowing with anger I didn't fancy looking him in the eyes, and I pretended to be tidying Jeffy up a bit, and examining the cut on his forehead. But I had no intention of doing what he said, not as long as Karl wished us to do the opposite. Although I thought Jeffy ought to be carried home, I wanted, I didn't know why, to obey Karl, not Growler. I felt I had to be on the same side as Karl.

Growler took a step towards us and tried again. 'You, Llewellyn,' he said, a change in his bass, booming straight at Charley. 'I know you are a sensible boy. We will not refuse our help to get our sick friend to his mother, now. We will not fail him, and fail her, will we?'

Fair play for old Charley, he didn't move or say a word, all he did was kneel there and look up at Growler miserable as a dog caught messing in the house, and finger the white handkerchief at his breast pocket in a troubled sort of way, the grooves of worry across his forehead almost as deep as the crinkles in his hair.

I wondered what Growler would do now. I hoped he wouldn't come any closer, or the bottom would be out of it completely for me. When Growler stood near you, even if he was behind you, you could feel him, some influence oozed out of his body and your own body was inside it, it stifled you, it was like the heat pouring out of a furnace, or a powerful smell, but he didn't smell much, except of rubbing-oil a bit in the winter.

'Pugh! Davies!' he said to Tom and me. 'We call ourselves Jeffrey's chums, don't we? So of course we will want to get him home to his parents. We cannot deny him that, a sick lad who urgently requires the love and attention of his mother.'

We all rose to our feet and what I was afraid of happened, he came right up to us. Sometimes, in school, when you tried to slip past him in the corridor without being seen, he would stop you and back you against the wall and ask to see your teeth. 'Open your mouth, wider, wider,' he would say, and then he'd whip off his glasses, and bring his heavy purple face close down to yours, with its holes in the skin and the strong stale smell of his breath, and the brown edging of bad-stomach scum round the corners of his lips—he would stare right into the back of your mouth, you could almost feel one of his eyeballs stretching out as though it was on a stalk, and going into the dark at the back of your gullet, and feeling its way about over your tongue, and round your teeth, and up against the roof of your mouth, like a searching finger. It was horrible, disgusting, it made you tremble so that you couldn't keep your mouth open properly; and then after a few smudgy remarks about your dirty teeth he'd let you go, feeling a fool and a wet for letting him do it to you. I was afraid he might be going to do something like that now, I could see him, behind his glasses, lowering the slack bags of his lids, and feel his eyes boring into me, trying to hypnotize me as he stood so close against us I could feel the hot-blast of his thick breath upon my face. But Karl came round and stood between Tom and me with his hands on our shoulders. We stared hard at Growler, the four of us, and he glared back at us, his chest bubbling up liked boiled porridge, and his eyes travelling from one to the other along the line, trying hard by the look of him to find something or other in our faces. Then his own face began to work and twitch like a bush full of birds, and suddenly he said, a good bit quieter: 'What's come upon us all of a sudden, boys? Have we thought of the consequences of what we are doing?'

It was all over. Suddenly, like a flash, I knew the words meant Karl had beaten him. Until then I had felt worried and afraid, although I knew what I was going to do I was anxious all the time, but now I felt some slackness inside me, and around me. I was free, I didn't care anything at all for Growler, I wasn't afraid of him any more, and it didn't matter to me what he threatened me with now. I felt a bit sorry for him really, because although he was a headmaster he couldn't do anything at all to us, and he couldn't force us to do what he wanted. I was so excited and surprised and happy, Karl had to repeat what he asked for before I heard him. 'Fetch me some water, please,' he said.

I went across and got our frying-pan out of the cave. As I was leaving the platform I saw Karl picking Growler's sheet up off the ground, folding it and placing it for a pillow under Jeffy's head. I danced down the cart-track in the dark, delighted, I seemed to be bouncing down the road blown like a little feather. I smiled to myself at the wonderful thing that had happened, until I came to where the mountain stream crossed the track.

When I came back with the frying-pan full of water Jeffy was still lying by the fire unconscious, and Karl and Tom were kneeling one on each side of him. Karl was in his shirt-sleeves, he had taken his Norfolk jacket off and put it over Jeffy. Charley was busy dragging more branches from the pile of firewood across the grass for our fire. Growler had retreated, he had gone to stand by the entrance to the cave, he was writing something in one of the little notebooks out of his breast pocket.

'Isn't Urquhart's father a jeweller in Church Street?' he boomed across to us, but nobody answered him.

Karl slipped his jacket back on, took the handle of the frying-pan from me and chucked the water smack in Jeffy's face.

Jeffy came round at once and sat up, his brass eyes bloodshot and rolling and shining with the firelight upon them, and the water streaming down his head. He glared all about him in anguish like somebody out of his mind, he didn't seem to recognize us, or even see us. And then suddenly his whole skinny body began to shiver, his head steamed and his flesh trembled as though he was going to shake himself to pieces.

'Mama, Mama,' he screeched, trying to dash the water from his face. He screamed so loud it was a pity to hear him, he sounded hysterical, more like a frightened little girl in a lane screaming than a boy. And then, without any warning, he sprang up off the grass and ran round the fire yelling for his mother like somebody let loose. *Duw*, I thought, this is hurting me right to the back of my heart just to hear him. How are we going to catch him? He's always slippery to hold as a sopping bottle. He didn't seem to know what he was doing, or where he was going. He ran straight over everything like somebody off his head, or blind. I tried to get to the path before him, and Tom snatched at his coat sleeve as he passed, but he tore it away with the sound of ripping stitches and ran on. Growler disappeared inside the cave and then peeped out again, still writing. 'What did I tell you?' he shouted. 'He should have been carried home to his mother.'

The platform sounded hollow underneath the heavy pounding of Jeffy's feet, he charged across the grass screaming, but when he saw me standing between him and the path to the cart-track he doubled back to get to the road over the edge of the platform. Karl was in his way there and Jeffy ran blind into him as though he didn't even see him. Karl grabbed hold of him at once, he gripped him tight by the chest with both hands and shook him hard several times. Jeffy struggled like a maniac with his teeth showing, tearing at Karl's hands. 'I'll smash you, you bastard, let me go!' he screamed, but Karl took no notice, he held him firmly away at arm's length a second, and then gave him a terrific welt with his open hand right across the puss, he drew his arm well back and brought the palm down on the side of Jeffy's face with a sound like the crack of a gun.

'I won't have that,' Growler shouted from his hide-out in the cave. 'I will not have it, do you hear me? The boy ought to be home with his mother. A fine look-out, beating him.'

Jeffy went absolutely silent and rigid when Karl belted him. As I watched I saw his face for a moment twisting up in the fire-light, as though he was going to start his howling and shaking again, but Karl drew his arm back, threatening to give him a second crack, and that settled him. He went quiet. Then he gave a tremendous sigh, and calmly unhooked Karl's hand from his chest, and walked away to the fire and sat down on one of the stones. 'I'm sorry,' he said to Karl. 'I'm sorry, Karl.' One by one we all went and sat by him, Tom, Charley and me, and Karl put his arm round Jeffy's shoulders and gave him a big hand-kerchief to wipe his face and neck with.

'I must have fallen on my napper,' Jeffy said.

Presently Karl turned round to Growler. 'He will be all right now, Doctor Roderick,' he said, rising to his feet again and giving Growler a bow. 'Please do not worry any more. The boy will be safe.'

We all turned and stared hard at Growler to make him go. He stood at the doorway of the cave looking stuffed, like two cushions in one cover, not knowing what to do, and then he began collecting up his things off the grass, muttering all the time, but whether he was talking to us or to himself I couldn't hear.

'It happens to me all the time, sir, fainting,' Jeffy shouted across to him. 'You go on with your mothing, sir, I'll be all right now, sir.'

Growler nodded and coughed, and mumbled something else,

but we all thought so hard about his going that he rolled off into the high bracken so as to reach the cart-track. After a few paces we could only see his head with the big white hat on it in the fire-light, and then we heard him calling each of us by name. 'I shall want to see you all in my room first thing tomorrow morning,' he boomed. 'First thing! You will be responsible for bringing them, Anthony.' He seemed to be grinning now, the idiot, and tapping the lobes of his ears as though he had gone loopy all of a sudden. What was he doing that for? 'I'll break the club with a club,' he shouted. 'Defiance! Flagrant disobedience! Tomorrow morning! Remember!'

Then he turned round and went off, marching into the darkness of the trees with his butterfly-net held high in the air.

Karl bowed again in his direction. 'Good night, sir,' he said. Then he came to sit down with us. We all started laughing. Growler must be mad. A fat lot we cared now about him and his bell-oil and his lacings, we knew we were in for it, but tomorrow morning was a long way off. It was great where we were, round the big fire on the mountain, and it was nicer than anything having Karl with us.

That was the best night we ever had in our camp, although Jeffy hardly said another word, all he did was sit there chewing what was left of his finger-nails. Karl liked lying down full stretch with his arms under his head and his feet to the fire. He asked us our full names and we told him. After a bit he took a white china pipe out of his inside pocket and began to smoke it, it had red roses on the bowl and an amber stem. His tobacco, burning, made a sweet smell. As he puffed he said our names over to himself, nodding to each one of us in turn. He was wearing a black Norfolk jacket and long trousers and a cellular cricket shirt but no tie. Round his waist was the broad band of scarlet satin. His boots were the ones I had noticed on him the day my father got him out of the river, they had no laces and were like brown riding-boots worn under his long trousers. As he lay there puffing and showing his black tooth in a smile, his face was a golden brown, the warm colour of a fresh pikelet, and the cut-down hair of his head had the paleness of white grass and the gleam of new thatch.

We talked on about Growler. Dotard, was Karl's word for him, and the way he said it it sounded a pretty awful thing to call anybody. He wanted to know all about Growler, and we made him laugh telling him how nobody could ever understand what Growler was up to, and how he used to frighten the school to death in his rages, but how the boys used to spy on him all the same, and creep into his room and rob him. 'Fancy slaughtering butterflies for a hobby,' Karl said.

Tom said he didn't know Growler was a doctor. Karl replied he didn't know either. He hadn't seen any of us in school. What forms were we in?

I said: 'We saw you, Karl. When the bell went break time yesterday we were round the fives court and you were just going into school.'

'Charley thought you were the new chemmy master,' old Tom croaked.

Karl grinned. I was fascinated by that upper tooth in the front, it was pitch black, and at first I thought it was missing.

> 'Out of my head,
> Bear all the dead;
> Bury under grass
> Young Antipas,'

he muttered, half singing. 'I've seen your face before somewhere, Dewi.'

'Yes, Karl.'

'Where?'

'You fell in the Ystrad river. Remember? About two months ago. My father pulled you out. In our yard. Behind the factory.'

He leaned on his elbow and nodded. 'I remember,' he said thoughtfully. 'Do you know what happened that day? Honour bright! When I got out in the street do you know what I found? There was a water-rat in my trousers pocket.'

We all laughed and in the end Karl did too.

'How did you come to be in the river?' I asked him.

'What a lark! I lived in Venice for two years, and one whole summer I was in Amsterdam. And in, where was it, where we had the orchards of cocoa palms—and I never once fell in a canal. But I had only been in Ystrad a few hours when I nearly drowned myself. I never have any luck with water. Only fire.'

We all wanted to know how it happened.

'I was exploring the top end of this valley, a place of ashes and cinders in great mounds, and red mountains of furnace clinker, up near the ruins of the old ironworks—that's what they look like. Are they? Beyond the end of the town? Yes? A woman came out of one of the whitewashed cottages on the opposite bank of the river and started shouting across, because some boys were playing football on the waste patch of ground the side I was on. They were waking her baby, she said. The boys began answering her back and swearing, no doubt they thought they were safe with the river between them. But the woman went back into the house and presently a much older woman came out and ran down the front garden and on to the large iron pipe that crosses from bank to bank just there, she was shouting and swearing back at the boys at the top of her voice. You know this pipe? Very large? No? About five feet above the surface of the water and stretching across from side to side. In no time at all the old woman had run on to it and balanced her way right over. I could see it was not the first time she had performed this feat. But the boys, seeing her coming, had picked up their ball and disappeared into the ruins of the ironworks. The old woman made running across that pipe look very easy, and when she had gone, and there was no one about, I had a try at it myself. I tried running, like her, and I fell off into the river before I was half way over. The current carried me down into the tunnel, I suppose, and under the road. You saved my life, Dewi.' He leaned on his elbow and held out his hand to me, and I got up and went over to him and shook it. This gave me a wonderful warm feeling, I was very proud I had done this for him. I forgot it was my father who had rescued him and not me.

106

He began to talk to us about his school in Germany, or perhaps it was in Austria, or Poland, or the Balkans, I couldn't tell. He asked us if we would go back there with him when he returned, and all of us said we would like to. We had never heard of a school like that before. The building was huge and old, it was once the cavalry barracks of the imperial guard, it stood at the foot of the great snow-capped mountain barrier, solid rock with the crevices at the summit white even in summer-time. But the valleys all about the school were thick with green grass, cow-belled cattle munched in them, and the rivers were white as milk flowing through the emerald meadows. Karl's special friend was a boy called Moriz, a baron Karl said he was, and his father had a castle of red and white rock on top of a precipice above one of the ravines. Another pal was Rudi, his guardian was his uncle, Count Eugen, and when this uncle wanted to speak to the head-master he used to ride his tall chestnut gelding across the school yard amongst the boys at playtime, wearing his hat with a feather in it and his suit of green leather and velvet corduroy. Karl and Rudi used to spend their holidays with this count some-times, and there were fine sights to be seen where he lived in the middle of the dark forest—herds of wild horses and stags and fierce wild boars. The count had a pack of huge yellow hounds, he kept them for hunting, and he used to kill the peasants' horses to feed them on. His foresters chained the carcasses up so that they dangled from the boughs of the trees, and the savage dogs used to jump up at them and tear them to pieces, and eat them right down to the bones, so that in the end only the chained skeletons of the horses were hanging from the branches.

Karl said he belonged to a select club in that school and the members of it were allowed to wear a special dagger in their belts. Before you could join you had to break out of the school dormitory at night and cross the railway bridge, which was guarded by sentries, near by into the next country—underneath. You groped your way down a track on the side of the ravine to get amongst the girders, and then you went across by climbing from one girder to the next in the darkness. Karl said it was quite a short bridge, but there was a drop of about two hundred feet into the river underneath it. Luckily, he said, he always loved heights. To prove you'd been across you had to light a fire on a little hill on the other side, which the boys could see from the upper dormitory windows. You came back on the first train in the morning and climbed into school through a window left open for you. Once a boy got tight celebrating the other side with some gipsies, he tried to walk back over the bridge, but one of the sentries woke up and shot him.

We were all listening hard to Karl without saying a word, we had forgotten all about Growler and his mucking, he seemed unimportant, not real compared with what Karl was telling us. Karl said when he was coming out of the trees into the school yard, the morning after he had crossed the bridge, he ran straight into one of the masters returning from an early morning gallop. What he did was to fling his arms out in front of him and pretend to be sleep-walking. Karl was too cute to go back to the dormitory with the master following behind him, so he went up to the headmaster's front door instead and began fumbling at the knob, trying to get into the house. When the headmaster, wearing his sleeping-suit and nightcap, came down to see what was going on, Karl pretended to have some sort of fit, he kept pointing into the house and shouting: 'There's a tiger on the mantelpiece! Help! Help!'

'This is the special powder we always used for lighting our fires when we had crossed the bridge,' Karl said to us. He took a flat tin out of his pocket and opened the lid. From where I sat the stuff inside looked like grape-cork. Then without any more warning he threw almost the whole boxful on the fire.

The effect was tremendous, the whole fire exploded in a terrible blinding hot flash and roared up like a furnace into twice its size, filling the air with terrific heat and a sweet, important, chemical smell; the blaze seemed to swell out suddenly all round towards us, and to shoot up its flames at the same time into a huge height, crackling and roaring and throwing up millions of sparks sky-high. The heat coming out of it was unbearable, so intense we all tumbled off our stones as fast as we could and rolled and scrambled across the grass out of the way of it to where the air was a bit cooler at the edges of the platform. A strong smell of burning came with me and I looked over my clothes to see if they had been scorched, but the sudden brightness of the fire had blinded me and I couldn't see properly. When I looked at anything it became covered with blackness, and when I shut my eyes everything blazed. Where was Karl? I could make out Tom, and Charley, in the firelight, crouching down on the grass as far away from the furnace as possible, but Karl was nowhere to be seen. Or Jeffy either.

Then I heard Karl's voice coming from somewhere in the bracken. 'Good night,' he shouted. 'Look out of the window and see the mysterious fire in the sky.'

We could hear him running down the mountain road in the darkness. And the other footsteps must be Jeffy's. He was not to be seen anyway. The stuff Karl had thrown on the fire, whatever it was, had made the flames roar up, and filled the air with this strange, hot, chemical smell; but a few minutes later the blaze had sunk down to silence and a smouldering mass, and in no time at all it had gone out, quicker even than the time Jeffy had spewed over it.

When I got into our kitchen that night, I was so full of excitement at all that had happened that I didn't notice at first that there was anything wrong. The gas was lit and a good fire of binding coal was burning in the range, and my mother was there, and my granny and my auntie Bronwen had come over from their house, as they did all the time now since my father was dead. I never liked the first few minutes in the kitchen when I had been out, although it always looked cosy, I always felt all the eyes in the room were watching and examining me all over. I didn't want them to know anything about Karl, it was no business of theirs, if they asked me any questions about him I would tell them a lot of lies. I was determined to keep Karl to myself, just as I had kept his knife to myself for weeks and weeks.

My mother was under the gas at the kitchen table, using the sewing-machine. Any other time I would have been down-hearted at what I saw her doing, but after being up the mountain with Karl I was too excited to notice properly. She was stitching up some new pink flannel shirts for me. She did try to get the ones after my father to fit me, brand-new some of them, but they were too small, she couldn't get them near my neck, thank God. So she had to make these new ones. But she always cut the things much too big so that they'd last a bit. They had big balloon sleeves I couldn't get my coat over, and the tails were so long they used to work down the legs of my trousers, when I wore short ones, and show at the backs of my knees. I had long trousers now and I didn't have to worry about that, but I still hated the things, they were rough as sacking to wear, so picky I itched all day when they were new, and at night I spent a nice bit of time on the edge of the bed scratching myself like mad after taking them off. We had plenty of boys' shirts in stock in the factory, cotton, youths' size and all, and I was always on to my mother to let me have some of those, but she wouldn't, they were too skimpy, and too dear, and not warm enough for the winter, she always had some excuse or other. Clean and paid for, and patches are better than holes, that was always her talk, she didn't care how my clothes felt on me, or what I looked like in them. When I came into the kitchen she didn't stop machining, or say anything, but her eyes followed me round until I went to sit on the foot of the couch by the fire.

I wanted my granny and my auntie Bronwen to go, so that I could have my supper and get upstairs to bed and think about Karl. But they didn't budge. My granny sat on the couch breathing and puffing hard, her man's starched collar nearly strangling her by the colour of her face, and her thin black velvet tie rising and falling on her big bosoms. One thing I was thankful for. When I was smaller, and my granny didn't have anything special to do, she would place the palms of her hands flat one each side of my head and lift me off the ground like that. She was strong through breathing a lot, my father told me, and singing contralto, but it sounded more like double bass to me. But strong arms or not, that was all over now, I would never again have that terrible feeling that just when my boots were leaving the floor, my body would drop off at the neck and leave my head between my granny's hands.

The big fire in our range and the strong smell of scenty soap meant most likely my auntie Bronny had come over our house for a bath, because my grandfather's house didn't have one. My auntie was sitting by the table with her washed hair down her back, one hand under her in a special way she had, and the other holding one of the women's papers she was always buying. She did the Ystrad calls for my mother now since my father died. She looked pretty ordinary out in her collecting clothes, her long grey raincoat down to her boots like a midwife's, and her hood, and her man's umbrella on her arm, but on Sundays going to chapel she was a proper fashion plate. She walked up Commercial Street to Libanus in the latest of everything, so that people who didn't happen to know her used to stare at her big hat with red ostrich feathers round it like a cavalier's, and her thick chicken-wire veil, and her high umbrella no thicker than a walking-stick, and her long white gloves and laced-up boots with light cloth panels and high heels. If she was going to a concert or something like that she smelt nice as well, she wore a feather-boa necklet and bangles, and she used to tear thin leaves out of a little book she had and rub them on her face to make it pink or white with powder. She had masses of clothes in her bedroom, the latest, out of our pattern books, and all sorts of things for looking after them, rows of boot-trees and coat-hangers and sort of ebony scissors for stretching her kid gloves, as well as chains and brooches and earrings and a pincushion full of hatpins about a foot long, and all kinds of bottles and perfumes and scent squirters and that. She was my father's sister, or stepsister or something, and I never thought much about her, she was all right, she seemed smart to me, and pretty. But some of the boys in our form gave me a bit of a shock one day when they started teasing me about her. We were all ragging one another about nicknames in our formroom, and Jonno Nicholas said my father was known about the place as Jack the Dragon. Well, I'd heard that, and I was just going to tell Jonno people called his own father Africa Jack when Tosh Lewis interrupted and said my father wasn't the only one in the family with a nickname, everybody in Ystrad knew my auntie was called Bronwen Big-doors. When I asked him why he said he thought it must be because of the big double doors of the factory in Brewery Square. I told him I didn't believe it, but Jonno started up again. 'How does your auntie walk like that, Ginge?' he said to me.

I had never noticed she walked in any special way. 'Like what?' I asked him.

'Here's my head, my arse is coming,' Jeffy said, butting in and doing it across the classroom, and everybody laughed. Jeffy was a proper flamer like that.

But I looked at her specially the next time I saw her out, and the way Jeffy had acted was quite true. It made me blush to see her.

As I moved about the kitchen I noticed nobody was saying anything. And I began to notice as well my mother wasn't the only one there with bright eyes, my granny's were glittering too, they seemed to have a lot of sparkling water packed round each of them. And I caught her and my mother making shapes at each other behind my back and that woke me up properly, and made me think there was something the matter. I hated it when they were all quiet and watching me like this.

I said: 'Any supper, Mam?'

'Wherever have you been?' she asked me suddenly, stopping the sewing-machine and giving me a sharp-nosed look.

'With Tom,' I said. 'I called for him.' She never minded me going with Tom much although his father was a boozer. Tom's grandfather Griffiths was a deacon in our chapel and Tom and his mother and Betty, his sister, were in Libanus every Sunday. 'And Charley Llewellyn,' I stuck on when I saw she didn't say anything, but just went on staring at me and waiting for me to say some more.

'Who else?' she said. 'Was that boy Urquhart with you?'

'Oh, yes,' I said, as though I had only just remembered about Jeffy. 'Jeffy Urquhart. We went for a walk up Pantglas.'

My auntie Bronny had put her paper down and was sitting on both her hands now. I thought I caught a few more signals going round the room.

'Did he tell you anything?' my mother asked me.

'Tell me anything? How do you mean?'

'About his mother.'

'I don't think he did. Why? I can't remember.'

By the look of her I expected her to start lecturing my ears off about going out with Jeffy again, but she didn't say anything.

'What's up with her?' I asked.

She glanced round at the other two. 'She's gone away,' she said.

At first I thought she meant on holidays, and then it struck me perhaps Mrs Urquhart had gone to hospital somewhere.

'Where's she gone? Is she bad?'

'If he doesn't tell you, don't you mention it to him, mind. She's run away from home, and people say that lodger they had has gone too.'

Was that all it was? It didn't seem much to me. Mrs Urquhart was a pretty funny sort of woman anyway, never talking to you, and mooning about the house, and always staring out of the windows.

'What's for supper?' I said.

'Make him the cocoa in the kitchen, Bronwen,' my mother said, 'will you? He can cut the bread and jam himself. Take your hands to the bosh and wash them, remember,' she said to me. 'Or he can have what's over of the cold fish.'

I could see why Jeffy had been even more jumpy than usual, and wild and hysterical. On the way to the scullery I said: 'How do you know about Jeffy's mother? I don't think he said a word.'

'Mr Powell the insurance was here. He had his call up there in "Hawthornden" this morning collecting and she'd gone. And your auntie Bronwen heard as well. She left a note.'

I ate my supper standing up in the dark of the scullery. I didn't want to be in there with them in the kitchen with the light on me while I was thinking about what they had said. If Mr Powell had been in our house most likely he had spoken to them about Karl as well. Bound to have. I was dying to know what he had said but I wasn't going to ask. I could never speak to my mother and the others concerning my thoughts of Karl. If Mr Powell had heard about Jeffy's mother perhaps Karl knew too. Was that why he was so determined Growler shouldn't take Jeffy home? And I remembered Jeffy hadn't seemed a bit surprised to see Karl when he came round after his faint. '*Ach y fi*,' I could hear my mother saying in the kitchen, 'and that little Mr Urquhart such a good clean-living little man too.'

'A dirty old hoor, that's what she is,' my granny said.

I was sick of Mr Urquhart by then, I didn't care about his clean living or his dirty blackheads, all I wanted was for the lot of them to take their nails out of my feathers so that I could get away. My mother was like medicine to me, I could only swallow her bossiness a bit at a time, and as soon as I could manage it I got out of the scullery and went up the back stairs to my bedroom.

I took out my knife, and when I had undressed and got into bed I lay gripping it under the pillow. Usually I went to sleep at once, but now I couldn't, I lay there hearing the noise of our river rushing past outside. I hardly ever noticed this, I was so used to it, but after the excitement of listening to Karl it kept me awake, remembering all he had told us about the great grey towering mountains around his school, with snow in the gashes near their summits, and the pretty houses all over the green countryside with paintings on their outside walls. And I kept on thinking about Karl himself, about his thin silver earrings, and his golden-brown face, and his pale eyebrows, very thick and straight, but made of fine silvery hair, pure white against the sunburn of his skin. And about him crossing the ravine in the darkness on the girders of the bridge, and the wild river rushing along two hundred feet below him. Every time I was going to drop off to sleep I would be with him, and feel myself falling. What did he mean by saying we would see mysterious fire in the sky? I got out of bed and looked out of my bedroom window, but our house was low down, near the river, and surrounded by other buildings, and all I could see in the air were a few ordinary stars over our orchard so I went back to bed.

But the excitement was too much, and a little later I got out again and crept on to the landing and listened. There was absolute silence downstairs. My mother was very fond of her cup and saucer and most likely she was over my granny's by now with the kettle on the fire, and my auntie's latest tissue-paper patterns spread out on some dress material on the parlour table. I went along to the landing window, and sure enough there across the yard was a light in my granny's parlour. I slipped on my boots, got my overcoat from behind the scullery door and went outside into the yard. All the doors downstairs in our house were wide open. I crossed our yard towards the factory archway, and crept up the wooden stairs into our showrooms. Everything there was closed, but not locked, because my mother hadn't been round with her keys yet. I couldn't light the gas in case it was seen from my granny's, so I felt my way among the stands and cases and dressmaker's dummies in the dark until I reached the staircase to the top storey. I climbed it and pushed up the trap-door above my head.

From there, on the top floor of the factory, I could see the flames at once. The back window of the building looked out over the lower end of the town and down the valley. When I had cleaned the dirt off one or two of the panes I could see somewhere down there in the darkness, perhaps a mile or two away, a huge fire burning high in the sky, a sort of bonfire resting on nothing at all, hung blazing in the middle of the darkness like a tremendous planet, just as Karl said there would be.

4

THE next morning neither Karl nor Jeffy was in school, so Tom, Charley and I didn't know what to do about our orders to see Growler first thing. At playtime we watched his corridor from our classroom window, and when we spotted him leaving his room we went down to see him. On the way we were lucky enough to bump into Tossy English coming back up along Growler's corridor. 'The headmaster's out, boys,' he said to us, so we said, 'Thank you, sir', back to him, turned round and went out to the playground as safe as houses.

Anyway, he didn't send for us, although every time anyone came into the classroom with a message for the master teaching us we stopped breathing, and we grinned and made faces at each other afterwards with relief when nothing happened.

At playtime in the afternoon, when we were all larking about in the classroom, Jeffy walked in with a wide strip of plaster across his forehead, and we all cheered. He gave us long noses and plenty of lip, but he didn't say anything about his mother or about the night before and none of us asked him.

On the way home in the afternoon as we were dawdling down High Street together, who should we see ahead of us but someone who looked to me exactly like Karl. We shouted, but he didn't seem to hear us, so we hurried and caught him up just as he was turning out of Ystrad Square into Station Place. He smiled when he recognized us, but not much, and his eyes were like icicles, he said he couldn't stop to speak to us now, he had to catch a train down the valley. He looked forward to seeing us on Monday. He gave us a sort of bow that meant he had finished with us and hurried across the road to the station.

I was deeply disappointed. Everything seemed flat and dull and uninteresting at once with Karl gone. His politeness hurt me more than many a bitter row, or teacher's sark or bawling. I wondered whether it meant he had finished with us for ever, whether the whole thing between us was already all over.

That week-end I thought about him all the time. I worried because of that distance and politeness towards us in High Street, after the way he had befriended us and stood up for us before Growler, and stayed with us by our fire, and told us about his life abroad. I longed for Monday to come, and I dreaded it, because I would find out whether he still wanted us as his friends. Saturday and Sunday were long and unhappy. I felt lonely and restless, as though I were homesick, longing all the time to hear him talking to us again about the countries he had lived in, and all the unfamiliar people, the strange wild schoolboys and the masters, and the operas and the balls he had attended, and the great stables of the palaces filled with beautiful horses, and the hunting and the shooting in the forests.

5

BEFORE very long we began going about with Karl every chance we got, Jeffy, Tom, Charley and I, and oftenest, well into the autumn, we sat around our fire in the Pantglas woods listening to him telling us about his life, about the schools and the castles, with stuffed wild beasts' heads sticking out of the walls, about his dogs and horses, his friends, fencers and dead shots with revolvers, barons, huntsmen, gipsies, princes, smugglers, beggars, beautiful princesses with auburn hair and diamond tiaras, and deep collars of diamonds around their throats. 'When the time comes,' he would always end up, 'will you come there with me?'

Sometimes he wouldn't talk at all, all he wanted to do was sit barefoot on the floor in the top room of our factory, eating apples and playing us a few games of dix-stones. The game was new to him and he got us to teach him the rules. He was marvellous at it, he had long thin hands, one badly scarred across the back, and it was great to see his slender fingers, with the minia-ture snow-storms in all his finger-nails, creeping around the metal stones on the floor-boards, and tossing them up and catching them as though he'd been doing it all his life. It was fascinating to watch Karl doing anything, he seemed so clever even at things he had never done in his life before. I marvelled at him all the time, and wondered about him day and night, I got, after a little while, when I wasn't with him and watching him, I kept looking out for him, wondering with a sort of excitement, and longing, and dread, if I would meet him accidentally in the street.

After the night he carried Jeffy up to our fire in the woods we never saw him again with his earrings in. He didn't tell us, but we guessed Growler had stopped him wearing them. That was the old toad's way of spiting Karl for getting us to disobey him. Although Growler gave us a big row because of our manners a few mornings later when he sent for us all suddenly to his room, he didn't really punish any of us for what we had done up the woods. Or he pretended he didn't anyway. That was Growler all over, the foxy old crawn, because he got us all the same.

It was easy for him to catch me, all he had to do was come into the maths lesson and look at my homework book. When he came round the class and found I had 'Not S' four times running, he gave me a good belting supposed to be for that. Charley he got for not wearing his cap on the way to school, he had it stuffed in his pocket to show his waves off, instead of on his head. Old Tom was harder to catch, he was so good at his work, but by a bit of luck Growler got him too in time. Tom only had one joke. He used to take a pop-bottle into the lab when there was nobody about, fill it with a mixture of coal-gas and oxygen, half and half, wrap an asbestos towel round his hand and hold the mouth of the bottle to a Bunsen burner. You could hear the bang all over school. When Tom had done it he used to buzz off out the back way and join the crowd of boys and masters running down the corridor to see what had happened. One day as he was hurrying out of the lab after doing it, with his silent mouth wide open laughing, he walked straight into Growler who happened to be coming in through the back door. He got a real coating with Growler breathing hard. Even Jeffy had to have a few, although all he'd done was faint away and be with us. When Growler handed him back his blotty essay on the Balkans he gave him four of the best to go with it.

But the worst thing that happened because of that night in the woods was that Growler got to know us all properly, we could see his big glasses following us about in school, watching our every movement, and if one of us did anything wrong he never gave us the benefit of the doubt. Growler would never forgive anyone who got the better of him, he was a merciless old jacksy in having his own back. And he thought we were out to get the better of him all the time, but we weren't, all we wanted was a bit of quietness and for him to leave us alone. It was all right defying Growler up the mountain, that was one thing, but defying him in school was different, it was something none of us wanted to do, except Karl, of course, because in school he was like a maniac. It wasn't fair, the way he picked on us. Why was he like this to us? He never said a word wrong to flags like Rubby Evans and Dodger Quant, who used to rob him right and left. Dodger would go down Growler's corridor in lesson time with a broken nib in his hand and knock at the study door. If Growler was in he'd ask politely if he might have a new nib; if he wasn't he'd nip inside, shove a handful of rubbers in his pocket or half a dozen exercise books down his trousers and nip out again. And yet Growler kept on warning us every chance he got, calling us the Club, and threatening to disperse us to different forms, or report us to our parents, or even to expel us. Jeffy said what did he care about that, he wished he could get expelled. Growler had never been like this to us before we became friendly with Karl.

He was always on to Karl, whatever Karl did was wrong. He would never forgive Karl for besting him. We didn't have a bobby-greencoat in the grammar school to whip us in if we were absent, and mostly Growler didn't care if we came to school or not, he used to tell us if the more indifferent of our parents didn't wish us to be educated it was not his business to ensure that we attended school regularly. But every time Karl was absent Growler sent for him, and abused him, and gave him a couple of weeks' detention, and threatened to expel him. Karl used to come out of Growler's room after these rows looking pretty flushed, but he never wanted to tell us what happened. All we knew was that he despised Growler and Growler hated him.

But old Growler didn't have it all his own way, either. Once when Karl had been away from school for about a fortnight, Growler gave him a terrible row, and wrote a letter in his presence reporting everything he had done to the governors. We were up in the formroom when Karl was telling us this, it was dinner time and only the five of us were there, Jeffy, Tom, Charley, Karl and me.

'Let's get even with him, the old faker,' said Jeffy.

'How can we though?' we all wanted to know.

Somebody suggested sliding up and down his corridor a few times when he wasn't about, with our football boots on. That would make him mad. Or, Charley said, tie a piece of string to two trees across the mountain road in the dark and knock his fancy hat off. Jeffy's idea was for us to watch Growler coming out of his house, and if he started to walk down Commercial Street, to dodge up to the tramroad where the colliers' railway trucks were kept in their siding on the hill. These trucks used to run across Commercial Street at the level crossing below Iron Lane, and we could release the brakes just before Growler started walking across the railway lines unsuspecting.

'What if we killed him?' I said.

'Nobody could kill Growler,' Jeffy said. 'Most likely he'd only have his leg off.'

His eyes were so shining and yellow when he said this I wasn't sure whether he meant it or not.

But during the next lesson I felt a compass point in my behind and Jeffy whispered: 'I've got a brain-wave. I'll tell you play-time.'

One of the things Growler was always playing about with was the school time-table. He used to make it up on a huge squared-out sheet of oblong cardboard, six feet by four, laid out on the table in the corner of his room. He had little coloured cards, a few hundred of them, a special colour for each subject, French white, chemistry orange, geography blue, and so on, and he fitted these cards into the squares on the board, lesson by lesson, day by day, form by form, like a huge puzzle, until the whole board was completely covered. When Jeffy went into Growler's study for one of his lampings he noticed the time-table for next year on the table. Growler had nearly finished it. It was very windy that time of year, and Jeffy's plan was to go down to Growler's study when he wasn't in and open the two doors there, the outside one from the quad into the corridor, and then the one opposite it, from the corridor into the study. The wind would do the rest. Jeffy was willing to bet not one of the little cards would be in its place on the board when Growler got back to his room. With a bit of luck half of them would be in the fire. Hours, days, weeks, perhaps months of Growler's work would be destroyed. And the best thing about it was he wouldn't be able to prove that somebody hadn't left the door open by accident, most likely himself.

This seemed a good plan to all of us, and we decided to put some lift under the wings of it the first chance that came up. Dinner time was no good because we had heard Dodger Quant saying Growler locked his door at midday and went home with the key in his pocket. But we knew he sometimes went into the staffroom during afternoon playtime, we had watched him going there from our formroom, most likely to tell the masters to do something or other special the next day. He was never in there long, but Jeffy was willing to try slipping down the corridor to the study then.

But Growler mustn't see him about, or any of us, or he'd begin putting two and two together. We didn't tell Karl, and he wasn't in school the day Jeffy actually did it, we meant to give him a nice surprise when it was all over. Every afternoon that week the four of us spent our playtime in our formroom looking across the quad, keeping watch on Growler's corridor, hoping the high winds would go on blowing hard for a bit. And then, on Thursday, we saw him, about half way through playtime, coming out of his study, shutting the door behind him, and rolling up his corridor towards the staffroom just round the corner.

It was a beautiful day, everybody crossing the quad had their shoulders hunched up against the gusts and their heads tucked in on one side, and all the morning the storm went on sandpapering the roof of our classroom like mad. And on top of that, on our way to school, we noticed the gale in the night had put half our Rugby posts flat on the field.

The four of us nipped out of our classroom, along the passage, down the stairs and into the school hall. The corridor where Growler's study was, and the staffroom, led off from the hall, but nobody could get into it at playtime because there was always a special prefect guarding the swing doors into it. We were not noticed in the hall because it was such a cold gusty day that lots of kids were hanging about school to avoid going out into the yard to play. The prefect on duty at the corridor doors that week was Tusker Grant, and we knew we could never get past him. Tusker always did the job properly, and he was so dull he wouldn't let the Prince of Wales through the doors unless he showed permission signed by Growler. But we had luck every yard of the way. As we were wondering what to do, pretending to study the photographs of the school teams around the walls, we saw Lucas, our French master, coming across the hall from the lobbies with a tail of four or five little kids following him. Most likely he was taking them to the staffroom to hand them the French newspapers he had started selling the little form one-ers who didn't know any better. Quick as a flash Jeffy fell in behind them and went through the swing doors while Tusker was holding them open for Lucas and his kids to pass.

Tom, Charley and I drifted into the cloakroom to keep out of the way. We didn't see Jeffy again until we were back in our lines after break. Then up in our classroom he told us what had happened.

'Lucas went down the corridor and into the staffroom,' he said, 'and left the kids I was with standing outside. I slipped round the corner into Growler's corridor, I don't think those kids will cleck, I doubt if they even noticed I was with them, they were so busy sucking up to Lucas. I half crouched going down Growler's corridor in case somebody saw me from any of the windows over here across the quad. When I reached the end of the corridor I opened the outside door from the quad first, and the wind swept into school whistling like a tornado. I didn't actually open the door into Growler's study, there was no need, all I did was turn the knob a bit and the wind snatched it out of my hand and punched it in itself. There was a terrific crash as the door flung itself against a hat-stand inside and knocked it over, and I could hear the fire roaring up the chimney, and the rustling of the papers flying all about the room. When I was tiptoeing back up Growler's corridor, that was the worst part of the job. What if I met him face to face coming back from the staffroom? I made up my mind what to do. If I heard anybody approaching round the corner I was going to start bolting towards them and say, all breathless, I had just gone down the head's room for a new exercise book and found all the papers and things blowing about inside. I think I could get most of the staff to believe me, if not Growler himself. As I came back I could feel the wind blowing a gale behind me, snatching all the pictures away from the corridor walls so that they were jumping about like mad on their cords and banging the plaster on both sides of me. But I had wonderful luck and I didn't meet anybody. Lucas's kids had disappeared from outside the staffroom door when I got there. But as I passed I could see the sleeve of old Growler's gown caught in the door, he must have been standing inside with his back to the door talking to the masters, and a foot of his gown sleeve with the old brown acid stain on it was hanging out into the corridor.

'Just when I was passing the staffroom, wondering how the

devil I was going to get past Tusker and back into the hall, the handbell began ringing in the yard. Playtime was finished! Through the glass in the swing doors I saw Tusker the other side moving away to clear the hall. That was my chance. I slipped through without anybody seeing me. And then I mingled with the kids in the hall and came out into the yard with a couple of dozen others turned out of school, and I got into the 3A line.'

We were all very excited at what Jeffy had done, and a bit afraid too, wondering what would happen. Half way through the next lesson we could hear Growler roaring in the passage outside our room, the sound of his voice louder even than the storm, and we knew for sure the little cards were all over the room, and the big sheet of cardboard with them too most likely. We tried to do our graphs, but we could hardly calculate, we were so excited, we were prickly and a bit breathless. I could feel my heart pounding at the sound of Growler's voice out there in the passage. What would he do? We kept looking at each other, and swallowing, and listening to every sound, wondering whether Growler would burst into our room roaring and accuse us of opening the doors. But nothing happened. Most likely Tossy English persuaded him he had left the door open himself, and the whole thing was an accident. We never heard that Growler said a word to anybody in school about it, and we had the fun of having had our own back on him for once, anyway.

6

KARL was absent from school all the time, he didn't like being indoors, he said, and he didn't like our teachers much, or the boys in his form, 5B. We didn't either, the louts, Jeffy and I especially, we hated them. They were big show-offs, always pretending they were something special, they used to say 'Adios,' and called football 'kickers', and they walked about school arm-in-arm with their hair done up with water, and if you passed them in the corridor they would clip you or give you a boot up the behind for nothing at all. Sometimes we wouldn't see hide or hair of Karl for a week, or perhaps even a fortnight. It was no good asking Tally Powell where he was, although they lived in the same house I never saw them going anywhere together, or speaking, or even looking at each other in school.

Karl never told us where he went when he was absent, at least he didn't at the time, although when he could he usually brought us back a big bag of the special mint caramels we liked from wherever it was he had visited. But sometimes, later on, when we were in the factory, or our formroom, or up the Pantglas woods, keeping our fire going with branches and Jeffy's gramophone records, he would mention he'd been exploring up the rifle-butts, or he'd climbed down the air shaft, or visited the powder-house in the bracken high up on the mountain. And sometimes he told us about the things he'd seen over in the other valleys on both sides of ours.

One place he had been to, he told us, was a special patch of grass called the Nannies. Just below our town, spanning the Ystrad Valley at its widest from mountain to mountain, there used to be an old railway bridge, a sort of high viaduct supported on huge square pillars of purple plum-red brick. There had been about ten of these pillars, they stood in a dead straight line right across the valley, rising from the fields of Graig farm to a height of about two hundred feet, and tapering slightly to the top.

I had never seen a train crossing this viaduct because it had been closed before I was born. The railway track up there had become thickly grass-grown and that's why people called the bridge the Nannies, because it was the place Phillips the Graig kept his goats. He put chains across at each end of the bridge and let them feed on it. They dunged it up and the grass there grew like mad. Then, when I was small, the bridge was dismantled, and the pillars supporting it blown up because the whole thing was supposed to be unsafe. I could just remember playing by the river in our factory yard and hearing the back windows of the mill rattling every now and then as the bangs went off down the valley all the afternoon.

But something must have gone wrong with those bangs. Most of the pillars collapsed all right, they fell down in huge heaps on the Graig meadows, they were still there, in a row across the fields, great slabs and masses of purple brickwork, and mounds of broken bricks and mortar and rubble, each one piled up high like the ruins of a street of houses, like Quarry Row when the council pulled it down, only all in one heap, and every one of the ten mounds was overgrown with willow-herb, and ragwort, and tall thin grass. But somehow or other, the pillar half way across the valley didn't fall down, it still stood there right in the middle of the fields, an enormous square plum-red tower, solid and tapering, with a bit of the old bridge, an oblong platform supported on stumpy girders, still left balancing on the top of it, and a wide black crack running down it through the brickwork from the top almost to the ground.

This pillar, and the flat bit of bridge on the top, were what everybody still called the Nannies. I was used to it, usually I didn't take much notice of it, but Karl seemed to think it was pretty wonderful standing there by itself in the middle of the valley, lonely and isolated. Majestic, he called it, and mysterious. And one Saturday in the Christmas holidays he told us how he had climbed it.

We were upstairs in our factory, sitting on the cills, and, looking out from the back windows of the top floor, we could just see the flat top of it rising above the town roofs through the rain, a couple of miles down the valley. The mysterious impulse to tread that secret grass came upon him, he said, the night he had carried Jeffy unconscious into our camp in the woods, while he was yarning to us about crossing the bridge over the ravine near his school and lighting his fire in another country. And it was that same night that he had climbed the tower.

'The only way of getting up the wall', Karl told us, 'was to use that crack in the brickwork as a sort of vertical path, but the difficulty was getting up to the crack in the first place, because it came to an abrupt end about thirty feet above the field. But, luckily for me, the lowest section of the pillar wasn't built in a dead flat wall; when I passed my hand upwards over the bricks, I found, after every three rows, that the next row every time was set back a little, about half the width of a brick I should think, making a narrow step, and it was these small regular ledges, which seemed to be waiting in the darkness for my fingers, that I used as holds to climb to the bottom end of the fissure. My head was turned to the right so that my left cheek was against the brickwork. My chest and the whole front of my body were more or less flat against the wall, but my feet, like my head, were turned to the right, to make as much contact as possible with the bricks under the soles of my boots.'

He glanced round at us, got out of his cill seat and stood facing the whitewashed wall of the factory in the position he had been describing.

'Like a figure in an ancient Egyptian painting,' he said. 'You know what I mean.'

I had never seen an ancient Egyptian painting, but I began to picture Karl clinging high up there to the perpendicular face of the brickwork, stuck on in exactly the way I had seen him lying on his belly in our yard the day we pulled him out of the river.

'Wasn't it dark, though, Karl?' said Charley, standing up on the seat of the rope swing. 'How could you see what you were doing?'

Karl came away from the wall and went back to his place on the window.

'It was night-time, of course,' he said, 'but, if you remember, it was one of the warm still nights when, although there's no moon and only a few stars, the darkness seems full of some secret illumination and glistening. But really, I find climbing in the dark has advantages. No one is likely to see you from the ground, and interfere, and shout at you to come down. And you can't see the drop below you and how far you've got to fall. That is if heights frighten you.

'The hardest thing in this part of the climb was actually to get into the bottom of the crack when I had at last climbed about thirty feet of wall up to it. Because with my head still just below it, the recesses in the brickwork came to a sudden end. How was I going to move up into that fissure, showing black as ink above me, when I had nothing at all to catch hold of? I clung there fast in the darkness, thinking, afraid I should have to give up and come down again after all and try some other time, by daylight.'

'What *did* you do, Karl?' we all wanted to know.

'I stretched up as far as I could, reaching into the intense black in the bottom of the crack, I groped about in the emptiness there, and at last my fingers closed over a ridge of bricks that felt absolutely firm. I thought that if they would support me for just one short scramble, I would be up safely inside the crack. So I jerked—and a whole piece of wall, a huge heavy mass of bricks cemented together, came away in a loud rush, they shot out of the crack over my head and crashed past me in the darkness. I heard them thundering heavily against the brickwork below me, shaking the tower, and then landing with a terrible series of thuds and crashes in the field below. Then there was silence. They must have missed my head by inches. And, what was as bad, I nearly went down after them. Because my right hand lost its grip when they came loose, and then my right foot, and my whole body swayed slowly away from the wall; for a few seconds I couldn't stop myself, and my entire weight was left hanging out there in space by the fingers of my left hand, and the toe of my left boot. Nothing else.'

'Were you frightened, Karl?'

'No. Surprised. And annoyed, too, that the solid wall I was relying so much on had deliberately swung away from me like that without any warning, like a door suddenly opened inwards, just when you are going to knock at it. Luckily my grip held, and in a few seconds I was safe again, close and cosy, flat against the brickwork of the tower.'

'What did you do then, Karl?' we asked him.

'Well, I clung there a little, wondering what I *could* do. I

128

decided to make one more attempt at getting into the crack before giving up altogether, and again I groped about above my head, feeling for a firm hold. At last my fingers clawed their way into the roots of some bushes growing there in the darkness. "Fine," I thought. But the powdered mortar, and the soot, and earth under the roots began drizzling over my face, I was staring upwards at the time, and suddenly, after the dribbling, the stuff came down in a rush, I must have taken a couple of bucketfuls of it right into my face and my open eyes, by the weight of it. I almost let go with pain, perhaps I even cried out, I don't know, but I snatched my head away, and after a little the earth stopped falling upon me, and the rest of the matted roots held firm in my fingers. But the pain didn't stop. With a few frantic tugs I got right up into the beginning of the crack. Many, I dare say, would have been screaming by then, I also was in agony, mad with the pain burning like hot pokers into my eyes. I leaned back, squatting there a while, drenched with dirt, and the sweat pouring out of me, trying to clean my eyelids out with my handkerchief, and dusting the grit out of my hair, and picking the lumps of mortar out from between my neck and my shirt collar. Gradually the pain became less, although my eyes watered freely for the rest of the climb, and I started going up the crack towards the platform at the top of the tower. Another hundred and seventy feet to reach the girders.

'The easiest parts of that climb were where the crack narrowed to just a little more than the width of my body. But sometimes it became too small to hold me, and then I had to climb out on to the outside face of the tower wall, with a sheer drop into the fields beneath me, and there find holds on the edge of the crack as best I could. At other times the fissure widened out a lot, and whenever this happened I found a sort of vertical garden growing in it, the crack was choked up with plants and bushes, elder and lilac mostly, and a terribly strong type of stinging nettle that grows in this valley. I had to snake my way up through them, it was like burrowing among a tangle of torn sacks and thick knitting, mixed up with lengths of barbed wire. Several times, squirming up through those bushes and nettles, I sent masses of earth and rubble and broken bricks shooting down the crack behind me and on to the field below, and the thud of them landing took longer and longer to reach me through the darkness, as I went farther and farther up the tower.

'At last I got right up under the girders at the top of the crack. I couldn't go up any farther. My eyes were painful again, watering and burning from the lime in the mortar, and at times I could hardly see at all. And my hands were on fire, and bleeding badly, and the whole of my head—cheeks, forehead, ears, neck, all stung and swollen and inflamed. But I wasn't going to give up now, having climbed to such a height I was determined to set foot on the Nannies somehow or other.

'It was a problem. The platform projected out about three yards from the tower on every side, it was like a flat roof supported on top of the girders. How was I going to get out from under the eaves, as it were, and climb up on to the roof? I saw that a piece of the ironwork that had once had something to do with supporting the bridge, was running out just under the girders from a point in the brickwork quite near the crack. It was a rusty iron pipe, a bit thicker than bicycle tubing, separated from the girders above it by a gap of about four inches, and projecting a couple of feet beyond them at the far end. It looked to me as though my only chance was to hang down from that pipe, work my way out along it to the far end, and then climb up from there on to the platform above me.

'I looked from the crack where I was crouching out into the night, and wondered. Right above my head, set close together, the great black hulking girders, plastered with hundreds of rivet-heads, stretched out into space, and ended abruptly about ten or eleven feet away from the wall. Far, far down below, I could see the lights of the valley, the Ystrad lights on one side, and on the other the street lamps of the places farther away, I didn't know which was which then. I could hear quiet sounds, too, the train flying a small hushed shriek up from the bend in the railway line, with the minute red patch of fire glowing hot on the engine smoke. Everything seemed a terrible long way down, and small, it was almost as though I was looking down into a midget world, another world altogether. "Here goes," I said to myself.

'I stretched forward out of my crack and grasped the iron pipe projecting from the brickwork just above my head. It was very rusty and sooty, but firm as a rock. Slowly I swung myself out on to it, and let the whole weight of my body hang down over the valley. At once I was in agony. The pipe, under the coating of soot, was rough as a file, and the moment I began to slide my hands along it they bled into a raw pulp. Soon I could feel the blood from them streaming hot down my arms and across my chest. I had learned one lesson. I kept my eyes shut in case my hands, moving sideways along the pipe, brought down the dirt and the thick scales of rust everywhere coating the ironwork. As I hung out there, blind and bleeding, I tried not to think there was nothing under my body, nothing to save me, nothing at all, only the night, and a sheer drop through the darkness of two hundred feet, and more, into the fields on the floor of the valley.

'Slowly I began to move along sideways, inching my way in agony out into space. It was very dark at first, hanging high above the valley like a bat under those girders, but when I had been travelling for what seemed hours, I thought it had become lighter. I wondered how much more of the pipe was left, because my body was getting heavier and heavier on my arms, and my boots seemed huge, all my bulk had been pumped into them, and swollen them up, until they were tight and weighed like lead. And what worried me most was that the grip of my blood-sodden hands was weakening under my weight, I could hardly stop my fingers straightening and slipping off the pipe. When I opened my eyes I couldn't believe what I saw. Instead of looking up at the horizon, I could see it a long way below me, and the moon was down there, far down, under the level of my feet, and just rising. And then, when I began to move again, faster now, towards the end of my pipe, I had another shock. The tower wall was ten or eleven feet away by now, it was only a dark mass in the distance, and as I jerked sideways farther and farther away

131

from it, the pipe began to curve down under my weight, and then jerk up suddenly again, almost as though it had turned into a length of flexible cane. The farther out along it I moved, the more it bent downwards, and the farther it sprang up under the jerks of my body, until at last it was whipping up and down in an angry rhythm, swift and powerful. My body suddenly lost all its terrible heaviness and began being tossed about helpless as a rag in the wind. The pipe itself was slippery with blood by now, it jerked so hard I felt it was deliberately trying to snatch itself out of my hands and shake me off out into space. How was I going to keep my grip on it with hands almost helpless and sopping with blood? What if I dropped that height from under the girders? What if the pipe was so rotted with rust that it snapped off under my weight where it came out of the brickwork? For a few moments I tossed up and down, far out there, not moving forwards or backwards, just hanging helpless in space, clinging in agony to the slimy pipe as best I could, bobbing up and down under the powerful spring of it, hearing my money jerking about loudly in my trousers pocket. Then, when the movement gradually came to an end, I began to edge slowly along once more, trying not to start that awful whipping movement again, and at last I reached the jagged twist of snapped-off metal where it ended. This helped me, and in another minute I had scrambled up the end of the girders and was lying safe on the platform in the long grass of the Nannies!'

By this time it wasn't only Tom was staring at Karl with his mouth open, all of us were. We hung up there with him in the darkness, blood pouring from our hands and a sheer drop of hundreds of feet under us, and nothing to fall into except the dark fields and the solid Graig ground that would kill us. When I looked out of the window, at the real tower down the valley, I felt relieved and not frightened any more. But Karl didn't even glance at it himself, he seemed to be in some sort of trance, almost, he looked as though he had forgotten all about us.

'I crawled to the brink of the platform and looked down,' he went on, 'and what a sight it was, hundreds of feet in the air, and what a blissful feeling. I forgot all about my bleeding hands in the cool breeze there, and my boiling face. I saw that newly risen moon through the long stems of the hay, a new moon lolling back above the rim of the valley, misty in a fume of glowing lemon. Far, far below, the night lay deep over the earth, it was like looking down into the black waters of a mysterious lake, thick and dark and tranquil, between the sides of the mountains. Up the valley, all Ystrad was dressed with lights, the small intense seedlings of the roadside lamps stretched out in a vast rigid pattern upon the earth, and the little heaps of the town lights floated everywhere, small intense clusters glittering in the over-all phosphorescence, showing where the shops were, or the pits; I saw laid out upon the dark floor of the valley the fallen constellations, the crystal skeleton of Ystrad, the diamond anatomy of the town.'

Karl had slowly crossed the factory and was staring out of the window into Brewery Square below him. We could still hear the rain pelting heavily on the slates above our heads, and the melted buildings opposite were busy running down our window panes. He had forgotten he had anybody listening to him, he seemed to be murmuring something, almost talking to himself again.

> 'Bury me, bury me, bury me sound,
> And bury me deep in the golden ground,
> Or bury me under the sun-green grass,
> Where the showers weep, and the shadows pass.'

None of us knew what to do, we sat feeling uneasy and clumsy. At last he turned round suddenly to us, grinning. 'Will you come up there with me some time?' he asked sharply. 'You won't be sorry. We must choose a night like that one, dry and warm and windless. Will you come?'

We all felt brave with Karl's bravery, and we promised eagerly that we would, me and all, although I was frightened even when I climbed the lamp-post.

'When I came home—that night you're talking about, Karl,' I said, 'I saw a mysterious fire in the sky. About where the

Nannies are. I looked out from this window just here. Do you remember you told me to?'

Karl smiled again. 'Before I climbed down from the tower', he said, 'I collected a haycock of dry grass, and kindled a fire under it. And I left all the magic powder I had in my tin on top of it. While it was burning I came down, put my coat on and went back to Academy House.'

That night again I failed to sleep. Step by step, hold by hold, I groped my way up that terrible black crack in the tower with Karl, slipping swiftly down to my death again and again, feeling all the stinging and the burning and the agony he had described to us, and then moving out along the iron pipe to the terror of those slipping hands and the helpless dangle in the darkness. Several times I drowsed thinking of this, and woke up terrified as the whipping pipe flung me off into space over the Graig fields, and I began to crash down to my death on one of the great piles of rubble below. I wanted Karl to tell us about the secret things he had done, but I didn't want to hear about him in terrible danger as he was climbing the tower. I couldn't bear to think of him in danger now.

7

KARL never mixed with the other boys in school, only with Jeffy, Tom, Charley and me. The others didn't understand him. If Karl said something wrong talking to anybody, or by mistake swiped a boy he thought had given him cheek, he would always apologize in a very gracious sort of way, and do a nice bow, and that used to upset the 5B boys, or make them laugh at him behind his back, they were a rude bunch of rodneys like that, the lot of them.

I thought at first Karl liked Jeffy best out of the four of us. After Mrs Urquhart went away with the lodger Jeffy had a paper round delivering the *News and Banner* after school, and Karl used to help him with it. Jeffy wanted a bit of a hand because he was always missing houses, and finding he had half a dozen papers over at the end of his round so that he had to burn them.

Jeffy began to give Karl money to go on his mysterious journeys. The first time Karl said he wanted to travel right through the next valley, but didn't have any money to do it, we began thinking up schemes to get some for him. Jeffy said he would pinch the gold leaf off the electroscopes in the physics lab, and sell it to Sam the painter for gilding the names on the shop windows; or steal the blocks of gold and silver out of the case showing the natural elements. Or pal up to old Mrs Rickards, one of the women on his paper round; she lived by herself in a big house and was mad, she had given gold sovereigns to half a dozen boys he knew who had called in to see how she was getting on lately, they used to throw the money in handfuls down from the upstairs windows to their butties waiting to catch it in their caps in the garden below. In the end what we did was to collect up the old clocks that wouldn't go, and all the old-fashioned watches our fathers and mothers had in the drawers at home, and tell them Mr Urquhart Church Street would repair them cheap. Then we handed them to Jeffy, and unless there was something very serious wrong with them he would take them up to the workshop in the garden behind 'Hawthornden' and do the job himself. He had learnt a lot about the trade messing about in that old shed. The money our parents gave us to pay Mr Urquhart with we passed on to Jeffy, and apart from a few coppers for 'Black Cat' and chlorodynes, or spanish-root, he handed it on to Karl. Karl said that whatever was given him was only a loan, and one day when he had left Ystrad he would pay it all back.

I knew that Karl used to go up to Jeffy's, just those two together, and I was jealous when I found out. I thought I fitted in with Karl better than any of the others, because I always knew what he was talking about, and I understood best how he felt without his explaining. And I felt proud that I was the one who had his silver knife, and that he had never asked me for it back.

Tom Stiff never said much at any time, but when Karl was with us mostly he didn't say anything at all. He just stared at Karl through his thick glasses and listened with his big mouth open. Tom would never read anything apart from his textbooks, and he couldn't get over it that Karl had lived in many different countries and actually seen places we had pictures of in our geography and history books. One day when we were looking at a photograph of Venice in Renton's *Europe*, Karl pointed to one of the buildings that he called a *palazzo* I think it was. He said it was the consulate of Montenegro, and he and his mother had lived next door in a house just out of the picture. It had a lovely sunny garden, half roofed with vines, and a long room upstairs where he and the consul's son used to play squash against the end wall. We could only tell what Tom felt by the way he looked when Karl told us something like this, he never said anything at all, he just stared and his nose whistled.

But once or twice the yarns Karl told us had a funny effect on Tom. We were up the mountain in our camp one day and Karl began telling us about a sabre duel on horseback he had happened to see in the woods in Serbia, or somewhere, I think he said. Karl was crossing the field below the forest and, hearing the clash of steel, he looked up the slope, and there in a clearing, in the sunshine among the trees, he saw two cavalry officers duelling, one in a golden uniform on a golden horse, and the other in a pure white uniform on a lovely milk-white horse. Spaced out in a ring around them were black hussars, all sitting in dead silence, mounted on tall chargers of glossy black, their swords drawn. The officer in the golden uniform had slashed the head of the white horse almost in two, it was nearly off, a great mass of red blood dripping onto the grass of the forest.

When Karl told us that it sounded so sad and beautiful I could have cried. But Tom began laughing. Karl stopped. Then he began to smile too. In the end Tom was on his back on the grass, laughing like a hooter, and kicking his legs in the air. We had never seen him like that before, he was nearly always so quiet and serious, even when he laughed you couldn't hear him. But he seemed delighted with the idea of the white horse with his head a mass of blood and nearly cut in half.

Charley was the one for arguing with Karl. Charley would argue with anybody. If he got some barmy idea into his head it didn't matter what you told him you couldn't make him alter his mind. Like when he argued with us, all the way home from school, in form one, that the proper way to say 'filthy' was 'thilthy'. Another time he argued with Tossy English that the *Rape of the Lock* was by Shakespeare. Tossy went into the staffroom and brought back some big thick volume about English literature and that to show him this poem was by somebody else. But Charley said he couldn't help what that book said, he had it in black and white in his encyclopaedia in the house, it said '*Rape of the Lock* by Shakespeare'. He used to drive us mad with his arguing sometimes, we used to get him down on the grass and rumple his head-hugging hair, and pull his shirt out, and hold him there until he said he agreed with us. But as soon as we let him get up he would tidy his waves, straighten his silk tie, see all his pocket flaps were out, and then start arguing again.

Karl wouldn't argue with him really. He had another wheeze to keep him quiet. If Charley interrupted what Karl was saying to ask him what he meant, all of us used to shout and tell him to shut up, so that Karl could give us the rest of his story. If he went on with his fussy 'But . . . but . . . but' Karl would say: 'Don't argue, Charley. Sing us a song—"A motto for every man". We'll all join in the chorus.' Old Charley liked that, and soon he would pipe up, 'Now we will sing, and banish melancholy', and all of us would bawl about putting our shoulders to the wheel and doing the best we could when troubles came our way.

I never said anything at all about Karl to my mother and the others if I could help it, although I really wished to speak about him all the time. I couldn't bear to hear my mother and my granny talking about him, and saying who he was, and what he'd done, they always made everything sound so ordinary and common and *ystrydebol*. My mother hated Karl anyway, I think, although she tried not to show it, it was through rescuing him my father had died. She never mentioned his name, but if I spoke about him her eyes flashed. I don't know if she realized how much I thought about Karl. She ought to, because often when I was talking to her I was so absent-minded I called her Karl by mistake.

Occasionally Karl attended our chapel, because the Powells were members in Libanus, he sat with Tom and me on the gallery, and once or twice he came as far as the front door of our house to call for me. But he wouldn't come in. Karl never seemed to want to go indoors anywhere if he could help it.

My granny had seen me about with Karl, she was very nosy, and she was eager to tell me who he was, although I didn't want to know, not from her anyway. But my granny could say who anybody in the valley was related to, or she thought she could, she was always saying, 'You know who that one is, she's the butter-pat's daughter', or 'That's one of the Thomases the tea-shop, isn't it? Exactly like them too. Belongs to the Montishes he does, they keep the bakery on Beulah Hill'—and then you'd have to listen to all about the Montishes, a lot of boring stuff going back four or five generations to about the time of the Romans if she was in the mood. She was a big know-all like that, and bit by bit I had to hear it all from her. Karl's grandfather was a wonderful singer according to her, he had the finest tenor voice ever to come out of the valleys, and that was saying something. And he didn't have the bird-brains that go with a throat like that either, she said, or the figure, five foot high and five foot round. Far from it. He had gone abroad and become a great operatic tenor in America and Germany and France and Italy, and then a famous professor of music, in Germany I think she said it was. I could see a picture of him, the handsomest man there, in the dress of a Viking, if I looked among the portraits of the Ystrad celebrities on the walls of the public library. And there was a plaque outside a house somewhere or other, too. But as far as she had heard, and she had heard everything, Karl's parents had never been in the valley, she didn't remember anything about them except that they were both dead. I suppose her pal Titus

Powell, another know-all when it came to singing and music and that, I suppose he hadn't got round to telling her about them yet, even if he knew himself.

My granny ought to have been there when I told some of this stuff to Karl; that would have set her back a bit. He looked puzzled. And then surprised. 'Is that who they think I am?' he said. 'No one in the valley knows anything about me, Dewi.'

One day when I got home from school I found my auntie Bronwen in our kitchen with my mother, who was rubbing her stick of menthol across her forehead. 'Go to bed,' my auntie was saying to my mother. 'Go on, indeed, Carrie. I'll look after Dewi. Go on.'

'You've got your own work to do, Bronwen *fach*,' my mother said. 'I'll be all right by tomorrow.'

But my auntie persuaded her, and when I was having tea she told me if my mother wasn't better she didn't think she'd be able to do her drapery round the next day. After finishing my homework I was to call and ask Mr Raymond if he would mind coming down to the factory in the morning. This Mr Raymond would help us with our rounds, part time, if he was well enough, when one of our packmen was ill or something.

I had arranged to see Karl that night after homework, but I didn't say anything at home. And on the way up Commercial Street I met him coming down towards Brewery Square, so we turned off and went up the hill together in the direction of David Street where Mr Raymond lived. It was bitterly cold and I had my overcoat on, but Karl was in his ordinary jacket and trousers without even a waistcoat. Yet he had an overcoat, I had seen it, it was long and black, nearly down to his boots, with a wide astrakhan collar that would turn up high above his ears.

When we got to Mr Raymond's house Karl said he would wait outside. I wanted him to come in, it was dark by now and this bitter wind was blowing on the hill above the town. 'I'll stand in the shop doorway opposite, Dewi,' he said. 'I don't suppose you'll be long.'

It was lovely and warm in the Raymonds' little kitchen, they had the gas on and a huge fire of tarry coal blazing and flaring in the grate. Mr Raymond was an ex-collier, he couldn't work underground any more because of his chest. You could hear it wheezing all the time. He was a lovely-looking man, tall, with thick grey hair and moustache, and a nice smile, but he only had one ear, he had lost the other underground one day, he put his head out of a manhole just as the taut rope of the journey snapped off and shot up to the roof. It took his ear with it, it sliced it off lovely, as clean as a whistle, there was nothing left on one side of his head only the hole. He did odd jobs now like helping us in the Dragon Mills sometimes, and he could play the violin, and he earned a bit of money showing the working models of ships and engines he made, mostly out of odds and ends that nobody wanted. I always liked going to this house because Mr Raymond and his wife were very kind and interesting, they stopped whatever they were doing and listened when I said something, and they smiled, and they were never down on me. They had a son too, Tommy John, who wasn't quite all there; he was a grown-up man, but he never went out by himself because the boys used to mock him and throw clodges at him. Mostly he sat on the fender in the kitchen and purred like a cat until you said something to him. He couldn't speak properly, only make noises nobody could understand except his mam and dad, but if you smiled and nodded at him a bit, and asked him how he was, he would grin, showing his empty red gums, and twist himself around, very pleased and excited, and rub the palms of his hands together hard between his knees.

Mr Raymond said at once that he would be able to help my mother the next day. And then when I asked him if he was making anything now he said yes, he had just finished a model of a coal-mine. Would I like to see it? It was in the shed in the back. He took a big black key off a nail in the kitchen wall and out we went, Mr Raymond, Tommy John and me. Tommy John had flat feet, he wore laced-up boots without any heels like a boxer's, and as we went down the back yard they made a loud flapping noise on the flagstones, each step was like the lid of a box slamming shut.

It was pitch-dark in the shed, but Mr Raymond only lit the oil stove in the corner. Lying on the table under a black cloth I could see in the dim light of the stove a sort of box, about two feet high and about six or seven feet long, with a square tower at the end of it. Mr Raymond folded the cloth away and underneath it I could make out a long glass case, but the shed was too dark for me to see what was inside. Then Mr Raymond switched on the light, not in the shed, but only in the model itself.

It was a marvellous sight. Inside the glass was the main road of a mine, one side of it anyway, as though it had been sawn in half along its length; it was sort of half an arched tunnel of brick-work, with a row of tiny lights along the roof, and the headings branching off with little colliers in them, all dead still, some standing or stooping, some kneeling, holding picks in their hands, some lying on their sides in the narrow seams with their backs to me, all silent and motionless. And each one of them had a tiny little collier's lamp beside him with a bead of light in it. There were journeys of little trams with real lumps of coal in them, all hitched to ropes and ready to move off, and also pit ponies and hauliers, and small timber logs holding up the roofs of the stalls and headings. The tall square tower on the end of the model was the shaft of the mine, and there were two iron cages hanging in it, one at the top and one at the bottom, and two large grooved wheels to carry the ropes to the engine-room at the back of the shed. I thought it was all marvellous, and Mr Raymond smiled to see me so interested in it.

'Do you like it, Dewi?' he asked me, beaming.

'It's great, Mr Raymond,' I said. 'How long did it take you to make it?'

'About a couple of years, this one,' he said. 'But I got plenty of time, see.'

'Did you do it all yourself? The horses and the men and all?'

'Ay, ay, the men, though Mrs Raymond made the little trousers and the singlets. I got the pit ponies from a set of toy soldiers Tommy John used to have. All broken. If you look, you can see the leggings of the chaps that used to ride them still on the sides of the horses. See?'

I could hardly make them out because the horses were in the shadowy part of the mine. But Mr Raymond knew I was delighted with it all.

'Wait a minute,' he said, 'I've got something else to show you. Look hard at the model.'

While I was trying to do this I could see Tommy John bowing up and down with excitement beside me, grinning, and rubbing his palms together between his knees, and making whining noises like a dog, because he knew what was going to happen. Mr Raymond had slipped round the other side of the model and I heard a click. There was a whirring sound, and all the lights in the model flickered for a moment and almost went out; and then everything in the pit began to move: as the lights brightened up again the colliers struck the coal face with their little picks, the ropes pulled the journeys along the rails, the pit ponies took their trams into the dark tunnels and came round again into the light, and the cages, packed with the standing colliers, went up and down the shaft. It was the most marvellous thing I had ever seen, it was perfect, everything moved in the light of the little lamps, exactly as it would in a real coal-mine.

I could see Mr Raymond looking at me and beaming as I watched the model, he was delighted I liked it, and he was ready to talk about how he had made all the parts of it, and wired everything up to his batteries under the table.

'What are you going to do with it, Mr Raymond?' I asked him, very excited. 'You are not going to keep it in the shed by here, are you? You ought to let people see it.'

'I'm going to, *bach*,' he said. 'I'm going to have a stall in the market, and people will have to pay to come in.'

We talked about the model for ages, I didn't want to leave it, but at last Mr Raymond switched off the power and then all the lights. He lit a candle and showed me his work-bench in the corner with his sharp penknife gleaming on it, and his tube of fish-glue, and his pliers and scissors and the camel-hair brushes, and all the masses of wires and bits of material and wood splinters and fur all heaped together in a terrible jumble. He showed me a few other things he had made too, a full-size wheelbarrow, and a ship in a bottle, and then he blew out the candle and the oil stove and the three of us went back out into the yard. What a night it sounded out there, cold and rough by now, the wind rattling up the ironwork of David Street back gardens like an old bone-shaker. In the kitchen Mrs Raymond had a cup and saucer on a tray ready for me, and a plate with two slices of the lovely wet fruit cake she used to make. She poured me a sweet cup of hot tea, and I sat by the fire with Tommy John and Mr Raymond, talking about the model, while Mrs Raymond went up and down to the pantry smiling and trying to force me to have more tea and another slice of cake.

Mr Raymond promised again to come down the factory the next morning and do the round. Until he spoke about it I had forgotten what I had come for. At the front door, saying good-bye to Mr Raymond and Tommy John, I had my back to the street, and then I turned away to go home. It was dark, and the wind poured hard and cold up the narrow road between the two rows of houses. I had only gone a few paces down the hill, thinking about the wonderful lit-up model with everything in it moving, when I heard footsteps behind me. I knew in a flash who it was. We were right under the street lamp at that moment. Karl's face was white, like ivory, the way they always show dead men in the history books; he seemed to be shrivelled and frozen to death and his teeth were chattering. But he smiled at me as best he could, he poured a long steady unbearable look down into my face, and then he smiled.

I was in despair for those few seconds when I heard him coming behind me, and ashamed, but much more ashamed than despairing, ashamed that I had forgotten all about Karl waiting for me outside the house in the freezing wind, while I was enjoying myself in the warmth and the welcome, and the excite- ment of Mr Raymond's model. How could I have done such a

143

thing to Karl? I would have given him anything he asked me for, anything, or done anything at all for him, stayed out all night, or drunk puddle-water, he only had to ask. I had already made up my mind that if I ever found any gold sovereigns hidden in one of the old mattresses that floated down the river behind our factory, I would give them all to Karl at once without telling anybody.

That night when I went to bed I couldn't sleep, I died all night long because of my unhappiness. My mother still had a splitting headache my auntie Bronny had told me, but I didn't think much about her, she would be all right after a Seidlitz powder and a day or two in bed, that's how she always was. And I forgot all about Mr Raymond's wonderful model, all I could think of as I lay awake grieving in the darkness, was what I had done to Karl, wondering how much less he would like me because of it. I didn't believe he would finish with me, I couldn't bear to think of that for a moment. He hadn't complained at all of what I had done, he said it was only his duty to wait because he had given me his word that he would. But I wanted Karl for my friend more than anyone else in the world, I loved him more than anyone I had ever known or heard of, and the thought that I had forgotten about him ached and ached in me like a wound. I was so unhappy that I put my head under the bedclothes and cried scalding tears. And after that I drowsed a little and fell asleep.

The next morning the first thing I thought about was Karl standing in the shop doorway in David Street, and the wind tearing up the hill with the roar of a waterfall, and I thought about it with anguish. When I got downstairs I found my auntie Bronwen in our kitchen cooking the breakfast. I was so full up I could hardly eat anything, and my auntie gave me a row for taking my mother's illness so much to heart when she had only been unwell for one day. On the way to school I was miserable, but I kept looking out for Karl, hoping more than anything in the world that I would see him and talk to him. The parts of the world he had come from were sure to be warmer than our valley. What if he had caught pneumonia standing so long in that windy street? What if he were to die because of what I had done to him? My mind went blank with agony at the thought of it. I was so miserable I decided to go into the Swamp if anything had happened to Karl because of me.

But I saw him before very long, although not on the way to school, and he was alive, and well, and marvellous.

8

THE Rugby pitches in our school field were in sort of three broad steps, or terraces, down to the Ystrad river, where there was a wide strip of grass, and bushes, and a row of trees. From the river bank, if we looked up, we could see the school buildings, high, and square, all long windows and bright bricks yellow as cheese, on a bit of a green tump the other side of the main road running up through the valley. The morning after I had left Karl outside the Raymonds' house in David Street, nearly every boy in school was down there by the river, although the holidays were a long way off. Jeffy, Tom, Charley and I were sitting on one of the big old fungusy logs of rotting tree trunks in the middle of the crowd. It was still as windy as the night before, but not so cold; the sky was blue and there were large clouds lying about on it, white, and folded-in at the edges, like the Prince of Wales's feathers. The weathercock on top of our school dome had a teacher in his gown at one end pointing with his cane, a geography globe in the middle and a little kid crouching in a desk on the other. As we sat there down by the river I noticed the cane was pointing to the south-west.

I was still aching over what I had done to Karl, but I was not so worried as I had been because something had happened on my way to school to make me forget it a bit. Tom, sitting beside me on the log, had his watch in his hand, and we were all looking up the slope of the field at the school terrace the other side of the main road. At exactly nine o'clock by his watch, as the town clock struck, we saw Pegger Armstrong, our history master, coming out of the main gates of the school and limping up and down the terrace on top of the steps, and ringing the handbell as loud as he could.

There was a cheer and a bit of booing from the crowd around us, but no sign of any boys going into school. Everybody was just standing about in groups on the grass by the river, talking mostly, and swapping cigarette cards, although some kids were chasing each other, and a few were playing high-backs or *talu-pump*. We were all pretty excited down there because we were on strike.

The night before, the bobby-greencoat had called at our factory when I was up in David Street and told my auntie Bronwen that if there were any British school children in the house they were to stay at home the next day, he had to go round warning everybody, because there was an outbreak of typhoid fever lower down the valley. My auntie had mentioned this, but I thought so much about what I had done to Karl that I didn't remember anything about it in the morning.

I called at the Bon Marché for Tom, and we went up High Street together towards our school. And then, just as we were rounding the last bend in the main road before reaching the school steps, we saw some big form five boys watching us coming up the pavement, three of them, Hywi Jones, Dodger Quant and Willy Williams. We went wide, we didn't want to have anything to do with rodneys like them, but they spread out across the road so that we couldn't pass, not unless we ran.

'Come here, Ginge,' Dodger called to me, and when we stopped he came up to us grinning. He was a swarthy boy with a thick moustache and long oiled hair like wet feathers, and some said he used to sleep with his auntie when his uncle was on the night shift. 'Heard about the typhoid fever in the valley?' he said to us, as Hywi and Willy came up and joined him.

I said yes, I'd heard about it, and Tom said the same. We

didn't grin back, we were very wary and suspicious, wondering what Dodger was up to.

'You know all the kids' schools in Ystrad are closed, don't you?' he went on. 'Every one of them.'

We nodded again, suspicious all the time of jokers like these three.

'Don't you think we ought to be closed too?' Dodger said. 'Typhoid's a killer, boys. You know that, don't you? Ask anybody.'

None of them could tell by Tom's face of course what he thought about this, but I said I agreed we ought to be sent home at once. I grinned at Dodger and he nodded. I wasn't so much afraid of dying of typhoid, but I hadn't finished my maths homework.

'Good boy, *cochyn*,' Dodger said to me. 'We're all going down to the school field to discuss it. Take them across, Hywi.' He had spotted another three or four boys coming up the pavement and he darted off to have a word with them.

As we got near the entrance to the field we could see other form five boys standing about in twos and threes on the main road, and on the pavements, stopping everybody and talking to them, and guarding the wide-open gates at the bottom of the steps leading up to the school buildings, so that nobody should go past; they were Arf Price, Danby, Rubby Evans, Gwilym, Lofty Gittlesohn, Rhysie and those, and they persuaded everybody to go down to the river instead of up the steps and into the yard.

I looked round the field to see who was there. One I could make out in the distance was Taliesin Powell leaning against the railings by himself, reading, wearing an overcoat too small for him after my father. But there was no sign of Karl.

After a few more rings on the bell Pegger limped back into school, and at the sight of his back going in through the gates the cheering and booing started again. We all wondered what was going to happen next. Some boys wanted to go home straight away, but form five were not willing for that yet. I knelt down in the ground-wind by the log and started cribbing the rest of my maths homework from Tom's book in case we had school after all.

Ten minutes went by. All the form fivers had come in from the road now, they stood together in a group on the grass not far from the logs. A few boys near us started singing the part-songs Cooper taught us on Friday afternoons in the hall, 'The Sailors' Chorus' and '*Oes gafr eto?*', and that, as well as 'Who stole a bloater?' and 'There was a little sparrow'. Then Cledwyn and Boysie Edwards got up on the logs and began conducting, and soon half the school had gathered round bawling away, starting a second chorus before the first one was finished, and making a terrible din, like a lot of drunken rodneys, and I had a job cribbing in the pandemonium, with everybody pushing and shoving around me. Then somebody remembered Jeffy had his own words for a lot of Cooper's choruses, and everybody wanted to hear them, so he was shoved up on the tree trunk between Cled and Boysie, and everybody bawled and shouted to make him sing them; and the whole school joined in the choruses, laughing, the words were so daft and filthy, everybody kept on breaking down, laughing. And then, just as another chorus was going to pieces, I heard Charley beside me saying: 'Hallo, look who's coming.'

I stood up and saw over the hundreds of black and purple heads, Growler and Tossy English, the long and short of it, rocking, with the high wind in their gowns, down the playing-field towards the river. And about twenty yards in front of them was Karl.

Everybody else had cleared off the slope and the rugger pitches, almost every boy in the school as far as we could tell had gathered by now in this one great crowd by the river, many of them round the fallen tree trunks, we all stood there grinning and swallowing, afraid and excited, watching the three figures coming down over the grass towards us, Tossy and Growler like a couple of comedians, Tossy high and skinny, with his scooped-out whitewashed face, and his thin red hair blown upright on top of it; and Growler, his right trouser leg up to his knee, rolling about in the wind, his gown ballooning outwards, holding his mortar-board on sideways with the flat of his hand.

And there in front of them was Karl, tall and lean and fair. I had never seen anybody as handsome as Karl, you couldn't help admiring him at any time, he was so cool and wonderful, and now in his black suit, his golden hair shining with the polish of new straw, after what had happened, he seemed more marvellous to me than ever. And seeing him like this, I thought how much his appearance had altered. When we knew him first his face had been a warm brownish, a golden colour almost, and his short thick hair was sun-bleached white, it looked like a cap cut from the dense fur of the polar bear. But since coming to live in the valley his colouring had changed about completely, his face had lost its golden sunburn and he must have paled to one of the whitest boys in school by now; but at the same time his hair had grown out long into lovely irregular waves, it was no longer white but had turned a pale golden colour. Compared with the two teachers struggling behind him in the wind he looked almost like a god. I didn't care about the school strike, or typhoid fever, or anything, all I wanted was for Karl to come and sit with us, and for everything to be the same as it was before between us.

As Karl reached the group of form five boys in the middle of the crowd some of them spoke to him, they seemed to be discussing something, and then I saw him nodding and staying with them with his arms folded. Then, when he turned and spotted us, we waved and he waved back.

In a few moments the outside edge of the crowd parted as Growler and Tossy approached. The two came right into the middle of the crowd of boys and looked round about them, as though they were trying to find somebody to speak to. I couldn't understand why Growler had brought a wet like Tossy with him if he was going to try to persuade us to go into school. Nobody ever paid any attention to what Tossy said, he was so wit-wat, nobody liked him much and yet nobody was afraid of him.

I thought Growler would have his hair off at what had

happened, cursing us all in heaps and calling us wretched
youths and that, and having a long shout about what was going
to happen to us before the end of the morning if we didn't get up
the field and into school a bit sharpish. But he wasn't like that at
all. When we crowded round the form five boys to watch what
was going to happen, we could see him wearing a joky sort of
grin on his big face. I could hardly believe my eyes at first, but I
ought to have remembered that with Growler you could never
tell what was going to happen.

'Well, boys,' he said. 'Why aren't we all indoors, and at our
school tasks, eh? What's the reason, eh? We heard the bell,
didn't we?'

What a voice old Growler had, even in a high wind deep and
throaty, but very penetrating also, like the dame in a pantomime.
Whenever he spoke he always made all the other masters sound
pink and squeaky.

Nobody said anything back to him direct, there was silence all
round apart from a bit of muttering and growling far out in the
crowd. Now that he was standing right in front of the form fivers,
and speaking straight to them, they didn't seem to be able to say
anything, they were flummoxed, all they could do was stare down
at the grass to avoid Growler's eyes, and mutter and murmur,
and look awkward and daft. If Growler had told us all in his big
bossy voice just at that moment to get into school, and no more
nonsense, we would have trailed off up the field and through the
gates like a lot of sheep. But Tossy had to make a big bug of it
for him. 'You boys, now,' he said, looking around him, very
angry and fierce, 'you are all acting like a lot of fools. Like a lot
of silly fools. You know, don't you, more than half the school
are inside already having their lessons? You know that, don't
you?'

What everybody knew was that this was a big lot of lies, and
we all laughed at the top of our voices, and started jeering and
shouting. 'No they're not, sir. We're all here, sir, we've counted.
The school is empty, sir,' and that.

Tossy flushed, and looked startled and angry. He hadn't

expected anybody to shout like that, and Growler seemed pretty mad, not with us but with Tossy, because he knew Tossy had made a big bloomer, but he tried to keep on smiling.

'Tell me, boys,' he said, 'why is it we haven't come into school today? Now come along now, tell me, so that we can discuss the matter reasonably together.'

We had all been ready enough to shout and start jeering at Tossy, but as soon as Growler asked us a direct question we were all silent again. Boys like Dodger Quant and Rubby Evans, who always had plenty to say, didn't seem to be able to open their mouths with old Growler only two or three feet away from them, they just stood there with their gang, looking at each other, red in the face, but afraid to look down at Growler, muttering and mumbling in their deep voices, you couldn't hear properly what they were saying.

'Come along,' Growler said, 'speak up, boys. What are we trying to tell me? Why haven't we all gone into school today?'

'Sir, it's because, sir,' Mal Williams began, 'it's because, sir . . .'

He stopped and blushed very red.

'Yes,' Growler said, turning to him. 'Yes, Maldwyn. Because what?'

Mal began again. 'Because, sir . . .' he said. Then he stopped once more. We waited for him to go on, but he stood there like somebody suddenly struck dumb, his face working and turning into the dark red of ripe rhubarb. There was dead silence. 'Oh, you tell him, Hywi,' he said at last and battled his way sideways into the crowd behind him. Everybody laughed at Mal, blushing and dodging away like that, and Growler widened his wide frog's grin after him. And then, just as he looked more serious again, as though he was going to say something, most likely order us all out of the field and into school, we saw Karl moving up to the front of the form five boys, and bowing, and then standing there, looking very cool and composed with his arms folded, only a few inches away from Growler. The boys laughed when Karl bowed like that, they always did, but he took no notice, and when he began to speak there was so much silence I could hear a horse and cart passing outside the field on the main road.

'With respect, sir,' he began.

Old Growler's own grin disappeared altogether when he saw who was talking to him. His brows closed in on his eyes, and the savage lines came on to the old furnace-face at once, he looked as though he wanted to say something extra dirty to Karl. But all that came out of the sneer on his fat chops was the word 'Yes?' in his deep-down growl.

'This is why we are not going into school, sir,' Karl said. 'You are aware that an outbreak of typhoid fever has been confirmed in the valley?'

Growler didn't answer. You could see he hated being questioned, especially by Karl. He just nodded a bit, very unwilling to do even that much, as surly as could be.

'Sir,' Karl went on, 'the elementary schools in this valley have all been closed because of this epidemic. Is that so?'

There was dead silence for Karl all the time, not a sound anywhere, although a lot of the boys around us were still grinning, delighted.

'Well,' Growler began, 'I believe that some of them . . .' But he didn't get any further.

'All, sir, all of them, sir,' everybody started shouting. 'Not a few, sir. They're all closed, sir. From today, sir.' But Karl held his hand up and there was silence almost at once.

'If it is dangerous for some schools to be kept open in this valley,' he went on, 'would you not agree that it's dangerous for all? Under favour, sir, are not we as liable in fact to catch typhoid fever here, as the children are in the schools already closed?'

Everybody cheered this and laughed at the tops of their voices, and shouted, 'Yes, sir, yes, sir, we are, sir', and that, and some on the outskirts began dancing round on the grass in twos because Karl had spoken so well, and made Growler look for once as though he didn't know what to say. Karl let the cheering go on, but at last Growler held up his hand. No doubt he had

had time by now to think up some cunning argument to floor Karl with.

'We all know perfectly well,' he said, beginning to sound in a bit of a wax, 'we all know perfectly well that there are differences between a grammar school and the elementary schools . . .'

But he had to stop again with interruptions.

'Oh no there aren't, sir,' some of the boys at the back of the crowd started shouting. 'No differences for typhoid, sir,' and that sort of talk. When there was quiet after the hushing, Growler went on.

'For one thing,' he said, 'we are older in this school, and so are better able to withstand disease than younger children are. Also there is the question of time. We have, before us all, external examinations of the greatest importance to our future careers. We cannot shut up shop every time there is a scare of some disease or other in the valley. School must go on.'

There was a lot of excitement on all sides at this, some beginning to agree with Growler, especially the seniors, and others very loud and indignant against him. In the middle of it all Karl held up his hand again impatiently, and boys began to say 'Sh! Sh!' all around.

'I meant no disrespect, sir,' he said again, 'but my information is that age gives no immunity at all in this disease. As for the other question, sir, what concerns us now is, not the examination, but whether we will be alive to sit it.'

Everybody seemed to go mad when Karl said this, boys cheered and shouted and stamped on the grass and whistled and a few threw their caps in the air and danced about with their arms round each other's waists. Everybody made such a rumpus for such a time that old Beynon geogger was able to come down the field from school and through the crowd to Growler's side almost without our noticing him. He stood near Growler and Tossy, the three gowns in a huddle whispering together, and then Growler turned away and held up his hand for silence.

'Boys,' he said, when we had quietened down a bit, 'Mr Beynon has just brought me information which has come to school by telephone from the town hall. By an oversight, our school was not notified with all the others that we must abandon our work because of the outbreak of typhoid fever in the valley. The school will be closed from today until further notice. You may all now go home.'

The three masters went up the slope to school as fast as they could, while the cheering and dancing around broke out everywhere again at once. 'Three cheers for Mr Roderick,' Dodger shouted, and everybody hoorayed at the tops of their voices. A great crowd of boys made a rush for Karl, some shouting, 'Speech, speech', and some trying to shoulder him, but he broke away, and looked flushed and angry, and they left him alone, disappointed. But most were only anxious to get home anyway, and we could see a great stream of black and purple caps going up the field and out into the road through the gates.

As the four of us went up the slope with Karl, boys kept coming up behind him and patting him on the back saying 'Good old Karl', and then going away. Everybody wanted to know Karl now that he had stood up to Growler, although before that morning the only friends he had in the whole school were Jeffy, Tom, Charley and me.

All that Karl said was: 'I am sorry Mr Beynon brought that news just then. I wonder what Roderick would have done if he had not.'

9

THE last time I saw my mother alive she was lying almost flat on the bed with her eyelids closed, and my auntie Bronwen was wetting her lips with a feather dipped in a cup without a handle. 'Why are you giving me sea-water to drink?' she was muttering.

Ever since our school had closed and we had been on holiday, they all kept driving me out of the house, my auntie and my granny, sending me on messages and suggesting places I could go to with Tom or Charley. They made excuses for some time for me not to enter the bedroom to see my mother, but at last they allowed me to. There she was in bed, looking very long and thin, her face on the pillow like an eggshell painted with patches of cochineal, muttering to herself. I looked down at her astonished, I hardly knew her, I hadn't expected her to look sickly like that, I really thought of her as dressed always in her velvet hat and tight purple costume, stately, her face dark and her eyes flashing. My auntie brushed another featherful of water across her lips. 'What's the matter with our mam?' I asked her. 'What's she saying?'

'Nothing, *bach*,' my auntie said. 'She's delirious. You'd better go now. Go and get ready.'

I felt sad and frightened at the word delirious. I began to cry. I pulled my handkerchief out of my trousers pocket, and a big lump of stuck-together caramels shot out with it, and fell in the silence with a terrible hollow crash on the oilcloth. I went over to pick it up, and I was so clumsy that when I bent down I accidentally kicked it across the floor, and against the wardrobe, with an even bigger crash. I looked to see if the noise had made my mother's eyes open, but she had taken no notice at all.

'Get ready for what?' I asked my auntie, wiping my eyes.

'Go downstairs and *mamgu* will tell you,' she said.

'Theatricals,' I thought I heard my mother muttering. 'Gone with the theatricals.' Something like that. 'A clean-living little man,' she said, as far as I could catch. 'Poor boy. Poor boy. No mother. Nobody to keep his feet on the rock.'

I went down the back stairs, thinking my granny would be in the kitchen, but she wasn't there. I was glad. I went out into the orchard and inside the coach I sobbed for a bit, although I didn't want to so much now that I wasn't in the bedroom. When I went back into the kitchen, I could hear loud voices coming from the front room, so I went along the passage to see who was there. I didn't go in, I stood in the doorway of the little room next door, where my father had had his desk and the safe, and the ledgers, and piles of extra pattern books; I hid there listening, ready to slip inside and pretend to be looking for something if one of the speakers came out. The two voices belonged to old Rees Mawr and my granny, and they were quarrelling in the sort of hearth-Welsh they always used to each other.

'It's that damn river,' old Rees was shouting. 'I don't care what you say, it's that damned river doing all the damage.' He sounded thick, as though he'd had a drop too much to drink.

I wondered what that meant. I tried to think. But I kept on remembering that Rees would never have been in our parlour at all if my mother had her feet under her. Nobody went in there unless my mother went with them, not even my granny.

'There's no need for cursing and swearing,' my granny answered him. 'Of course it's not the river, or all of us would have caught it. But he's going away in any case. It's all arranged.'

'And I bet I know where he's going,' Rees said, making a sort of snorting noise. 'Up to the Powells, isn't it?'

There was no answer and I could hear some drawers being pulled open and shut, and a box or something heavy being put on the table.

'Fancy sending him there,' Rees went on. 'The Powells! They're no better than a lot of savages-o, the lot of them. They've lived on strap as long as I can remember——'

'Don't talk ridiculous, will you?' my granny interrupted him, sounding very angry. 'And mind your own business too. Go on, I expect you've got plenty to do in the warehouse. Go on. And it would pay you to keep your foot off the brass rail in working hours, by jobe it would.'

'I wouldn't put a dog of mine with those Powells,' he went on, taking no notice. 'They won't leave the boy nails to scratch himself with. Why don't you send him down to his auntie-o? That's healthy enough down there. In the pub. And it's not far away.'

'It's no drop of joy to me to send him anywhere from by

here,' my granny said. 'And anyway, it's too late to think of that now. I've spoken to Mr Powell.'

I knew by now they were speaking about me. Stay with the Powells! With Karl! That couldn't be true. It was too marvellous. To live in the same house as Karl, and be with him all the time. Rees was trying to stop it. And my granny wanted it. She always thought the world of Mr Powell. I didn't care about Powell, all I wanted was to be with Karl.

'Indeed to God,' Rees said, 'you'll come from by there. He's a madman-o. Look at the way he raises them children, disgusting, half starved, white as maggots, filthy. How can you do it, woman? Sending your own flesh and blood to a murderer, that's what you're doing!'

'Hush,' said my granny. 'Hush. Hush. How dare you! You must be drunk. Go back to your work. Go on.'

'You know it's true,' old Rees continued. 'As good as. Him keeping that Lizzie of his a prisoner for ten years, and more. She didn't ought to have been having children at all, the shape she was, the doctor told him plenty, let alone what he was doing to her, filling her up every twelvemonth and then him coming by here crying to Jack and Carrie every time she lost one. *Yr hen fochyn* Carrie called him more than once. I heard her. The dirty old pig, she said, and she was right, too. "*Ach y fi,*" she said, "that old Titus Powell." She didn't have any looks on Powell, not Carrie didn't. And now you're sending the boy to live there. I don't know! I don't understand you-o.'

I could hear my granny limping on her stick towards the door of the parlour, so I slipped down the passage, through the kitchen and back to the coach in the orchard. I couldn't face my granny after what I had heard. My mind was full of all sorts of strong feelings, they were in high waves charging across one another, like a rough sea sweeping in among rocks. What did it mean about Mr Powell being a murderer? That couldn't be true, old Rees must have been drinking. A murderer was always arrested and hanged. Besides, Mr Powell came to our chapel and led the singing. Was he a madman, like Rees said? Was that why he stripped, and washed his trombone in the bath? But a murderer! Had he murdered his wife? Is that what Rees meant? How had he done it? Stabbed her? Or kicked her to death like that navvy in Lower Row we read about in the paper? What was the matter with my mother? I had never seen her looking like that before, or heard her talking when she didn't know what she was saying. Who was she talking about? Theatricals? Mrs Urquhart was it? She must have thought a lot about her. More than I had, although I was supposed to be Jeffy's friend. I never thought about her running away, I forgot all about it after a bit. One day, when Jeffy wasn't with us, Charley said to Karl: 'Jeffy's mother was a proper old shove, everybody in Ystrad knows that.' Was that true? And Charley claimed he saw her on the landing in 'Hawthornden' one afternoon with her arms round the captain's knees, begging him to sleep with her or something. My mother looked so ill. Delirious. I always hated the word 'delirious', it was like 'ghost' and 'funeral' and '*marwolaeth*'—the terrible Welsh word for death. What did it feel like being delirious, unconscious, talking daft, not knowing what you were saying? Soon, if my granny had her way, I would be living with Karl. In the house of the madman and the murderer.

10

THAT same night Rees in his bronze hat and an overcoat, for once, strapped my father's old Gladstone bag filled with clothes and groceries on the carrier of his bike, and the two of us wheeled it up to the Powells in Academy House, Edwards Terrace.

He didn't want to go, I heard him telling my granny at first he wouldn't do it-o, and then he said he'd never go inside the house, never, only to the door, not a step beyond. She said all right then that would do, she was going to call up the next day in any case, with Bronwen, to see that everything was all right. As far as the doorstep would do.

I felt excited helping Rees to push the bike. It was getting dark and the light on the bicycle lamp was dim, glowing no brighter than a cigarette end. What would Karl say because I was going to live with him? We could go to school and come home together every day. Perhaps on a Saturday we could take the train through the tunnel to one of the other valleys, or climb the Bryngwyns, or go down to the sea. I wondered how long I had to stay there. Until my mother got better, I supposed. I didn't care about the way the Powells lived, no cloth on the table, always bread and dripping, bare stairs, the floors only tiles and flagstones, stains everywhere, and smells. Karl and I would be together, we'd put up with everything, we'd eat on the mountain, or have meals in my granny's, or most likely Karl could cook anything we wanted. All the way up the hill Rees was grumpy and didn't say a word.

It was pitch-dark by the time we reached Academy House. Edwards Terrace was a row of old stone houses raised up a bit off the road, with long narrow gardens in front, and low walls decorated with huge ugly lumps of grey pumice stone. At each end of the terrace was a much larger house and in one of these the Powells lived. It overlooked the railway, and that's why it had the big Van Houten's cocoa adverts on the pine-end, for people to see them from the trains. It was double fronted, and quite high, and I could see a light in the attic windows up in the pointed gables. The downstairs bay windows seemed pretty ordinary but the two upstairs ones were held on to the front of the house with heavy black timbers that leaned up against them out of the garden. I hadn't been in the house since I gave up my music lessons.

We left the bike just inside the gate. Rees knocked at the door with the heavy brass knocker and the first thing I noticed was the loud hollow sound, as though the house was empty. But soon we heard somebody coming along the bare boards of the passage, and a girl's voice saying: 'Who's there, please?'

Rees looked at me and nodded, and I said: 'It's me, Dewi, from the factory.'

The bolts were shot back and the door opened. In the dark of the passage stood Buddug, with a candle in her hand and a Scotchy's tommy-shanto on her head. When she saw us she let out a funny high giggle, like a pony neighing, only politer. 'Come in, please, will you?' she said.

Old Rees had told my granny he wouldn't set foot in the Powells' house, but he came in all right, carrying the Gladstone bag. Our footsteps resounded right through the house, it was so empty, it was always a terrible building for echoes; as we followed Buddug down the dark passage, her candle-light fell on the torn-off wallpaper and I noticed Mr Powell's top hat on its peg. The place stank like a gut. In the back kitchen the gaslight was on, and Buddug carried the candle through to the scullery and stayed out there with it. Mr Powell was standing with his back to the fire, smoking his pipe, smiling, and holding his hand out to us, his tight red hair shining, and the scarlet lines of sealing-wax dribbled in a network across his pale nose glistening prominently in the gaslight. Instead of his frock coat he had a black velvet jacket on, with a big quilted collar covered with dribbles and food droppings, and all the velvet worn off at the elbows. 'Welcome, welcome,' he said in Welsh, waving his arms. '*Croeso, croeso, 'nghyfeillion i.* Welcome, my friends.'

There was supper ready on the table and it looked nice for once. I glanced around for any sign of Karl, but saw none. Nor of the Powell children. When I was smaller and I used to call here with my father and mother sometimes, that's how it was then; you came into the middle room and sat down to talk, and there were no children to be seen anywhere. But as time went on, and Mr Powell got into some yarn or other about himself, you'd see the children creeping out one by one from behind the furniture where they had been hiding, and sitting on the oilcloth and listening without a word. But there was no furniture in the kitchen where they could hide, only the fastened-on sideboard and a few chairs with broken-off backs that the Powells always called stools.

Mr Powell, Rees and I had supper by ourselves, and Buddug served us. She was a pretty ugly girl, skinny, about seventeen I think she was, with a very short neck and a big head, and thin knock-kneed legs. Her hair was in dirty-looking masses of old-fashioned curls all round her face, and spread out down her back, but what made her really ugly was the top lip of her puffy face, it was thick and fleshy, and sticking out, and a good bit longer than her nose. She smiled all the time, but she would hardly ever say anything, only flutter her eyelids if someone spoke to her, and make the short sharp whinnies of the pit ponies smelling their oats, that was supposed to be a sort of girl's giggle I think. She went in and out of the scullery all the time we were eating, she cut bread and butter for us by the light of the candle.

We had a pretty good meal, it was the black pudding that I always liked, although my mother would never have it in the house, and cold potatoes and spring onions, with bread and butter and tea. Never mind what old Rees had said about the Powells the day before, he ate like a horse, he sat there crashing through the jibbons and saying hardly a word, helping himself, wearing his old overcoat buttoned up under his beard, and his copper-coloured Panama still on his head. Mr Powell was in a good mood, he talked non-stop about his insurance round, and Libanus, and his choirs in America, and he urged us all the time to eat more. As soon as the meal was over Rees brought the Gladstone bag into the kitchen and left us, with hardly a word, at the front door. Mr Powell picked up the bag and began to carry it upstairs, with me following behind him, but by the time he had got to the first landing he was puffing so much he couldn't go any farther. Fair play, he was a pretty fat man, and very heavy, and not only that, the old Gladstone was solid leather, you could hardly lift it up off the floor empty, let alone with all the food and clothes my granny had packed into it. So he said:

'You go up to the very top of the house now, Dewi, right to the top, and knock at the door on the right-hand side up there. You'll see light coming under it, most likely. That will be your room. Vaughan will look after you, and get you anything you want. Good night now, *bach*. Good night now.'

He went bumping back down, and I struggled up the dark stairs to the top landing. 'Who's Vaughan?' I thought. 'Is he somebody staying here with Karl?' Or one of the Powell kids I'd never heard of? There in the darkness at the top of the house I saw the narrow bar of light under one of the two doors, I saw it with so much excitement I could hardly breathe. I put down the portmanteau, waited a few seconds to get my breath, and then knocked.

'Come in,' said a voice, after a bit of a pause. With joy I recognized it as Karl's.

I opened the door and saw before me a very low and narrow passage, wallpapered, with three steps leading up from it into the full light at the far end. I walked along stooping, and when I had climbed the steps I found myself in what looked at first glance like a huge tawny-coloured tent, like one of those long, wide, all-roof ones filled with a warm yellow glow that Florence Nightingale had for hospitals in our history books, during the Crimean War. There was a small crucifix facing me on the pointed wall at the far end. The smell there, it was one of the first things I noticed, was sweet and rich after the stale damp and pee-niffs on the stairs, like cigar-smoke, and the air for closeness made me think of our chapel packed on *cymanfa* night, so warm and thick it would hardly go up my nostrils, lovely. By the amber glow of the lamp in there, burning warm and low on the table, I could see the sloping yellow roofs, supported by short thick posts, coming down to the floor, or nearly to the floor, at the sides, because the walls of the attic were only about a foot high. The yellow paper had bulged loose from the ceilings with damp, and hung beautifully into the room, curving down everywhere like a slack roof-canvas. Only the zinc water-tank at the far end, and a couple of triangular window recesses, showed I was at the top of a house and not camped out miles from every-where in the middle of a field.

Between two of the sloping posts hung a hammock. Karl was lying in it, doing nothing as far as I could see, and when I got to the top of the steps he tipped himself out and came forward smiling. I looked round for Vaughan, but there was only Karl.

'I've been expecting you, Dewi,' he said. 'I'm delighted to see you. Have you had supper? Welcome to our tent. Put your bag down. Here's your bed. I was just having a terrible night-mare when you knocked. A faller. Or rather a slider. Do you ever get those? They're horrible.'

My bed was a little narrow workhouse one in the corner, but I didn't care about that. While I was unpacking, Karl went down the steps and bolted the bedroom door at the end of the passage. Our room covered half the whole space of the house, he told me. Next door was Mr Powell's room. The rest of the children slept on the first floor, the one underneath ours. He rolled up the paper blind, opened the window and called me over to look out.

'Let me show you how to get in and out of Academy House any time you like,' he said. On the wall right below us, outside in the cold air, I could see the top ends of the balks of timber that held the front of the house on to the sides, sloping down into the garden from just underneath our window cill. I knew Karl would love that, climbing along the balks in and out of the house at all hours, but me, I didn't fancy it at all. Karl could tell what I was thinking and he closed the window smiling.

'Who's Vaughan, Karl?' I asked him.

'Vaughan?' he said. 'I am. Didn't you know? Karl Vaughan Anthony. To Mr Powell I'm always Vaughan. He likes that.' Yes, he had painted the large coat of arms and the eagles on the wall facing the door, and the crossed foils and the fencing helmet opposite it. He took down the Red Indian head-dress of eagles' feathers hanging from the hook of the clothes-line and put it on me; and he let me have a go with his dumb-bells and his chest expanders bolted to the post in the middle of the room. He took me round on a journey of inspection, showing me the way he lived, indicating the sink in the corner, the gas-fire, the gas-ring, the cupboards, one for food and one for books—poetry, travel, philosophy, books about art and heraldry and history. He told me how convenient everything was for the two of us, and how comfortable we were going to be, and the way he spoke made me feel calm and happy and very excited at the same time.

He had been climbing in his nightmare he told me, on his hands and knees, up an enormous coal-black mountain, almost vertical, a wall of soft black earth; he had to get to the top, where he knew somehow he would find a huge, terrifying crater on the plateau. He just had to get there in his dream, he knew that. Up and up he went, his hands and knees sinking all the time in a soil soft as brown sugar, but black, and very clammy and yielding. At last he reached the top, and had his first glimpse of the annihilated landscape there, a vast crimson plain of endless marl and furnace gravel, glaring and black-shadowed under a bitter red light, the whole immeasurable territory barren, pock-marked everywhere into craters like gigantic sunken acorn cups, and humped with harsh mountainous masses of red ash and slag and monstrous clinker. And right at the edge, so that his climbing fingers curled over the rim of it, the enormous crater he had expected to find, vast and black and bottomless, with steamy clouds floating slowly across the dark depths of it below him; so immense and black and mysterious, the majesty and the remoteness and the horror of it overawed him, and he turned his face away, terrified and overwhelmed. But when he could bring himself to peep over the edge again, he found the whole of the inside slopes of the bowl transformed; the secret crater, no longer black and hideous, was now brightly illuminated by a dozen invisible suns, it was made of soft sweet earth vividly coloured in shades of the utmost warmth and intensity, large irregular areas like gigantic fields of purple plush, and deep blood scarlet, and velvet black, and sun-grass green and orange covered it, the shapes contained and separated from one another by broad white borders like paths of pure soft snow. Karl was uplifted with delight at the beauty of it, he wished to gaze at it all the time, but he found himself constantly slipping down a short distance from his high position on the crater's rim, and having to struggle back up the soft earth again before he could have another glimpse of the overwhelming loveliness of those colours, so warm and brilliant inside the bowl. He turned to speak to the person with him, he couldn't tell when he woke who this person was, but during his climb he knew very well it was one of his friends. In doing so he lost his grip again, but this time he was unable to recover it, and he slid, grabbing frantically for hand-holds all the time, down the side of the mountain, his speed increasing and the wind rushing cold past his ears, but before he had reached the bottom I had knocked at the door and woken him up.

By the time he came to the end of his dream most of my clothes were lying across the divan, and the pikelets and the tins of apricots my granny had packed for me were in the crockery cupboard. I felt sleepy with the heat and the excitement. In the flap pocket of the portmanteau I had placed my dagger, and when the time came for me to take it out I could feel my heart pounding with emotion. I didn't know whether to show it to Karl or not. I had never mentioned it to him since the day I had found it in our yard, and he had never once asked me about it. It was like a secret between us that both of us wanted to keep. In the end I failed to bring myself to open the pocket and fetch it out into the light. But I made up my mind to let it be seen by Karl in the morning.

I went and lay on my bed with my arms under my head, listening to Karl. Now I felt drowsy and happy, and because the lamp on the table was level with my glance I shut my eyes. Karl was talking about his school, a college, I think he called it, in a *château* in France, and about the boy there who was supposed to have put one of the village girls in the family way. After a bit I got off my bed, undressed, said my prayers, and lay down under the clothes. Karl by now was swaying his hammock, pulling at the rope he had rigged up in the roof and puffing at his pipe, the smoke giving a sweet rich smell. This boy's father was a wealthy merchant, he owned the Yvetot vineyards, a huge fat man with a red face, a loud voice, and a lot of jewellery. He was blind in one eye, Karl said, and he always wore an all-gold monocle to hide it, gold ribbon, gold rim and the curving lens of solid gold. He wanted his son to be a good shot, and a rider, and a swimmer and that, but Victor, that was the boy's name, wasn't happy in the school, the thing he cared about had nothing to do with horses and pistols and dogs. It was painting. He always wanted to stay in his room in one of the turrets of the *château*, putting on paper and canvas the scenes outside the windows, and reading poetry. He went off a lot by himself drawing and painting in the country-side, and the other boys began to hate him, they felt insulted by his refusal to join them in their shooting parties and in having hinges tattooed on their elbows and that, they thought it meant he despised them. Every year on the feast of St Denis there was boar-roasting in the middle courtyard of the school, a huge bonfire was lit on the cobbles, the spits turned by means of wagon wheels, and the boys sat round on benches until late into the night, singing and drinking mulled wine, and eating bread with hot slices of pork-meat on it. One of the boys noticed that Victor Yvetot was absent. Up to his room in the tower they went, half a dozen of them, Karl with them. Karl's idea was to stop the boys doing anything violent to Victor whom he liked to talk to very much, and whose painting gave him so much pleasure. Victor was inside his room with the door bolted. He refused to open. Karl didn't want him to shout anything defiant to the boys, anything to make them angry and perhaps cause them to break his door down and beat and scratch him, so he called out asking him if he was feeling better. There was a pause and then Victor said yes, he was a little better, all he wanted was to be left alone to sleep. Karl got the boys to go back to the courtyard, where the fireworks had started by now, and after that he and Victor Yvetot became great friends.

Victor began visiting a family in the old walled town near the school. That town, Karl said, was an evil place, full of violence and horror and all sorts of terrible wickedness and confusion.

166

One of the women there had been with a forest bull, the huge black fierce ones they had in those parts, and had given birth to a hideous monster, black and powerful and deformed, she kept it imprisoned and chained up upstairs in the attic because it was dangerous, it had killed a little girl and a farmer already; you could hear it howling sometimes, and banging for hours on the walls wanting to get out; and you could see the thick iron bars over the attic windows to stop it escaping. Some of the boys had met the woman's father and brothers taking it out in the lanes after dark, with cart-ropes around its head and waist, it was huge and revolting and covered with thick black fur, it couldn't talk, but every now and then it jabbered to itself, and let out a loud bellowing sound. It had a man's voice, but much louder.

The family Victor visited pretended to be interested in the paintings he used to show them, but they knew who he was, and who his father was, and they used their daughter, Jeanne, to trap him. One day when he went there they told him Jeanne was going to have a baby, and that he was the father. Victor denied it, and ran out of the house and back to school to tell Karl. Karl said they would have to consider what to do. The next day the two of them set out together for the town to see Jeanne's parents with a plan ready.

The town, Karl said, was built on top of a hill, and outside the walls on the side facing the sun was a vast slope, bare and treeless, made of dried-up brown clay, like the waste patch behind David Street on Ystrad hill. Fields of rye and barley began on the plain below the hill and ran down to the Ystrad river. As Karl and Victor, crossing the fields from the *château*, looked up the slope at the town, they saw something there that greatly astonished them and brought them to a standstill. At each end of the town wall were large, high wooden doors. They had never seen these doors open because all the trade of the town used the gateways on the north wall. But on this hot summer afternoon those doors stood wide open, two large black squares in the long blank yellow of the sunlit stonework. And as the two boys stood there in the barley, staring upwards, wondering what the reason was, they saw a row of lovely girls and young women, six or seven abreast, coming out of each of the doorways, they advanced into the sunlight at the head of a pair of great identical columns; from each of the two exits hundreds and hundreds of girls, all of them beautiful, and dressed, they seemed to be, for the chapel outing, poured out on to the slope, talking and muttering threats about what Victor had done, and sometimes shouting aloud. Karl was puzzled and astonished at the sight, and so was I, I had never seen as many girls as that in Ystrad before, and I didn't know any of them, not one. The columns advanced on to the bare slope at an angle to each other, still the same length and shape; the girls kept pouring out of the two doorways without a pause, and soon they had made an enormous V on the barren hillside. And at that they all stood dead still and screamed and screamed Victor's name with such a terrible sound of hate and vengeance that I was terrified, if Karl had not held me I would have run away and hidden by the Ystrad river. But they didn't stop for long, the leaders of the two arms of the letter moved forward again, and mingled together, and came down towards us in one single column, so that the V became an even larger Y before our eyes. When this happened the girls gave up walking, they began screaming and rushing wildly down the hill towards Karl and me, still in the form of the letter, as though they meant to tear us all to pieces.

I don't know where in Karl's story I fell asleep, and how much of it I dreamt, but I came upright in my bed with that terrible screaming in my ears. Everything was pitch-dark. My heart was going like a hammer. I couldn't understand where I was. Then I realized the screaming came from outside the room, on the stairs.

'Karl,' I shouted across to him. 'What was that? Who's that screaming?'

'What?' he said, as though he was just coming awake too. 'Oh, don't be alarmed, Dewi. It will stop presently. Good night.'

After a few more yells there was silence in the house, apart from a whimpering sound, and presently that stopped too, and I fell asleep again.

PART THREE

I

EVERY Saturday morning I took the train down from Ystrad to see my granny and my auntie Bronny, who, soon after I went to live with the Powells, left the Dragon Mills and moved in to lodge with the Richardses, their tenants in 'Tegfan', a villa they had rent from in Tremartyn, farther down the valley. As soon as Mr and Mrs Richards could find another house they were going to take 'Tegfan' over completely themselves, and then I was to go and live with them for good and all, and travel up the valley to school in Ystrad every day by train.

The night after Rees took me to the Powells they arrived at Academy House together to see how I was placed, and my auntie Bronny climbed the stairs up to the room Karl and I shared at the top of the house to examine it. She told me my mother was still ill, delirious, and I could see by the way she said it she meant she was worse. I was worried. Delirious. That word for me of awful foreboding again. Every time I heard it it seemed to fill me with terrible uneasiness, and worry, and dread. Everybody I had ever heard of being delirious had died not long after, mostly at midnight, with only a night-light burning in the bedroom. I asked her if I could come down Brewery Square some time to see her, but she said no. But before I had been in the Powells' a fortnight she had to call for me and take me over to the factory to try another new Norfolk suit on from our showrooms, youths' fitting, black serge, because my mother was dead. I had to have a fresh suit because the one I had worn at my father's funeral my mother had tacked the price tickets back on to, and put back in stock.

The night I was down there in the Dragon Mills fitting-room, in the middle of all the powerful smells of newness I liked so much, with the hoarse green gaslight filling the little wooden room, I couldn't believe my mother was lying dead in the house

171

across the yard. The smells of the new boot-leather were strong and fragrant in my nostrils, and of the camphor and the dressing in the clothes all around; I could see, hiding the walls in the greenish light, the big brass-handled boxes of shirts, and men's flannel drovers, stacked one above the other on the wooden fixtures, and I thought about her making me wear flannel shirts that hung down below my trousers, and scourged the backs of my bare knees red, and nearly drove me mad. But one thing I had always wanted I was going to have now at last, for the funeral—swanky best boots like the ones Tom and Charley wore for Sunday, the uppers of soft black kid like funeral-glove leather, and with thin soles you could bend about all shapes. My mother always liked me to wear brown boots, yellow she called them, she must have thought they looked nice with my ginger hair. She got them out of stock from the factory bootroom on the other side of the passage from where I was standing fitting my suit, they always had iron tips on the heels and patterns of nails embedded in the thick soles, and a loop of royal blue tape at the back for the name of the brand, and for pulling them on with. She wasn't partial to me tucking these loops inside my boot-tops, or tying them down tidy with my laces, she liked me to leave both of them sticking out behind so that people could read the printing on them, 'Young Chieftain', and see what a high quality brown boot we sold in our factory.

In the weeks after my mother's funeral, living up there in the Powells', I thought more and more about her. I remembered her regular soldier's march to chapel, and the new hat my auntie got her to wear when I was very small, a kind of crimson helmet, the latest fashion, it had a huge golden hatchet trimming fastened in the front, and every time she nodded I thought it threatened me, what with her black looks and her crackling eye it made me think she was going to chop my face in two. I remembered her papering, and her cleaning, and the floorboards under the oilcloth that she scoured every year, and our brass spittoon in the parlour so bright that when Morgan the butcher called in to see my father he said: 'Take it away, indeed, Mrs Davies, or I'll be sure to spit in it.' One day, not long after my father died, when she knelt down in the kitchen to reach the shoehorn under the couch, I saw one of her legs in a brown stocking, from her wide black garter just above her knee down to her elastic-sided boots, and I had a big surprise at seeing that, because I never really thought about my mother having legs at all, not higher up than the tops of her boots. Sometimes when the sight came into my mind suddenly and unexpectedly I blushed, although I didn't know why. And I remembered my uncle Walter Lloyd in Abergarth describing her running out into the snow in her nightdress when she was a little girl. I couldn't think of my mother being a little girl, or dead either.

I didn't see her dead, although when I was going down the passage the morning of the funeral I heard a loud click-clicking noise coming from the back room, the one we used for an office. I knew my mother's body was in there, and when I looked in through the crack I could see the noise was made by two of James the undertaker's men fastening the lid down on the coffin with a couple of long screwdrivers. I saw my father dead and he looked all right. He was in an open coffin, laid across between an armchair and the harmonium stool upstairs in the Vaughan Arms, where they had brought him from the Abergarth cottage hospital; he was wearing a long white shirt with a line of crimson buttons like loganberries hidden in the frill down the front, and a pair of white cotton gloves. In the dim light of the upstairs parlour of the pub, with the street curtains closed over the windows, his face looked ordinary, his eyes were shut, somebody had parted his thin sandy hair in the middle and put oil on it, and waxed his moustache out long and sharp as darning-needles. My mother was in the dim parlour with me at the time, but after a bit she seemed to have forgotten I was present. I saw her putting her hand down into the side of the coffin and gripping my father's gloved hand in there. I watched her standing beside him, holding it, and gazing down at his face. Everything was quiet in the room, in the whole pub, and in all the sunlit streets of Abergarth outside the windows. I was afraid to move in that silence. 'He often took my hands,' she said to herself, but out loud, and her voice ended in a kind of sob. I felt frightened, and I had a big job to stop crying, it was so pitiful. I didn't want my mother to say anything like that, not in front of me. Suddenly she turned round, and I saw at once there was no sign of tears on her cheeks, or in her eyes, and the old angry look was upon her face again; when our glances crossed I could hear in my head the sharp hiss of steel like swords clashing together. At her funeral my face was white as chicken-skin and the tears bounded out of my eyes, but only because my granny was crying, and my auntie Bronwen, and my auntie Mag. I couldn't imagine my mother being dead.

My auntie Bronwen and my granny could never run the Dragon Mills alone, they said. Soon after my mother's burial they had a white board fastened to the front wall of the factory, out there in Brewery Square, saying in letters of red paint that the whole property was for sale, the factory, the two houses in the yard, the orchard, the stock, the trade fixtures, the goodwill, everything. I didn't care at all. I was glad. I never wanted to go near Brewery Square again. I loved it in the Powells', living up there in the attic with Karl. It was like a holiday all the time, alone in our tent, camping out on the mountain or up the woods. But every Saturday I went down to Tremartyn to my granny and my auntie, to take my washing and darning, and fetch my pocket-money and my board and lodgings to pay Mr Powell.

When the term started again after the typhoid was over, Karl and I went to school together every day, that is every day Karl decided to be present. We cut our sandwiches for dinner time, and had our breakfast, in the big bare back kitchen of Academy House, the two of us together, before the Powells were out of bed; we cooked it ourselves, and we often left without seeing any of them, or only Mr Powell, perhaps, coming in from the back dubliw and wetting his little stump of indelible pencil to put a puce cross on his calendar hanging by the fireplace. The Powells' middle room was full almost to the ceiling of chests of the left-over dandelion coffee Mr Powell had tried to sell one time, and that's what we drank at breakfast every morning, Karl had found out a fine wheeze to use it, and while I was cleaning our boots in the scullery, he was boiling it up thin on the gas-stove, with plenty of condensed milk, so that it didn't turn solid the way it used to when my mother was buying it. It was nice done like this, very sweet, like liquid strawberry jam, only hot, and when I went to Academy House first the smell of it boiling was one of the things that used to make Mr Powell look happy.

Although Karl never said anything about it, I could see as time went on that he always wanted us to keep out of Mr Powell's way; but once or twice when I went there first the old man caught us in the passage as we were coming into the house or going out; the door of his room, the one I used to have my music lesson in when I was small, would open suddenly, as though he had been just inside listening and waiting for us. He invited us into his room, his music studio he still called it, and told us about his great concerts, in the old days, in Ystrad drill hall, and in the chapels of the valleys; packed out the concerts were always, with people fainting right and left in the crush, he told us. And he described his trips to America with his choir, and how they sang other times in Europe, before the Crowned Heads. And he opened the doors of the sideboard cupboard, and showed us one or two of his ivory batons and some of the silver cups and the shields he had won, pretty dented and tarnished they looked to us, battered about as though the Powell kids had been allowed to get at them.

This music studio was the only decent room in the house; well, there was a lot of furniture in it, anyway, most of it shabby as an old cuff if you looked into it, all scratched and broken down and with the stuffing coming out. The fancy wicker chairs were dry and powdery and gradually uncoiling, every time I went in there I snapped off a couple of yards of the brittle binding-cane myself, just for something to do. There were faded cushions everywhere, almost white, faded carpets, faded pictures; and faded curtains so ripe-looking you were afraid to touch them. And there in the middle of the room was the big black grand piano that Mr Powell taught his pupils on when he had any. Ninepence a lesson he charged, he told us, a very reasonable sum for the quality of instruction he was able to offer. Whenever he managed to get us into his studio that's what he did, he sat there in his velvet jacket, or his frock-coat with the gravy stains on the silk front, his feet in their cracked boots and brown spats on the piano stool, and he told us about the wins of his choirs in the big *eisteddfodau*, how he used to hear the sound of money in their voices in those days, and the great singers from all over the world who had performed in the oratorios under his baton, and the way everybody pleaded with him to stay over there in America conducting. He had the illuminated address on the wall over the fireplace to prove it. But after a bit he began to be so changeable towards Karl and me that we avoided him, we felt sure he was going off his head.

If Karl and I didn't see much of the Powell children we heard them often enough, even from the top of the house. For noise-making they were all in the same bundle, the whole lot of them. But sometimes they were dead silent for ages, the whole house was like the grave, although we knew for sure all the kids were in there somewhere. I found out the reason one night when Karl told me to creep downstairs and to peep in through the glass door of the kitchen to see what they were up to. All the kids were inside sitting round the table drawing in silence with their little tongues out, Buddug had emptied all the rubbish from the drawers in the sideboard and the kitchen dresser in a heap on the hearthrug, and the children were all drawing with wax crayons on the clean wood of the drawer bottoms. But they were not often like that. They had a game called *voting*, and they used to go marching round and round the house dressed up in old hats and curtains and tablecloths and things, and singing at the tops of their voices and banging saucepan lids together.

'Vote, vote, vote, for ——'

somebody or other, they sang, marching up and down the stairs, and they repeated the thing over and over again until they nearly drove us mad.

Sometimes the row didn't come from them all, but from just one or perhaps two. Little Eben, it may be, howling and frothing in a fit against the kitchen wall, or Myfanwy, the little girl twin, screaming because Mendy was teasing her. Mendy was the one with two thumbs on one hand and short legs curved like a corgi's, and all his organs on the wrong side. One night soon after I went to Academy House he crammed a tin po on the little girl's head, and she screamed and screamed for a couple of hours although all of us were trying hard in turns to get the thing off, turning and twisting it all shapes, and rubbing goose-grease round her head and neck to oil her a bit. In the end Karl and I took her to doctor J. J., the Powells were too ashamed to go themselves, we walked her down town hand in hand, the po still on her head, with a towel over it. But half way there she sicked up and we had to use the towel to wipe her.

All the Powells were terrible quarrellers and pouters, it was agony to have a meal with them because they cheeked one another and argued and answered back all the time; and one of the kids would push his dinner away and sulk because all his potatoes were not whole ones; and another one wouldn't drink his broth because there was no fat floating on the surface of it. The only thing I liked at their table was to see their teapot pouring, a battered old silver one it was, gone nearly black, but it was a beautiful pourer, the tea came out of it in a lovely slim curve like a curlew's beak. We always made some excuse if they tried to get us to eat with them. The kids couldn't use their knives and forks properly anyway, the snobby-nosed lot, and they messed their food up eating it and got it all over their faces enough to make you heave.

Sometimes when Karl and I were sitting up in our room in the lamplight, talking or reading, or playing dix-stones, we'd hear two or three pairs of feet thundering hollow up the wooden stairs below us, and then a struggle on the landing with the banisters making loud splitting noises, and then screaming, or perhaps gasping and whispering, as though somebody was being strangled; or sometimes there were terrible loud slaps on bare flesh, and screeching after them, and weeping and sobbing out loud. At first I was frightened by this but Karl would go on reading or playing, in silence, as though he couldn't hear anything out of the ordinary, and in time I got used to it too. Although one night the screaming was so terrible, and it went on such a long time, that we went out of our room to see what was happening. Down there in the darkness, on the landing below ours, we could make out Buddug sitting on the top step and screaming, and bowing her body up and down with agony like somebody demented, and beside her Myfanwy, not doing anything at all, only standing there, with her fingers stuck hard into her ears at right angles because of the yelling. We went down, carrying our oil lamp, and by the light of it we saw that Buddug's dress was ripped off her back almost down to her waist, the dirty curls of her hair were spread out like unpicked sacking, and underneath them her skin looked exactly as though it was covered with a pattern of overlapping Bass adverts, as though somebody had dipped his hand in red dye and pressed it again and again, this way and that, all over the skin of her back. We couldn't get any sense out of her, she was howling and shaking so much, nor out of Myfanwy, but at last we managed to persuade Buddug to go to her bedroom. There we could see more raw marks, this time deep red ones around her throat. When we got back up to our room Karl wouldn't talk any more, he blew out the lamp and went into his hammock without a word.

Luther was the big trouble maker as far as we could see, the one that upset everybody, including his father. He was about fourteen and in standard six in the elementary school, a big, heavy, dull-looking lout with black meeting eyebrows and a heavy black moustache that went round the corners of his mouth. He could hardly say a word because of his stammer, but that didn't stop him being dirty and objectionable and acting filthy. He was the one who had shown me his bare bottom from the plum tree in our orchard when he was little, and he was just the same now, or worse. He used to make gug-gugging noises in his throat for you to look at him, and then he'd pull his jacket up at the back, push his bum out and stick his thumb against it; or in hot weather he'd point to your feet and hold his nose. Whenever anybody new came to the house they would feel sorry for him because he stood in front of them trying hard to speak, and all he could do was gulp big mouthfuls of air into himself and go blue in the face, and fail in spite of all his struggles to get a single word out. People would sympathize with him and be kind and patient, and he'd bring something to show them, they thought he was doing it because he couldn't talk. My first real night in Academy House, the night my granny and my auntie came up to see how I was getting on, he brought his walking-stick into the kitchen, grinning, to show them, a long black thing it was, shiny and knobbly, and he got my auntie and granny to handle it, and smooth it and say how nice it was, and my granny used it to hobble up and down the kitchen with once or twice instead of her own stick, just to humour him. He made me blush doing all this, and the first excuse I could think of I got out of the room, because I knew he'd tell them in a rush if he could get the words out that what they were handling was made out of a bull's jontomus. He was always trying to make people blush like that, and feel awkward, and another thing he had for doing it was a long brown lump of rock, like a dollop of solid stone, some animal's droppings it was really, fossilized, he had pinched it out of the science case in his school. And the first time the Abrahams' little mongrel bitch from next door trotted in, soon after I went to Academy House, he played a trick on me with her; he snatched her up off the floor and beckoned me after him out into the back garden. Karl was with me at the time and I saw him looking away, but I was dull enough to follow him by myself, although I couldn't bear looking at the garden really, it was like a wilderness of high canes, and rubbish-mounds, and heaps of wet ashes. He went into the outside dubliw, knee-deep in torn-up newspapers, where the kids had pulled the wooden seat off and hung it on the wall like a horse-collar. There he held the

179

little bitch over the pan, and he began to make a murmuring sound to her until she did her little business down the hole. Then he laughed like a maniac and put her back next door over the garden wall.

Buddug did the work in the house, cooking the food and washing the clothes and that, but usually the place looked and smelt as though nobody had ever done any work in it at all. The kitchen ceiling was black as coal, and unless the fire was lit the grate was high with cinders as though somebody had delivered a load of them down the chimney. There was hardly any sign of paint on the woodwork anywhere, that was black too, like the wallpaper, or dark brown, and a lot of the glass in the windows and the fanlights was cracked, or broken, or boarded up. And the washing Buddug put out on the line in the back garden, especially the sheets, was always a deep grey more than white, the bed-clothes had stains all over them, patches of brown blood and the remains of all sorts of muck. I found her a pretty *didoreth* housekeeper after a big white-limer and bucket-basher like my mother used to be down the factory.

Buddug was too ladylike really for housework, mostly she was very superior and refined, especially in front of Karl and me, she smiled in her prim sort of way and fluttered her eyelids at us. I didn't like her much, though; when she stood near you she gave out a strong smell of ear-wax, and ill-favoured was Karl's word for her. There were one or two crayon drawings of cats on the walls of her father's music-room that she had done in school, and a poem she'd written once about pets, although they didn't have any in Academy House, had been printed in the *News and Banner*. She thought she could sing, too, because she was one of the famous Powells, soprano, but her top notes always sounded pretty jackeracks to me, her tremolo shook them out like tapioca. But ladylike or not, she could scream like all the Powells if anything upset her, and curse and swear, we could hear her from the top of the house sometimes, especially on Sunday mornings, swearing at her brothers at the top of her voice when she wanted to go to early prayer-meeting in Libanus, and she couldn't find her proper chapel clothes because the boys had been in her bedroom looking for something and messed the place up.

Luther was the one she hated most, she couldn't bear the tricks he played on people, or anything like that. She was refined, and I think she wanted Karl and me to know it. One day, before I'd been in Academy House long, she came right upstairs to the attic and knocked at the door of our room. She had a book with her, *The Art Treasures of the World*, a big thick volume full of coloured reproductions of the famous paintings to be seen in the galleries of Paris and Rome and that, and she asked us if we would like to look at it. Luckily she didn't stay when she had handed it in to us, because it made Karl and me helpless laughing. Buddug was so refined that what she'd done was cover all the tuppences of the naked little boys in the paintings with blacking. The funny thing was that after that whenever we were talking to her we began to think about coppers, and we were terrified we'd have to say a sentence with 'tuppence' in it. We couldn't have said it, I couldn't anyway, Karl was different, I would have gone hysterical first.

Old Mr Powell was the one that really puzzled us. Sometimes, especially when I went there first, he was jovial and talkative, wanting us to go into his room, and smiling in the mornings to see us using up the coffee, but oftener and oftener after a bit he was silent and morose and nasty, he wouldn't show himself downstairs in the house for days, and he would pass us on the road even in Edwards Terrace without a word. And the longer I stayed there the grumpier he got. He was the most moody man I had ever seen, you couldn't understand him at all. He had a big plumber's calendar on the kitchen wall, an advert, covered with thick purple crosses in indelible lead, a cross for every time he went to the dubliw, none sometimes for nearly a week and then three or four big ones in the same square. And yet, although he was feeding the children on soup and vegetables all the time, if one of them farted when he was about he would clip them and carry on. He was complaining a lot, too, he still looked pretty big and fat to us, and a good weight, but he was worrying all the time about his health, staying in bed up there in the attic for days at a time, and keeping little Eben home from school to hand him the po. His bedroom was up the top of the house, next door to ours, only a narrow passage separated them, but more and more I think, he kept out of our way, and we kept out of his for sure. For one thing, he had got you could smell him before you could see him. For another he began to make me, anyway, feel awkward by the way he behaved, like leaving his front buttons open and that. One morning when Karl and I came downstairs we found him fallen down in the passage with his head on the bottom step. Karl said he thought he'd been drinking. Another time I was looking at him from the gallery in Libanus as one of the deacons handed him the silver bread-plate in the communion service. Instead of choosing one little lump of bread and waiting until everybody else had one too before eating it, what Mr Powell did was grab a handful of the pieces off the plate and cram them straight into his mouth, so that half of them fell out and stayed tangled in his beard.

2

EVERY Saturday, as soon as I got back from my granny's, Karl and I went off together, it was marvellous. Sometimes Jeffy, Tom and Charley came with us, or one or two of them, but usually we went by ourselves because we could stay out as long as we wanted to, not like them, and there was nobody to badger us about where we'd been, and who was with us, and what we'd had to eat, and when, and that. We went out at night as well, sometimes, when we were supposed to be in bed, and Karl used to mesmerize me before we went down the timber balks, because whenever I had to climb anywhere my head began to buzz as though a few thousand bees were among the blossoms inside there, and it got so swimmy I couldn't move. But after Karl had passed his hands in front of my face a few times, and muttered some special incantations he had, I always felt brave, I would have gone goating up the Nannies after him then if he'd told me to.

Karl loved travelling about, he always wanted to walk out of Ystrad over into the next valleys, or up the Bryngwyns, or go down by train to the sea. He spoke about his life abroad, and about what we would see when we were living there together, and about what we saw and heard around us now. Growler was supposed to be the big Ystrad naturalist, but Karl talked in a way Growler never did. He would lie on his belly on the grass sometimes up the mountain, or in the woods, and stare in front of him, I didn't know what he was staring at. Once on a hot sunny afternoon we were in the disused railway cutting, and the shadows of the railings at the top of the grassy bank fell in rigid black bars down the slope, the stripes were close together and the grass between them glowed like a fur of green fire. I couldn't see anything much in it at first myself, but Karl kept on staring, he said if we watched hard enough we would see the whole pattern on the bank moving very slowly, and hear the heavy shadows grating across the hot grass. He used the word *grating*, that puzzled me, although I liked it very much. I didn't hear anything myself but I was willing to believe that Karl could, because he noticed all sorts of things every day that went by me as though they passed in the dark; the sun glittering and trembling on a crag of granite; winds blowing into the great yawn of a tree; bead-bunches of hard dung dangling on a cow's tail, giving out a rattling sound; the stickiness of hoar-frost on the pavements under our feet; from the end of Edwards Terrace the early morning like yellow fiord-water filling up our street from wall to wall; the midday sunlight falling in a runnel of brilliant water across the shiny cobweb bellying in the breeze. He was fed by his eyes, he told me, and he always used to stop and look at the holly trees, he seemed as though he couldn't get over the light grey bark on them, with the tiny wrinkles in it; where a branch came out of the trunk, especially a small branch, the bark was

183

often wrinkled around it, he said, there was a mass of fine curved lines and wrinkles, small and elegant and close together, beautiful as the bunches of lines around the eyes in human skin. Beautiful! But I began to look for them myself after a bit, and for other things I thought would please him. Between us we made up something about the little wing of an insect we found abandoned on a stone, it was like a tiny leaded window, the transparent parts iridescent, coloured bright red and blue and purple, like the stained glass of a cathedral, and between the tiny panes, rigid as iron, was the delicate black framework of veins that held the wing together. The little leaves of the bush in front of Academy House, too, on a frosty morning, used to halt him, the tiny flat leaves, themselves clear green, but each one white-edged with a little braid of hoar-frost.

Karl asked me on the mountain: 'Do you know anything about women, Dewi?'

'Course I do,' I shouted at him.

'What?'

'Plenty, boy.' But just then I couldn't think of anything much I *did* know, except that they had babies. 'I know where babies come from, if that's what you mean,' I said.

'And how they got where they come from?'

'Course.'

'Who told you?'

'Oh, everybody. Everybody tells you that. Tom told me most.'

'How did Tom know?'

'His mother told him.'

'How did she come to do that, Dewi?'

'One day just after we got to the grammar school his Queenie died, she was the big fat bitch they had before Pincher. Tom heard the vet saying she had an abscess on her womb, and when he asked his mother what her womb was she put him off. But you can't get rid of old Tom like that, not if he really wants to know something, so a day or two later he got the armchair and he said to his mother: "Ma, sit down there. I've got something to ask you." And he asked her everything, and she told him the lot.'

I stopped, but Karl didn't say anything.

'Charley told me some, too,' I went on. 'He knows all about being on heat, and serving, and castrating and that from the farm, he's seen all the animals mounting each other, and the young ones dropping out of their mothers, pigs, lambs, colts, calves.'

We talked a bit more about girls, and Karl told me he had no interest in them really, because he was married already, or as good as, his *fiancée* was a foreign princess, her family were poor, they lived in exile on a beautiful island, I think he said it was in the Mediterranean. I wanted him to tell me more about this princess because she sounded pretty strange, and beautiful, and queerer than any girl I had ever heard of, but instead he began to describe how he had helped the family to escape through the sewers of the city. As they hid in the darkness, crouching at the side of the wall, waiting for their guides, they saw to their horror thousands and thousands of small red eyes creeping slowly towards them, a great river of rats they realized it was, advancing in a murmuring silence, filling the floor of the tunnel from wall to wall. As the front row came nearer, they could see an enormous powerful grey rat out in front leading, and other giant rats almost as huge spread about here and there in the moving mass. Karl and the family of the princess pressed themselves back flat against the wall, almost fearing to breathe, watching in fascination and horror as the great murmuring river advanced, and then began to flow by, lapping their feet as they passed. They thought the flood would never end, and Karl said that if the party had killed one of those rats, or even pushed one off their boots in disgust, the whole sewer-full would have turned upon them in fury, and swarmed over them, and torn them to pieces.

Karl described to me the opera houses he had been in abroad, the great crystal chandeliers in the high domes, the boxes all round the walls framed with lights, tier above tier filled with officers of the white-uniformed imperial guard, and glittering countesses, the red plush, and the soft lights, and the perfume of flowers, and the string music. We went to the Ystrad Lyceum where my mother had never allowed me to visit, to see the variety turns, singers, dancers, conjurors, comedians and that. The side street and the roadway outside the theatre were filled with a crowd, they were mocking Sam Bomper Central Cottages, dressed up like a general and parading to and fro on the top step shouting: 'Early doors to all parts.' We pushed through and bought our tickets in a tiny lit-up hole in the wall. Inside it was magnificent, more wonderful than anything I had ever seen before. I walked the thick red carpets along the corridors, over my head in perfume, there were crimson hangings of plush everywhere, and dim red lights behind shades of rose silk. The auditorium, although almost empty, was just the same, dark and stuffy and scenty, the deep carpets soundless under our feet, and our smooth velvet seats giving under us softly as we sank into them. Everywhere the air surrounding us seemed sweet and unhealthy and lovely, and with every breath of it we drew in beautiful waves of a warm musky smell like the sultry inside of a man's hot hat.

Surely nothing that Karl had seen was more beautiful than this. There was only one gallery in the Lyceum, but on the dark red walls all round were long windows closed up with heavily tasselled curtains of crimson plush, and between them large round golden shields were placed with jewels flashing in their rims, surmounted by golden helmets and with spears, and swords, and war-axes of gold, sticking out all around their edges. Almost as soon as we sat down the orchestra began playing a loud brassy tune, they sat behind a partition a few feet in front of us, and above them rose the ample red velvet folds of the curtains closed over the front of the stage, decorated with golden smocking, and enormous tassels, and thick ropework of gilt, and rows and rows of heavy golden fringes near the hems. Yellow glare from the footlights oozed upwards into the curtains so that the deep folds were either bright crimson or almost black.

When the people entered, after Sammy Bomp had shouted 'Ordinary doors' outside, the theatre became crowded. The orchestra played fast and loud enough to deafen you. I had never been anywhere like the inside of this opera-house for size and magnificence and wonder. I could have stayed there for ever, breathing the warmth of that vast audience, and the sweet scents, watching the glitter, and listening to the loud human murmur in the dimness all around me. The lights began to lower, but before they went out I caught a glimpse of the chandeliers hanging from the dome above us, a ring of gigantic crystal bowls encrusted with white pearls, and suspended by ropes of enormous diamonds. My heart felt full of light and joy and thankfulness to Karl.

The curtains split up the middle and swept to each side showing the stage so bright I could hardly bear to look at it. Venice was on the backcloth, the Rialto, ethereal in the glare. The prow of a gondola slid on to the stage behind a low quay wall as the orchestra subsided, and a handsome young man, dressed in the bright clothes of a gondolier, stepped out singing a tenor solo and playing a guitar. Everybody clapped and cheered and the young man bowed and smiled at us, I had never seen such brilliant eyes or such glittering white teeth on anyone before. With his foot on a bench he gazed up the vine-draped wall opposite, and at the first notes of his song a beautiful young woman came out on to a balcony above him. She wrapped round her shoulders a long-fringed shawl of all colours, that hung on the balcony railings, and with a spotlight on her sang in a high soprano back down at him. After their duet she left the balcony and appeared on the stage dressed like a gipsy, wearing golden ear-hoops and the fringed shawl and red shoes with very high heels. She was the most beautiful girl I had ever seen. Her shining jet-black hair was parted in the middle and pulled back, hiding her ears, into a large bun at the back of her head, her skin was white as milk, and radiant, somehow, and intense, and her red lips were bright as the blood fresh from a cut on a white handkerchief. Her eyes glittered all the time, too, as if they had

187

some special light shooting an endless sparkle out of the darkness surrounding them, and when she smiled her teeth flashed wet and brilliant from her scarlet mouth. I wanted to watch her all night, I didn't care about the other acts to come, she was so beautiful and wonderful I could have run away with her, all I wished for was to see her face and hear her voice and to serve and worship her for ever and ever.

The next time the curtain went up we saw a bedroom on the stage and a little man very much like my father, but red-nosed, came running on with a beer-bottle in his hand, chased by a tall woman about my mother's height carrying a rolling-pin. He dived under the bed, and when the woman had gone off he climbed on top of the wardrobe for safety, and began to drink the beer up there. Presently a beautiful curly headed girl came on to the stage, opened a Japanese screen and began to undress behind it. We couldn't see her doing it but we knew what was happening because her bare arm kept appearing, tossing out underclothes and stockings and things on to the chair beside the screen. And we could tell even better by the antics of the red-nosed man on top of the wardrobe. He was watching her undressing and he turned and twisted and writhed in excitement, and his eyes bulged out of his head every time another garment was flung out from behind the screen. It was so funny my throat ached laughing at it, I wished it would come to an end, although I couldn't bear to look away. In the end the man squirmed and capered so much he fell off the wardrobe, and the girl screamed and pushed the screen over in her fright. She was fully clothed, she hadn't been undressing at all, only getting things out of a chest of drawers to pack them in her portmanteau, and the turn ended with the little man walking off the stage on his bottom.

Then when the troupe of beautiful long-legged dancers came on everybody stamped and whistled. All the girls were smiling as they pranced to the front of the stage in a line, but one of them, after a bit, the prettiest she seemed to me, began smiling straight at Karl and me. She was lovely, she had long slender legs in golden trousers, and a yellow bodice covered with spangles, and upright ostrich feathers nodded on her head. I smiled more at her, and she noticed it, and when I waved my hand she waved back. It was marvellous, I sweated and my head began to sing with excitement as though I'd had a big kiss on the ear. I didn't know what to do for joy.

That night I couldn't sleep, I sat until the early hours in one of the theatre boxes overlooking the glaring stage, sometimes it was in Karl's opera-house, or it might have been a balcony of the imperial palace, watching the troops parading down the blinding boulevards, the soldiers in platoons like wire brushes moving along the middle of the road. Their officers came into the box off the stage, wearing white gloves, and medals, and golden sashes, and speaking all sorts of wonderful languages, and the perfume drenching over us all seemed thick and refined as the scent of a rick of honeysuckle. Beautiful smiling dancers were there too, and a silent mysterious princess, and gipsies, and gondoliers sometimes, and every time I was about to drop off, the glare of the boards and the thundering band woke me up, and I was bowing to the beautiful women again, or trying to behave properly to the high-class nobles surrounding us.

★　★　★　★　★

'Fancy Bowen geogger thinking of taking fifty of us single-handed up the Bryngwyns,' Jeffy said to me one day. But when Growler got to hear of it he thought he had better come too. We didn't fancy having Growler in our laps all day, but we had given our names and we couldn't get out of it. Bowen wanted us to reach the summit of Pen Bannau, the highest peak there, about three thousand feet it was, the highest mountain anywhere near our valley. There were marvellous views from the top on a sunny day, everybody said, you could see about half Wales, and the faint horizontal fume of the sea blue in the distance.

We went in a little train to a halt called Pontelin at the foot of the mountains, miles from anywhere, and then we began to walk up a sort of rough path leading to the top, although the track disappeared after a few hundred yards. The weather was marvellous, bright and clear, and the farther up we went the more we could see, the dim smoke-smudge of Ystrad far behind us in the distance, and then a thousand fields hung in the vast hammocks of the hills, dun, or frosted, or a sad green, or jersey-green in the gusty sunlight and gay as a ganzy; and a couple of blue lakes were right beneath us too, and the dark wide woods, and a yellow lake of corn; and all around us the sun and the shadows of the clouds lying motionless and clear as stains of water on the dusty velvet of the scentless mountains.

After a bit, in spite of the lovely weather, things began to go wrong. The boys wouldn't keep together, they started wandering off in groups ahead up the grassy side of the mountain, and soon we heard somebody screaming for help behind us. We ran back round some huge boulders we had just passed and found Boysie Edwards floundering about in the middle of a hairy bog, and before we could reach him he had fallen flat on his face in it. When he came out his clothes were soaking, but Growler didn't seem to care, he had climbed so fast to keep up with us he was purple and bulge-eyed behind his glasses, as though invisible hands had found his windpipe and were slowly throttling him. But he was still cocky and full of his coat, and on his face was a very cheeky expression all the same. Nobody could ever make head or tail of Growler. In the end Boysie buzzed off back to the station when Growler wasn't looking, and Jonno and about half a dozen others did a bunk with him.

A bit farther up we found a sort of turf platform where we could eat our sandwiches. Jeffy didn't have any, only a bag with two or three fairy-cakes in it, and while the rest of us were eating he was wandering about looking for something to do. At last he came across a workman's shovel in a ditch, a rusty broken old thing, how it got there I don't know, and he began chucking it down the slope for Tom to catch. Jeffy got wilder and wilder, he could never play anything like that tidy, he always had to start getting mad and hysterical. Tom couldn't see very well looking upwards and after a bit he missed his catch, and the rusty edge of the thing took a groove of flesh out of his hand from his thumb right up to his wrist. He bled like a pig and we all gathered round.

Although Growler was supposed to know all about hygiene and that, he didn't seem to have any idea what to do, and neither did Bowen either, it was Karl who lifted Tom's hand above his head, and put handkerchiefs on the wound, and a couple of coat-belts strapped tight around his arm. A bit later when Growler and Bowen slipped behind a rock to water the pony Tom and Jeffy buzzed off too, back to Pontelin, which we could still see from time to time in the trees miles below us at the foot of the mountain.

We were climbing Pen Bannau the easy way, just walking up at a leisurely pace over the turf-covered slope. The mountain gradients were steep in places, and sometimes we came upon unexpected dips, empty rush-covered valleys right across our path, but mostly we just climbed up and up at a steady pace. And then, when we had reached what must have been about two-thirds of the way to the top, the weather changed suddenly. In no time at all, it seemed, we were in the middle of a thick mist. We stopped walking and Growler got us all huddled together at the foot of a long black wall of rock, a low cliff about twenty feet high. As we sat there and watched, the mist got rapidly denser. The top of the little cliff disappeared up into it, and the greyness hung round in a semicircle in front of us like drape after drape of steamy and impenetrable butcher's muslin. Karl pointed to our clothes, beginning to be covered with a coating of tiny glass beads. He hated sitting there, trapped and hemmed in, he said, with Growler around he always felt as though he were fighting for air. Was I willing to slip off and risk reaching the summit on our own? I said I didn't mind if we could get away without Growler seeing us. Be ready then, he told me.

We got our chance when one of the boys the other end of the group suddenly found he was sitting practically on top of a horse's skull. We all crowded round and there it lay spread out on the turf, the perfect skeleton of a mountain pony, the hoops of the ribs, the thick backbone straight down the middle, the big skull and the tail in line with it, and the legs stuck out rigid like diagonals on each side; every bone in perfect order, and all picked clean and rain-washed white as though they'd been boiled. Growler began making some sort of speech about it and while everybody's back was turned Karl and I slipped off together into the mist.

The stuff by now was packed around us dense as fine-meshed cheese-cloth and before we had groped very far Karl said: 'Dewi, stop a minute. We can't go on together like this, it's too dangerous.'

'Why, Karl?' I asked.

'This mountain's treacherous. It's famous for it. In bright sunshine there's no danger, but under mist it's different. There are cliffs and precipices all over it, some not deep, some vertical for hundreds of feet to the bottom. But even the twenty-foot drop we sheltered against was enough to kill the mountain pony.'

'Do you mean you want to give up, Karl?' I asked him surprised.

'Oh, no,' he said. 'What I mean is I intend to go on ahead alone. You can follow me. If I disappear suddenly with a loud cry you'll know I've gone over the edge and you can go back for help.'

I looked at Karl and he was grinning, and the next moment he was away up the slope and standing right at the blurred edge of the grey visibility He waved me on, and that was how we climbed to the top, Karl like a dark, silent, uncertain spectre, hovering in and out of the mist ahead, stopping a moment and then beckoning me forward across the clear space between us, while all around the dense grey thickened over thousands of vertical cliff faces, and rocks, and mile-high precipices.

We seemed to go on like this for hours although it couldn't have been, and at last Karl's phantom ahead of me stood still and signalled me up to his side. It had, during the last few hundred yards, begun to get a lot lighter, the mist was moon-white and thinning in the breeze, and some pale illumination flooded it like opal. 'I think we're right at the top, Dewi,' Karl said. 'Stay near me. Right on the very top.'

At our feet the turf covering the mountain ended in an abrupt line as though it had been chopped off, and everything out below it, or beyond it, if there was anything, was still hidden in the unspooling of that vast cocoon of greyness. Gradually, right below us, we began to make out an enormous rough stairway of black rock descending into the mist, like steps disappearing into a vast cellar from just below the brink of the turf, three, four steps became visible, but the rest was hidden below us in a sea of shifting steam, restless and impenetrable, and pallid as hoarfrost. Karl turned me away and pointed across the slope. There the mist was completely broken up, and the breeze streamed it off the tops of the mountains all round, and above us in the sun floated the beautiful shiny masses of fleecy cloud, huge in size as mountain ranges themselves, but pink, or milky and silver, and weightless as cotton grass, moving on the floods of air like mountains of gleaming silk and bubbled ivory. I could see it was true, we were right on the summit of Pen Bannau, and the sun was shining brightly in the sky again, its brilliant gusts flooding the grass around us green. And we could see the whole line of the Bryngwyn summits rising into the clear air before us, Pen Owen, Pen Carn, Carn Leiaf, Cader y Llyn, with the wrecks of the great clouds sailing away from them into the blue emptiness on one side, and another vast armada of shining masses spread out in endless flotillas across the heavens bearing down upon them from the other. It was the most magnificent sight I had ever seen, I had never known anywhere such limitless expanses of air and sky, such grandeur, and freshness, and universal radiance as this I saw all around me through following Karl. My body could have broken into a thousand mouths to shout my joy or gone galloping across the mountain grass in ecstasy. But Karl had me tight. 'Look, Dewi,' he said.

I almost fainted with horror. What he had done was to turn me round and show me what was right beneath our feet. There too the mist was gone. Below the four black steps of rock that a few minutes ago had disappeared into it, there was nothing, they ended abruptly in mid air and the whole mountain fell away below them in a vast black sunless amphitheatre, like a gigantic crater with vertical sides dropping eight or nine hundred feet sheer into a valley of black rocks below, and a black tarn. I sank on my knees, shuddering, too giddy to stand, and crawled away, afraid I was going to be sick.

★ ★ ★ ★ ★

It was marvellous being out at night with Karl. We had glowing tips of clinker in Ystrad that had been smouldering and steaming for about a hundred years, and one night Karl took me to see the tramps asleep in the little hollows among them. The tips were always warm and comfortable for homeless people on cold nights, but the fumes they gave off were poisonous, and sometimes by the morning the sleepers were found to be dead. I was afraid going over the burning ground in the darkness, and through the glowing steams, and looking at the men lying down asleep in the hollows. What would happen if we wakened one of them? And was it possible I was looking down at men who were already dead? But Karl said we ought to pity them and not fear them. Another night we watched the meth drinkers under the arch of the railway bridge where they lived, we peeped in through a bolt-hole in the corrugated zinc they had for a wall, and saw one of them sitting on a box cooking something in a tin over a fire. By its glow we could see the men lying about on the ground drunk, dressed in rags and with torn-up newspapers all around them. We knew two of them, Harry Roberts, and Conno, who used to frighten us, when we were little children going to school, by his staring eyes and the bad language he used to mutter at us. But Harry was harmless, and once about midnight we found him hanging over the wall of the Ystrad churchyard, drinking from his meths bottle and shouting to his wife buried inside: 'I won't be long now, *cariad annwyl*, I won't be long.' He had fallen down and his hands and face were covered with blood. We tossed the bottle and the packet of cloves into the graveyard and got him to walk with us arm-in-arm to where his son lived. The doctor said he was killing himself, Harry told us, with all the smoking he was doing, but he didn't care any more. He began to cry and then he struggled a bit to go back to the burial ground, but we managed somehow to get him to the house.

Before I started to go out with Karl I believed everything in Ystrad came suddenly to a stop when it got dark or it was time to go to bed, but I think we saw more things going on at night at last than in the day. Once or twice we went round with Olly John the deaf-mute for a bit, he wasn't all there and he prowled the Ystrad streets and back lanes every night, flashing his bicycle lamp here and there and putting what he found in the sack hanging over his shoulder. We saw the lights on in the bedrooms where people were ill and dying; we stood at the door of the dark and cosy bakehouse and watched Mr Protheroe the night baker kneading the bread by the dim light of the bat's-wing burner, up to his elbows in dough; we looked in over the frosted glass at the back of the post office and saw the yawning men getting the letters ready for the next morning. We stood silent and motionless under the hoarse or blub-blubbing street lamps, and saw the colliers going to the pits in groups with white faces, or coming home pitch-black; we saw the policemen, the bad women, the *News and Banner* printers, Herbert the milk meeting the morning train. Ystrad was alive every night with silent people, while above our heads, under the moonlight and the moon-sheeted blue on the slates, thousands slept and knew nothing of it, nothing of the darkness and the silence and the solitary lights on in town, and the soft whir and pounding of machinery behind closed doors, and the night creatures wandering the streets, the rats, the stray cats and dogs, the sheep and the little mountain ponies.

Often we went up to our camp in the woods at midnight, until Charley's father became bankrupt, and gave up the land, and went away to England to sell his sewing-machines. We wandered the mountains on both sides of our valley, on starless nights we looked back into Ystrad to where the little towns had laid down their mounds of diamonds at the bottom of the darkness, each under a faint glow of golden breathing. Sometimes, as we returned in the mornings, we saw the valley like a vast cup of darkness filling up with rain, or the lights paling, and the sunlight in a long bed of steaming gold behind us in the sky, casting the stretched-out shoes of our morning shadows upon the mountains. We loved the calm still nights on the slopes, with a full moon torn into shreds of silver in the stream at our feet, and the same moon at the same moment hanging motionless and assured in the sky before us, flooding the whole night with the blue silver of her illumination. But we loved the windy nights best of all, watching the huge masses of cloud crossing the clear sky; or instead we made, for a change, those dark charging tons of darkness stop dead, and we let the moon swim out far into the open blue, and we loosed the small stars and sent them whippeting across from cloud to cloud. It was lovely to watch this in the dark on the mountain, crouching together, and the air pouring over us as though we were stones lodged at the bottom of a torrent, listening to the wind rushing upon us as it pushed itself shrieking through the holly hedge. But often when I got back to Academy House again I couldn't sleep, I thought of the moon bright on the mountainside, and the circling stars, and I wondered why anything was, why the stars in their millions existed, and the people of flesh and blood, and myself; I lay in bed often gripping the mattress, because when I thought like this for a little time my mind seemed to reel, I felt as if I was becoming faint and unconscious with the swirling mystery around me, as though I was slipping overwhelmed into everlasting oblivion. When I told Karl about the vastness and the terror of my thoughts he smiled at me, and nodded, and patted me in a comforting way on my back.

3

BEFORE we had been back in school long after the typhoid, Growler sent for Karl again.

Everybody in school was interested in Karl by then, after the way he'd argued with Growler in the playing-field, and beaten him. When Jeffy and Charley and I, before the holiday, used to talk to the boys in our form, and other kids we knew, about Karl, and tell them the marvellous way he'd gone up the Nannies in the darkness, and how he'd stood up to Growler before, one night in Pantglas woods, and describe to them some of the adventures he'd had abroad, they weren't interested enough to listen, or else they didn't believe us. But now we heard stories about Karl that we didn't even know ourselves. But if you thought about these stories a bit you could see they were something like what we had been saying a few months back, but they were all mixed up and exaggerated, you couldn't imagine Karl doing half those things at all. But with everybody talking about him, and blabbing about what he was supposed to have done, Growler must have got to hear things about him too. Anyway, one day at playtime Karl told me not to wait for him after school because Growler wanted to see him in his study at four-thirty.

I went home alone. In Academy House Karl and I had a signalman's enamel jack each for carrying our tea or coffee about. I collected mine in the kitchen and went straight up to our room. When I had finished my bread, and scraped the jam-pot, I began my homework, but I couldn't do it properly for thinking about him, and wondering what Growler wanted him for this time, and what he would do to him. At nine o'clock he still hadn't come home so I had my supper, a packet of dragees and a cup of water from the bathroom on the floor below. I couldn't eat any more. Soon after ten o'clock I heard Tally Powell shooting the bolts of the front door. Tally would do anything for a couple of coppers and I wondered whether I should go down and tell him Karl was still out, but I decided I would stay awake and let him in somehow myself.

I lay there on my bed in our attic, reading one of Karl's books, a historical one about the adventures of a Russian count whose face and voice were Karl's, trying not to fall asleep, wondering and dreaming all the time, remembering the livid scar across the back of Karl's hand torn by the beak of a Serbian falcon; and the sight of that hand mastering the bridle of the horse he used to

197

hire to gallop round the Ystrad back streets on, and up the mountain, on a Sunday morning; Francis the coster's old race-horse it was, with ribs like a corrugated roof; and about his black tooth that had decayed suddenly the time he died. Karl had been killed a few years ago in Spain climbing the cliffs to reach an eagle's nest, he had fallen from a dizzy height on to crags sharp as fangs at the foot of the precipice. He lay dead in the apartment of his aunt, and his uncle the admiral, for three whole days, with the shutters closed. The doctor signed the death certificate saying his neck was broken, Karl still had the paper somewhere. But his aunt never gave up praying for him, and then, minutes before the funeral, he suddenly came back to life. The blood began to move in his veins again and his whole body recovered, except for that one tooth that had turned black at his death, and remained black and dead ever since.

I put down the Russian book and began to let my fingers feel over my face, wondering if I was getting to look a bit more like Karl. I wished I could look like him. When I lay on my back on the bed like this, and drifted my finger-tips over my eyes and my nose and mouth, I often persuaded myself I was favouring him more and more. Especially when I put a haughty expression on, or pulled my cheeks in to look a bit more refined and intelligent. But always next morning when I studied myself in the glass in the Powells' bathroom I couldn't believe it. Karl's hair was wavy, a pale straw colour now, with a flare of red in it like ripe grass, but mine was ginger, a low-down metallic colour that Jeffy used to tease me about, although a bag of bones like him ought to be the last one to shout about the way people looked; Jeffy said if I stood out in the rain without my cap on the trickles coming down my face would be green. Karl's eyes were large and clear and a vivid blue, but mine were nothing like that. One was a sort of greenish grey and the other was quite different, it was a kind of spotted green. All Karl's teeth were lovely, except the one that died in Spain, very white and wet and regular. But when I grinned at myself in the looking-glass what I saw was a row of black dumb-bells, the teeth were all right at the top and the bottom, but the middle of every one had been eaten thin by decay. I expect I had chewed too many sweets, my auntie was always bringing them home for me from the sugar boilers behind her workroom. One thing I did have like Karl—a white face; but as soon as the sun shone a bit Karl would turn a warm, golden, pikelet colour, while I'd only be a mass of dark freckles again, like a sandy beach with the first raindrops of a shower starting to dot it black all over.

It always used to get very stuffy up there under the roof with the oil lamp lit for hours and the gas-fire on, and some time or another I must have fallen asleep going over Karl's adventures when he was in Russia and that. One night, out in the middle of winter, he was lost, miles from everywhere. He trudged on hour after hour across the flat endless wastes of virgin snow, seeing nothing but darkness, and the icy stars mocking him above, and the flat snow stretching out around him, endless, in all directions, to the very end of Russia, and hearing nothing but the wind and the distant howling of the hungry wolf-packs for their prey. Every now and then he stopped and listened, wondering whether the wolves had picked up his human scent, and he peered around him, searching the darkness for any glimmer of light, but he found none. And then, suddenly, behind him, after many weary hours of trudging, the clear jingling of harness bells! Karl stopped, and presently, as the sound drew nearer, two yellow dots of light shone into view through the darkness, travelling in his direction. He ran back towards them shouting. The large elegant sleigh of ebony and silver, drawn by three snorting horses, beautiful black bloodstock, pulled up as he approached. The occupants were two, the pipe-smoking driver muffled up on his box, and behind him a handsome bearded young man heavily wrapped up in rich furs. He invited Karl to sit beside him and loaded him with scented furs also. At his feet lay two beautiful snow leopards, with broad golden collars on their necks, attached to golden chains which the young count held in hands gloved and magnificently jewelled. The two animals snarled fiercely at Karl, but without making a sound. The driver cracked his whip and the sleigh moved swiftly on again to the jingle of the silver harness-bells, and after some time they found themselves on the hard snow of a long straight road, with snow-covered hedges on each side. Presently, ahead, two smooth white hills came into sight, like the bent knees of some gigantic figure buried in the plain, and right across the road, from hill to hill, stretched a high spike-topped wall, with a pair of vast iron-studded doors set in the middle of it. The doors were shut, completely barring their way, but at the approach of the sleigh-bells and the lamps they swung silently open without anyone appearing to touch them, and Karl found himself in a spacious courtyard, brilliantly illuminated by the countless chandeliers pouring their lights down from all the large unshuttered windows of the prince's palace surrounding it, and by the enormous bon-fire burning in the middle, and the torches stuck in their sconces on the courtyard walls.

The next thing I remembered was waking up in the darkness with my heart pounding. The lamp had burnt itself out. Some-body seemed to be tapping at the attic window. I jumped off the bed and drew back the curtains. Karl's face, smiling in at me, the whites of his eyes glittering like silver paper, showed at the glass with the red glare of the sky behind him. I opened half of the window and there he was with his elbows on the cill, standing on top of one of the sloping balks of timber that held the front of Academy House on to the sides.

'Let me in, Dewi, will you?' he whispered. 'The front door's locked.' And in a minute or two, after I'd relit the oil lamp, we were sitting together on my bed, eating condensed milk with a teaspoon and sharing the barm cake Karl had brought in with him in a paper bag. He looked terrible, but handsome, very pale, his lamp-lit mop the foggy gold of barley fields, but under his eyes were dark patches. He was smiling and happy, and he began to tell me what had happened between himself and Growler after school.

'What do you think Growler wanted me for, Dewi?' he said. 'He told me first he'd been learning a lot about me lately, and little of what he heard was to my credit. He wanted to speak to me because he was concerned that what he called the more deplorable of my accomplishments might be bringing the name of the school into disrepute. Was it true, now, he was anxious to know, that I had achieved the imbecile feat of climbing that remaining pillar of the viaduct arches in the Graig meadows? Was it? I said, yes, it was, but I couldn't see how that could get the school a bad reputation because nobody saw me doing it. He said he couldn't allow that sort of thing to pass and he meant to punish me for it. I would be removed from 5B for the rest of the term and placed in the form below. Good afternoon.'

'What did you do, Karl?' I asked him.

'Well, I didn't go out of the room as he expected me to, I stayed there and tried to reason with him. I pointed out with respect that it would be very unwise to punish me in that particular way, since my age indicated I should already be in the upper sixth to begin with. He could almost certainly not expect the support of the governors if such a move were brought to their notice. In fact it would be an ill-advised proceeding to punish me at all for anything I had done in the Graig meadows. How could he? Because what I did in my own time was no concern of his. In school, certainly, and going to and from school, possibly, but not in the holidays or the evenings. We argued and he began to lose his temper and to make general accusations against me. Jeffy's prank with the time-table, you remember, must have been going round and round in his head because suddenly he made reference to it, he said he suspected I was directly involved in scattering the time-table cards about the room some time ago, on the, let me see, he said—when was it? He dived into one of the drawers of his desk and brought out the school log-book. As he was fumbling for his key to open it I spotted in the glass cupboards behind his head a pile of last term's form registers, tied up in pink and put away, so I nodded to them and said: "The evidence of my complete innocence of that charge is on those shelves behind you, sir."

'He was taken aback at that, wondering what I meant, but I

made him pull the registers out and compare the dates of my attendances in the 5B register with the date the time-table was scattered as recorded in the log-book. He only grunted when he saw I was absent on that day, but he didn't apologize. And then, because he had failed with the other charges, I suppose, he brought out what he thought no doubt was his trump card. He accused me of organizing the school strike! The school strike! At first I couldn't think what to say, the accusation was so completely monstrous and fantastic. "Organizing, sir?" was all I could say to him. "So far from organizing the strike, I am prepared to give you my solemn word of honour as a gentleman that I knew nothing at all about it until I saw the whole school already gathered down by the river the morning it took place. If you remember, sir, I arrived in the field at almost the same moment as you and Mr Thomas. Just a little before you, sir."

'If it was true, he said, that I wasn't behind the whole thing, how did it happen that I had all my arguments in favour of it cut and dried: and how was it I was the one who spoke up every time the boys were wavering under his persuasion, and were just preparing to move off into school?

'I told him what he called my arguments were only expressions of ordinary common sense, and the message from the council offices ordering the closing of the school was surely a clear confirmation of their correctness.

'He said he couldn't accept what I had said as truth. If I knew nothing of the strike beforehand my interference was mere impertinence, an impudent and rascally attempt to challenge and undermine the authority of the headmaster in the presence of his pupils. And since this was not the first time this had occurred, and since my general behaviour, added to my complete indolence, was most unsatisfactory, most unsatisfactory, I would go down a form, pending a decision concerning my future in relation to the school. Good afternoon.'

Karl laughed.

'Will you go down, Karl?' I asked.

'I shan't be here long now, Dewi,' he said, smiling happily.

His words hurt me like a deep stab. Not be here! I was unable for the first time to return his smile. Where was he going? What was to happen to me if he left Ystrad? I couldn't bear to think of it. I felt frightened and abandoned and in despair. I felt my eyes filling with tears. 'Don't you like being here, Karl?' I managed to get out at last.

'I'm very homesick, Dewi,' he said.

'Homesick? Homesick for where?'

'I hate everything about my life here, this madhouse, Growler's paltry school, the valley, everything. I am homesick for nobility, and honour, Dewi, weary of the pettiness, of all that is common and vulgar, and the small satisfactions, do you know what I mean?—parched for a glimpse of the mysterious brightness burning at the back of the sun. That world is my home. If you hadn't come to live here, I would have gone already. Will you come with me when I go?'

'But where will we go, Karl?' I asked him.

'Back to Europe! Or round the world! We'll sail in triumph round the edge of the world! I saw a man in Ystrad today who gave me a splendid idea. He was walking round the world! Have you seen him about? He has a huge wooden globe on a pair of cart-wheels with him, with a black and white map of the world painted on it. He pulls it behind him, and there's a curved door cut in the side so that he can live inside it! How marvellous! He walks round the world by day and sleeps at the world's secret centre at night. Will you come with me, Dewi? Let's go together! To Europe first! To Europe!'

He got up and started marching up and down the empty spaces between the attic furniture, singing in a whisper a sort of chant: 'To Europe! To Europe! We'll sail away to Europe!' When he passed me he said: 'Come on, Dewi, get up and join me. To Europe! To Europe! Europe over the blue!' And he got me marching up and down behind him, buzzing in beat because I didn't know the words he was making up. It was daft, and childish, and very exciting. In the middle of it all I heard the

203

town hall clock striking. I stopped dead. 'Karl!' I said. 'What time is it?'

He took out the watch hanging in his breast pocket and grinned. 'Half past two,' he said.

'Half past two!' I couldn't believe it. 'Are you sure?' I asked him. 'Where've you been till now?'

'Climbing,' he answered softly, and smiled again. And that was all. 'Come on, Dewi,' he went on. 'Let's turn in.'

He went over to his hammock, and I lay down in my bed. But again I couldn't sleep. His talk of going to Europe had disturbed and excited me. Every so often he had letters from abroad, some with coats of arms on the backs, but he never showed me what was inside them. And one day when I came home from school, what did I see standing outside Academy House but Jamesie Davies's cab from the rank at Ystrad station, the one my mother and father used to hire for the morning we went on our summer holidays. Jamesie the cabby was up on the box smoking, and the old piebald was dreaming with his nose on the road. Inside the house, as I was passing the music studio, I heard loud talking going on, which was a thing I had never heard there before. 'Can't you believe the evidence of your own eyes?' a man's voice asked loudly just as I passed the door, a foreign voice I thought it was, nobody I knew anyway. I didn't hear any more because I went straight on up the stairs and towards our room; but on the first landing I met Buddug crouching behind the banister, and peeping out through the bars. She had her finger on her lips.

'What's up?' I whispered, nodding back down the stairs.

'Somebody in the studio come to see about Karl,' she answered. 'From abroad. Two men.'

I thought at once they meant to take him away. 'What do they want?' I asked her.

'I don't know,' she answered. 'They're in there talking to Datta.'

'Where's Karl?'

'He's in there with them. They've been ages.'

I went on up to our room, greatly disturbed. After some time

204

I looked down into the street from the attic window, and there below on the pavement outside the house I saw Karl talking to two important-looking men in top hats and long black over-coats with astrakhan collars; one of the men was tall with a white pointed beard and a sword-stick, and the other was shorter, his face yellow, and he carried a very shiny black bag in his gloved hand. They bowed to Karl, got into the cab, Jamesie woke the old horse up, and off they went down Edwards Terrace towards Ystrad station. I often thought about these mysterious-looking foreigners visiting Karl, and the money he had for a long time after they'd been, but I was too shy to ask him about them at the time, and after a little I was afraid, in case I had dreamt it all and it had never really happened.

And now tonight, after his talk of Europe, I remembered it again, and thought a lot about it. And then I began worrying about Karl and Growler, imagining in different ways the scene with Karl in the headmaster's room. Growler was behind his desk, panting and puffing in anger like a huge purple-faced bull-frog, wearing bird-catching boots, and Karl faced him, his back to the door, slim and tall, his skin white as silver and his hair like solid gold. Growler was bawling and waving his glasses about, the veins in his neck thickening above his collar as he denounced Karl, and his bare eyes bulging out like basin bottoms until nearly the whole of each eyeball was visible outside his purple eyelids. In size he often became immense, nearly filling his whole study, so huge his shoulders were pressed up against the ceiling and the back of his head was along it, with his face glaring down at the floor. His arms became so long his elbows rested on the carpet. In the corner of the room stood the trestle table where the time-table lay on its vast sheet of cardboard. The sun blazed in hot through the study windows. 'Jackass, jackass, jackass,' Growler screamed, 'I'll trim your comb, you jackass.' Karl bowed and said something I couldn't catch, but whatever it was it made Growler slump back suddenly into his chair, his purple face pale to the lips. Presently he dropped his head on to his desk and started to weep, asking Karl over and over to forgive him. I kept on imagining this scene, sometimes in one way, sometimes in another, and waking up terrified every time I was just dropping off to sleep. The last thing I heard was a clock somewhere striking four.

4

WHEN I woke up in the morning Karl had gone. He had left a note pinned to the bedroom door which said: 'To the Bryng-wyns, perhaps! Tonight!' I felt cross at first, but then I remembered that I didn't know what he had to do and see to, when he went off in this way. So I got dressed, ate my breakfast in our room, and went off to school.

I didn't pass Tom Stiff's Bon Marché now, coming down to school from Edwards Terrace, and when Karl wasn't with me I usually walked by myself until I got to the Tiger *gwli* which led out into High Street. Charley had told me the day before that he was going that night to see Mr Raymond's model coal-mine, now on show in Ystrad market, and as I walked up the tramroad I made up my mind what I was going to tell him about another model of Mr Raymond's I had seen. It was a fire brigade, all little dwarfs in huge Britannia helmets and blue and crimson uniforms, the tallest only two inches high. At the back of the case Mr Raymond kept for them was a pretty little cottage, a sort of doll's house thatched with bottle straw, it was night-time and the moon was up, and as you watched you saw smoke oozing slowly from all the windows of it, and then red tongues of fire leaping out here and there the size of match-flames. Women holding children like jelly babies in their arms lean out of the upstairs windows. Soon a crowd of undersized little people gathers outside. The alarm bell begins to ring loudly, and on to the grass in front of the house dashes the fire-engine pulled by four little fiery white stallions. Out jump the stumpy firemen with big moustaches, and begin setting their ladders up against the house, and squirting thin water-pistol jets at the windows. Their tangled hose-pipes gleam like pipeclay, white as the laces of canvas gym shoes. In the end all the people are rescued, the fire is put out, and the cottage saved. This was all lies. Mr Raymond didn't have a model like that at all, nobody could, and I didn't know why I took the trouble to make it up just to say: 'Ever been had?' to Charley. I started thinking about it because I found the brass end of the poker-handle in the passage on the way out of Academy House, it looked a bit like a fireman's helmet, but not much, but it was enough to start me making up all this daft guff about Mr Raymond's model just to floor Charley, and make him believe for a bit I'd seen a better model than he had.

Going up the last slope of High Street before coming to the school gates I saw Jeffy and Charley ahead of me waiting. 'Heard the latest?' Jeffy said, gnawing his nails and his eyes giving out their special glitter. 'Where's Karl?'

'What latest?' I asked him. 'Gone up the river.'

'Fire in Growler's house. Burnt to the ground.'

'Burnt to the ground?' I said. 'When?' The news was like something terrible you read about in the history books, it was a shock and terrible, you could tell that, but it was a happening that had nothing to do with you, and you couldn't imagine it.

'Last night, they say.'

'This morning,' Charley said. 'Early. Ivor's got it on his placards. In the square.'

Jeffy lived the nearest to Growler's house. 'Have you seen it?' I asked him.

'No,' he said. 'We're going up tonight. A click of us. Coming?'

'How did it happen?' I asked.

'Nobody knows. Mystery. Started in the roof.'

A mystery, I thought! Started in the roof! My ears almost burst with the jerk of my heart at the realization of what these words meant. I went cold, icy from my inside right out to my skin. This news really was terrible. Not because Growler's house had been burnt down but because suddenly I didn't know whether Karl had caused it, and because I dreaded the cruel things that would be done to him if he had.

'Where was old Growler?' I asked for something to say that would hide my panic. 'Was he hurt?' I continued, cold as a stone, and unless I kept my eyes down I saw all the streets of Ystrad blazing in huge sheets of flame around me.

'No. Rescued in his nightshirt. And Mrs Growler. It's in the *News*. The only thing saved was one teaspoon, silver.'

'Will there be any school today I wonder?' I asked, dazed. I hardly knew what I was saying.

'Are you daft?' Jeffy answered. 'It would take more than his house being burnt down to make Growler close the school.'

'It *is* more than his house,' said Charley. 'A lot more too.'

'What?' I asked him.

'His butterflies. And moths. All gone. Not a single case saved, according to the paper. You know what the fire brigade are. They didn't arrive until the house was practically coke.'

'Growler's life's work gone up in flames, the paper said. He kept his bugs up in the long room under the roof.'

I didn't know what to do, I felt desperate and sick, and my head was swimmy. As soon as they had begun telling me the fire was a mystery I thought of Karl, and what he had told me of his interview with Growler; and the knowledge that he had been out late, climbing, as he said, confused and frightened me. Should I tell Jeffy and Charley Karl hadn't come in until two o'clock in the morning? We had all sworn to be his friends for ever, but would they be faithful to him if they knew what I knew?

'Where's Karl?' Charley asked again as we were going up the steps to school. 'He won't half be pleased when he hears about old Growler's butterflies. Good job, too, the steamy old crap. I'd like to see him in his nightshirt.'

All day I walked about and sat in the lessons in agony and bewilderment, and when from time to time the anguish lessened I felt numb and cold and lost. What ought I to do? I longed for

208

the evening to come so that I could see Karl and speak to him alone, and ask him what had happened. The same burning thoughts seemed to go round and round in my head, all day my mind went on hissing without a stop like the iron cistern in the Powells' dubliw. I didn't know who to speak to, and I didn't want to speak to anybody, only Karl. No one saw Growler all day, he couldn't have been in school. I was glad too, because if he had looked at me through those frog's-eyes glasses he would have seen at once I knew something about his fire.

5

WHEN I got home at tea time Karl wasn't there but I found a letter waiting for me on the table in our attic. It had arrived after I went to school and was from my auntie Bronny. She wished me to go down to 'Tegfan' as soon as I could but she didn't say why.

I didn't know what to do. I wanted to wait in Academy House for Karl, to find out what he knew about Growler's fire. I had no homework I couldn't crib dinner time so when he didn't come I left, hoping to have tea in 'Tegfan' and to return immediately after.

It took me half an hour to reach the house by train from Ystrad and when I got there I could hear my granny retching in the bedroom from the front door. She was in the middle of the bile again and my auntie couldn't leave her. What she wanted me to do was to take the keys of the Dragon Mills, and of the two houses, up to the office of Simonds the sand and gravel next door in Brewery Square. They had promised to hand them out to anyone wishing to inspect the place. And my granny wanted me to go in and have a look round the factory to see that everything was all right there, she was afraid the tramps might have broken in and started camping in the building.

All the time my worry went on roaring loudly underneath everything I said and did like a subterranean river. I couldn't listen or answer properly. While my auntie and I were eating our tea she asked me about Ystrad, and school, and the big fire in the headmaster's house, and how Karl and I were getting on in the Powells'. I said it was great in Academy House—but I didn't tell her anything about the sort of indoor camping life we had organized by now up there under the roof—living by ourselves and hardly ever seeing the Powells; making nearly all our own food, over our ankles sometimes by the bosh in scraps and potato peelings; fighting the dizzy flies that were so thick they made the room look like the air above a gnatty brook; standing on the furniture to clap our hands at the cobwebs festooning the roof thick as Christmas decorations; waking up every morning at one time dotted all over with masses of red flea-marks until we bought special powder for the bedclothes. All the same, she said, she was determined I shouldn't stay there much longer, as soon as the Richardses moved out I must come down to 'Tegfan' to live and travel up to Ystrad every day to school as one or two boys were doing already.

After tea she showed me the keys. They were in a large leather bag so heavy I could hardly lift it off the table. Inside there was a key for every lock in the mill and for all the rooms in the two houses. Must have been. Big old heavy iron things some of them were, and nearly all were covered with a thick powder of dry rust that got all over your hands. We sat down a bit tying labels on the chief ones, I had to run upstairs every now and then to show a key to my granny and ask her where it belonged. When everything was in order I said I would take the bag round to Simonds's after school the next day because the office would be closed by the time I arrived back in Ystrad. My auntie gave me my train fare and a bob and a bag of Welshcakes she had made on the bakestone.

When I got back to Academy House the whole place was in

darkness. As soon as I turned the front door knob and put my foot in the passage, although I was thinking all the time about Karl, I sensed something was wrong. For one thing I could see straight through into the kitchen where the light was on, because the frosted glass in the door at the end of the passage was smashed to pieces. Buddug must have heard me at the front door because she came out of the kitchen peeping around under the stairs. 'Is that you, Dewi?' she said. 'I thought perhaps it was Luther back.' Then suddenly she burst out crying. 'My father is very ill,' she sobbed. 'Very ill.'

'Ill?' I said. 'What's the matter with him?' I didn't know what to do or say to her.

She hesitated a moment. 'I don't know,' she said, looking for a dry corner of her handkerchief. 'I've sent Luther with a note for doctor J. J. but he hasn't come back. I expect it's surgery time.'

I still couldn't think what I ought to say. As I turned to put my bag of keys on the stairs she said: 'I think he's had a kind of fit.'

'A fit? How a fit?' I thought it was only children had fits.

'Come here,' she said. 'Look at this.'

She led me along the passage to the open door of the middle room. The gas was lit inside there too, and I could see the chests of dandelion coffee piled one above another to the ceiling all around the walls. She pointed to one of the long wooden panels in the door. It was split from top to bottom, there were deep cuts in it, fresh ones, showing the light right through the woodwork as though somebody had been sticking a sharp instrument into it with very powerful blows.

'How did that happen?' I asked her.

'Come in and sit down,' she said. 'I was resting in here on the couch reading,' she snivelled. 'It was washing day and I was very tired. Suddenly I heard Datta in the breakfast-room raising his voice to Luther. I don't know what he had done wrong this time, but I expect you have found out by now how annoying our Luther can be sometimes. I didn't take much notice to be candid, because Datta often has occasion to correct him, but in a minute or two I heard a scuffle and loud shouting in the kitchen and the sound like a chair going over. Then the passage door banged, it slammed with such force that the glass in the panel smashed to smithereens. Perhaps you noticed it was broken as you came in. I jumped up in fright at that of course and went to see what was happening, but before I could get out into the passage Luther rushed in here as white as a sheet, he slammed the door behind him and turned the key in the lock. He was crying, almost hysterical with fright. "He'll murder me, he'll murder me, he'll murder me," he was stammering, terrified. "He's got the carving-knife, I tell you. He's going to murder me!" Something like that he was trying to say. A knife mind! and I knew it was like a razor because only yesterday the grinder was in the street sharpening it. The most Datta had ever used on Luther before was a stair-rod, or a lath of the rotten wood in the trellis out there in the garden. Luther wouldn't come away from the door, he kept leaning hard against it and beckoning me to do the same, although he had locked it. By then my father was outside in the passage, trying to get in, he kept shouting terrible things at Luther, that he wasn't his son and things like that, horrible, and digging the carving-knife into the panel of the door. I was terrified myself by now to hear the blows, and to see the sharp point of that knife every now and then coming right through the wood, and to hear my father shouting those dreadful insults at Luther, and every now and then putting his shoulder to the door to break it down. What would he do if he got in with that terrible sharp knife in his hand? I was sure he would cut Luther's throat with it, or stab him to death. But before he could burst in I heard Taliesin coming into the house through the front door from the town library. When my father saw him he dropped the knife and leaned on him and began to cry. We took him upstairs to bed, and he's quiet now. Taliesin is with him.'

'Is Karl in?' I asked her.

'Karl? I don't know,' she said. 'I don't think so.'

'Wait a minute,' I said. 'I'll see if he is. Your Datta's in his own bed now, is he?'

'Yes. Upstairs. In his bedroom.'

I went up to our room and found Karl fast asleep in his hammock. I woke him up and told him what Buddug had told me.

'Come on, Dewi,' he said. 'We'd better find out if we can help her.'

When we got down into the kitchen the doctor had arrived—fat doctor J. J.—and Buddug was telling him what had happened. He didn't go up to see Mr Powell, he was too stout and asthmatical, and most likely from the smell he breathed over us he didn't fancy that long climb in the dark with only the swaying Academy House banisters to catch hold of. He handed Buddug a box of soothing pills he had brought with him to give to her father in a drink of tea or something, and then he went off puffing.

Karl asked Buddug if we could go up and relieve Taliesin a bit and she said yes. Karl boiled up some coffee in his special way first in the back kitchen, and we carried it upstairs with the pills in it, and that must have been the nicest smell that had been on those stairs for a long time.

Mr Powell's bedroom was the same size and shape as ours exactly, like a large, bare khaki tent, all roof. The only light there came from a night-light in a saucer of water placed in front of Mr Powell's cuffs on the chest of drawers; the room was so dim all we could see at first was a pyramid of night-clothes in the middle of the bed and what looked like a man with two heads rising out of it. Tally was leaning up against the chest of drawers trying to read a textbook by the night-light, and because you couldn't see his blackheads and his pimples and his dirty shirt in the little flame he seemed nice-looking. The smell in the bedroom told us somebody had just been sick. Mr Powell was sitting up in bed in his red flannel nightshirt, hollow-cheeked, the big untidy bundle of his nose carried in its scarlet openwork of veins, and his huge bald head shining smooth and whitish grey like a solid head of candle-grease. Beside it, capping the brass knob of the bedpost, was his red wig. There was a china bed-pan on his lap, a badly smashed one repaired with a sort of poultice, for him to be sick into. He must have thought he was going to be sick again, because just as we came up the steps and our eyes got used to the dimness we saw him taking his teeth out and holding them smoking in his hand. All the time he was crying bitterly to himself.

'Hallo, Mr Powell,' Karl said. 'How are you feeling now?'

Mr Powell shook his head, sobbing, he couldn't say anything.

'Drink this, Mr Powell,' Karl went on. 'Dandelion coffee. Come on, done the way you like it.'

He went on rocking his head from side to side and sobbing, his face all twisted up and the spittle dribbling down his beard, but after a bit of coaxing he pushed his teeth back into his head and started to drink the coffee. But he couldn't manage more than a mouthful or two and then the big bald head began shaking again, he handed the cup back to Karl so that he could go on with his crying. We looked at each other and at Tally. Loud noises began to leap about in the old man's belly like a lot of acrobats.

'Have you got any pain, Mr Powell?' Karl asked him.

He nodded his head. 'Chronic, Vaughan *bach*,' he said, sobbing, 'chronic.'

'Where, Mr Powell?' Karl asked him.

'Where? Here, right in the groin,' he snivelled, feeling with both hands under the bedclothes up into the small of his back.

'Would you like to sleep?' Karl asked him.

He didn't say yes or no, he just went on crying, so we got him down in bed and arranged the clothes and the pillows comfortably for him. He didn't want the night-light so we blew it out. We said good night to him, and then Tally went downstairs for Buddug, and Karl and I crossed the landing to our own room.

In the excitement of what had been happening I had forgotten for the first time since the morning about Growler's house being burnt down. But although I had longed all day to ask Karl what he knew about the fire, now that we were alone in our room I found I couldn't. I didn't know how to start speaking about it.

Instead I fetched my leather bag of keys and showed them to him. Presently we heard Buddug coming upstairs to her father. She knocked at our door first and handed in the evening *News and Banner,* asking if we would like to see it. She often did this although I could never bother to read the thing, and all Karl did with it was glance at the foreign news. The report of the fire, with a picture of Growler's house in ruins, was in the middle page by that edition.

'Karl,' I said, 'see this? Growler's house burnt down.'

He stared at the paper for a few moments, without saying a word.

'Did you know?' I asked him.

'Yes,' he said. 'I heard about it in town this morning. We ought to go and see it, Dewi.'

He stared again at the paper.

'That's a pretty terrible thing to happen to anyone,' he said at last. 'To have all one's life's work destroyed. But then, Growler is a pretty terrible man. By the way, Dewi, I found out an interesting fact about him today. You think, don't you, he's called Growler because of his voice. But he isn't. It's because when he came to this valley first as a young science teacher, he cycled everywhere on a very large and decrepit bicycle that made a loud growling noise when it was ridden. That's how he got his name. You ask your friend Rees Mawr, he'll confirm that what I say is true.'

Karl had beaten me, although I didn't know if he had intended to. I couldn't bring it up again then, the mood was all wrong for it, about the fire breaking out, nobody knew how, the very night he had come in at two o'clock in the morning after quarrelling with Growler. When I went to bed I was in misery, I couldn't sleep. Sometimes Mr Powell in the next room shouted out or groaned for a long time on end, and we heard Buddug or Tally in there with him. I tossed and turned, dreading what would happen to Karl if they found out what he had done; and the next minute feeling ashamed that I had suspected him at all of doing such a thing.

215 Obsessed.

Day after day went by after the fire and Growler didn't appear in school. Everybody wanted to have a look at him to see how he'd behave after all that had happened. The school was full of rumours about him and about his fire. Some said he'd had a heart attack and was in Ystrad hospital, others that he was staying with Tossy English, others that he had gone to his wife's relations in the next valley suffering from shock. And everybody had an idea about how the fire had started too—a candle, or Growler's carbide lamp left alight in the attic some said; or a spark from the train going over the mountain behind his house; or Conno the meth drinker who lived in the coke ovens and had disappeared from there about the date of the fire; or Growler himself, to have the big insurance after his moth collection. Anyway, according to the *News and Banner*, presents of rare moths and butterflies began to arrive in Ystrad from moth-catchers all over the world, so that Growler could begin his work again.

Karl never went to school now and with Growler absent nobody seemed to notice. During the day-time he painted outdoor scenes and coats of arms on our ceiling, or sat reading at Mr Powell's side in the bedroom. The pills the doctor had given Buddug made the old man doze all the time, but when he did wake up properly he cried so that nobody could stop him.

All the time, day after day, I wanted to ask Karl about the fire, but he never seemed to give me a real chance to do it, not without my sounding as though I had deserted him, or was condemning him, or wanting to betray him. I didn't care at all in a while if he had set the house on fire or not, all I wanted was to be on his side whatever he had done. But as time went on, and there were more and more rumours in school, I worried day and night about what would happen to him, I was haunted by the fear of it as though strange footsteps were following me all the time along a dark street. My ears were very thin to the mention of anything to do with him by then, and one morning when I was sitting in the cloakroom at playtime with Tom and Jeffy I began to hear a group of boys on the other side of the wire mesh partitions talking about what had happened to Growler. They were half

216

hidden by the overcoats hanging on the pegs, but I could see Bleddyn Reynolds was there, whose father was the chief constable of Ystrad. I listened with one ear and soon realized Alcwyn, Bleddyn's brother, was in the group, too, although I couldn't see him because of the coats. But I would recognize his hoarse blow-lamp voice anywhere and what he was saying made me forget Tom and Jeffy and give him all my attention. The police knew, he was telling the boys, that Growler's fire hadn't been an accident, they were absolutely certain of it, although they couldn't give their reasons yet. And they had a description of the man seen outside Growler's garden the night of the fire, they knew who he was, in fact, and they were just collecting a little more evidence before issuing a warrant for his arrest. And then everybody in school was going to have the biggest shock of their lives.

'What's the matter with you, dog's dung?' Jeffy said to me. He meant my face being so white.

'I'm all right,' I said. But I wasn't. The police! All the time I had been worrying about Karl I had thought only of Growler finding out who had set fire to his house, and about the rest of the staff, and the boys in school, and perhaps the Powells, and my auntie and my granny. But the police! And a warrant for Karl's arrest! That was something that had never occurred to me. It meant that Karl would be tried and convicted and sent to prison. What would I swear to, I thought with dread and dismay, if I were taken to court and examined by the judge on my evidence about Karl? Would I be such a funk as to speak the truth and convict him to prison? Or would I have enough guts to stick to him and remain staunch and loyal and go to prison with him? Whichever I did I saw before me only terror and the agony of betrayal, either of Karl or of myself. For the rest of the day I lived under an unbearable weight of terror and anguish, tormented by a great longing for peace, for escape from the knowledge I possessed and from the agony of decision.

That night I went to bed early, long before Karl was in. When I heard him coming up the stairs, about nine o'clock, I pretended

217

dubious level of friendship

to be asleep. I listened to him humming softly to himself as he undressed. I longed to spring out of bed and rush across to him and tell him all I knew and all I had suffered for him so that we could be friends again in the way we used to be. When the room was again dark I wept scalding tears into my pillow and after that I must have fallen asleep.

My head was swimming when I woke up. I was standing in the Powells' bathroom with the light on full-float. I couldn't believe my eyes. I had no idea how I had got there, I couldn't remember getting out of bed and coming down the stairs at all. I stared bewildered at the brass door-knobs the Powells had for bath-taps, and I was struck by how like prancing horses' hoofs the taps themselves were, curving over the edge of the bath. Suddenly I realized Karl was there with me. 'Come on, Dewi,' he said. 'Let's go back up.' He began leading me up the stairs to our attic. 'How did I get here, Karl?' I asked him puzzled, staring round me.

'It's all right, Dewi,' he said in a soothing way. 'I think you must have come down to the bathroom for a drink. Come on, let's go back upstairs. I'll fetch you a cup of water in a minute.' He led me up to the attic where our lamp was burning, and tucked me up in bed. He blew the light out, locked the door and got back into his hammock, but every time I moved I could hear him half sitting up, and listening, and looking across at me.

motherly? Karl in control, prisoner like?

6

A FEW nights later I woke up suddenly hearing, so I thought, some terrible loud thud, although I wasn't sure what I had heard.

'What was that, Karl?' I said, sitting up in bed. I could see he was awake too.

'Was it in the house?' he said. 'Or outside? Not Buddug, was it?'

I was certain what I had heard wasn't anything like Buddug screaming, but before I could say it Karl was out of his hammock and down the steps to the bedroom door. He opened it and stood there listening. 'There's somebody groaning,' he said. 'Come here.'

The sound didn't seem to be coming from Mr Powell's room. We both put our overcoats on over our sleeping-suits and went out on to the landing. It was dark, but not cold. Karl went across to Mr Powell's room and listened by the door. He tried the knob. The door opened and he went in. In a second or two he was out on the landing again. 'Come on, Dewi,' he said. 'The window's wide open and he's not there. He must have fallen out into the yard.' He began hurrying down the stairs. 'You call Buddug and Taliesin,' he said. 'Don't tell them what's happened.'

I stopped a few seconds to knock at the two doors and to whisper through the keyholes that something was wrong. Then I went down the stairs full pelt after Karl.

He had gone out to the back yard through the kitchen, leaving all the doors open after him. There I had a glimpse of him kneeling by the side of a huge bare body stretched out on the paving stones covering the yard.

'Go in and light a candle, Dewi,' he said.

When I came back out with it I could see Mr Powell lying naked on his face on the flagstones under the open window. If it was he we had heard groaning, he wasn't groaning any more. He was lying absolutely still and silent, except for low breathing and noises like chewing gristle in his belly; with his nightshirt wrapped round his head, he was a big fat lump of flesh like a huge soft slug of hairy white soap swelling up off the pavement. He had a tremendous fat behind and across both cheeks of it was a deep dark weal, as though he had had a cut with an outsize cane on his bottom. I didn't know what this was at first and then I remembered the Powells had a rusty wire line about eight or ten feet up across their yard, for hanging bunches of herbs and that on I think it was, and most likely Mr Powell had sat plumb on top of it when he fell out of the window. Karl and I tried to get him on his back but he was so huge and solid and heavy it was like turning a cold horse over. We managed it at last and unwound the nightgown from his head, and held the candle up to his face. He must have landed on it. It was a terrible sight, as though it had burst open and spilled out a lot of red jelly that hadn't set properly. We heard somebody coming through the house. 'Put your coat over his privates, Dewi,' Karl said.

Taliesin, fully dressed, and Buddug in her dressing-gown and her hair wilder than day-time came out into the yard.

'Datta, Datta,' Buddug started screaming when she saw her father, going down on her knees beside him. 'Oh, Datta *bach*, what's happened to you?'

Taliesin came towards us and bent down to lift his sister up. When he saw his father's face in the candle-light he sighed loudly and fainted on top of him.

'What's up?' came a voice over the garden wall. It was Mr Abrahams next door, so I shouted down the garden to him and asked if he could come over and help us. We left Taliesin lying on the yard, and with Mr Abrahams's help we carried Mr Powell into the house and laid him on the couch in the coffee-room with as many coats and cushions over him as we could lay hands on. We got Luther up out of bed and Karl wrote a note for him to take up to doctor J. J.'s and he made Buddug calm down with a lot of pretty awful threats, and told her to see to the younger children, especially Eben, that he didn't go off frothing in a howling fit. With Buddug out of the way Karl whispered to me: 'He's finished, Dewi. The doctor's no good at all now. He went in the yard between our fingers.'

In a few minutes, it seemed, the house was full of people, although it was only between four and five in the morning, there were neighbours, mostly women, in all the rooms, half Edwards Terrace seemed to be there, people I had never seen before were out in the kitchen making tea and sitting down chatting and crying and carrying the Powell children wrapped up in blankets out through the front door. The whole place was like a fair in no time, and Karl and I could see they were going to get on fine without us so we just put a kettle of water on the gas and carried the soap and flannel into the middle room ready to wash the blood off Mr Powell and clean him up a bit.

Before the water was boiled doctor J. J. had arrived. He took one look at Mr Powell and grunted. He was dead. Karl told him what had happened and he said we had done fine. We saw the neighbours carrying the body out of the middle room and into the music studio and placing it on top of the grand piano, with a bedsheet from upstairs under it and another one over it, because there was no couch in there. When this was done I went to speak to Karl, but he seemed to be missing. I climbed up to our room by myself, looking for him, but he wasn't there. I opened the window and looked out. Shabby daylight drizzled over the town. I lay on the bed thinking about him and about all that had happened, fingering the scabs spreading on my belly since I had begun worrying about him and his row with Growler, and finding my scabs worse made me worry even more.

7

IN SCHOOL the next morning when we were gathered in the hall for morning assembly, I had a tremendous surprise, all of us did. Tossy English always led the masters on to the platform now that Growler, so they said, was dying of shock, but when the staff corridor door swung open who should come bobbing through it first but Growler himself. Tossy was behind him and all the other masters followed. Everybody gasped with astonishment seeing him there in his mangy old gown, and the whole school went absolutely silent. He looked terrible. His clothes always did bag about on him even when he was fat, but now he had a fallen-in look, as though some huge mass like the bodily core of him had been lifted out of the middle of his bulk. His face used to be purple, but it had gone a darkish grey, a bit like greasy pewter, and there was something the matter with it, it had a distorted look as though we were seeing it through a sheet of faulty glass. Even his voice had changed, it seemed to have gone down a couple of octaves compared even with what it had been before. He took morning assembly and it was embarrassing to listen to him, his deep voice kept on skying up into a tremble all the time as though he couldn't master it, and I was afraid that any moment he might break down altogether and burst out crying. That was the way he sounded.

Then, when we thought the service was all over, instead of leading the staff back down off the platform he stood there trying to control himself, and coughing non-stop like a cow. It was awful, it made you damp listening to him, but after a drink of water he began talking to the school, mumbling and growling at us, more like. We couldn't make head or tail of it; I couldn't, anyhow, and I noticed some of the masters sitting behind him on the platform glancing across at one another and looking uneasy. At last I began to realize he was talking about Karl. Karl! I went hot and angry at the thought of it, and some painful dread filled my heart up again. Why didn't he shut his big ugly mouth and leave Karl alone for a bit, the crapping, mucking old toad. Anybody could see he wasn't properly solid any more, mumbling and growling and sweating on the platform like somebody half daft, and working himself up into a furnace-face with rage. I felt so sick at what he was doing I wasn't listening properly, and the next thing I saw was Karl leaving the form five line and walking swiftly and alone up on to the platform with a face like white-wash. Growler must have called him up, although I didn't hear him. And that must have been a signal too, because at the same moment the swing doors from the staff corridor opened and Tusker came into the hall carrying Growler's three-tailed strap. I couldn't believe it. Growler wasn't going to try to strap Karl, was he, before the whole school, he couldn't be that mad. Karl would die ten thousand deaths rather than be strapped in public, by anybody, let alone somebody he despised and hated as much as Growler. There was dead silence in the hall now, and intense icy excitement, you could feel it moving like electricity, only cold, all over your skin; not a sound anywhere except for Growler's double-bass voice hammering and echoing against the rafters, bawling at Karl to put his hand out for punishment, rising from time to time into hysterical screams as it accused him of all sorts of wickedness and crimes.

Karl stood there silent, looking down at Growler, his white face unmoving and his arms folded. 'Put your hand out, you ugly frog, you *bwbach*,' Growler bawled at him. 'Put your hand out, do you hear me?' But Karl didn't budge or alter a hair.

Growler seemed to go mad. He brought the thick strap up with a rush back over his opposite shoulder as though he was going to slash Karl a back-hander across the face with it. Still Karl didn't flinch, and before the strap could touch him his face became radiant, glowing like lit-up silver, and three livid red weals burned themselves diagonally across his forehead and down his cheek. Everybody gasped. Growler stared, the strap half way to Karl's face, and then he crumpled up and went limp and empty. The strap fell from his hand and he began feeling behind him for a chair. How marvellous! Karl was safe. I didn't care about Growler, I hoped he'd have scabs and worms on top of it. Several of the staff jumped up and hurried towards him and got him to sit down and drink some water, they stood all around so that we couldn't see from the hall floor what was happening. Tossy English stepped forward and nodded Karl down from the platform and sent us all to our formrooms. Everybody suddenly started talking and the prefects went round clearing the hall.

Up in our formroom all the boys were excited, wanting to talk about what had happened. It was a mystery. A burst of sunlight had saved Karl, that was obvious, but was there anything behind it, that was what I worried about. Did Karl know somehow that the sun was going to blaze out of the clouds just then, and did he stand so that his face would receive it full force? I wondered again if Karl really had some powers that nobody else possessed, and whether he could perform magic. When I saw those burning weals across his face I was sure he could. If not, how was it that so many strange things were always happening to him? How marvellous that the red bars in the coat of arms should have fallen so exactly across his face, and the opal shield fitted over him as well. Evans our history teacher had taken us round when we were kids in school and told us about the coats of arms in the hall windows, but I couldn't follow him. They belonged to the people who put up the money for our school first a couple of hundred years ago, I remembered that much about them.

Jeffy was sitting on the inside window cill of our formroom, turning his pockets inside out and brushing the tobacco on to the floor. He looked a sight, his yellow hair tangly as if it hadn't had a comb through it for days, his mortar-coloured corduroys could have done with a good wash and his boots were so dried up they looked like suède leather. My thoughts were disturbed by his words and I realized he was jealous again, and trying to make me mad, but I wasn't having any.

'Don't listen to what Dewi says about Karl,' he told the other boys, 'he thinks he's a flaming magician.' This made me blush because I hadn't said a word, I had only thought it to myself. 'Tell them about the time Karl made you put your ear under the water, Dewi, to hear the fishes talking. Go on. Don't be narky. What did they say? Tell us.'

This was all lies, Jeffy had made it up, so I turned away and said to Jonno: 'Snitch Urquhart for me, will you, Jonno?' I opened my desk and arranged my books, but I could still hear him making the boys laugh round the window. 'Do you know what Karl told us once?' he said. 'The ship he came over to this country on was so big it had three farms on it. You can laugh, but it's as true as that I'm swinging from the roof. You ask Dewi. I told Karl I knew it was all jonuck because my old man had a job on a ship like that once, he was the master of foxhounds.' Jeffy's expression changed suddenly: 'God bless the Prince of Wales,' he said, pointing out of the window. 'Look down there, boys.' We all gathered round, and beneath us in the quad we could see one of the cabs from outside the station drawn up below Growler's steps. After a bit two or three of the younger masters half carried Growler out, the battered old brown trilby over his eyes looking as though it had been on the peg with an overcoat on top of it. They put him inside and Tossy got in after him. The cab went round the grass circle and back out through the school gates, and that was the last time any of us ever saw Growler in Ystrad Grammar School.

I didn't meet Karl again until that evening. When he stepped off the hall platform he went straight down the corridor and out of school.

When I got home at tea time who was waiting for me in the kitchen but my auntie Bronny, dressed up like a duchess, wearing the frozen sloping-out cape down to her middle that made her look as though her head was coming out through the top of a roof, and with so much eau-de-Cologne on her you couldn't smell Academy House within yards of her. They had heard down in Tremartyn about Mr Powell's accident or whatever it was, and I had to leave at once, it wasn't right for me to go on living in a house without a grown-up in charge. I couldn't stay with her and my granny, unfortunately, they only had two rooms in 'Tegfan' themselves, I would have to go to Abergarth to my auntie Mag's in the Vaughan Arms. She was going to write directly she got back home. Meanwhile, for a night or two, they would try to manage to put me up in 'Tegfan'.

I didn't want to stay in 'Tegfan'. I knew hardly anybody down there in Tremartyn and I wouldn't see Karl either, not if he'd given up going to school. I didn't think my auntie wanted me there much, really, not yet anyway, before she had a proper bedroom for me to sleep in, and a parlour where she could push me off to do my homework and that. But she was determined to

225

get me away from the Powells. I said the best thing would be for me to stay where I was for the present, until she'd had a reply from my auntie Mag, and in the end she agreed and went away.

They were expecting a pretty big funeral for Mr Powell, everybody in Ystrad knew him because he had done so many different jobs. All the week relatives kept arriving, they slept in the Powell kids' beds, and the kids slept on the couches or with the neighbours. It must have been these relatives who paid for the funeral, because there was no money in the house. Tally stayed at home all the week and went through his father's rooms, the bedroom and the music studio, to see if Mr Powell had left any money about, hidden somewhere or other in the house, or perhaps some insurance for himself nobody knew about. All he found were packages of caca wrapped up in newspaper in the chest of drawers in the bedroom, as well as a few bundles of it behind the pictures and the big illuminated address in the music studio. Somebody must have paid for the ham Buddug boiled for the funeral, too, that smelt so lovely all over the house, and for the wallpaper Karl put up in the studio to brighten the place up a bit. When I went in after school to find out how he was getting on, I saw Mr Powell's coffin on the undertaker's trestles in front of the fireplace, and Karl standing on top of it with a paste-brush in his hand, looking very happy as he fixed over the chimney breast the new frieze he had bought in Ystrad.

I had no word from my auntie Bronny until after the funeral. And then one day a letter arrived, not from her, but from my auntie Mag in Abergarth, telling me I was to come down as soon as we broke up for Easter in a week's time. If I let her know the time of the train Myrddin should meet me.

I was disappointed at this because I had hoped my auntie Bronwen had forgotten about getting me away from the Powells, or had changed her mind. But it was better in the Vaughan Arms any day than in 'Tegfan', I didn't mind it so much, and perhaps Karl could come down with me before he went away. That's what I thought about at once as soon as I had my letter.

226

8

THE day before I was to go down to Abergarth I was upstairs in our room packing my Gladstone bag when Karl came in.

Whatever happened, Karl was always calm, he seemed as though he knew what to do, doesn't matter what happened. Even when old Mr Powell died almost in his arms he was unmoved and swift in everything he did, and he always made me feel the same. I could always sense Karl's feelings, where he was concerned I could read where there was no writing, and now, although he was calm, extra calm, there seemed to be something the matter. He got out his pipe and sat smoking it with the back of the chair against his chest.

'Stop packing a minute, Dewi,' he said.

I did. 'What's up?' I asked him, trying to sound off-hand.

For a few seconds he didn't reply, he just went on puffing quietly. And then he said softly:

'Growler's dead.'

I went cold, as though at one icy drench, and my loins seemed to shrink up into my belly with terror. I sat down on the bed.

'Dead?' I repeated. 'How do you know he's dead, Karl?'

'I've seen him,' he replied. 'I found him dead.'

This was awful, I dropped my face into my hands, overwhelmed, I didn't know what to do or think. For Growler's house to be burnt down was bad enough, but for Growler to be dead, and for Karl most likely to be the first to know about it, was something nobody could take in properly, or understand, or grapple with. I could do nothing, I felt helpless, and frightened, and overborne, like on the night of the great thunderclaps, when the whole sky turned molten above Ystrad, and we watched in terror on the shaken mountain as it dropped in one vast rushing sheet of golden lightning around us, pouring fire into the glass woods of Pantglas. What had really happened? Karl wouldn't say, not just then. All he wanted was my promise to help him. Would I give it and trust in his word?

I said yes of course I would. But what could I do? School had broken up, and I was going down to 'Tegfan' in a few minutes to say goodbye to my auntie and my granny before travelling to Abergarth the next day.

'When you arrive back in Ystrad station tonight after your visit', he said, 'I will be waiting for you. It will be dark by then. Will you come with me? Swear it, Dewi?'

I said again I would, I gave my word of honour I would, but it didn't seem to satisfy Karl. 'What will you swear it on?' he asked me, putting his pipe away. 'Where is your dagger?'

I hadn't thought about my dagger for weeks but I still had it safely hidden in my Gladstone bag. This was the first time Karl had ever mentioned it since he left it behind stuck in our factory yard. 'Bring it here, Dewi,' he said, seeing me hesitating.

I got it out of the inside pocket of the bag and handed it to him. I still had never seen a more beautiful dagger in my life, every time I looked at it I felt again how marvellous it was, and how strange that such a splendid weapon, all gold and silver, should have been given to me. 'We'll use this to swear by,' he said. 'Give me your wrist.'

I held back, wondering what he was going to do, but he rolled up his own jacket sleeve and the cuff of his shirt, unnoticing. When his left wrist was bare he pressed the point of the dagger into the skin in the front, and presently a dark little bead of blood rose up at the spot. When I had bared the wrist of my right arm also he did the same to me. Then we pressed our wrists together, so that Karl's blood, he said, was now in my body, and mine was in his for ever and ever. With our wrists pressed against each other I swore again to go with him wherever he wished me to, and to be faithful to him from now on and for ever whatever should happen to us.

We walked up to Ystrad station together in heavy rain. I said hardly a word, I was so deeply shaken by what had happened, and remembering all the thunder and lightning, good and bad, that had been in my life since Karl first appeared. I wasn't far from crying, although I could never show Karl this. At the station I left him and got into the train going down to Tremartyn, to say goodbye to my granny and my auntie. Those two lectured me until I was sick of hearing them, about what I was to do in Abergarth, what I was to eat, and what I was to wear, and how often I was to write and when I was to come to visit them and that. But my mind was all the time on what Karl had said in the attic, smoking his pipe so calmly, sitting on the chair the wrong way round, and I couldn't pay any attention to what they were saying. No doubt that was why they told me everything about ten times. But it didn't matter at all, I could think of nothing but of my oath taken in blood, and Karl's terrible words, they were like a great ton weight pressing upon my heart. All the while my auntie and my granny were jawing and jawing I was longing to get away to endure my agony and terror alone and undisturbed and as soon as they handed me my train fare and my pocket-money I was off.

Karl was waiting for me as he had promised, sheltering from the rain far back in the doorway of the fruit shop opposite the Ystrad station. The lamps were lit in town by then. Over his shoulder hung a twenty-eight-pound flour bag with what sounded like some glass bottles inside. We went along the tram-road behind the main street of Ystrad, and running parallel with it, and before long I found we were leaving the town and going up the old parish road towards our camp on the mountain. We hadn't been there at all lately, not during the winter, it was too cold, and the grass there was always soaking wet.

'Where are we going, Karl?' I asked him, breaking a long silence.

'You'll see, Dewi *bach*,' he answered. 'Come on. You'll see.'

It was dark on the mountain with the trees overhanging us from both sides of the cart-track. The rain had stopped, and presently a good round moon began to tear shining across the clear sky. We went on up the road in silence and crossed the flooded little stream, and when we came to the path leading off to our camp Karl began to follow it. I stopped, for some reason I sensed there was something wrong, I felt suddenly a sense of dread and foreboding at having to enter that path, like that night we found the smoke going up from our fire in the long grass, and our camp deserted. I thought in desperation of something to say which would prevent our leaving the road. 'Karl,' I said, 'you know Charley's father doesn't own this land any longer. We'll be trespassing if we go off the road.'

'It doesn't matter,' he answered. 'No one will know. And whether they know or not, we must go now.'

We squelched along the old bracken-track and climbed the slope through the long wet grass. When we got up on to the platform where our camp was, to my surprise I saw a fire burning there, a small one, with Jeffy, Tom and Charley sitting round it. But everything about seemed smaller and shabbier than it used to be, and the turf had grown long and untidy. I noticed by the light of the fire that our cave of branches in the far corner had collapsed, and the ends of the iron tramlines were sticking out in a cone above the ruins like a wigwam.

The three round the fire got up when they saw us coming towards them over the grass. Jeffy stood there in the firelight biting his nails, holding the middle finger of his left hand hard against his teeth with his right hand and gnawing away, looking puzzled and anxious for once. When we reached them, Karl took the bag off his shoulder and brought out of it not bottles but two glass jam jars with long string handles, and a stump of candle stuck in a thickness of grease at the bottom of each. He put the jars down on the grass and spoke to us.

'Jeffy,' he said, 'Tom, Charley, Dewi, do you remember the first time we all met here? Many months ago now. Do you remember?'

He looked from one of us to the other, and we all nodded in turn.

'Who was the other one present that night? You all know. Headmaster Roderick. Growler you called him then I remember. He is here tonight also.'

We looked round into the trees, myself, unthinking, with the others, although Karl had already told me Growler was dead. There was no sign of him anywhere. What did Karl mean? The others looked at him, waiting for him to explain, but he said nothing, he just stood there very white in the moonlight looking back at us.

'Where is he, Karl?' Jeffy asked at last.

'He's dead,' Karl answered.

Dead! Although I knew it already it sounded terrible up there on the side of the mountain, in the darkness and the moonlight, only five of us together and miles from anywhere. I felt as though a slow chill was rising around us, and my skull began to stir. The others looked queer too by the firelight, very pale and strained and frightened, especially Charley. Most likely he was the most worried to begin with, because we were lighting a fire on this land his father no longer owned.

'Dead!' they all gasped. They couldn't believe Growler would be dead, and neither could I, not even then.

'When?' Jeffy said. 'He was in school a couple of days ago.'

'Tonight is our last meeting,' Karl went on without answering him. 'Tomorrow I shall be leaving this valley and returning to the world. But before I go I have one thing to do. And to do it I require the help of my friends. You have all promised to give that help. If for any reason you have changed your minds, and do not now wish to be concerned in what I have to finish, all you need to do is to say so, and then, when we have shaken hands, to walk down that path and on to the road to Ystrad. If you do that we will still part as friends and comrades.'

Although we were all afraid we couldn't leave Karl. He looked from one to the other. None of us moved.

'What I am going to tell you now', he went on, 'I swear on my word of honour to be true. You may question me on any statement I make. Let's sit down.'

We went round the fire and sat on our caps on the wet stones, and because the fire was only a small one we were close together.

'Yesterday,' he said, 'just before it began to get dark, I came

231

up to this camp to look at it for the last time, because I had already made up my mind to leave the valley. Dewi knows that, since I told him of my decision and asked him to accompany me. I walked around the border of this platform and looked over the edge, there where I first came across Jeffy lying half stunned in the bracken, that night, before he fainted away completely. You all remember it. When I was passing the doorway of the cave I stooped down to take a last look inside, and it was at that moment I had one of the greatest surprises of my life in this valley. Because sitting on the grass facing the entrance with his back against the farthest wall was Growler. I stood staring at him for a while, I was too astonished and perhaps puzzled, at seeing him sitting there so oddly in dead silence, that I didn't think of saying anything to him. And before I could make a remark it struck me he looked very strange, unnaturally still and remote. I thought he must be ill. Instead of speaking to him I went inside the cave and placed my hand on his shoulder. At my touch he fell sideways to the ground. He was dead.'

Karl stopped. We all stared at him in fright and fascination and horror. Where was Growler's body now? Karl said Growler was present. What could he mean? And what could he want us to do?

'A little while ago,' he went on, 'as you know, the head-master's house was burnt to the ground in very mysterious circumstances, and his unique and world-famous collection of moths and butterflies destroyed. My name was under suspicion at the time, I was suspected because my enmity towards the headmaster had become well known. When I found Growler dead in this way I realized immediately what my discovery would mean. So I am asking you to give me—what do you call it here? —secondy offers?—another chance to escape. Will you?'

We were all silent, but we nodded to him mechanically one by one as he looked at us. 'What do you want us to do, Karl?' Jeffy asked. I was surprised to hear what sounded like his teeth chattering.

'I want Growler's body to be hidden until I can escape right out of the country. Will you help me to hide it?'

'Where, Karl?'

'Near here. In the Pantglas level.'

We all looked around at each other, puzzled.

'It's not far,' he went on. 'There will be no work there for a few days because of the holiday. We can carry it inside, one of you at each corner of the bier I have arranged, and with all due reverence and respect place it across the first tram we encounter inside. There it will be discovered when work is resumed in a few days' time, but by then I shall be in Paris, or Lisbon, and in safety.'

For a time there was dead silence. Then Tom said: 'Where's the body now, Karl?'

'Over there, under the branches of the cave,' he answered, waving his hand towards it. 'I pulled the cave down over it, a sort of rustic burial mound, to afford it shelter. I hope you can forgive me for destroying your handiwork. Let's go and see.'

Karl jumped up and moved away from the firelight towards the heap of branches in the corner, that was all that was left of our cave. We went after him, slower, Charley shivering in the rear, all of us reluctant and fascinated and appalled, avoiding each other's eyes. Karl began pulling the wet branches away and handing them back to us, and we threw them behind us on the grass. At the bottom of the heap we saw some clothes with shining buttons on them, and then the body of a man lying stiffly with his arms crossed on his breast. We all moved nearer in silence, trembling and frightened, but determined. The moonlight showed us the man could only be Growler, dressed in his mothing outfit, his big boots and dark dungarees, and the wide brim of his hat throwing a deep shadow over his face. From the middle of his breast protruded the golden hilt of my snake-handled dagger.

Tom stepped closer and bent down, peering at the body through his thick glasses. 'You didn't tell us about this, Karl,' he said, pointing at Growler's breast. 'Look! A dagger! He's been stabbed!' When he turned back towards us his mouth gaped wide open like a seam with horror and bewilderment.

As Tom was speaking Jeffy bumped down on the grass shivering like a leaf, his teeth chattering out loud, his arms across his face. I thought he had fainted. I could hear Charley behind me beginning to sob. Karl looked pale against the dark trees, his face seemed to be bright and clear with the moon full upon it, as though a silver beam had been turned on inside his skin and was shining out powerfully through it. I noticed for the first time he had his silver earrings in again.

'What I have told you is the truth,' he began, but he was interrupted because Charley burst out into loud crying, he began shouting at Karl, I was too dazed at first to understand what, and then I heard his words. 'Murderer! Murderer!' he shouted in a sort of hysterical shriek. My skin began to creep up my back at the sound of it. He ran up to Karl with his fists in the air, I thought he was going to attack him by the sort of frenzy he was in, but all he did was spit in Karl's face. Then he raced off the platform with the spittle he meant for Karl still swinging from his chin, and ran squealing down the path leading to the road, we could hear the platform hollow as a drumskin booming under his feet as he pounded across it, and then his wild hysterical screeches getting farther and farther away in the night. It made me cold to hear him.

Jeffy struggled to his feet up off the grass and half ran, half staggered, over to the edge of the platform; there he sank down on his knees again and began spewing, making a terrible whooping sound, his whole body convulsed like a dog vomiting after eating grass. Tom went over to him. 'You will stay with me, won't you, Dewi?' Karl whispered.

I felt as cold as ice. I couldn't move or even speak. My heart was beating powerfully, as deafening as three in my ears. What was going to happen next? In a moment or two Tom came back, his head huge under the little cap, and his hands and feet gone enormous. 'I don't know, Karl,' he said. 'What I saw in Growler's chest wasn't Scotch mist. Goodbye. I must take Jeffy home. I suppose I'll never see you again. Too bad.'

Karl bowed, but he didn't seem to notice the huge white hand

234

Tom was holding out to him. Tom turned away looking hurt and clumsy, and went at his stiff awkward walk across the grass to where Jeffy was still retching and dribbling, and helped him to his feet. Then the two staggered down the slope at the edge of the darkness, the way Karl had brought Jeffy into the firelight on our first night together.

At first I was unable to speak at all, and then I managed to say: 'Karl, what are we going to do, what are we going to do?'

'You do not intend to leave me, Dewi?' he said. 'Good. My plan to carry the body with reverence into the level we must now abandon. When Charley reaches Ystrad his mother will report what he tells her, and a search of the mine will be instituted immediately. I had intended my four friends to act as bearers of the bier, one at each corner, Jeffy and Charley in front, so that they would not have to look into the face of the corpse, you and Tom at the rear; and leading the funeral procession, myself, bearing the candles into the silence and darkness of the level. That would have been a splendid burial, Dewi, dignified and impressive. But two of us alone cannot carry this out, the distance is too great. The only thing to do with the body now is to burn it. Come on, let's make a real fire, the biggest fire in the world, a mammoth ritual conflagration! Come on, Dewi! Help me!'

Burn Growler's body! The words struck me with the shock of a sudden heavy blow, I seemed to stagger under the weight of it, and yet I felt a thrill of joy and a glow at the same time. I had wanted to begin crying before Karl said these words, but they brought me to life, and once I started helping him I forgot it. We carried all the boughs still left near the cave over to the fire, shook the rain out of them, and threw them on, and then we collected the other branches we had strewn about the platform and did the same with them also. Soon we had a great blaze crackling and throwing up red steam like a boiler, blazing so hot we couldn't go near it. 'Come on, Dewi,' Karl said again, full of excitement. 'Let's turn the feet towards the east.'

Growler now lay on the grass in the middle of the ring where our tent had been, with the rails of the tramlines rising in the skeleton of a cone around him. Karl pulled a couple of these rails up out of the ground, laid them about two feet apart on the grass near the body and placed a few branches over them from side to side. He showed me by signs that we were to lift Growler's body from where it lay and place it on top of the boughs so that we could carry it across to the fire.

We went over and stood ready to raise up the body, Karl at the head and me at the feet. The dead face gleamed black at us in the moonlight like gun-metal. I wanted to ask Karl for my dagger, but I was afraid to. When at last I brought myself to catch hold of the legs to lift them I found the boots and trousers sopping wet, and then I saw all the clothes were soaking as well, the body must have been drenched to the skin in the heavy rain that had fallen during the night. With a great struggle we got the body on to the home-made bier, it was like trying to lift up a full sack of something, say concrete, stuck fast in thick mud. Then we placed ourselves between the rails as though they were the arms of a stretcher, and staggered over the grass to the fire with our burden on it. Although Growler had gone so thin he wouldn't have been heavier if his whole body had been solid through and through, and made of cast iron. Or perhaps it was the steel rails under him that made him such a weight. Karl looked up at the stars to find out which was the right direction, and then we advanced, sideways on, to the blaze. We slid the body and the rails on top of it, with the big soles facing the east. The fire blazed up like mad to twice its size with the fresh branches under the body, and the water sopping the clothes hissed and steamed up like a wash-house, only red. All the boughs and twigs and the old wood we could find about on the grass we threw on the blaze on top of the fiery body, and we had to throw from farther and farther away because of the heat. Growler's straw hat blazed up and fell off at once, and the whole of his long, brushed-over hair vanished in one flash. Before long his boots sticking out of the other end of the fire began to burn blue. Karl went round the blaze, as near as he could get, with the flour-bag in his hand, throwing his special grape-cork powder into the flames, and every time he tossed a handful in there was a terrific explosion, and an outburst of the sweet smell, and the flames flared out of the blaze like angry dragon-fire burning towards him across the grass. When he had been round two or three times almost nothing of Growler could be seen because of the size of the fire, it roared like a furnace all around him, the blaze was so terrific I was glad to crouch down on the slope from the heat of it.

Karl lit the two candles in the jars and placed them one where Growler's feet were and the other at his head. 'Rest in peace,' he said, and made the sign of the cross high in the air. 'Come on, Dewi,' he went on, 'come on, we must get away.'

We hurried down the path through the ferns and out on to the road. The moon hung now like a glassy ball, and through the trees by the light of it we could see the surface of the Swamp, phosphorescent as milk. We met nobody at all, keeping to the dark back-streets of Ystrad, but when we got to the top end of Edwards Terrace Karl said, 'I must leave you here, Dewi. I mustn't be seen in Ystrad.'

'But Karl,' I said, 'where are you going? You can't go anywhere tonight. Come back to the Powells'. Nobody'll know.'

'Goodbye, Dewi. I shall see you again, and soon. I shall sleep tonight in the safest place in Ystrad.'

'Where's that, Karl?'

He only smiled in answer and said, 'Goodbye', again. And then he was gone. And I hadn't asked him anything about Growler's death, or about my dagger. How would I see him again soon? When? I was going down to Abergarth the next day. How was it possible for us to meet if he was going abroad? I couldn't understand what he meant.

I went home to Academy House bewildered, dazed by the memory of the great hot furnace which I could never forget. I had to sleep alone in the attic. I left the blind up, and the moon shone in across Karl's book cupboard and his empty hammock.

I got into bed and crouched there shivering, although the night was warm. My thoughts would not clear, they were full of confusion and leaping flames. Suddenly I remembered the safest place in Ystrad for Karl would be the Nannies. In the middle of the night I woke up heaving, and was sick time after time on the floor. I cried burning tears into my pillow, because I felt lost and lonely and abandoned, and I had no one at all to turn to for help and comfort.

9

THE next day when I reached Abergarth Myrddin was waiting for me in the station with his iron truck, and he wheeled my Gladstone bag on it through the High Street to the Vaughan Arms. He had new china teeth instead of his old brown saw-edged ones, but they were so long and thick and false, and the gums holding them were so massive, he couldn't close his mouth properly over them. He began telling me about his mother again, when he was born she had so much milk she used to sell it. This time she had been a servant in the Vaughan Arms, and he had arrived in this world when she was standing on a chair in the High Street, stretching up, cleaning the fanlight over the front door.

In the pub my auntie had put her best clothes on and laid the tea in the upstairs parlour, and I had a bit of a surprise to find my uncle Walter Lloyd there too, with his thin cap flat on top of his head, and his big round face looking hot enough to burn you if you touched it. My auntie was washed and shaved and shining, her dark chin like charcoal, she was wearing a new white hair-net and she cried a bit when she saw me. For a moment I didn't remember why, all I could think of was being separated from

Karl, and what I had seen the night before, the great fire, and Growler burning in the woods, and the candles lighted, and the sign of the cross high in the air.

During the meal I learned my uncle Lloyd had given up his mucky cottage, he was living in the Vaughan Arms altogether now. His right foot was huge, a black woollen stocking with a white toe and heel covered all the bandaging swelling it up, and he crept about on a couple of walking-sticks. He didn't say a lot at the tea table to either of us, he complained to my auntie about the cockerels waking him early; he was going to take a chopper among them, he said, and as soon as my auntie opened the tap he struggled downstairs to the bar.

I had nothing much to do that evening so I wandered about the pub, in and out of the parlour and the bar and the snug, listening to the men talking, and carrying drinks around for them from the tap; but my auntie didn't like me doing that, much, I could see by her expression, and after a while she sent me out for a walk, down to the river, she said, or I was to go and see who I could find in the park.

I got my school cap and pretended to do what she told me but when she had gone back to serving I slipped upstairs to my bedroom, I thought I would lie down up there and think in peace of all that had happened until it was time for supper.

The bedroom was my old one right at the top of the pub, looking out over the stables and the yard at the back; I could see the sloping fields behind the High Street from the window, and the Garth river at the far end of them. As I went along the landing I noticed the door of the room where my father and mother used to sleep was open. On the bedpost inside hung a pair of armlets for keeping your shirt-sleeves up if they happened to be too long, they were the sort that always fascinated me, not the elastic ones my father had, but metal, like a spring coil, only flat, and made of a silver-like wire. Karl had had a pair like that and I always liked playing with them in Academy House, looping them through each other like the links of a chain, and

239

pinching one into the other, and twisting them into figures-of-eight and that. When I saw them there gleaming around the bed-knob I suddenly longed to handle them and play with them again. I listened at the door and then I peeped inside. The room was empty. From the boots and clothes scattered about and the row of flagons in the grate I guessed this was where my uncle Lloyd slept now. I knew where he was, in the bar, and I thought by the look of him he'd take the best part of half an hour to climb up here to the top floor, and I would hear him coming right from the bottom. So I slipped inside the room and began fiddling with the armlets. They were a cheaper sort than Karl's, made of thicker wire, and stiffer, but they were fine stretchers. I tried putting them on my arms on top of my coat. And then with a bit of a struggle I got them over my boots and up on to my trousers. I walked about the bedroom wearing them first of all like garters, and then I slipped them below my knees, so that I felt like a high-class navvy in silver yorks. I forgot everything playing with these armlets, it was like when I was a kid, and at last I put one on each bedpost at the bottom of the bed and tried to stretch them across and make them meet in the middle. They stretched fine when I tugged, and they nearly did meet, but when I let them go suddenly they didn't spring back as I expected, they just dropped down where they were and hung on the bedposts limp and lifeless; instead of springy compact armlets they had become all of a sudden just long straggling stretches of wire kinked into wide zigzags. I felt panicky. I didn't know what to do. I sat on the bed and started pushing the kinks back towards one another, one zigzag at a time, but the wire was stiff and springy and slippery, and I couldn't do it. And then I heard somebody climbing up the stairs. I bundled the armlets up and chucked them under the bed, and got into my own room without anyone seeing me.

I worried all night about what I had done. What would my uncle Lloyd say when he found the things on the floor all stretched out and useless? He seemed a pretty grumpy sort of old man, with his fierce red face and his long silences, perhaps if there was drink in him he would be nasty. Presently, as I sat fretting there in my bedroom, I heard him moving about in the next room, I expected him to knock at my door all the time, looking very angry, perhaps shouting, pushing the bunch of armlets at me in his temper; but nothing happened. When I thought supper would be ready I went downstairs trembling, ready to confess at once what I'd done, and to apologize and to offer to pay for another pair next Saturday. But only Auntie Mag was in the kitchen, there was no sign of my uncle anywhere and I didn't mention him.

After supper I said good night to my auntie and hurried back up to my bedroom. It was dark by now, and I took with me one of the three or four candles she always kept lit on the table on the first floor after dark. I hoped I would get to sleep before I began to hear all the creaks coming from the roof above my head, as though something heavy was dragging itself about on it, and the fluttering noises, and the loud scratchings in the walls, and the breathing under the bed that used to frighten me when I slept alone in the darkness of the Vaughan Arms. I lay there wondering if it was all true, had I really seen Growler burning, was it a dream that I had carried him dead and placed him on the fire, and seen his slack lips open as I did it, and his tongue coming out thick and black, with ridges along it, like a fat slug backing out of his mouth? But I must have slept, because the next thing I knew after blowing out the light was waking up to hear all the timber around me creaking as though the whole house was suddenly filled up with wind. And sitting on the side of my bed, smiling at me over the flame of the candle, was Karl.

For the moment, waking suddenly like that in the bedroom, I wasn't surprised, this had happened to me so many times before. And then everything came back to me, the memory of all my worries about Karl and what I feared he had done; but in a twinkling again none of this mattered, I was overjoyed to see him, to see his face in the candle-light looking as it had done that first night in the Pantglas woods, when he dragged Jeffy up the slope into the light of our bonfire.

He put his finger to his lips.

'Hallo, Karl,' I whispered at him, smiling.

'Hallo, Dewi,' he answered. 'Did you hear me striking the match?'

'I don't know. I just woke up, I think.'

'You were fast asleep when I came in.'

'How did you find me, Karl? What's the matter with your eye?'

He was wearing a black patch over one eye with a black tape going round his head.

'Never mind that now,' he said. 'I've had a bit of a struggle. You said you were coming to the Vaughan Arms, and I knew this place already. I climbed up here off the roofs of the stables down there at the back. There was an old man snoring in the first room I looked into, he had a huge bandaged leg resting on a pillow on the rail at the foot of the bed. The second room was yours, so I had to look no farther. I have come to see you before I go. I leave the country tonight.'

'How are you going, Karl?'

'By boat. Will you help me, Dewi?'

'Yes, I will,' I said, getting out of bed. 'Of course. What can I do?'

He didn't answer for a moment, he just let a long intense look stream out of his candle-lit face into mine. Then he turned away. 'Will you come with me, Dewi?' he asked.

I felt my heart trying to break away at his words, leaping up strong and painful, bucking fiercely like a frightened pony on the end of a halter. 'When, Karl?' I asked him. 'Now?'

'Yes,' he said. 'I have a plan for leaving at once. Will you come? For ever, Dewi.'

I thought of the marvel of travelling with Karl, but I found it hard somehow to say outright I would go. And then I remembered the spoilt armlets on the floor under my uncle's bed next door, and the dread I had felt all night of having to face him. That determined me. 'Yes,' I said, 'I'll come. Let me get dressed. Why do you have to go so suddenly?'

'Come here,' he said, moving to the bedroom door. He opened it and beckoned me out after him into the dark passage. Almost opposite my room was one of the windows in the front of the pub overlooking the main street of Abergarth. Karl tiptoed up to it and pointed down. Under the street lamp opposite I could see two tall men all in black standing motionless looking across at the Vaughan Arms. Back in the bedroom he said: 'Those two are following me. There's a warrant out for my arrest in Ystrad. Charley reported, as I foresaw, that I had stabbed Growler to death. After running away from our camp he met the chief constable's boys in Ystrad High Street. What are their names? In your form.'

'Bleddyn and Alcwyn.'

'Yes. He told them everything he'd seen, and they took him to their father to repeat his story. The police went up the Pantglas woods to see if what he said was true. But Growler hadn't burnt, Dewi, as I intended. His clothes were too wet, and it takes a lot more fuel than we had collected to consume a human body. Never mind. Come on. We must get away. Have you any money?'

'Wait, Karl,' I said. 'Charley thought you had stabbed Growler. Tell me if you did. I will come with you whether or not if you want me to, but you must tell me the truth.'

'Growler was dead when I got to the cave,' he answered. 'He must have been out mothing and gone in there to rest when he felt ill. His face was purple, almost black. You saw it.'

'But the dagger,' I began. But I had no heart to go on. What did I care how Karl had got hold of my dagger, or whether he had used it on Growler or not? I didn't care. I hated questioning him, as though I no longer trusted him, as though he was on trial, my enemy and not the only friend I had. 'Oh, never mind, Karl,' I said. 'Come on, let's go.'

He held out his hand, smiling, and I took it. 'Sit down,' he said, placing the candle between us, 'because you've got to climb to the ground.' He fixed his one eye steadily on mine, passed his hands a few times in front of my face and muttered the

243

words that always made me not afraid of climbing any more. 'Follow me,' he whispered when it was all over. 'Bring all the money you've got, will you?'

He blew out the candle and climbed out of the window. I watched him standing on the sort of wide string-course running like a stone ledge along the wall just below the cill, and then reaching sideways to get hold of the open shutters of the next window, my uncle Lloyd's. I put my head out into the night to watch how he would do it, and I heard the cracked iron clock in Abergarth church strike three. There were many handholds up there on the rough back wall, old shutter brackets and rusted iron bars driven into the stones, so that what Karl was doing looked easy. Beyond my uncle's room, on the corner of the building, was a downpipe. Karl slid down this the short distance on to the slate roof of the lean-to shed below, where Myrddin kept the chaffing machine and the feed bins for the horses. Here he waited for me, and when I had joined him we crept together across the roof to the far end, walked along the top of the back wall of the Vaughan Arms yard and dropped down into the field outside. Here Karl picked up a bulging cotton bag, similar to the one he had carried the jam jars and the burning powder in a few nights before. 'This way,' he said.

We went down the slope in silence and across the fields in the direction of the Abergarth castle, which was only the back halves of a couple of short towers really, with a bit of curtain-wall between them, the whole lot held upright by a rug of thick ivy. Around the castle was the little Abergarth park, containing a place for the children to play, and a bowling-green, and an artificial lake for boating, not a very big one. There were no railings round the side of the park we were on, only a high thick hedge of rhododendron bushes. Karl pushed his way into them and I followed. When we came through we were inside the park, and he said: 'To the lake, Dewi.'

We crossed the children's playing-field, and when we reached the lake we found all the rowing-boats drawn up out of the water on the sloping asphalt enclosure in front of the little pavilion, they lay there tilted on their sides, about a dozen long narrow skiffs, very light and easy to row, their oars lying along the thwarts and their rudders on the bottoms.

'This is what we want, Dewi,' Karl said.

I was puzzled. I thought he meant we were going for a row on the ornamental lake at that time of the morning. 'Help me,' he said. 'Go at the back end and push.'

'What are we doing, Karl?' I asked.

'We are getting one of these boats out of here and on to the Garth river,' he said. 'And then we are going down the river in the direction of the sea. I'll tell you the rest of my plan when we get there. Are you ready?'

He started tugging at the front of the boat he had chosen, the longest one there, called the *Silver Princess*. I did as he asked me and pushed. We slid the boat across the enclosure and up to the gate in the iron railing surrounding it. There the two of us lifted the bows on to the top bar, went to the back together and pushed until the screeching keel was balanced half way across; and then, while I held the stern up, Karl jumped over the gate and began to pull the bows forward, and finally to lower them on to the grass. Soon the two of us were tugging our burden across the children's playground towards the outside railings of the park. We got the boat over these in the same way as we had crossed the enclosure gate, although they were higher, and then we slid it down the grassy slope outside the park and on to the wide meadows leading down to the river.

It took us a long time to cross the meadows although it was downhill all the way, the boat got heavier and heavier to push. Often we sat down on it blown and perspiring. We tried carrying it, but it was much too heavy, even when we put it on our heads as we had seen Indians doing in pictures, but at last we reached the bank of the river, and Karl said the first part of our task was over.

Behind us, on the low hill above the meadows, stood the town of Abergarth, silent in the moonlight, not a light showing anywhere. Before launching the boat into the river we went back to the enclosure two or three times and carried down two pairs of oars, the cushions and the rudder. Where the river bank was low we slid the boat in and I got aboard and placed everything in position, holding on to the branch of a willow tree growing out of the bank. When all the gear was arranged in order I looked around for Karl, expecting him to step into the boat, but he was nowhere to be seen. I sat there waiting, listening to the river sounds, the water tinkling past the boat and the night birds squeaking. I didn't like to shout, it seemed the wrong thing to do in the silence and the darkness of the fields.

Presently I saw two red lights floating slowly just above the earth towards me, coming steadily nearer down the path beside the trees planted along the bank of the river. The iron church clock struck four. Presently I recognized Karl carrying two lanterns with red glass windows. He stopped on the bank above me and handed them into the boat one at a time. They were heavy road lamps smelling strongly of oil, the sort old Davy Rice the roadman used to clean and light up in his cottage. Karl tied one of them to a stripped willow branch and hung it out over the front of the boat, and the other he hung in the same way over the stern.

We pushed off from the bank with the oars and got out into the middle of the river. It was wide there and flowing swiftly. Karl told me he had seen a barrowful of the lamps unlit up near a hole the workmen had begun on the road to the bridge. Fire was what he loved, he said, not water, he had used water to escape only to throw his pursuers off the scent, in case they had bloodhounds as well to trace him. He sat half way along the boat rowing, and I worked the rudder in the stern. The red lights of the lamps fell vividly on to the black waters, and the elastic swirls of the current stretched them out and unravelled them, and then let them fly back together again, until once more for a moment they burnt in intense and undivided fire beneath their lanterns. The night was warm. The river flowed so fast that Karl had hardly any need to row, he just dipped his oars in the water and leaned slowly back against them.

Soon we were away from the park, and on top of the banks on both sides of us, although we couldn't see them, stretched the flat fields of the countryside beyond the town. There were no lights anywhere, only the crimson reflections spilled by our lanterns on to the water. Out on that plain the river was sunken and twisted a lot, we kept running between high banks, going around endless curves and bends, thinking we would never come to the end of the turn we were in, and that we would never again see more than a few yards ahead of us. But the straight reaches came again, and the dark trees crowded down on each side of the water, and the fish jumped. The moon came up huge and round, a warm golden colour, but it gave no light. In spite of the excitement, I began to feel sleepy. Karl noticed it and told me to give up steering and to lie down on the long cushions which I could place on the bottom of the boat. I did this, and soon he was describing to me the beautiful sunlit town of white he had once floated through on a foreign river as we were floating now down the narrows between the high white rocks. The water branched out among the houses and made islands of them, white islands, the whole town was soft and milky in the brilliant sunshine. When we reached there we would see the quays gleaming white, their walls built of beautiful marble-white pebbles and mortar, and all the ships tied up alongside them thickly painted in a shining whiteness, their sails, and all their rigging, and their ropework, and their tackle, radiant as snow. The walls of all the cottages beside the water were warm and whitewashed, and their roofs, and the roofs of the villas, were smooth in the sunlight, flat as fresh pages for writing on, the only darkness we could see in that town were the shadows of the snow-lit sea-birds moving over the roofs, and among the milk-white cattle in the fields, and upon the gleaming roadways. Farther along, as the river carried us into the centre of the town, we saw the great high icing of the glittering palaces on both sides of us, all of the palest marble, with the terraced gardens coming down to the water, and the beds of milk-white flowers fragrant in them, and shrubs heavily laden with blossoms, and great clusters of snow-berries and

247

feathery trees, and white statues along the moon-pale walls. Above our heads the great white birds circled again in the sunshine, and drifted down among the palaces like large snow falling off the roof of the world; and ahead of us a slender bridge of white marble curved across the river from bank to bank, an unarrowed bow of ivory drawn against the heavens, and upon it stood three beautiful figures in robes of white fur. As we drew near everything darkened and became cold and terrifying, and the three figures grew to twice, three times, their size. They leaned over the bridge to catch us as we went under, they were many in number, huge and ugly and savage, their flushed faces lined and knobbly, the sheeting of their white robes was solid, looped and festooned down their bodies like the sides of candles dripping wax. I ducked down to escape their clutching fingers as we went under, and into the endless darkness, and I moaned aloud and struggled in my sleep.

10

I AWOKE with the sapling above me dividing the dazzling sun among its branches, and the warmth and light streaming down upon my face through the frail oak leaves of lemon and gold. At once I smelt the sweet smell of fire. I tried hard to think where I was, and what had happened, and why Karl's coat had been placed over me. Then I remembered the river of our flight and rose on my elbow to look at it, and Karl waved to me from the edge of the wood where he crouched stripped to the waist and still wearing the black patch over his eye. He was preparing to cook something in a tin. The tall trees sat up motionless in the sun in a half-ring round the edge of the little clearing, begging like waving bears, and spread out beneath them was the gloom of their purple shadows, with the golden holes in them, and the green-smouldering grass. I looked the other way again, out across the full broad river under my elbow, and saw the watery surface of it everywhere dark and shining, the sunlit glister of a tarred door covered the water right to the buckled cliffs opposite, and the hills above them, where the fields spread over the sunlit land were golden, or earth-purple as foxglove, or, when sunburnt brown, reaped and ridgy as the canework of a chair. Through the clear water immediately below me I watched another stream flowing, a silver current of little fishes moved glittering down the glass-like water close to the bank. But of our rowing-boat there was no sign anywhere.

I got up and walked across the grass of the little clearing to Karl. He had a hot invisible fire going with bacon beginning to sizzle in a tin on top of it. I couldn't remember getting out of the boat the night before, or this morning, or whenever it was. I wondered what point along the river we had reached. We hadn't crossed the sea in the darkness, we weren't already on the Continent, were we? The river was very broad in front of us, we were bound to be near the mouth of it, with the tide coming in fast. This grassy little clearing on the bank was a fine hiding-place, it had thick woods in a complete semicircle around it. 'Where are we, Karl?' I asked him.

'We won't be long, Dewi,' he said, smiling up. 'Come on, let's have something to eat. We'll soon be safe now.'

He tipped the bacon out on to two thick slices of bread, and the fat soaked in. It was lovely, and the hot food smell was right in the clear sunlight, although different from it. Karl said we were eating our dinner, not our breakfast, I ought to be able to tell by the sun it wasn't morning any more. He was surprised I couldn't remember coming ashore because I had argued with him about Buddug having a baby. 'Come on, I'll show you,' he said when I asked him where the *Silver Princess* was.

We went across the grass towards the river, carrying our bread and bacon. At the edge, about twenty yards below the spot where I had woken up, stood a clump of trees with their thick branch-like roots standing out black from the soil of the bank, and disappearing into the clear water. Sunk on the bed of the river beneath these trees lay our boat, with the two red lanterns swaying about in the current at her bows and her stern. She was full of stones, and holes seemed to have been bashed in the bottom of her. I was so surprised I didn't know what to say. 'How did that happen, Karl?' I asked him.

'I did it,' he answered, chewing.

'Why?'

'We can't reach Europe in a thing like that,' he said. 'We must get another boat, a big one, to put out to sea in.'

I walked back up to the fire in confusion and sat down. I thought of all the trouble we were in, Growler's home burnt to cinders, Growler dead, Karl in flight, and pursued by mysterious watchers and bloodthirsty dogs. And myself his accomplice in everything that had been done. And now Karl was talking of taking another boat to carry us abroad. Could all this have happened? Was it true, was it real, or only a dream? I knew the brown scabs covering my belly like a cake-crust because of it all were real, and the swollen ankle-pad of a boil in the middle of my cheek. But all the time, whatever happened, I had at the back of my mind the belief that soon everything would be all right, that Karl would meet someone rich and powerful he knew who would be proud to have a chance to carry us across the sea at a word from him, or that some prince or nobleman related to him would be meeting us in secret with his yacht, or that we would hide aboard a liner as stowaways. But Karl was going to take a ship from somewhere, belonging to someone else, and sail us across. I felt homesick and sad at the idea. Where was he going to get the ship from, that was one question. And when were we going to attempt our flight, that was another.

The weather got hotter and hotter all the afternoon. We lay down by the fire helpless, smoking, and dozing, and talking. Every time I woke up I sweated more, and I felt happier and forgetful again, trusting Karl. The ship he had chosen for us was a beautiful white sailing yacht, he told me, long and slender, lying tied up at the wharf a quarter of a mile farther up the river, a ship as lovely and graceful and light as a great snowy sea-bird, called *Tir na n'Og*, painted dove grey and white, and the inside daffodil yellow. A deck covered the front half of her, which had a brass bell on it glittering like gold. High on the front of the mast was fastened a bright red lantern, and a pointed flag of royal blue flew at her masthead, and her hooter gave out a soft note. Karl sensed I had been worried, and spoke to me about what we would do abroad, but lying on the grass I was soothed as much by our talk of the Powells, Tally trying to cadge a penny ha'penny each off us to buy fags, Mendy picking his nose with the button-hook, Luther at the dinner table dipping his hair in the broth pretending to wash it, Mr Powell collecting the pennies from all the public dubliws and the boys in school ragging Tally he was a son of one of the copper kings. 'Don't worry, Dewi,' Karl said to me. 'I will do this alone. You stay here and I will pick you up as I pass down the river and out to sea. No damage will be done to the ship, we will borrow her to get abroad and then abandon her on some safe beach, high and dry on the other coast. What are you thinking about?'

All around us were the high trees with solid masses of green leaves in the sunshine draped over their branches like displayed velvet. With the blood boiling beneath his feathers a thrush sang endlessly in the little lemon-leaved oak. The night had left the perfect pearl-shine of a moon behind hanging over our heads as we lay on the grass, marble white and dry, but fragile as a bubble, and transparent, and the gulls sailed round over the river, and over the trees, and in a great ring out over the sea; or they came dropping down with their wings curved, as though they were bringing us huge bundles carried under their arms. I thought waking and sleeping about Tom and Charley and Jeffy, and wondered where they would be on a hot afternoon like this. Had Jeffy tried to get a ram's horn for us to call our club together? Had he stood on the wall up the mountain and dropped a brick on to the head of the old big-horned ram, hoping to hit one of the horns off? The ram was still lying on his side unconscious when we came back down the mountain two hours later, but when we went to examine him he got up and ran away.

When I woke up everything was changed, it was pitch-dark, and cold, and the fire had gone out. The first sound I heard was what I thought to be rain creeping in the grasses about my head like mice among paper. I sat up shivering and afraid in the darkness. A fast icy wind came pouring down the river and turning aside into our clearing, and at my waking every tree in the forest around me rocked with it, roaring like a steep waterfall in a struggle with its own storm. Before I could stand up the rain came down upon me in torrents, hissing through the darkness, not falling, but forced hard sideways, splashing and battering against everything growing on the earth. There was no sign of Karl. No dogs, not even bloodhounds, could follow our trail on a night like this. I ran down as best I could in wind and rain and darkness to the river bank to look for him, and after a few steps I found myself splashing over my boots in water. The river was in flood, and its banks had burst, a great depth of water was already swirling among the trunks of the trees and lapping half way up the grass of the little clearing. But somehow I had to find a place where I could watch for Karl coming down in the yacht, so that he wouldn't pass me in the darkness. I went on into the frothing water, over my knees, up to my waist in the cold, I splashed on until I came to an isolated mound with a clump of trees on it rising out of the flood and making a little spongy island away from the bank. Here, with the swirling river rushing all around me through the night, I crouched for shelter behind the trunk of a frightened birch among the bushes growing there. I listened to the wind and the rain together lashing the branches of the trees on the bank behind me, and then suddenly the lightning came, like a flung bottle of liquid gold smashed against the darkness. By its splashed brilliance I saw the river in great waves rolling along past me, and a whole tree upon it, tufted as though it had torn out half its hair, rising up glittering on shifting roots to its full height, before crashing down again as though it had been felled at one blow, and disappearing into the water. The birch above me gave me no shelter and soon I was wet through to the skin, but I didn't care about that. Where was Karl, what could he be doing out alone in a storm like this? How could we cross the Channel in the darkness, and the pouring rain, and the waves mountainous in the wind? How would we know the way? What if Karl had been captured? And taken away? He would never tell them I was with him, he was too honourable, but what would I do without him? Without Karl I didn't feel as though I lived at all, not even existed, all my thoughts were of him, I couldn't imagine my life if I were not able to turn to him for strength and courage. I shivered in the rain without stopping and my throat ached with my tears.

I felt the body of the birch move against mine all the time with the frantic rhythm of the wind, and then, when the lightning came again, the whole tree awoke, it was alive and screaming with fright, it reared wildly in the gusts, shying back like a plunging stallion upright against its leading-rein. The glare hung pulsing over the whole sky, spread out suddenly like a wild stampede of golden lizards flashing in streams of terror to the edges of the cracked sky, and this time, by the throb of it, I saw an upturned boat riding the waves, and then some large drowned animals, perhaps they were dogs or ponies, swirling down after it. The gale-goaded trees stretched gibbering and metallic along the river bank in the glare and, suddenly, just as the flash was coming to an end, I saw rounding the bend a good way up the flood the white prow of a yacht, rising and falling violently on the waves, the pale mast bare and slender and carrying no sails, and with no light in its lantern. And holding the little wheel at the stern a drenched bareheaded figure. Karl! It was bound to be Karl. Only a glimpse and then the darkness, blacker than ever, shut down like a slammed lid, and the blows of the thunder followed almost at once, a deafening brutal sound shaking the ground of the island under my feet, searching me out. This darkness showed Karl's boat carried no lights. How was I to get aboard? Even with the river over its banks Karl would not be able to bring the yacht near my island. But as soon as he was abreast of me I would jump into the water however deep it was, or however dangerous, and somehow wade or scramble or swim out to him, nothing would be able to stop me reaching him, not winds, or deep water, or storm, or darkness, nothing could come between us and keep us apart any more. The clap of the thunder that had shaken the earth went farther and farther off, banging the doors of the heavens one by one behind it. And then I heard only the deep-throated hiss and gurgle of the river pouring down through the darkness, and the wind lashing the trees. I stood crying with cold but my heart was filled with hope now and the excitement of being soon with Karl again.

A faint white smudge appeared lunging about in the darkness a little distance up the river, well out into the middle of the current. It must be the yacht, no other boat could have reached there, Karl was going to bring the vessel close in to the bank, so that I could get aboard. I jumped into the water and began to wade out into the river to meet him, and just then the lightning glared again, gilding like a map all the throbbing roadways of the sky with its juddering illumination. I saw the yacht clearly, heeled well over, and pitching with great violence, quite close in now, and running diagonally at a high speed across the waves towards the bank, the blue flag at the masthead tinned rigid in the wind. Behind her, rounding the bend, followed another boat, a small black steamer with the smoke from her chimney hauled into the air and then flattened down with gusty blows into the river. The flash lasted only a few seconds, but it was enough for me to see this, and to see Karl's yacht come shooting in under the trees fifty yards above my little island. I saw the tall mast hit the overhead branches and snap off level with the deck, making a loud agonizing wrenching sound that I couldn't hear. I saw Karl at the little wheel in the stern throw up his arms above his head to protect himself, but before the falling mast could strike him the scene was plucked back into the darkness again. What had happened? 'Karl!' I shouted, wading farther out into the water towards the boat. 'Karl, Karl! Here I am! I'm coming! I'm coming!'

I groped about in the water for what seemed hours, weeping and calling out to him. The steamer farther up the river had a powerful beam on its pitching deck, which kept sweeping to and fro over the water searching for something. I longed for another flash of lightning. The rain was heavier than ever, and the darkness so thick over the river I could see nothing. Then again the great glare of the golden lightning hung clinging to the sky above the river for a moment, like a massive high-tide breaker exploding, smashed against the sheer cliff-face of the darkness, and dripping golden from its ledges. It lit up Karl's yacht stranded against the river bank above my island, tilted on its side under the trees, the deck sloping into the water and the snapped off mast lying overboard. Karl was nowhere to be seen. The lightning crackled, it was deafening, I was standing in the sidings and miles of iron railings crashed from a height on to the railways around me, staggering the ground even at the bottom of the river. When it was over the steamer hooted far out, and in her beam, when the lightning stopped, I caught sight of Karl floating rapidly on the current, his body rising and falling on the surface of the water as the flood carried him on towards the sea. Soon he would be past me, and gone for ever into the darkness. I waded out to intercept him, moving through the wild current as fast as I could, stumbling in the mud and the stones covering the bottom. Then the pitching of the steamer swivelled its beam away from Karl's head and I lost sight of him. I began to cry again and to shout out. On I went across the current, getting deeper and deeper into the water. Soon I was above my shoulders and the waves splashed about my face. The steamer swung her beam frantically around, sweeping the waves, but no sign of Karl was to be seen. I had moved so slowly he must be a long way down beyond me. 'Karl!' I screamed after him. 'Karl! Karl!' I tried to swim down but I had all my clothes on, and my boots, and I couldn't do it. When I let myself be carried along the water all the time swept me into the bank, and not out into the current where

255

Karl was. Where an arm of the bank jutted out into the river I scrambled ashore, meaning to run ahead and try to find him and intercept him lower down the river. I found myself in the middle of the woods with mounds of brambles everywhere. 'Karl!' I screamed again, 'Karl, Karl! Don't leave me. Karl! Karl!' The lightning burned, it jigged and throbbed in the heavens like an unceasing agony pulsing through my flesh. The brambles held me fast although I struggled, and in the lamps of my pursuers I saw the green rain falling cold, my rescuers had landed from the steamer and were in the woods all around me.

'Karl! Karl!'